THE RED LEDGER REBORN

VOLUME ONE
PARTS 1 - 2 - 3

MEREDITH WILD

THE RED LEDGER REBORN

VOLUME ONE
PARTS 1 - 2 - 3

MEREDITH WILD

WATERHOUSE PRESS

TABLE OF CONTENTS

For Sean, my little writer

THE RED LEDGER

LEDGER

part 1

1

ISABEL

Rio de Janeiro

Carnaval saturates the streets like a thousand tiny rivers of excess and desire. Heat and music and the ebb and flow of revelers create an undeniable pulse of excitement. It exists in the balmy ocean air, settles on my skin, and sizzles against my nerve endings. I feel like I could drown in it.

"Do you want another drink?"

Kolt's American accent stands out in the cacophony of the open-air bar.

I don't need another drink. The alcohol from the few caipirinhas I've already had flows through my bloodstream, making me horny and impulsive. I meet his gaze and consider where I want the night to go.

"We have to work tomorrow." I'm not sure if that will discourage him, though.

"Then maybe we shouldn't waste all night here."

I smirk. "What are you trying to say?"

"I've been staring at you in that dress all night. And right now, I'm willing to do just about anything to have a couple hours alone with you."

With his soft brown eyes, he rakes me in, betraying his desire. He's smooth-shaven with lightly tanned skin. His short, dirty-blond hair has grown out just enough to curl naturally at the ends—as close to rugged as he'll ever look.

I swirl the ice in my glass. "A couple hours?"

He rests his hand on my lower back and presses his lips to my bare shoulder. "You know I want a lot more than that."

I tense. I care about Kolt. Deep down, I know he cares about me too. But every time I sleep with him, I feel his grip tighten on me as if I'm becoming more his. He doesn't understand I'm not his at all. I can't give him more.

But I can give him tonight. One more night.

"Let's go back to my place," I say, silently promising myself I'll indulge the physical attraction one last time.

His eyes widen a fraction before returning to normal. He gets the attention of the bartender with his broken Portuguese and pays him quickly. He makes no effort to fit in here. Most days he looks like he should be strolling the grounds at Harvard, the very place that shaped him through undergrad and another shaky year in grad school.

Kolt's on vacation from his life. It's been six months. In another six, he'll go back to it, and I know as surely as I know my own name that he intends to bring me back with him. I tick off all the boxes. We have chemistry. If we both ignored my inability to love him, I could fit into his life nicely. He's rich and driven, and every time he looks at me, I know what he sees. A pretty fuck. A prize to be won. A match.

But I'm not on vacation. I'm running away. The urge to thrust myself into a future unknown was so powerful, it landed me in Rio. In the center of this chaos is exactly where I want to be—until I can find the truth. But the truth is like this overwhelming place. It's much easier to get lost than to ever find what you're looking for.

"Let's go." Kolt slips his hand into mine, and we're off.

He leads the way, walking quickly through the boisterous crowd. His eagerness has my heart beating faster, momentarily overwhelming the sensations of the celebration around us.

I'm mourning the decision to leave the festivities the second we turn onto the quieter Rua Lopes Quintas. Shadows play in my periphery as we head toward my apartment. Relief and unease curl inside me with Kolt's possessive embrace around my midsection.

"Thanks for walking me home," I hedge, already anticipating his disappointment, because I don't think I can go through with it. Not tonight.

We're at my door, and he turns me, squaring our bodies. He weaves his fingers into my hair, caresses over the dampness at the roots, and guides my mouth to his. I accept. Because if we're not lovers, we're undeniably more than friends. And even though I refuse to give him everything he wants, I still crave contact. His taste is a mirror of sugar and citrus on my tongue. He slides his other hand to the back of my thigh and inches up, pressing his groin to the center of my physical desire. But his desperation barrels over his sensuality.

I close my eyes and reach for what I want… A memory. Silvery-blue eyes flash in my mind. Full lips mark my skin, and then the memory takes me away. In my mind, I'm pinned under hard thrusts that threaten to shatter my body and my heart. Reckless lust and love I want so hard to believe was pure.

A rush of desire hits me. I gasp and answer Kolt's persistent groping with an infinitesimal shift in my hips. With a hungry growl, he pushes me back against the rough stucco of my building. My eyes open to his perfectly chiseled features. I turn my head, disconnecting our mouths. Undeterred, he latches on to my neck instead.

"Kolt…not tonight."

He hitches the tight fabric of my dress up like he means to take me here in the street but stops short of baring me indecently. "Why do you do this to me?" His voice is low, gritty with need.

I wince because I really don't want to do this to him. "If I gave you everything, you wouldn't want it."

He pulls back to stare at me for a quiet moment. "That's a goddamn lie, and you know it. I want you all the time."

He can't want the person he's never truly seen. I trace my fingers across his lips, wishing I could tell him the truth. That I'm incomplete. Still utterly broken. And he doesn't have what it takes to put me back together. Somehow I know if I told him all that, he'd try to talk me out of it. Either way, the answer isn't the one he wants.

"I drank too much. It doesn't feel right." I offer the half lie that gives him no choice but to leave me alone.

He may be cocky and entitled, but Kolt is still a gentleman. His shoulders soften, and his touch falls away. "At least let me walk you up."

I shake my head. "I'll be fine. I promise."

"Are you sure?"

He's only being half genuine, giving me one last chance to give in. I consider it one more time. I lean in, close the small space between us, and kiss him softly on the mouth.

"Good night, Kolt," I whisper against his lips.

He reacts, taking the kiss deeper, molding his hands over my ass and yanking me against him. I pressure him back gently because we're riding a dangerous edge when it comes to self-control. I still have plenty, but I'm not sure he does.

Finally he lets our bodies separate. His breath comes in uneven pants as he looks me over like every inch of my bare skin burns him.

"Good night, Isabel. I'll see you tomorrow."

Tension lines every plane of his face as he turns and takes brisk strides down the street. He disappears into the shadows I have learned never to trust. I reach for my key, quickly turn it in the lock, and bolt the door behind me.

TRISTAN

Sweat beads down my back. My heart beats slowly, like the pendulum on an old clock. Adrenaline rushes don't come easily for me. As I circle to the rear of the building, memorized details project onto the bright-white screen of my mind.

Isabel Foster. American. English teacher. Aged twenty-five.

Marked for death, she'll be extinguished within the hour. I register the faintest measure of relief that her lover—or the man who desperately wanted to be—is now out of the picture. Collateral damage isn't uncommon, but I prefer to avoid it if I can. God knows I have enough blood on my hands.

I scale the metal stairs in the darkness, mentally mapping my journey from a brief assessment of her living arrangements days ago. The week of Carnaval is already loud and dangerous. Her death will be one of dozens of others reported by the morning.

I peer into her apartment through the glass doors that open from her second-floor balcony. Nearly every light is on. I withdraw my gun from the holster hidden under my shirt. With practiced deftness, I spin the silencer onto the end until it's secure.

Opening the door from her balcony, I pause when a low sound comes from the bedroom. After a beat, I slip inside, leaving the door open a crack for my inevitable departure. I glance around the living room that leads into a small kitchen. My brain captures snapshots that my photographic memory will store forever, whether I want it to or not. A thriving bromeliad on the window sill. A framed photo of her with her parents. An old purple crocheted blanket strewn over the back of the couch. None of it matters. Tonight will be the last night she draws air.

With that final thought, I move toward her nearly closed bedroom door. The gap reveals my target, but instead of taking action, I halt my advance. Where I didn't care about the sounds of my approach seconds before, now I still my breathing and freeze my motions to become totally silent.

She's on the bed. Her chestnut hair fans out on her lavender pillow, and the sheets are tangled around her ankles. With one hand, she's massaging her breast through the sheer black fabric that clings tightly to it. The other hand is hidden under her panties. Her position reveals details I couldn't have appreciated when I watched her from afar—graceful, toned legs, a line of unreadable text inked along her rib cage, and a smooth, firm stomach decorated with a tiny silver ring pierced through her navel. The pinched look on her face is one I haven't seen before. Not even with her boyfriend. A fascinating mix of anguish and rapture.

With her eyes closed and her position on the bed, she can't know I'm here watching her pleasure herself. The pendulum of my heart swings a little faster at my predicament.

Her beauty doesn't give me pause. A nagging instinct that I know her from somewhere else doesn't give me pause either, though perhaps it should. My weapon hangs heavily at my side now as I entertain both a slow burn of arousal and a rare moment of empathy that I'm about to end her life in the midst of her ecstasy.

I trace my fingertip over the cool metal trigger and attempt to rationalize my hesitation. Then I swiftly resolve to correct it. But not before Isabel's body arches. She wraps her fingers around the edge of the mattress, taking a handful of sheet with her. Her movements quicken, and she sucks in a breath. I'm growing hard, cursing myself with every passing second for my inaction.

Fuck this.

I grit my teeth and lift the gun, lining the barrel up precisely to ensure a quick, painless end.

Her body undulates unevenly as the orgasm rolls through her. She trembles and moans, and my groin betrays the pleasure it's giving me too.

Her lips part with a loud groan and then...

"Tristan..."

My name leaves her lips and fills the room like a gunshot.

I freeze, and the pendulum stops.

JAY: Please report on the status of Isabel Foster.

I chew on a thin red stir straw, rest back into the office chair that sits behind my desk, and stare at the text cursor on my screen. I'm still in disbelief. I've never hesitated like that. I sure as hell have never had a change of heart. I simply have no heart to change.

This was curiosity, pure and simple.

I mash the straw between my molars and quickly type a reply.

RED: In progress. Need a little more time.

Jay's response comes quickly. I sense her displeasure before the words appear on the computer screen. We've spoken in person only once in three years, and the details are still foggy. She provided only the information that she felt I needed to go into my new life. There was a time when this unnerved me, but now I take solace in it. The less I know, the better. Everyone, including me, is likely safer that way. Except for my marks, of course.

JAY: The client is eager. Is there a complication?

I hover my fingertips over the keys, weighing my reply. Complications are rare and historically have never required her intervention. Still, I remain irrationally protective of my error, and I want to ensure enough time to fully investigate the source of it.

RED: She has a boyfriend. Waiting to get her alone so I can keep it clean.

JAY: When will it be done?

RED: Within the week.

I hesitate and follow the answer she doesn't want to hear, trying to allude to inevitable closure on the subject of my living, breathing mark.

RED: Where to next?

JAY: Take care of this and I'll let you know.

Jay knows I prefer to disappear for a while after a local hit. Rio is vast and crime is rampant, but corruption is being confronted more vigorously, and at least some of the many homicides will receive the thorough investigation they deserve. In addition to being American, Isabel Foster is the daughter of a Pentagon official. Chances are extremely slim, but not impossible, that her death could be linked to my face, my untraceable fingerprints, my unregistered and unmarked car, or my apartment. All in all, incarceration would be easier to avoid if I were nowhere to be found.

After wrestling with my total fuck up all day, I turned my focus to research and compiled a more thorough profile of the girl—an exercise that offered no enlightenment. As far as I can tell, our lives haven't intersected in the past three years. The Tristan on her lips could easily be someone else.

I try to reassure myself that she could be important, even if I don't understand why yet. Then I remind myself that Isabel Foster is a beautiful woman who shouted my name as she brought herself to orgasm, and there is not a single iota of importance to that odd coincidence. I am being idiotic, male, and uncharacteristically human. Yet I stare at the photograph before me, and all of my instincts—all the ones that have kept me alive through God knows how many situations that certainly should have left me dead—tell me unequivocally that my hesitation has merit.

I blink a few times and type into the protected chat that allows both

Jay and me anonymity, never knowing each other's exact whereabouts. We deal in death wishes and wire transfers, with not a shred of trust between us.

RED: A hint?

I try for humor, knowing Jay has none. Still, having something to look forward to would be welcome. Rio is becoming intolerable. Sensory overload. Easy to blend in, impossible to tune out. I've had the strong urge to move on for months. Perhaps now is the time. Now, when I've faltered so irrationally, risking everything.

Yes, I'd move on after this. I'd take Jay's next assignment, scout my next stop, and say goodbye to Brazil for a while.

JAY: How is your Russian?

I smirk. Jay's reply is both humor and insult. She knows my language skills are shit and I hate the cold. I've never said no, though.

RED: Flawless as always.
I'll be in touch.

I close out the chat and pace the largely empty living room. Nearly every square foot of my apartment is dedicated to my work. The space contains an old teacher's desk covered with connected monitors. A leather chair sits in the corner. The walls are cluttered with notes, all currently dedicated to the inauspicious woman who is hijacking my thoughts at the moment.

I have no need for couches or formal dining areas. Or friends, family, or lovers. I've never had a guest, and I suspect I never will.

I'm going to find out why Isabel Foster's face feels like it's been tattooed onto my brain. I'm going to eliminate her. And then I'm going to leave this country without a trace.

2

ISABEL

"I'm going to the store. Can I get you anything?"

I overenunciate each word and take in the wide-eyed stares from my classroom of students. They attend the Horizonte Centre to learn English, and I have the unfair advantage of being fluent in their native language as well as my own.

Ramona, a teenager from a nearby secondary school, raises her hand. "Can you get for me a loaf of bread?"

I smile because she's progressed quickly in my class but also because I recognize my drive in her. That drive to excel, paired with an affinity for language, had in some ways saved me. Language had healed me. Ultimately, it had given me a ticket to run away.

"Of course. Anything else?"

I glance around the room for other participants. I sense someone's eyes on me and turn my head. Kolt is standing in the doorway. He looks fresh wearing his expensive blue jeans, a pale-blue collared shirt, and a cocky grin, as if I didn't blatantly shoot him down just hours ago.

"*Bom dia, amigos.*" He flits his gaze around the classroom and then nods to me, his smirk deepening. "*Senhorita Foster.*"

I want to be mad, but he makes it difficult. I can only muster mild annoyance. "English only in my classroom, Mr. Mirchoff."

"Lunch?"

I want to admonish him for clearly flirting with me in front of my students. They smile and share knowing looks. I think they enjoy this pretend romance that most of the school and its staff believe we have. I think they also enjoy when I play hard to get.

"We have ten more minutes of class. I suggest you get back to work. *Tchau.*"

I flip my hand in his direction and move to the whiteboard to highlight some new vocabulary.

"Now, who brought their recipe homework today?"

Twenty minutes later, I'm sitting across from Kolt at the outdoor café. I'm devouring my sandwich while he picks at a pastry beside an emptied cup of coffee.

"How are you feeling?"

I look up, wide-eyed. "I'm fine, why?"

He follows the curve of the cup with his finger. "Well, after all those caipirinhas last night, I thought it might be a rough morning for you."

I pretend like I don't hear him. We both know the truth anyway.

"Can I take you out tonight? Dinner maybe?"

I shake my head. "The city is too crazy right now. Maybe next week sometime after things calm down."

That would also buy me time to figure out what to do with him. Because a real relationship isn't in the cards for me right now.

He works his jaw and stares at me intently. I'm worried he can read my thoughts. I've never been great at schooling my features.

"Isabel, what's going on with us? We work together. We're friends, and we messed around a few times. Now I don't know what we are."

I swallow hard and avoid his gaze. "I don't like labels."

"Fuck buddies?"

I glare at him. "Stop."

He shrugs his shoulders. "Sorry. I'm not trying to be an asshole, but I can't stop thinking about what I want this to be." He gestures between us, his expression softening.

"Kolt…" I sigh because it's safer than forming words. I like our easy friendship. I enjoy the low hum of our attraction. But I can't get entangled with him.

"Is there someone else back home?" Concern shadows his eyes.

I shake my head. "He's gone."

His lips tighten. "Who is he?"

"Nobody. An old flame. It was a long time ago, but he's not the problem. I'm the problem."

"You're perfect." Affection and determination wrap around his words, tugging at my heart.

At this moment I hate Kolt for being sweet and charming. I hate myself for not being able to embrace it, because if I could, that means I could be normal. I could fall in love, make love, and carve out a normal future with a man like him. But I'm not healed all the way, and I'm not certain I ever will be.

"I'm so far from perfect, you have no idea."

I distract myself by watching the people on the street. Every walk of life. Every wild and passionate inclination fueled by this week's celebrations. I belong to this city more than I'll ever belong to Kolt. Even though it challenges me and scares the shit out of me sometimes.

On the other side of the street, a man dressed in black is leaning against the building. In black jeans, black T-shirt, and a faded green jacket, he seems to be the only one not in motion. I can't look away. Something about his face commands my attention. The longer I look, the faster my heart beats. So fast and so loud that I can't hear Kolt speaking above it.

I'm riveted. I'm in disbelief.

"Isabel?"

I tear my gaze away to meet Kolt's. "What?" I snap at him, because I can't help how annoyed I suddenly feel by this conversation and his untimely distractions.

He leans in and reaches for my hand. "All I'm asking for is a chance to talk this through over dinner."

"Fine, dinner." I pull my hand away and look back to the man in the street. Fear seizes my heart. He's gone.

No, no, no.

How could I have lost him? Seconds have gone by. Only seconds. I grab my purse and throw some bills on the table.

Kolt frowns. "Where are you going?"

"I'm sorry. I just have to go." I push up from the table and walk away. I scan up and down the street. My breath hitches when I catch a glimpse of the man's green jacket disappearing behind a group of partiers several feet away.

I don't think. I move as quickly as the crush of the street traffic allows.

"Tristan!" I yell, garnering a few looks from passersby.

He doesn't look back. My heart falls.

It has to be him. It has to be. Otherwise I'm crazy.

My thoughts whirl and stutter. Maybe I have lost my mind. Maybe that's how badly he's broken me. That's how desperately I want him back. I've dreamed him up so many nights, he's going to haunt my goddamn days now too.

The seconds seems to grow longer as that last thought passes through my mind. He's disappeared again. No matter how hard I look or fast I move, he's nowhere to be found.

My gut is telling me he's close. My whole body is telling me I need to find him again. Except I feel like I'm running out of time.

I pass salons and stores and run-down nothingness. I scan faces and peer down alleys. I don't know how far I've gone or how much time has passed, but as hope dwindles, a familiar pain stabs at my heart.

Loss. Regret. Utter loneliness.

I should turn back. I should go back to my life and forget the dream…banish the memory…heal my heart.

TRISTAN

I'm rioting inside. She knows me. She screamed my name down the street, for fuck's sake.

Determined to prove my gut was all wrong about Isabel Foster, I decided to see her up close. Resolve once and for all that there was nothing special about her so I could kill her and move on with my plan to get out of Rio and on to my next assignment. I had no idea I'd be tempting fate.

I've been traveling the globe for three years. Working, blending in, and then getting out of sight. No one's ever given me a second glance. No one's ever known my name. I'm a ghost, and with one look, this woman has pulled me from a life of anonymity. I don't know how to wrap my head around this new reality. It's both terrifying and too tempting to deny.

If she knows me…

God, the possibilities are endless. My life is a book ripped in half. The first few hundred pages forever lost. But what if they aren't?

I can see her clearly from inside the restaurant I ducked into moments ago. She's stopped in the middle of the busy street, only a few feet away, wringing her hands and looking everywhere. *Looking for me.*

She turns her back to me. Her shoulders hunch. I can almost feel her ready to give up. I should let her. I should finish this, but there's no way I can now. In the space of a few seconds, she's graduated from a mark to the most fascinating person I've ever known.

I step out of the shadows of the restaurant and onto the sidewalk. She spins as if she senses me there. Our gazes lock. She says my name again, and another explosion of panic detonates. I can hardly fucking breathe.

I pivot quickly, continue up the street, and turn into a narrow alley. Darkness closes in on me the farther I walk. The alley is empty, quieter than the busy street. I can hear her footsteps behind me. Then her voice.

"Tristan!"

I turn back, and she halts a couple feet away. I've been watching her from afar for days. Being this close to someone I'm supposed to take out typically means they're about to say their last words. This is different. So very different.

"Oh my God. I never thought I'd see you again." Her eyes are glassy, and her voice trembles. "It's me… Isabel."

She reaches for me, and I'm ready to jump out of my skin. I cover her mouth with my hand and press her to the alley wall. She puffs rapidly into my hand, confusion washing her beautiful features. Her stormy hazel eyes are red-rimmed, but she doesn't struggle against me.

"Who knows about me?"

I drop my hand so she can speak. Her rose-colored lips part, but she remains silent. Is she in shock? Why do I want to kiss her? Why does seeing her cry twist something inside me?

Not knowing fills me with renewed frustration. The muscles in my jaw tense, and I grit out the next words. "Tell me. Who knows I'm here?"

She shakes her head quickly. "No one."

I exhale in relief. "No one can know."

As I say it, I realize I can't trust her to stay quiet now that she's seen me.

"Are you in trouble, Tristan? Is everything okay?"

A shockwave jolts through me every time she says my name. It's making me edgy. This woman's presence had me unsettled from day one. If I don't find out why, she'll haunt me forever. I need to find out what she knows about me. I need more time. Except every day she's breathing is a day we're both at risk.

I've given her more time than she deserves. She's supposed to be dead. I'm not about to let her get me killed too.

Back on the street, pedestrians stream by unaware and unconcerned with us. I have to make a decision. Kill her now or satisfy curiosity about my past that's never burned this fiercely.

3

ISABEL

Tristan's voice is like cold velvet—rich with texture, void of feeling. I'm a trembling mess, but his eyes are calm.

He's bigger than I remember. His clothes hint at the solid muscular frame beneath. He's changed, but I'd know him anywhere. Those piercing eyes, opalescent blue orbs that I could stare into for the rest of my life. His hair is the same dark brown, short and unstyled. Stubble lines his jaw, making the ridges of his full lips stand out. Worry lines crease his forehead and the edges of his eyes.

We've grown. We're not the same.

A thousand thoughts blur together as I convince myself he's not a dream. No longer just a memory.

He's Tristan Stone. The love of my life.

He takes a step back, and the separation borders on painful.

Instinct drives me next. My fingers become ten tiny magnets. I reach for him, drawn to his flesh, determined to prove he's not an apparition. Before I can make contact, he takes my wrists in a firm grasp, holding them immobile in the horrible empty space between us.

Those few inches are made up of years of missing him. Of not knowing if he was alive or dead.

"You're looking at me like you hardly know me." I choke on the last word because every emotion is tearing its way up my throat.

His expression never changes. He's unreadable. "I know who you are, Isabel."

I let go of the fight in my muscles, feeling foolish and broken all over again. He doesn't love me anymore. I'm so far in the past, how could he have possibly hung on to those feelings like I have?

"We should go," he says, releasing his hold on me.

I drop my hands to my sides, confused and reeling from everything that's happening between us. True enough, this alley isn't the safest place for a reunion.

"Where do you want to go?"

"Your place. I'm parked nearby. I'll drive us."

I swallow my doubts and follow him down the alley to the congested street. He tugs me behind him until we get to his car. He opens the passenger door and shuts it after me without ceremony.

Seconds later, Tristan is whipping through the streets. I can't imagine the reason for his urgency.

"How long have you been in Rio?"

"A while." He glances into the rearview mirror, seeming distracted.

I nod and try to ignore the sting of his tone. I remember a gentler Tristan. Always tuned in to my feelings and needs. The man I met in the street is frighteningly intense and completely unreadable.

He stops at the end of my street, puts the car in park, and turns to me.

"How do you know where I live?" My heart starts racing again at this new revelation.

"There's no time to talk. Not here. I need you to pack a bag for a few days away," he says.

"A few days? I can't just leave with you. I have a job." I can no longer hide the panic in my voice.

He stares at me silently for a moment and then speaks slowly and calmly. "I know it doesn't make sense. I have a friend outside the city. We'll stay with him, and I can explain everything there."

I blink slowly, trying to process his proposal. "Then we'll come back?"

He nods wordlessly. I don't completely believe him, but I'm not willing to let him disappear again so soon.

"I need to call work."

He opens his palm. "Give me your phone."

I reach into my purse and hand it to him, expecting him to make a call with it. Instead he puts it into his coat pocket.

"You have five minutes. You can make your calls on the road."

My throat tightens, and my eyes burn with fresh tears. "Tristan… you're scaring me."

"Five minutes." His voice is clipped. "Go now."

I reach for the car door, feeling numb but propelled forward by Tristan's inexplicable urgency. He pulls out his phone, and I step out just as he begins to speak into it.

"Mateus. I need a favor."

I hurry to my apartment. My hands are shaking as I turn the key in the lock. I rush up the stairs and pull a backpack out of my closet. I glance at the clock, and the urge to cry is almost too strong to resist.

What the fuck am I doing? Tristan just crash-landed back into my world. After the most agonizing goodbye of my life when he joined the army all those years ago. After one last heartbreaking letter saying we were over. After years of nothing but silence and heartache.

He's a stranger, yet he never could be. Not after everything we went through together. And now we're thousands of miles from a home we once knew, and I'm agreeing to leave with him. It's only a few days, but this is insane.

I keep moving through my doubt as I stuff clothes into the bag. A few toiletries. I kneel to the floor and open the lockbox under my bed. I empty it of my passport and some cash and put both into the backpack.

I scan the bedroom and living room briefly. Why does dropping everything and running off seem justifiable when the love of my life is idling at the end of the street, waiting to drive us into a future unknown?

TRISTAN

All my loose plans for leaving Rio just firmed up. I can't let Isabel out of my sight, so the only option is to bring her into my world. Doesn't matter what she ends up seeing anyway. Her days are numbered. Hell, at this rate, mine are too.

We drive away from her neighborhood toward the condo-lined strip of Ipanema Beach. We pull into the parking lot of my building and take the elevator to the penthouse condo in silence.

She takes one step inside and freezes. "You live here?"

"I mostly work." Not a lot of living happens inside these walls. I shut the door behind us and shift both deadbolts to the side. As if in a daze, she wanders toward the sliding doors that lead to the oceanfront balcony. I register faint regret that it's probably the last time I'll have this view. The waves crash silently on the beach below as I eye her warily. So far she's gone along with everything, but I have a feeling the window of her compliance is closing.

I go to my desk and start moving through my mental checklist. I remotely back up my files and wipe the machines. I pull papers and photos pinned to the wall and stuff them into a folder.

In the bedroom, I find the lever inside the chest of drawers that rests along an accent wall. The large mirror above it angles up, and I push it open the rest of the way, revealing a hidden compartment that stores possessions I wouldn't want anyone knowing about. I pull an array of weapons off the pegs that display them and throw them into a bag. Beside several bricks of cash in various currencies, my passports are bound with a thick rubber band to a worn red leather notebook. I collect what I need, grab clothes, and make my way back to Isabel.

Except she's no longer there. That, and the room *feels* empty without her in it somehow. The folder on my desk is open, revealing pictures of her, her boyfriend, her work schedule, and a few other documents I collected.

The door is open. *Fuck.*

I grab the folder and my bags and say goodbye to the apartment and everything in it. In the hallway, numbers illuminate above the elevator bank. She's on her way down. I hurry to the stairs. I won't beat her, but she's got nowhere to go.

Heat and ocean air hit my lungs the second I emerge from the building. I'm parked close, and Isabel's already at the car, struggling with the door. I come from behind.

"What the hell are you doing?" I force myself to keep an even tone.

She whips around. Her eyes are wide, and her pupils are dilated. "Let me have my things."

I open the trunk and deposit my bag. "Get in the car."

"I'm not going with you."

She's practically screaming, so I take her firmly by the arm and lead her to the passenger side. She struggles, but I won't let her go. A few more feet and we'll be on our way without making a scene.

"Why do you have all those things about me? How could you be here, this close to me all this time? I need answers, Tristan!"

I open the door, but she fights me.

I lean her against the car and take a handful of her hair, tilting her face up to mine. Before she can say anything more, I'm kissing her. Her hands go to my shoulders, but she's no match for my strength. I kiss her until I feel her fight go.

A small sound escapes her, disappearing in the melding of our lips. My eyes barely close, because I don't trust her, or anyone. As her tongue seeks mine, her flavor floods my senses. Sweet and fresh. Soft surrender. She holds nothing back, so neither do I. I kiss her deeper to take in more of her essence. As I do, my eyes close.

Then she's on the bright-white screen of my mind. The visual is overexposed, like a memory. She's under me. Her body moves with mine. We're fucking. I can feel her everywhere. She's overwhelming all my senses. The fantasy takes hold and arousal prickles my skin— everywhere we touch and everywhere we don't.

Except it all feels too real. Feels too good to be a fantasy. In seconds, my body begins to respond to the closeness of hers. Which is just fucking great.

I can already see this will be yet another distraction I can't afford. I was hired to kill this woman. Now I'm about to kidnap her and keep her until she can tell me things I'm not yet sure I want to know. And all I can think about is getting inside her.

There's no time for this.

I break the kiss and try to mentally erase the disturbing erotic image. But Isabel replaces it in the flesh, breathless, her eyes hazy. She looks how I feel. Overwhelmed. Confused. Ready to fuck.

The pulse at her neck beats rapidly. She might be turned on, but she's scared too. And even if she thinks she knows me, she's too smart to give me her trust. I only need a little of it to get us out of here.

I brush her hair back off her face. I'm not accustomed to charming my way to a desired end, but I manage a small reassuring smile. "I need you to trust me. Okay?"

She softens, but I keep my hold on her.

"I want to," she utters.

It has to be enough. I don't ask, and I don't tell her again. I simply guide her into the car, shut the door, and move back to the driver's seat.

As I start the ignition, I'm anything but relieved.

Two hours go by, and already the drive is too long. Isabel's presence dominates the small space of the car and every crevice of my mind. She chews her lower lip and wrings her fingers as the city turns into jungle and the road narrows. Her fear and uncertainty don't affect me. The longing in her eyes does. Her confusion seems laced with an affection I can't comprehend.

She has questions, and so do I. I have no idea how I'll answer hers. I wasn't prepared for this. I grip the wheel and cycle through my options.

Killing her would have been so much easier. I've built this new life on the surety of the kill. The simplicity of it. Nothing is simple now.

I keep my eyes straight ahead. "We know each other."

A statement. A question.

I could spend days coaxing the truth out of her, pretending to know about whatever connection we share. But if I have to kill her anyway—and despite my strong urge to fuck her, I *will* have to kill her—the truth can do no harm. I realize this in a moment of sudden clarity.

I brave a look in her direction. She stares back in confused silence. "Of course we do."

I break the stare and focus on the road. "How?"

I refuse to meet her gaze again. The late-afternoon sun is setting ahead of us, turning the sky orange and mauve above the trees as we pass through town after town.

"You know…"

I shake my head slightly. "I have gaps"—I swallow hard, pushing down the unwelcome feeling that comes with the truth—"pretty big gaps in my memory. I recognize you. I just have no idea why."

I can feel her gaze hot on me. The air between us is thick with emotions neither of us can fully understand. I turn, and the tears in her eyes confirm the pain I've inflicted with this admission.

"We were in love," she utters, almost too quietly to be heard.

I curse inwardly. Another complication I don't need.

"When?"

"It's been six years since you left."

"Since I left?"

"You joined the military right out of high school. I went to college, but you never came home."

I nod slowly. She's an old girlfriend. From high school, for fuck's sake. Nothing. She's nothing. Lovesick and naïve, thanks to a narrow, privileged existence. If she were important, surely she'd have been *somewhere* in my memories. Somewhere in the dreams or nightmares, the smallest flashes of remembrance, the blurred darkness that is my past.

My stomach clenches. My grip tightens around the wheel. The urge to dig through those clues and learn more is dangerous. For years, I've existed for no other reason than to breathe, point, and shoot. Even if

Jay hasn't all but promised it, inherently, I've always known that reaching beyond that basic state of being is inevitably painful and likely to end in death. Not others' for once, but mine. Yet here I am, seeking out my past. Drawn to the irresistible beacon of Isabel Foster and the things she knows about me.

"If you don't remember me...how did you know where to find me?"

I make a turn onto a dirt road and ease off the gas. Outside of Jay and the people whose light left their eyes at my hand, very few people know exactly what I do. Mateus knows enough to be an ally. I trust him because I did him a favor once, and now he owes me about a thousand in return.

Ahead, a pristine white stucco house is set back on a large lot protected by several feet of well-kept gardens and a wrought-iron gate. I slow at the entrance and dial Mateus's number.

He answers after the first ring. "Tristan?"

"I'm here."

The call ends and the gates, armed by guards on either side, slowly open. I pull through and drive up the winding path to the house. Every inch closer brings an unexpected calm over my rattled nerves. A momentary reprieve is what I need, and I'll find it here.

4

ISABEL

I've never been this far outside the city. Every instinct is shouting at me. It's the same voice that keeps me on high alert when I'm in uncharted territory or edging outside my comfort zone. Tristan leaves the vehicle and pops the trunk, while I hold on to the door handle with a white-knuckled grip. What if this was all a terrible mistake?

I want to trust him. I told him so, but that was two seconds after he kissed me like the Tristan I remember. The second our lips touched, an avalanche of memories rushed in. Stolen moments, heated touches, and forbidden nights. Everything precious that clung to the hurt he'd caused me, making him impossible to forget.

In my periphery, a man descends the white stone steps that lead to the grand entrance of the home. He smiles warmly, and I hear his muffled greeting to Tristan from inside the car. I take a deep breath, gather my resolve, and step out.

"It's good to see you, *meu amigo.*" The man's gaze shifts swiftly to me. "And who is this?" His accent is thick and brusque.

"I'm Isabel." I smile weakly and take his outstretched hand to shake it.

In one fluid motion, he brings it to his lips and brushes a kiss against my skin. The warmth in his dark eyes chases away the discomfort the gesture should give me. The man has charm, and even though my entire life changed a few hours ago, somehow I'm grateful we're here and not someplace even more frightening.

"I'm Mateus da Silva. *Muito prazer em conhecê-la.* Welcome to my home."

"*Obrigada*," I mutter.

Tristan's eyes darken as he hauls our bags over his shoulder. "Shall we?"

"Of course." Mateus hesitates a moment before easing away, nodding toward Tristan, and leading us toward the house.

We step inside onto a well-worn Persian rug that stretches into an expansive living area. The walls are covered with dozens of paintings of varying sizes. Each is trimmed with gold leaf and light dust. Antique furniture hugs the walls and completes several small entertaining areas. The tables are decorated with ornate lamps and bronze statues.

The guards at the gate and the heavily barred windows tell me whatever he keeps in this house is worth protecting. I'm telling myself it has to do with the wall-to-wall antiques and nothing to do with the danger that Tristan insists we're running from.

"Are you hungry from your travels? I can have a meal prepared."

"We'll eat in the room," Tristan answers quickly. "Where are we staying?"

Mateus motions us to follow him down a hall. He seems unaffected by Tristan's grim mood. A sinking feeling washes over me. If this is normal behavior for Tristan, who has he become? Is there anything left of the man I fell in love with so many years ago? I can't think that way...

We pause outside one of the doors, which Mateus pushes open. "The honeymoon suite," he says with a smirk.

Tristan frowns but doesn't reply. He only guides me into the room that matches the rest of the house—rich textures and deep colors. The bed is draped in a red satin bedspread, its ornate metal headboard pressed to the wall like a piece of art in itself.

"I will have Karina bring you dinner. I'll be in the den if you need me, Tristan."

"Thank you," Tristan says after dropping our bags to the floor. He meets Mateus's gaze briefly, and I swear something passes between them. An understanding, a wordless exchange.

"Good night, Isabel." Mateus bows his head before retreating, leaving us alone again.

I walk to the window. Through the bars, all I can see are trees and the winding drive up to the house. I wrap my arms around myself and turn to face Tristan.

"Are you going to give me my phone now?"

My first two requests were refused, which only ramped up my panic on the ride here.

"Not yet."

I tense with renewed anxiety. Then I remind myself that I know Tristan. Maybe he doesn't know me, but once upon a time, he was a man I could trust. A good man.

"I left with you without telling anyone. I have a job and a life and friends who—"

"I'm sure your boyfriend can live without you for a few days." He stands in the middle of the room with his arms crossed. The muscles in his jaw tighten, and the air becomes thick with tension I don't understand.

Then I remember the photos of Kolt and me together in his file. "Are you talking about Kolt?"

He shrugs slightly. "The American who can't keep his hands off you."

My cheeks heat like I've been caught doing something wrong. "Kolt isn't my boyfriend."

He lifts an eyebrow but otherwise maintains an inexpressive countenance. In an instant, I want him to be jealous, because it means something still exists between us. He was so possessive once. So convinced that we were meant to be together, two halves of a whole that no amount of time or distance could keep apart.

I drop my hands to my sides. "Would you care if he were?"

"No," he says flatly.

His blunt answer lashes back at me, reward for an indulgent moment of yearning for his affection again after such an absence. "What do you want from me, Tristan?"

He stares at me a moment before turning toward the crushed-velvet couch that lines one wall of the room. He sits down and drops his head into his hands. "I'm still trying to figure that out."

For the first time since he kissed me, I sense his vulnerability. I fight the urge to go to him and wrap my arms around him. My fingers itch to touch him. But what good can my touch do when he doesn't know me? I still can't fathom that our entire history has been erased. A part of me refuses to believe it's true.

I swallow over the painful tightness in my throat. "What really happened to you?"

"I don't know very much," he says. "When I woke up… Everything was kind of a blur. Jay—" A deep groove cuts between his dark brows. "I had been on a tour overseas, on a special ops team. A mission went wrong…really wrong. I guess it was bad enough that my life in the military was over and my freedom would be in jeopardy if I didn't disappear. Someone on the inside pulled strings to give me a second chance. A chance to start over as someone else."

"When did this happen?"

"Three years ago. Everything before that…it's just flashes. So small that I can't tell if it's real or just my imagination. Kind of like a dream you can't fully remember."

The last letter from Tristan had come to me six months after his enlistment. Long before this incident occurred. When he said goodbye and ended things between us, he had his memory. Six agonizing years compound onto my heart. The emotional pain turns physical as my chest constricts and pinpricks cut into my palms.

He looks up at me, his eyes clear and wide. For the first time, I'm convinced of the emptiness of his memories. I push my pain away and reach for compassion. If he brought us here to fill in the gaps, I'm probably the only one who can help.

"Why did you bring me here?"

His lips thin and his features tighten. "It's not safe for you in Rio. Not anymore."

I jump at a knock at the door. Tristan rises as a beautiful young woman arrives with a tray full of dishes in her arms. He relieves her of it, and she closes the door. He sets the tray on the table by the bed and gestures toward it.

"Eat." He turns away and shoves his hands into his pockets.

"Aren't you hungry?"

"No."

I huff, cross my arms, and ignore the pang in my stomach. I powered through my lunch, but the stress of the afternoon and the hours passed have me starving. Still, bigger issues loom. I'm not ready to accept his silence and avoidance.

"You need to talk to me, Tristan. You can't leave me in the dark."

He spins back, his eyes narrowed. "In the dark? My past is pitch black, Isabel."

I hesitate, momentarily thrown by his anger. "I'm sorry, but—"

"You're sorry? You have no idea who or what you're dealing with." His tone is low and, if I didn't know better, threatening. "And I don't need your goddamn pity. Eat your dinner."

My temper flares at his words. In an instant, I forget that Tristan is essentially a stranger off the street. I push to my feet and get so close our faces are mere inches apart.

"You either talk to me or I'm going home. I don't care how dangerous you say it is."

I expect anger, but his expression flattens into a hard calm. Somehow that's even scarier.

"You're not leaving here, Isabel."

There's something final about his tone, nearly knocking the wind out of me.

I maneuver past him and go for my bag. Before I can get to it, he's between me and the door.

"I don't think you heard me. You're *not* leaving."

I place my hands on his chest to push him away, but the second I attempt it, I'm stumbling backward. He bands his arms around my torso, dragging us toward the bed. My hands are free, so I pound against his shoulders and struggle against his massive strength.

"Let me go! Let me go, or I'll scream!"

I'm already yelling, but he doesn't seem to care. My heart is racing, and hateful tears burn behind my eyes. Inside, I'm at war with my innate trust in him and the fear he inspires.

Any possibility of escape is squashed when I realize he's got me entirely immobile—hands around my wrists and his hard, heavy body pinning me flat to the bed, my legs kicking feebly off the edge. He repositions my wrists into one of his hands, reaches behind his back, and retrieves a sliver of plastic.

I scream and pray that Mateus's earlier affection might save me now.

But he never shows, and Tristan has deftly cinched each wrist to the metal bedposts. The cable tie is thin enough to sting me when I test it but thick enough that I don't have a chance of breaking it without really hurting myself.

As quickly as he secured me, he lifts off me twice as fast.

He paces once around the room.

"Why are you doing this?" My voice is weak and watery. I can't fight him now. I can only appeal to his humanity.

He stops and pivots in my direction. His eyes are ice. No shred of the man I knew. A second later, he's out the door and I'm alone. I cry and then I scream. I scream until my throat burns. Until the sky fades into a black night and sleep overwhelms me.

TRISTAN

"Who is the girl?"

Mateus shuffles barefoot toward the sideboard that holds a few bottles of his favorite liquors and a set of cut glasses. His linen clothing hangs loosely on his short and stocky frame. His calm expression and easy movements are perfectly relaxed. He's at home, appearing so comfortable that I have no choice but to feel at home myself, as much as I ever could.

Part of Mateus's gift is his ability to put people at ease. That's also what makes him lethal. No one ever sees him coming.

"No one of importance, as far as I can tell," I say.

An old girlfriend. I chastise myself for this new fact as a smirk curves Mateus's cheek.

"You don't expect me to believe that, do you?"

He brings me a tumbler of clear liquid muddled with limes. One sniff, and I identify the local brand of cachaça. The essence of sugarcane fills my mouth, but the lime clears it away, inviting me to another taste. I swallow, welcome the sensation, and exhale a sigh.

I close my eyes and think about her taste. The way it consumed me when I had it on my tongue. Then doubt and rational thought wash it away.

When I open my eyes, Mateus is sitting on the adjacent couch watching me. Tan leather cracked with wear and use slides under his palm as he rests it on the arm.

"She is very beautiful," he says.

I nod. Isabel's beauty is indisputable. I just wish it was the only thing drawing me to her.

"She looks at you like you are precious to her. I had no idea such a creature could exist in your world."

I take another swallow and weigh my next words. Everything about this situation is uncomfortable for me. My past is foreign soil, a battleground I've never seen before. I'm unarmed and completely unready for it.

"I knew her once," I finally admit.

"And now you are protecting her?"

"The opposite, actually."

I don't need to say any more. Mateus can put the pieces together. He frowns, and his lips form a wrinkled line.

"I see. So why have you brought her here?"

"I need time. She knows things…" I pinch the bridge of my nose, still uncertain how long it'll take for me to explore this newfound curiosity about my past. "Someone will notice she's gone soon enough. Probably her boyfriend or her coworkers. Then her family back in the States will know something's gone wrong. I don't have much time. You don't have to worry. We won't be here long."

He sweeps his hand in a gesture between us. "You can stay as long as you need to."

"I won't make this your mess. Not in your home."

He lifts an eyebrow and cocks his head. "If you must, you know I will oblige. Even if it costs me this refuge. My debt has not been paid."

"I'm in no rush for you to pay it." Calling Mateus's debt over this would be foolish. I may have left Rio in a rush, but I still have time and space to maneuver.

Mateus sighs heavily. "Perhaps one day, if the devil doesn't take us too soon, you'll tell me your story."

I muster a laugh. "Perhaps if I knew it, I'd tell you."

Mateus's eyes soften with understanding. We've hardly bared our souls to one another, but he knows my past is beyond reach. Oddly I think he counts my anonymity as an asset to our friendship.

"If your past is dark, how do you know who she is?"

I pause and relive that moment of recognition as she sat in the café this afternoon. Life had been different seconds before.

"She recognizes me. She knows me." I frown hard. "We were lovers. She hasn't forgotten, and I have no way of remembering."

"*Meu Deus*, Tristan! How can you let her go?" Mateus's cool calm breaks as he leans forward, resting his forearms on his thighs.

I shrug. "It's her or me."

He cusses under his breath and rises to his feet. He crosses the long room, opens a drawer at his desk, and returns.

"Here," he says, pushing a blackened silver frame into my hands.

I open it like a book, and it parts stiffly. Inside, two ornately trimmed ovals reveal faded photographs. On each side, a woman and a man are dressed in clothing from a couple generations past.

I lift my gaze to him. "Your parents?"

He nods. "My sister raised me. My father opposed the regime, so they burned down our home. My parents were tied down, brutalized while my sister and I sneaked away. We couldn't save them. Days later, we found this in the rubble. A miracle." He's silent a moment, his gaze on the frame. "Their enemies wanted them to disappear. No body, no voice, no grave beyond the ashes of our home. But this…" He leans in and drops his thick fingertip onto the center of his mother's photograph. "This is a memory they could not destroy."

When he pulls back, I close the frame gently and hand it back to him. "You're lucky to have found it."

He whips it from my grasp. "And you, *idiota*, are lucky to have her. She is your memory. She is your living and breathing miracle." He shakes the frame at me once more before returning it back to his desk, slamming the drawer firmly shut.

He returns and drops on the couch. I marvel at Mateus's break in composure. I've only seen him beyond reason one other time. Those were memories neither of us wished to relive. But this is different. He's emotional over memories he holds. I have nothing like that.

"She's going to get me killed," I finally say. Suddenly, despite everything I've told myself, I know this to be true. Isabel is difficult and impulsive. No reasonable person would leave her life behind on a whim to come with me—a stranger. She's unpredictable and far too attached to the person I once was. And already I can feel her reaching for more.

Mateus rests his empty glass on the table beside him and spins it rhythmically.

"People are always wishing away their bad memories. *Meu Deus, I wish I could forget. Make it go away.* Ah!" He flicks his hand. "They only wish away the pain it brings them. Me? I would rather die than live as you have, Tristan. Nothing but death to drive you forward. If hers will keep you on this path, you have nothing to live for."

I hold my teeth together, bearing down against the impact of his words. "And what do you live for? Vengeance? How is that life better?"

Mateus's expression relaxes a fraction. "Tristan... You are vengeance for hire, for those who don't have the heart or the *colhões* to pull the trigger themselves."

I down the rest of my drink and rise to my feet. I pace around the room, chasing the flurry of thoughts that accuse and contradict and provide no true answers. Mateus is perhaps my only friend, and he could be right. If Isabel dies, by my hand or any other, her memories of my life die with her.

I shove my hands through my hair with a pained sound. Why do I fucking care? Living with darkness might not be a life worth living, but it was vastly simpler. Nothing is simple now.

"Tristan."

I turn as Mateus speaks. His eyes are soft with understanding, but everything else—his posture, the tension that lines his shoulders— speaks of his newfound determination to guide me through this.

"Go to her. She has the answers."

5

TRISTAN

A small click and the pelt of rain against the windows are the only sounds as I enter the room. Isabel is asleep. Her body lies diagonally on the bare bed. The satin bedspread and sheets have been kicked to the floor. Suspended by the restraints, her arms are stretched above her, obscuring her face.

I switch on the lamp beside the couch. The tray of dishes remains untouched, and I'm momentarily grateful Karina didn't return for them while I was gone. Isabel would have begged to be freed, unknowing that Karina is also Mateus's lover and would never betray him.

I circle the bed without a sound, gaining a better view of Isabel's face. Dried tears streak her cheeks. Her lips and eyes are puffy. I don't enjoy the misery that's only just begun for her. She's trapped here, but so am I.

Every hour that passes with her in my world awakens compassion I didn't know I possessed. I resent her for it, even if I can't deny it.

I retrieve a knife from my pocket and cut through the plastic bonds. Her eyes open wide. She scrambles away from me the second she's free enough to move. She glances around the room and then down at her wrists, which are red and will likely bruise by morning. She rubs them but says nothing.

"I'm sorry," I finally say.

She laughs roughly. "You're sorry?"

"If you understood the danger we're in, you'd know leaving here without me is impossible."

She swallows but doesn't meet my eyes. "If you explained why we're in danger, maybe I wouldn't have wanted to leave."

I reach for her, but she flinches back. She slides her stormy gaze to mine. Slowly, I take her hand, tracing the grooves at her wrist with my thumb.

I slide my hand into hers. I don't know why I do it. But the contact, palm to palm, sends a shockwave over my nerves. It's not the vague familiarity I've experienced before with her. It's something more... something primal...deeper.

Her gaze settles there. Her lips part, as if she feels it too.

"You have something valuable of mine," I say. "I have to protect you, even if that means protecting you from yourself sometimes. You'll have to forgive me because I'm not in the business of protecting anyone. You'll just have to learn to trust me."

She doesn't show acceptance in any way. She only stares at me. The mix of concern and devotion passing over her features is troubling, making me feel like a stranger in my own skin.

Exhaustion tugs at my body. Knowing she could run, or worse, will make it difficult to drift off, but the thought of lying down beside her promises something soothing.

"Come on. Let's get some sleep."

I get up and replace the blankets on the bed. I kick off my shoes and untuck my gun, placing it on the bedside table nearest to me. I hear Isabel's sharp intake of breath before I catch the fear in her eyes.

"For protection," I say, reassuring her. And myself.

I take life day by day, hour by hour. Everything could change tomorrow. But right now, she's safe with me.

⊕

I move around the tiny kitchen. She'll be home soon, and I'll have food ready for her before I head to school. She's been working all night.

That's when I hear it. Gunshots. The familiar sound freezes me in place. My heart stops beating. They're too close.

I fly to the door. Her car is parked in her usual spot, a few spaces down from the entrance to the house. The driver's-side door is wide open, but she's not getting out.

The distant sound of shoes scuffing swiftly on pavement tears my attention from the car. Gray sweatpants and hoodie… Running down the street. He's too far away, going too fast. There's no time if…

I run to the driver's side of the car.

I can no longer feel my body. I'm dead inside, because in that instant, I know she is too.

No hope. No praying. Her body is punctured with wounds. All I can see is red. Her neck is twisted awkwardly, no longer able to support the weight of her head.

Her purse hangs from her lifeless arm. The possessions of her purse are scattered on the street.

She wouldn't let it go.

I reach for her and pull her into my arms. Her weight is too much. I fall to the ground with her. She's gone, but she's still warm. The last of her life weeps from the holes he shot through her body. For the contents of her purse.

I hold her. I can't let her go. I can't leave her when this is all we have. Seconds…

Our silence gives way to sirens in the distance. Shouts and cries of people who mean nothing to me. Because she was everything. The beginning and the end.

Then all I can hear are screams. The screams are mine, and even as they pierce the air, I know they're not enough to bring her back.

"Mom! Mom!"

ISABEL

Tristan's low, painful moans cut through the night.

The lamp is off, so the faint moonlight through the window reveals just the basic outline of his still-clothed body. We're only inches apart on the bed.

I'm afraid to move or touch him. The past several hours in Tristan's presence has taught me at least one thing. He's unpredictable. Even though he's asked for my trust, I'm not sure I can give it. Not until he proves to me that he's capable of being the Tristan I once knew. With his memory gone, I fear that's an impossible dream.

I toyed with the prospect of escape as we fell silent in the darkness hours earlier. But I thought better of a renewed attempt, and eventually sleep overtook me once more. Now, no matter what logic and self-preservation shout at me, my heart is breaking at Tristan's nightmare.

His voice belongs to the old Tristan. The boy who shared his tears and racking sobs only with me in the days after his mother's tragic death. I know the source of his pain. The thought that in consciousness he may not tugs at my growing pity for him and his situation.

To the point where I can't stay away.

I roll slowly toward him so my front is barely pressed to his side. His breathing catches, and then he stills. Unsure if he's awake and aware of me, I don't dare speak. I press my nose against the collar of his shirt. I couldn't forget that smell in a million years. The smell of Tristan in my arms, in my bed.

As his breathing evens out, I ease my arm across his torso. As soon as I'm there, his hand is wrapped over mine, tucking me tight against him. I tense at the sudden contact and then relax, melting into his warmth and unexpected affection.

"Sleep, Isabel." The command is almost tender in his sleepy rasp.

"You were dreaming."

He's silent for several seconds. "I'm awake now. Get some rest."

I lift my head from his shoulder and take in his shadowed features.

Indeed, he appears fully awake now. Any vulnerability from the dream has fallen away.

I inch my palm up, resting it over his heart. Its rapid beats don't match his measured breaths or guarded expression. If only I could reach into this man and find the lover I once knew. What would it be like to escape into the deep, haunting bliss of our bodies finding perfect harmony?

His shadowed gaze offers no consolation, no promise that he'll ever be more than the kind of man who can tie me to a bed and leave me screaming for help without a second thought. Yet having him near—blood and heat and his inexplicable intensity humming against my skin, searing me despite our clothes—is both the answer to a prayer and the beginning of what I fear could become a nightmare worse than his disappearance.

I withdraw my touch and turn from him. Far enough so I can no longer feel his heat. I close my eyes and hug my pillow. Wanting anything more from him is dangerous. In less than twenty-four hours, he's simultaneously turned my world upside down and ripped me from it. I need answers. I need rest. God knows what tomorrow will bring.

The sound of the shower running wakes me. I blink against the late morning sunrays blasting through the barred window. This isn't a dream. I'm still in Mateus's home, which means Tristan is in the adjoining bathroom.

I'm furious to find that he's bound one of my wrists to the bed. I survey the room, wondering where he keeps his stash of zip ties. I kick the sheets and prepare to start screaming my head off again, when my foot touches something cool and hard on the side where Tristan slept. I grasp it with my toes enough to draw it into view. It's the pocket knife he used to release me from the ties last night. He must have forgotten about it in the moments after.

I nudge it up the bed a few inches at a time.

Water crashes in the shower, competing with the loud drumming of my heart in my ears. Every second that passes seems perilous, knowing Tristan could return before I have a chance to cut myself free.

I twist and maneuver until I can reach it. Finally I'm able to unlatch the blade. The simple act releases a shot of adrenaline to my system. The hit is so strong, I can hardly think through what I need to do next.

I'm trembling but manage to cut the thick plastic zip tie. I roll off the bed swiftly, my muscles charged and my head buzzing. With the weapon in my hand, I have options I never had before.

Tristan is only a few steps away. The man I never stopped loving. The stranger he's become.

I'm at war with his contradicting interactions with me. His unexpected tenderness mixed with his unforgiving tones and domineering behavior. But this could be my only chance to break free during daylight.

All I can do is act. Run.

I put on my shoes and grab my backpack. I quietly exit the bedroom. My heart hammers in my chest anticipating Tristan's reaction when he finds out I'm gone. Will he try to find me? Somehow I already know he will. But for how long?

The more pressing question is how the hell I'll get out of Mateus's compound. I reach the front door and remember the armed guards who manned the gates down the path. I know nothing about this place or Tristan's so-called friend, but I'm guessing leaving undetected may not be as straightforward as waltzing out the front door.

All too aware of the dwindling moments before Tristan discovers I'm missing, I venture into other rooms of the house. The foyer opens into a sitting room with several accent chairs around a coffee table. I walk along a wall of bookshelves without making a sound. I peek through a doorway into a kitchen decorated with hand-painted tiles. Karina's back is to me as she chops food facing the farthest wall.

I step back into the sitting room and consider the double doors that open to the back of the property. Carefully I slide open the door, step onto the patio, and glance around. The gardens behind the house are vast, lush, and mercifully empty of people. I move quickly, eager to reach the perimeter of the property, when a familiar voice stops me.

"Isabel. It that you?"

Panic seizes my breath. I turn my head. Mateus is coming toward me from some hidden place in the gardens. He doesn't rush. His gait is casual and comfortable, as if all of this is perfectly normal. Tristan's knife is hidden in my fist. I ready myself to use it, an anxious tremble taking over my limbs once more.

But as Mateus slows before me, his countenance is so easy and warm, I can't help but relax a little. I exhale shakily. Maybe he can help. Maybe he could be a friend…

"Isabel. Where are you running to?"

"I have to leave." I try to keep my tone even and calm. Like I'm not a prisoner on the run. Like I'm a free woman with the right to come and go as I wish. I fear I'm anything but.

He assesses me quickly, his eyes lighting on my backpack slung over my shoulder and then my closed fist.

"Where is Tristan?"

His tone doesn't change. But in his question lies another… *Does he know you're trying to leave?*

I shake my head. "Please. Just let me go."

His gaze drops again to my closed fist. "What have you got there?"

I swallow hard. I grip the knife tight again, but my palms are so slick with sweat, it slips from my grasp, rattling on the pebbled stone patio.

I curse my foible as Mateus bends to retrieve the knife. Straightening, he rolls it around in his palm, eyeing it carefully.

"Is this yours?"

I clench my jaw and lower my voice. "It's Tristan's." I pause a moment. "Can you help me leave?"

His gaze is like a tractor beam on me, full of knowing. Not unkind. A hint of compassion, maybe a touch of humor, but nothing that tells me he'll help.

"You may already know that Tristan is a very dangerous man. He's also my friend. I would never betray him."

"But he's keeping me prisoner here." I can barely contain the outrage in my voice. No one's been able to hold me against my will since… I clamp my eyes closed and reason that the emotional prison of my youth is nothing like the situation in which I now find myself.

"I keep my treasures locked away as well. You must be very important to him."

"He doesn't seem to think so."

The humor flees Mateus's features. "He does, Isabel. You are a miracle. The key—"

"To his memories. I know." I toss up my hand and try to ignore the burn of the truth.

"It hurts you," he says with a cadence that feels like a direct hit, "that he doesn't remember you."

"How could it not?"

"Do you think you can get him to remember again?"

I shrug. "I have no idea."

He gazes at me silently, as if in challenge. I've been so busy making sense of our mad dash from the city and his odd confession that I've hardly considered the possibility. Could I really make Tristan remember what he's lost? Could I possibly have that much power?

"Isabel! Where are you?"

I jolt back at the sound of Tristan's voice bellowing through the house.

Precious seconds pass, and then he's at the sliding door. He looks around the garden but doesn't notice us right away.

"Right here, friend," Mateus says loudly but with that even quality he possesses that seems to lull one into believing everything is as it should be.

Tristan is there a moment later, and then I have two men staring at me like I've just committed a cardinal sin. Tristan is wearing only his black jeans, a dark T-shirt twisted in his fist. His skin is flushed, and his wet hair sends rivulets down his neck. A few travel down his chest, journeying across a map of scars that mar at least a dozen points on his skin. Most are white with age, ghosts of the pain inflicted upon his flesh. Some are clean and straight. Others are jagged and ugly, raised and broad from lack of proper suturing. Each one is a fresh tear in the inner fabric of my being, claiming space on the landscape of my own invisible scars.

"Tristan…" I whisper his name as heat burns behind my eyes. Who did this to him?

"What are you doing out here?" He darts his gaze over me, no doubt arriving at the same conclusions as Mateus.

I tighten my grip around the strap of my backpack and speak as calmly as my clenched jaw will allow. "You can't keep me here against my will."

Mateus's raised eyebrow answers for him. Still, my focus is on Tristan. I cling to the anger that motivated me to run. But his scarred body has me in knots, the compass of my will spinning wildly.

Mateus offers the knife. Tristan swipes it from him and jerks his thumb toward the house.

"Inside. Now."

"Karina will have lunch for us shortly." Mateus hesitates a second. "Or perhaps you should go into town. Explore a little," he says coolly as he turns toward Tristan. "You have things to discuss, after all."

Hope springs in me at the prospect of escaping the property, even with Tristan, but his grimace dashes every ounce of it.

"We're not leaving."

Mateus squares his body with Tristan's a fraction more. "Why? Petrópolis is big enough to get lost in. You said yourself you have time."

I still at the firmness in Mateus's tone. I care less about his cryptic challenge than the fact that he's facing off with Tristan, a man he's already admitted is truly dangerous. Can Mateus set him off as easily as I seem to be able to?

"Is this your way of asking me to leave?"

"You know it isn't."

A moment of silence passes between them, and I resist the urge to back away and give the two men space.

"To capture what we most desire, sometimes we must first learn to let go," Mateus utters quietly.

Tristan is silent, his body a physical representation of his mood, rigid with frustration.

He looks at me, jerks his shirt over his head, and punches his arms through the sleeves. He motions for my bag. "Leave your things."

I don't move. My grip tightens on the bag. My identity. Money. I'm wary to part with either under the present circumstances.

"Isabel." His sharp tone nips at the edge of my control.

I sling the bag at him in one sudden motion. "*Tristan*," I hiss.

I pass him and return to the house, but not before catching the curl of Mateus's lips and a flicker of mischief in his eyes.

6

TRISTAN

I scan the busy street, up and down and back again, committing it all to memory. Petrópolis is vastly smaller than the metropolis we came from, but Mateus is right. It's big enough to disappear in, for a little while at least, and the Carnaval celebrations don't hurt. The people gracing the streets are raising no alarms, but I can't escape the feeling that could change at any moment.

"Are you looking for someone?" Isabel sits across from me.

We're at a little restaurant on the edge of town that Mateus recommended, but she's barely eaten. Instead, she's staring at me as if she'll find a doorway to my soul. Too bad there's no chance of that.

"I am," I say.

"Who?"

"Someone who might be here for the wrong reasons."

She sighs and leans her head to the side, as if all of this has become an exhausting game. "Who would that be?"

I look around again, seeing no one of concern. Still, I take nothing for granted. "Your guess is as good as mine."

"I doubt it. You've been acting like someone's been chasing us since we got here."

"If they aren't yet, they will be."

She glares at me, her expression falling somewhere between panic and skepticism. "Tristan, what the hell is going on? Why would you say that?"

We live such different lives. We've been sitting here less than twenty minutes, and I've already grown tired of dancing around her innocent questions. I look her square in the eye, readying myself for the real panic to set in after I say what I need to.

"Someone wants you dead."

She exhales, her breath audibly rushing past her trembling lips. "How... How can you know that?"

"The important thing is that I know. Because I do, I can make sure they don't get what they want."

She stares into her lap and grips her paper napkin tightly.

"Is it the same people who put those scars on your body?"

I shake my head slightly. I don't know where half my scars came from, but I'm certain they're not the same bad guys who want Isabel knocked off.

"Different people," I say a little softer, sensing the heaviness of this subject might send her into an emotional fit—one I'm not especially eager to deal with in public. The last thing I need is for Isabel to make a scene.

"Why would someone want me dead?"

Her question has merit. I'm not paid to care why someone needs to be taken out, but I'm confident Isabel hasn't done anything to deserve a death wish. She's a revenge hit. Her death will send a message, maybe a warning, to someone who cares about her. If I had to guess, that person is her father.

"I'm not exactly sure why yet," I finally say.

"Then how do you know they want me dead? You're talking in riddles, Tristan."

Her voice is edging on hysterical.

"The less you know, the better. I'm only telling you so you know how dangerous it is to run from me when I'm the one trying to keep you safe. And right now, I am the *only* one who can keep you safe. Do not doubt it," I say with finality.

I run the words over in my head, convincing myself of them too. I need to keep her safe. Need to figure out a plan that will get us out of this mess alive.

Or you could skip the mess and end this now. Do your job. To hell with the past.

I wince and take another scan up and down the street.

"If that's all true, I suppose that explains why you've been so… determined." Her voice is steadier now. She juts her chin out almost defiantly. "So what happens now? We can't hide out at your friend's house forever. I have a life back in Rio. I'm sure you do too."

I stir my coffee and lift the tiny red straw to my lips. I trap the tip between my teeth and contemplate my next words.

I have a few options, most of which I'll never tell her. I could attempt to stay in Jay's good graces and do the job I was hired to do. Except now I've taken Isabel out of the city, no doubt raising suspicions about my ability to follow through. Then there's Mateus, who's become inexplicably driven to unearth the memories Isabel and I share.

"You know things…"

"About your past," she finishes the thought. "And now you expect me to be able to fill in all the blanks while we're here."

"I'm resourceful. I just need a place to start, and I can figure out most of the rest."

She swallows without making eye contact. "Why did you kiss me?"

I gnash the straw a few times. "I needed you to cooperate," I admit.

"Right. It's not like we were in love or anything." Her voice gets softer as she speaks, like she's no longer talking to me.

But her words are an invitation I'll never be able to accept. Whatever she still feels for me has to fade out. I'll never be the boy of her dreams or the lover who stars in her fantasies. The mere thought of it scares me enough to believe that stealing her away from Rio was a horrible idea.

"I'm not in love with you, Isabel."

She nods tightly and looks out the window. A few people walk into the shop on the corner. Her focus is fixed on the church across the street, though. Streaks of dirt stain the stucco below its windows. Three thin crosses mounted on the roof's round arches pierce the blue afternoon sky.

"I think this is a nightmare," she whispers.

"You have no idea," I mutter, regretting it immediately.

She looks back to me, her expression pinched with pity. Of all the things we don't know about each other, I don't have to explain my nightmares now. She was a firsthand witness to the effects of last night's horrors. God knows what I said in my sleep.

"I was with you after she died, you know."

"My mother," I mutter matter-of-factly, though I'm certain a deeper pain exists somewhere inside me.

"She was a really sweet woman. You were close. I stayed with you for a couple weeks after she died. My parents were pissed, but I didn't care. I couldn't leave you alone."

When Isabel's soul-piercing stare creeps under my skin, it's my turn to gaze at the church. The bright cerulean blue fence around it matches the sky, a vibrant distraction from the darkness of my dreams. Whoever my mother was, I know she died in my arms. If the recurring nightmare hasn't confirmed it, Isabel just did.

If these are my memories, who needs them?

"Maybe my nightmares are better than the truth. I should just be happy with an abridged version, the version my mind lets me remember."

"For what it's worth, you don't seem happy at all."

I laugh at the ridiculousness of her statement. "I'd agree with you if I had any sense of the word."

"You never feel joy."

I shake my head, feeling nothing as I do. "I survive." *I try not to get killed.*

The glimmer in her eyes seems like it might spill over into actual tears. She blinks them away rapidly and points toward the church. "I'm going over there for a few minutes, if that's okay."

My immediate response is *Hell no*, but I can't get the words out before she rises and gets several paces ahead of me. She leaves the restaurant and crosses the street to the gate that separates the building from the curb. I chase her and catch up as she reaches for the latch on the gate.

"Wait." I cover her hand with mine, trying to ignore how the smallest touch affects me.

"Wait for what?"

There's peace in her eyes. Sadness and confusion too, but under it all is a layer of stillness that I can hardly understand.

"I'm not going in there," I say firmly.

She stares steadily at me. "Are you afraid?"

I grimace, both at her question and the odd twist of emotions it inspires. Afraid? Of a church? It's all I can do to hold back the nervous laugh that wants to break free.

"No, but I'm not letting you out of my sight, which means you're not going in there."

I curl my fingers over hers, reveling in the silkiness of them as I struggle with her request. "Let's just go back—"

A door creaks loudly. "*Posso te ajudar?*"

An elderly man steps down from the entrance toward us. He's in black garb, and a string of rosaries dangles from his neck. His skin is mottled and lined with age. One eye is clouded white. Both lower when the high noon sun catches the silver circle at Isabel's neck.

"*São Paulo*," he says with a kind smile.

Isabel fingers the delicate pendant of St. Paul that rests at her clavicle. I noticed it before, briefly. Noticed it first when she was moaning my name two nights ago. When I was a reflex away from ending her life. I haven't given it much thought until now.

I can see her pulse ticking beneath the thin chain. The charm interrupts the bare beauty of the woman who wears it. Her skin shimmers like a sea of Moroccan sand. The sharp line of her collarbone slopes to her shoulder, disappearing under her shirt.

I memorize her. Desire I can't understand inspires dangerous visions. Trapping her against me in the middle of the street. Declaring war with the barriers of her clothing. Baring her. The rest of her perfect skin. Inch by inch, I unveil her in my mind. The sounds she'd make under me. The fear and desire I'd recognize with a single taste.

Something tightens in my gut at the memory of her taste. Something beyond the eagerness of her kiss. The desperation. The asking in it. No, the pure taste of her. The melding of our mouths. The familiarity of it. The way I knew her lips were mine the minute I felt them. And her tongue. The hot and greedy cavern of her perfect mouth.

I'm ready to turn the wanton cravings into truth when her rose-colored lips curve into a soft smile for the old man. In that moment, I force myself to see her as he does. Innocent next to the likes of me. A beautiful young girl. Full of life. Clinging to faith. Hope.

"*Me chamo Antonio. Qual é o seu nome?*"

"Isabel."

He nods, rests his gaze on her for one thoughtful moment before lifting it to me.

"*E você. Qual é o seu nome?*" he says, as if I can be lured in with such a simple request.

The warmth I felt a moment ago in my visions of Isabel and all the carnal things I yearn to do to her crashes like a deluge to the ground beneath my feet, leaving me cold and sober.

I'm me again, and I have no business here.

I step away, dragging my hand away from the gate latch, disconnecting from Isabel's defiant hold on it.

"Tristan," she says. "His name is Tristan Stone."

Isabel's eyes storm when they meet mine, like some sort of mystic who knows all my darkest secrets. Or just a beautiful woman who knows my name…

ISABEL

Any fleeting comfort I felt on the doorstep of the church is swiftly ripped away when Tristan takes my hand, his grasp firm, and pulls me away from the half-blind father who would have welcomed us with open arms. I don't know what drew me there. Perhaps a moment's peace, but that's become impossible now.

I glance back at the old man, gulping down emotion I fear has no place in my current predicament. The priest draws his hand up toward the gate latch, lingering there, his eyes wide and more alert than they'd been moments ago. Tristan doesn't give him a chance. We're down the street. I'm tucked into the car seconds later. And we're off, speeding through town.

I stare at Tristan, regret and misery lodged in my throat. "Who are you?"

"No one you know." He jerks the gear shift, lurching us forward at a faster speed. "If you knew me, you'd know that's the last place I belong. And what in the *hell* were you thinking? Do you think this is a joke? Do you think there's a chance someone isn't out there right now on our scent, trying to figure out where I've taken you?"

"He's a priest. He's harmless."

"Everyone can be bought. *Everyone.* I don't care how compassionate or kind you think they are. Everyone has a price."

"You really believe that."

He stares blankly ahead. "Words to live by. It's not a hard lesson. I'd suggest you learn it before you get us killed."

I shove a hand through my already tousled hair, incensed. "Tristan, why don't you just take what you want from me and let me go home? If you don't already know who my father is, believe me when I tell you that he can protect me."

"The people who want you dead don't care about your father's security clearances in DC."

I hesitate a moment. "If we're not safe here, then send me home."

My panic climbs with his silence.

"Tristan…"

He turns onto the dirt road that leads to Mateus's compound. My prison.

"No," he says firmly.

The rumble of the car quiets beneath the thrumming of my blood in my ears. I'm afraid and angry. And I'm suddenly aware of what might have possessed my mother when she fought with my father. Late at night when they thought I was sleeping, I would hear her words flying—a mix of language, her voice imbued with the kind of rage I could never comprehend. Then, sometimes, I'd witness her violence. From the upstairs hallway, hidden by darkness, I'd watch my father restrain her, calm her. Beyond that, he never retaliated.

Until this moment, I never believed I could be capable of such intensely negative emotions toward the man I loved. As I dig my fingernails into the car's seat, I imagine doing the unthinkable. I have to get away.

I reach for the door handle and unlatch it.

"Isabel!"

We swerve as Tristan reaches across the seat to pull me back. He slams on the brakes and eases the car onto the side of the narrow road.

"What the hell do you think you're doing?"

His proximity and anger should frighten me, but I'm too fired up. I match his furious stare and yell, "What do you want from me?"

His nostrils flare. "For starters, I want you to stop trying to jump out of the goddamn car."

"Why do you care?"

"Because I'm trying to keep you safe." He yanks the door shut tightly and leans back, putting space between us again. "If I'd known you had a death wish, I would have kept you tied to the bed or—"

"Or what?"

"Never mind."

My heart thunders in my chest. Something in his voice changes when he talks about keeping me safe. Something that niggles at my instincts. I still love him, even if it's just the memory of him. But the more time we spend together, the less I trust the man beside me.

"What. Do. You. Want?"

He turns off the ignition, letting silence settle around us.

"Tristan—"

"My mother. Just…" He closes his eyes and swallows. "Just start there, okay? It's the most vivid memory I have."

A few minutes pass between us. Our breathing slows. Gradually, the fury between us turns into something else.

"Her name was Grace. She worked as a nurse in Baltimore. She was coming off the night shift at the hospital when it happened." I hesitate, reliving the sadness. "It was awful. The police had a couple leads but never caught the guy who did it. I often wondered if they had, if things would have been different."

He looks up at me, silently asking for more.

"You changed," I say quietly.

"How?"

I exhale slowly, taking myself back to that time. The tragedy had changed us both.

"Something went dark inside you. At first, I didn't think it would change *us*, because we were closer than ever. Unshakable. But plans we'd made began to shift little by little. When we were together, sometimes it felt like you were somewhere else. I worried that you'd never make peace with it."

"And then I left."

I nod. "We'd both applied to a few schools. I got acceptances from some Ivy League schools, so my parents were obviously breathing down my neck about that. But we both got into UCLA. It was kind of like our little escape plan. You wanted to get away from your past. I wanted to get out of DC."

"Let me guess. The plan changed."

"We were ready to send in our acceptance letters when you changed your mind. An army recruiter reached out to you right around then and started filling your head with all the possibilities."

"Then what happened?"

"I ended up staying close to home for school. I felt tethered to DC, like if I went too far I'd never see you again. Didn't end up mattering, I guess. You left for basic training. I remember you kept saying, 'I've got to do this. It's the right thing to do.'" I close my eyes. "If you want to know the truth, I think you needed to take your revenge out on someone, and it didn't matter if it was your enemy or someone else's."

My thoughts spiral down into the agony that followed. The long months apart. The calls that came less often. Then the letter that ended everything.

Why couldn't I let him go? Why couldn't I move on and live a normal life? Have friends. Be happy. Be with someone like Kolt, who's probably wondering where I am now, along with my students and the staff at the school. I've been missing for close to twenty-four hours.

I exhale a rough sigh.

"I just couldn't let you go when there was still a sliver of hope that you'd come home. I tried to move on. I came here…"

"You came to Rio to forget me."

"I wasn't in a good place for a long time. I needed a change. Something big. Something…dangerous."

"You came to the right place."

"I suppose I did," I say, gazing out the window.

The sound of the engine revving back to life brings me back to the present. Tristan is eerily silent as he drives us back the rest of the way. We pass through the gates under the watchful eyes of the guards, climb the white stone steps of Mateus's home, and I excuse myself to get cleaned up.

I take my time in the shower, eager to let go of some of the tension and uncertainty that's taken hold of me. I towel dry my hair and put on a white sundress I packed, my thoughts tripping over our earlier conversation and his odd behavior at the church.

Maybe it'll all be worth it in the end, when Tristan can find the truth I'm still not convinced he wants to know. Maybe the people who want me dead will give up, and I can have a normal life again. *A normal life.* I didn't come to Rio to have normal. I came to shock myself out of my own malaise, brought on by missing Tristan to the point of inescapable daily pain.

I gaze up into the mirror and judge my reflection. My eyes are tired, my hair leaves much to be desired, and the dress still holds faint wrinkles from being jammed in my bag. What will Tristan see? I don't know whether to trust that our kiss was a ploy to get me to leave Rio with him. I can hardly believe that the passion crackling between us when we touch is only mine.

Venturing beyond the room Tristan and I share, I follow the sound of voices murmuring in the kitchen. I'm hit with the most amazing cooking smells, and then the sight of Karina with Mateus's arms wrapped around her waist as they whisper and laugh.

I hesitate in the doorway—hoping I can step away unnoticed—when Mateus turns to me.

"Isabel." He smiles warmly.

"Sorry. I thought Tristan might be in here."

"He's in the den. We were just getting things ready for dinner."

"It smells delicious. Can I help with anything?"

"Actually, if you could help Karina, I need to attend to a few things."

"Go. I can finish up," Karina says, nudging him away with a coy smile.

He shoots her a heated look before leaving us alone.

Karina dices what look to be fresh chives from the garden. "Mateus says you went into town today. How was it?"

I open my mouth to speak and realize there's nothing I can say about today that doesn't sound completely crazy. I snap it shut and shrug with a smile.

She huffs out a little laugh. "I was wondering if Tristan was any different with you. I suppose not."

Her familiarity with Tristan sparks my curiosity. Karina is more than the household staff. She's obviously Mateus's lover, and she may know the new Tristan better than I do.

"You know him well?"

She sprinkles the chives into a large pot and bangs the wooden spoon on the edge a few times. "Not well. He's Mateus's friend. He doesn't pay anyone else much attention."

Even though I've just witnessed her and Mateus's embrace, a little prickle of jealousy edges its way into my thoughts. Why would she desire more of Tristan's attention?

"He doesn't seem to want many friends," I finally say.

She cocks her head. "That's probably true."

"How did he and Mateus meet?"

She shoots me a suspicious look but covers it up quickly by turning her attention to the oven.

"I don't know all the details. I don't expect I ever will. All I can say is that Mateus is in his debt. Not that he minds. Tristan is always welcome here."

Karina pulls out a tray of nicely browned *empadas* from the oven and rests it on the granite counter. Only now do I realize how little I've eaten since leaving Rio. I'm starving, and for the first time, I feel relaxed enough to eat.

"Can I help?" I'm willing to do anything to expedite dinner or steal a bite.

Mateus returns just then. "Isabel. Come. Tristan is waiting for you."

I sigh and follow him deeper into the house until we reach the den. Tristan halts mid-pace and looks me over, his expression unreadable. I glance down and tug at the sides of my dress.

"Sorry. I didn't pack much."

He comes toward me. "You look fine."

I try not to cringe at the word *fine*. Even though it perfectly describes Tristan. Now that he's not dragging me from one place to another and I'm not trying to leap out of a moving vehicle, I can actually appreciate the physical man. His corded neck and arms that test the fibers of his black T-shirt. His narrow hips and muscular thighs. His fearless stance before me, close enough to touch.

I lift my wandering stare, only to get lost in the cool assessing eyes that have seen more than I can possibly know.

"Is everything okay?"

I swallow and pretend like I'm not blatantly checking him out, even though a little part of me still feels entitled to.

"Is black the only color in your wardrobe?"

He shrugs. "I just try to blend in."

My defenses come down a little with his honesty. "You could never blend in, Tristan."

"I do a pretty good job of it, actually."

A small smile curves my lips. "I'd find you in a crowd anywhere."

"Or on a busy street, as it were."

Thank God I found you...

As if he can hear my unspoken words, he averts his gaze. In the corner, a round, mahogany table is set for two. Several candles burn in the center. It feels oddly intimate—between the rich colors of the room, the musk of leather furniture, and the candlelight.

"Hungry?"

"Starving is more like it," I say.

Karina walks in with two steaming plates right on cue.

"Then let's eat," he says.

7

TRISTAN

Mateus arrives on Karina's heels and places two glasses of wine beside our plates. "*Saúde*," he says with a wink.

Isabel smirks as he leaves. "Why do I get the feeling he wants us to get along?"

"He likes to meddle. I had no idea how much until I brought you here."

"How long have you been friends?"

I tense at the warmth she attaches to the term. It's both foreign and uncomfortable, much like the way she makes me feel.

"Almost as long as I can remember," I finally say between bites.

Isabel is quiet for a moment. "So not long, then."

"We met a few years ago. Right after I came to Brazil. Things were different then."

"How?"

I internally berate myself for opening the door to her question. But the more we share with one another, the less I seem to worry about the vulnerability the truth creates. Our days may be numbered. If she doesn't die by my hand, Jay's people will get to her. What does it matter what she knows?

"I was figuring out my life here. I accepted his friendship before I realized how inconvenient they could be."

"Friends?"

"Friends. Lovers. Essentially anyone who knows my name becomes a liability."

I laugh to myself at the sudden irony that, until a few hours ago, I didn't even know my own surname. I was reborn as Tristan Red the second my boots hit the ground in Rio for the first time. I have official documents with a dozen aliases, but Red is how most of the people in my world know me.

My given name is like my past. Good to know but largely irrelevant. I can never be Tristan Stone again. Isabel has to finally believe this now.

"I go by Tristan Red, by the way. I'd appreciate it if you didn't introduce me to random strangers though."

Her cheeks redden. "Sorry."

I point to her full plate. "I thought you were starving."

She exhales a deep breath and nods. We spend the next few minutes devouring Karina's masterpiece. I shouldn't feel so unguarded, but between the heavy meal and the atmosphere, I'm feeling at ease. Relaxed, even.

As we finish, she gestures to the couch and offers a hopeful smile. "Do you want to sit?"

"Sure."

Together, we move to the other side of the den where Mateus scolded me only a night ago. I refill our wineglasses, unable to stop from dwelling on the photos he showed me.

Meanwhile Isabel sits in an adjacent chair. I cross the room as she tucks her legs under her. In her flowy white dress, she's nothing short of a miracle. An impossibility.

She sips her wine and holds it on her tongue before swallowing.

"Do you like it?"

She smiles. "I do."

I sit on the couch and try not to feel like the silence is a physical thing, creeping in, beckoning me to break it and ask Isabel all the questions I should be.

"So," she says, "what should we talk about?"

Her voice is tentative, and I don't blame her after this afternoon. I should rip the Band-Aid off. Get this over with so we can both move on.

"You said my mother worked in Baltimore. If your dad works at the Pentagon, we were nowhere close. How did we meet?"

Her eyes light up. "I was your tutor."

I blink. "Excuse me?"

"I took a bus twice a week to tutor English and Spanish at an inner-city high school in Baltimore. I was trying to rack up community-service hours for my college résumé. That, and I was looking for any excuse to get out of Alexandria."

I can't hold back a laugh. "You were my tutor?"

"You were failing English before you met me," she says. "By the end of the year, you were on the honor roll."

"I suppose you think you had something to do with it."

She bites her lip with a smile. "I motivated you."

I try not to get hung up on all the ways she could have inspired my good grades. I'm guessing the eighteen-year-old version of me would have crawled across hot coals for an hour under her tutelage.

Because Isabel is more than a beautiful woman. She's fierce and kind, and I'm certain those are only a few of the layers of the person before me. She can't seem to say much without hitting a nerve, but I'm beginning to appreciate the reward. The truth. Even her dangerous affection for me is something I've found myself looking forward to experiencing during our brief time together.

"So your parents must have loved that. Falling for a boy on the wrong side of the tracks."

She traces her fingertip around the rim of her glass. "At some point, I decided to just do what I wanted. Even if it was a little scary. Even if it made my parents furious. It is my life, after all."

"It was puppy love, Isabel. Hardly worth upsetting your parents."

She narrows her eyes. "It was more than puppy love. A lot more. And it *was* worth it. Even though it nearly broke me."

I clench my jaw. We're edging into territory I'm not used to. Feelings. Heartache. Love.

"We were young," I say.

I'm not sure if I should end this now. Every exploration into my past seems to trip over the inconvenient truth that Isabel and I were once in love.

Before I can come up with a better diversion, Isabel rises from her chair and walks to me. I stare up at her as she stands before me. I can't decide if she's more angel or goddess at this moment.

"We still are young, you know."

Her knee nudges mine. Playfully, suggestively. I'm drawn to her so completely, I can't stop myself. I feather the tops of my fingers over her soft skin. The contact reverberates through me, dares me to do more, feel more.

Before I can, she leans in and sits astride me, sucking the air out of the room as our bodies meet. Her hands on my chest, her warmth covering me... I've never known this kind of temptation.

"Isabel..." I consider pushing her off but stiffen my hands into fists on either side of my thighs instead. If I keep touching her, I'll never stop.

"It wasn't that complicated, Tristan." Her voice is soothing, echoing through me like an old song. She looks into my eyes like she knows me. *Really* knows me. In ways I don't even know myself. "Boy meets girl. Boy falls for girl. Girl decides she'll break all the rules to be with the boy." Sadness hits her eyes. "Boy breaks girl's heart. Girl never recovers."

"Girl was probably better off," I whisper.

"Probably. Doesn't change the fact that I'll never be able to love another man the way I loved you. Doesn't change the way you destroyed me, Tristan. Or that I'd do anything to feel it all again. *Anything.*"

Her lips are a fraction away from mine. I attempt a sobering breath but get her essence instead. Then her lips, her taste, as our torsos and mouths melt together.

I inhale as her tongue flickers over mine. God, it's all too fucking good to resist. And her scent… Something about it hits my senses in a new way. It's familiar. Cocoa and vanilla and something else. Something I can't quite reach with my thoughts until a field of deceivingly innocent red flowers projects onto the bright-white screen of my mind.

Poppies. As far as the eye can see.

She glides one hand along my neck and into my hair, fisting gently as her body undulates above me.

I open my eyes abruptly and break the kiss. "What are you doing?"

"I'm remembering you, Tristan," she rasps against my lips.

I swear every solitary sound that comes from the woman decimates my better judgment. Even as my brain screams at me to stop this madness, I answer with a fevered kiss. Because I can't resist the way she says my name, like a siren song luring me closer to her, deeper into the sensations.

My fists ball and release a few more times before I can't fight it anymore. My fingertips meet her ankles and trail up her calves. She lifts the bottom of my T-shirt and slides her other hand up my bare chest, triggering everything else. My blood. My cock. Even my pendulum heart, racing like a fucking fool.

I close my eyes again, and suddenly we're in a dark room. Cold, save the scorching press of our bodies. She's naked, covered in shadows. Her fingernails dig into my flesh as I rock into her.

"Touch me. Tristan…please."

I can't tell if it is really her or the echo of a memory. I open my eyes and flood the vision with the golden glow of Isabel in the candlelight. Pure carnal lust drives me as I palm her knees apart, forcing her wider over me. She whimpers, and that single sound punches through the wall between reality and my hazy past. I make the final journey up her thighs, cup her ass, and haul her hard against me.

She gasps and grinds down on me, eliciting a groan that tears from my chest and rumbles inside our next kiss. It's rough and desperate. It's a flood of her perfect taste. I tease my thumbs along the edges of her panties. My head buzzes with the promise of tasting more of her… All of her. Every inch.

She's moaning my name. Clawing my bare skin and nipping at my lips like a kitten demanding affection. I'm ready to give her all I have when I hear a sound that isn't Isabel's.

Karina's figure hovers in the doorway. "Oh. I— I'm so sorry."

She disappears as quickly as she appeared, but I'm frozen, jarred by Isabel's ability to distract me so completely. Her lips are parted and swollen from my rough kisses. Her touch is no less divine, no less addictive. And deep down I know we're reliving a memory so potent I'll never be the same if I get inside her.

Against every base instinct, I draw my hands away.

"We can't do this." My voice is tight with lingering desire.

I will my palms to relish the worn leather over her silken skin. I can't feed this fantasy. I can't get this close to her.

I don't know how or when, but I feel like I've endured torture less painful than the act of pulling away from her. Gradually, I unwind, withdraw, let go…

Pushing her aside, I rise to my feet, not feeling entirely in control of myself. I'm out of breath and my body is fucking rioting. Nothing has ever felt so dangerous. I pace away and shove my hands through my hair.

"Tristan…"

Turning back, I see her flushed, perched on the edge of the couch, her dress bunched up around her thighs. An intoxicating mix of lust and anguish play on her features. Both turn me on in equal measure.

"We can't," I say firmly.

"You feel it too. I know you do."

I clench my jaw, refusing to show her how true her words are. If she knew what a single touch did to me, she'd never stop pushing for more. She'd push until I break, and I'm ready to fucking snap. This has to end. Here and now.

"You have no idea what I feel. I'm nothing more than a stranger. Do you fuck strangers, Isabel?"

She flinches like I've struck her.

"You're not a stranger. I know you…"

I take a couple steps toward her. She stiffens but doesn't recoil the way she should. She should fear me more, but I'm not sure our history will ever allow it. I stare down at her, ignoring the way my fingertips heat and prickle to touch her again.

"The Tristan you knew died years ago. He was shot full of bullets, brought back to life, and never thought about you again. I never stayed up late at night wondering what you were doing or if you were hurting. I didn't get off to thoughts of us. You were nonexistent to me. Nothing." I draw in a steeling breath that burns my lungs. "And that's never going to change."

Her cheeks bloom a deeper shade of poppy red. Her jaw falls open slightly and shuts again. Silently I beg her to believe me.

ISABEL

The muffled sound of Tristan's voice wakes me out of a restless sleep. I blink a few times. He's somewhere else in the house, probably talking to Mateus. I'm relieved and instantly heartbroken.

I went to bed alone last night, reeling from his confession. Every word cut into me like a blade. The emptiness in his eyes offered no remorse.

I mean nothing to him, and I never will. I'm the key to a locked door. A means to an end. Nothing more. All I can do is leave, lick my wounds, and wish I'd never left Rio with him. The anguish of it all has me wide awake again, despite the latent fatigue.

Morning has brightened the sky beyond my barred window. My heart sinks knowing I have to face this day. Tristan's rejection is fresh, lingering in my psyche the way his touch lingers on my skin. I kick away the sheets with a frustrated sigh, embarrassed for coming on to him in the first place. What the hell was I thinking…

I wasn't thinking. I was only feeling, reaching for magic we once had. For those few intoxicating moments, wrapped in each other, I believed we were the old us. And I was flying without a parachute, high on the way he responded to my touch, the sounds vibrating through our bodies, the familiarity of it all.

I groan and roll into my pillow. Doesn't matter if he still kissed me like he wanted to swallow me whole or touched me like he might tear me apart with the passion he felt. In the end, none of it mattered.

It never will.

I rise slowly and change into clean clothes. I look down at my bag, messy from living out of it for the past couple of days. Maybe today will be the day Tristan lets me leave. How many more memories will he pull from me before it's enough? How much deeper can he push the blade?

In the back of my mind, I think of Kolt. I miss his friendship and the way he always made me feel safe when he was near, even if I could never give him my heart. I took what I wanted and rejected the rest. I let him chase me and feel more for me than I could ever return. Worse, I disappeared without a trace…

A draining kind of discontent burdens my steps as I go down the hall toward the voices.

"We should consider leaving."

Mateus's words slow my approach outside the kitchen.

"We? You mean me?"

"No. All of us. I have a bad feeling."

"Why now? Have you heard something?" There's an edge to Tristan's voice that wasn't there before.

"You know I have eyes and ears everywhere. No signs of trouble, but—"

"Is there something you're not telling me?"

Mateus laughs nervously. "No one is ever safe, Tristan. You know that. They'll be here before we know there's trouble. I have a place a few hours south of here. We can stay there until we know more."

I hear someone shuffling around. I hold my breath and stay still. Silence. Then the sound of a coffee pot sliding out of its cradle and back again.

"You can't keep a roof over our heads forever," Tristan says. "You need time with her."

Tristan is quiet for a moment. "I think I have all I need now."

Mateus makes an exasperated sound. "Already?"

"I can figure out the rest on my own."

"And what about Isabel?"

When Tristan falls silent again, my skin chills.

"Don't be stupid, Tristan," Mateus snaps.

"Don't be stupid? I'll probably be dead in a month. The people who want her gone won't give up. Not if we leave here. Not if we find a hundred other places to hide out. They'll want me a thousand times more than they want her for everything I know."

"And you know their tricks. You can outmaneuver them. You can keep her safe."

"Maybe," Tristan mutters. "Maybe not."

The chill morphs into a wave of sickness twisting in my gut. Someone wants me dead. And the love of my life doesn't even care.

"Karina saw you together last night," Mateus finally says.

"I know."

My cheeks heat, knowing we'd been caught.

"You care for her."

"I want to *fuck* her. It's animal attraction. Nothing more. And last night was a mistake I have no intention of repeating. I was relieved that Karina interrupted us. I can't seem to…"

"What?"

"Nothing." Tristan's voice is barely audible.

My heart starts to race. Last night's humiliation feels even more raw now. I should go before they find me eavesdropping on their conversation. But Mateus's sense of urgency has me planted where I stand, desperate to learn more and find out our next steps.

"Do what you wish. You know what I think. Be ready at noon if you want to come with us."

I don't wait to hear more. I retreat to the bedroom. My thoughts sprint through what I need to do. Pack what little I have. Find Tristan or appeal to Mateus. Maybe he'll take me with him. I can't trust Tristan's heart.

I throw my toiletries in my bag with the few clothes I brought. The sound of a vehicle rolling over the gravel in the front drive draws my attention up. I glance through the window as a black Hummer idles near the gate. The armed guard is speaking to the driver obscured behind the vehicle's tinted windows, but I can't hear what they're saying.

Then the guard's head jerks back violently with a sharp pop, and he collapses onto the ground. I slap my hand over my mouth to mask my scream at the sight of his wound gushing onto the chalky white stones.

The second guard lifts his automatic weapon and gets a few shots off before he's given the same fate—a single answering crack of the air that sends his gun and limbs flailing. He drops like a ragdoll to the ground only a few feet away from his post. My shaking hand closes tightly around my pendant. I try to scream, but I'm frozen in place until the Hummer lurches into motion toward the house.

"Tristan. Tristan!"

I grab my bag and run to the kitchen to find him, but he's gone.

"Tristan!"

I spin around and run into the sitting room, finding it empty too. I scream his name again, unable to control the violent shaking of my limbs. Finally the back door opens and Tristan is there, his eyes wide with concern.

"What's wrong?"

"They're here. They killed them. The guards. They're dead. Oh my God, Tristan. They just shot them both."

He grabs me by the arms. His eyes turn from blue silver to dark steel. "Who? Who shot them?"

I can only shake my head and swallow over my tears. "I don't know," I whisper. "But I think they're coming for us."

Mateus rushes into the room, eyes wide.

Tristan looks up. "We have to go. Right now. Get Karina."

Mateus exhales in a rush. "She's gone… She went into town to get a few things before we left."

Tristan hesitates. Precious seconds pass as he quietly assesses the other man. "Who the fuck did you tell?"

Mateus pales. "No one, Tristan. I would never put you in danger. Not after what you did for me."

Tristan pulls a gun out of his waistband and points it square at him, shoving me to the side. "You're lying. I know the price on her head. What's mine?"

Mateus takes a tentative step forward, halting when Tristan cocks the gun. My heart lodges in my throat.

Mateus speaks quietly. "That's not what happened. You have to trust me. I would never betray you."

"I don't trust anyone, and you know it."

Mateus lifts his hands in surrender. "Money will never turn my alliances. I have no reason to bring harm on you."

Tristan's jaw is tight. "No? Getting rid of me wipes the debt. And it's a pretty big fucking debt, if I recall."

Mateus doesn't move. His expression is steady. "A debt you've never called, friend."

I jolt at the sound of two car doors slamming in close succession, but neither men flinch. Voices outside. Footsteps on stone. Then I can only hear my own heartbeat pumping blood and adrenaline through my veins. My throat tightens with panic. I don't know who to trust, but the bad guys who want at least two of us dead are mere seconds away.

"Tristan. We need to get out of here."

"She's right," Mateus says evenly. "If your comrades make it through the front door, none of it will matter. They'll kill us all."

Comrades?

What the hell has Tristan gotten us into? The phantom demons he's been talking about have suddenly become real. If I thought I was living a nightmare before, I'm certain I've just arrived at the gates of hell.

Tristan grimaces tightly. "Where's the car?"

"Downstairs. Keys are in the ignition."

Tristan gestures with the tip of his gun toward the hallway. "Let's go. Move."

I manage a relieved exhale as we move together through the house. Tristan pauses at a second bedroom, where he retrieves his bag and slings it over his shoulder.

"This way." Mateus opens the door to a basement stairway that leads us to a dark and dingy garage.

In it sits a cream-colored classic car that looks like it's decades old but in mint condition.

"You're kidding me," Tristan says.

"It's fast," Mateus assures him, slipping into the driver's seat.

Tristan tugs my backpack off.

"No, I need this," I say, my voice trembling badly.

"I know you do. But you need to go with Mateus." He rounds to the back of the car, pops the hatchback open and, after a few seconds, closes my backpack in it, slinging his own bag over his shoulder again.

"What are you going to do?" I ask shakily.

My breathing is ragged as he walks toward me. I feel like I could pass out. When my fingers start tingling, I worry that I might. Tristan seems eerily calm, though.

"I'm going to stay here and take care of this," he says.

I shake my head violently. "No. Come with us. You have to get out of here. They'll kill you."

"Not if I have anything to say about it. I'll meet you after."

Mateus looks up at us through the rolled-down window. "There's a safe house in town where we can stay until the coast is clear. It's near—"

"Fuck your safe house." Tristan's anger breaks his calm but eases when he looks back to me.

My brain whirls and stutters until it lands on at least one place I'd rather be than here under siege.

"I know a place," I say quickly.

Tristan stills, his gaze locked to mine.

"From yesterday." I touch below my right eye, hoping he picks up the hint.

He nods slightly and looks down at Mateus. "Drop her at the

edge of town. She knows the rest of the way." Then he curves his hand firmly at my nape, forcing me closer. His voice drops to a whisper. "Don't let him follow you. And don't fucking talk to anyone. Blend in. Understand? I'll meet you there."

"Okay." I can barely get out the next words. "What if something happens to you?"

I can't lose you again...

"I put your phone and some money in your backpack. Get out of Brazil as fast as you can. If you can't talk your way out of it, don't be afraid to get creative. Bribes always help."

My eyes threaten to bulge out of their sockets when he presses the gun into my hand. "Take this. Feel free to shoot him if you need to."

"Tristan, I can't."

"You do what you want, remember? You're braver than you realize." His hands fall away. "One more thing. It's important."

"What?"

His expression hardens. "There's a red notebook in your bag. If I don't come back, give it to your father. No one else."

Another bang sounds from upstairs. My heart nearly flies out of my chest.

"Now get the fuck out of here."

He steps away, and I rush on shaking legs to the passenger side, joining Mateus in the car. He starts the engine and rests his hand on the gear shift.

"Mateus."

He looks up through the window. Tristan simultaneously leans in.

"If anything happens to her—"

"I know, Tristan. Trust me...I know." Mateus looks away, presses the garage opener, and stares ahead. "Take care of yourself, my friend."

8

TRISTAN

I pull a second handgun out of my bag and peek under the door as it opens. Mateus can nearly clear the opening with the Envemo as I catch movement by the Hummer. Then a man in black whips around the back of it and aims for the windshield. My heart slams against my chest as I get a shot off. He drops limp to the ground.

Mateus peels out, barely missing the body. I watch only long enough to see them speed down the road before I turn back for the house, every sense on high alert. This is nothing like a hit, but nothing I can't handle. Sometimes it's complicated. Of course, that was before Isabel. Before I signed myself up for a lifetime of ducking extinction—mine and hers.

Jay had messaged me twice this morning asking about Isabel. I should have known it was a warning shot. Maybe Mateus's gut was right, or maybe he just offered me to Jay's backup plan on a silver platter. I hoped it wasn't the latter, since he was Isabel's only chance to get out of this bullshit alive.

"Red!"

The hairs stand up on the back of my neck because I know the voice booming through the house.

"Come on, Red. Where's the girl? I know she's pretty, but you gotta give her up now."

I move up the stairs without a sound, sliding my back along the wall as I go. All the while, I'm cursing Jay. Of all the people to send…

I make it to the hallway and move toward the sound of his loud footfalls. He's still a big fucker.

"Boss isn't happy," he calls out. "But we can figure this out, man. We just need the girl so we can get this done."

I round the corner and find him in the foyer, pacing casually. I aim for the back of his crew cut when he turns. His face splits with a crooked smile.

"There you are," he says, making no effort to draw his weapon.

"Crow. Long time, no see."

He chuckles. "Yeah. I'm hard to miss too."

He lowers his big frame onto the edge of one of the accent chairs. I'm surprised it doesn't tip under his weight. Crow fits his name. Black hair and black eyes and, if I had to guess, a black heart to match. Big and loud and there's no vermin too indecent to fatten his wallet. Not that I'm one to judge, except he has a penchant for pissing in my backyard from time to time.

"Jay's wondering what you've been up to. Your trigger finger broken?"

"Not remotely," I mutter, my aim more than steady.

I'm ready to push Crow for more information when I spot movement in my periphery. I knew he wouldn't be alone. The third party is stone-faced and leaner than both of us, edging his way into view from his hiding spot in the entryway. His eyes are round and glassy, like an owl who sees everything. I'm not sure he's blinked since I noticed him.

"Drop it." His voice wavers.

"Have you met Hogan? No?"

Crow lets out a shitty, condescending laugh. Despite it, I decide to play nice and let the gun fall with a thud on Mateus's expensive Persian rug. Thankfully I don't need it to fuck Crow up and take out his helper. Crow's overconfidence has gotten him into trouble before, and I'm more than ready to take advantage of it. Just as soon as I find out a few things.

"How did you find us?"

Crow draws his gun and points lazily to the chair. "Have a seat."

"No thanks."

He grins. "I insist."

I sit as he grabs his phone and talks into it walkie-talkie style. "Otto, we have him upstairs." Silence and a few crackles. "Otto."

Crow's distracted and he's about to get bad news, but I'm more worried about Hogan on my right, who's either sleep-deprived or high as a kite.

"She's gone," I say. "So is Otto."

Crow's expression melts into a displeased snarl. He straightens and comes closer to stand directly in front of me. "Where. Is. She?"

"Couldn't say."

He crosses his arms and stares down at me, no doubt enjoying his perceived position of power. "What happened, man? You had to hit it a few times before you put a bullet in her? That's some weak shit."

"Not sure it's any of your business."

"Kind of my business now, don't you think? Where's she going?"

"Probably driving back to Rio right now. You know who she is. Feds are probably hot on this and working with the police to find her and get her back home."

His eyebrows jerk upwards. "Feds? You've got a red dot on your fucking head, and you're sending her home to Daddy? What the fuck for? You in love with her or something?" He pauses a beat. "Aren't the Feds the ones who tried taking you out to begin with?"

I hate that Crow knows anything about me at all. But we all come from somewhere. I was a special ops mission gone wrong. Crow's mob boss family created a protégé killing machine who made better bank on private assignments than TVs falling off trucks.

"If you found us, so can they."

"I've been tracking you for days, Red. Didn't get the go-ahead from Jay to move on you until this morning, otherwise you'd have seen me the day after you *didn't* pop the girl." He shakes his head. "This was easy money too. I don't get it."

He knows better than to question my ability. He's right. Killing Isabel would have been an easy hit. Controversial maybe, but hardly a challenge in execution.

He leans closer, bracing himself on the chair's arms. It's a precarious position for him if not for the all-seeing eye a few feet away. Crow knows this, so he's being cocky. He's daring me to make a move. Under normal circumstances, I would. I'm not afraid of getting shot. I'm not sure I'm afraid of dying either. What scares me now is the prospect of leaving Isabel unprotected. Because once Mateus drops her off, she will be.

I curse inwardly, harnessing some calm. "Why is she so important?"

"We're not paid to ask questions, Red. Point and shoot. Don't get killed. You know the drill."

"Maybe she's worth more than the price on her head."

He cocks an eyebrow. "Worth more alive? Doubtful."

I shrug. "Suit yourself."

He hesitates, but I know he's got money-hungry running through his veins.

"More than the cost of getting put on Jay's naughty list?"

I offer him a million-dollar smile, hoping he takes the bait. "Why don't we have a drink? I'll tell you what I know."

He laughs and straightens. "Sure, why not. What's the rush?" He walks toward the bar and looks toward his comrade. "Want something?"

Hogan lowers his gun and nods. Junkie. He'll catch any high he can, even if it means taking his eyes off me.

"If he gets out of that chair, shoot him," Crow barks as he pulls two glasses down from the bar.

I laugh to myself. Crow's cocky, but he's not stupid. Most men who turn their backs to me end up dead.

I stare down the barrel of the gun trained on me when another face appears over his shoulder. Karina steps into the house.

No. I feel the blood drain from my face.

I don't have time to rethink Mateus's betrayal, because if Karina dies like this because of me, he'll never forgive me. The junkie swivels, turning his back to me. In a fraction of a second, I lift from the chair and map my steps toward her, already knowing I won't reach her in time.

Then her face changes into something wild, and I see the gun. She lifts it and fires, sending an explosion of blood out the back of the man. His gun swings limp around his finger as he brings his other hand to what's left of his neck.

I dive for my gun and turn it to Crow, but he's ducked out of the room.

I fire randomly down the hallway, where he's likely waiting for his opportunity to fire back, as I make my way to Karina.

She's still wild-eyed and shaking, clutching the gun tightly in her hands.

"Nice shot," I say in a hushed tone.

"I was aiming higher."

My mirth fades when a bullet whizzes by, narrowly missing me and shattering one of the paintings on the wall. I duck farther into the entryway, feeling less than safe behind a few layers of drywall.

I push Karina over the threshold. "Get out of here. Mateus went into town. He'll find you. Go now."

She doesn't acknowledge me, but she obeys, disappearing out the door. I slam it shut and peek around the corner for any signs of Crow. I have a vantage of the empty hallway, and the huge shadow spilling out from one of the extra bedrooms tips me off. Two down, one to go.

"How's this going down, Crow?"

"You tell me. I thought we were talking."

I can hear him reloading.

"Tell Jay I got away with the girl. I'll loop you in after we get out of the country."

"Like hell you will. This is a death wish and you know it," he shouts.

"Your loss."

Silence falls on the house.

"How much?"

I bend and grab the dead man's gun, tucking it into my waistband.

"This is your last chance to pique my interest, Red. Then I'm coming for you and it's fucking over. Tell me how much she's worth."

"Everything," I grit out, knowing the sound will never reach him. I leave the entryway and move silently down the hall, gun raised and ready.

The pendulum swings in slow motion.

I shoot the first thing I see.

"Fucker!"

I turn the corner into the bedroom, and he's pushing back by his heels, cradling his bloody hand against his stomach. He only hesitates a second before he raises his left and begins firing, nearly emptying the chamber.

I hiss as one drills through my upper arm. I duck back into the hallway and curse under my breath.

"You left-handed?" I push hard on the wound that's already saturating my shirt with blood.

"I am now, you piece of shit. Show me your face, and we'll finish this."

I clench my teeth against the pain, but something in me doesn't want this to end the way Crow thinks it will. I need to get back to Isabel, but I need to send a message too.

"Seems like a waste, doesn't it?"

Crow answers with a barrage of gunfire through the doorway, punching through the drywall near me. I scramble down the hallway. Mateus's master bedroom is a dead end.

Hurriedly I cinch a handkerchief on the bureau around my upper arm. I'm not overly concerned about the wound, but I'd rather not pass out before I have a chance to send Crow back to his maker if I need to.

Between his lumbering steps, I hear him crash into the wall before continuing down the hall toward me. How he sneaks up on anyone

I'll never know. I do know I'm at an advantage, though. Crow has one good arm and only a couple of shots left. I decide to give him a target and hope he wastes them. I pivot into the doorway and aim for his shoulder. *Crack crack.* I duck and dodge his answering shots, the last he has, but his steps don't slow. He turns into the bedroom, his eyes wild with murderous rage. I hit my mark, but the gushing from his shoulder doesn't seem to faze him at all.

He advances on me. Goddamnit, I didn't want to kill Crow. I back up and ready myself to put his name on the list that's already too long.

"Do you want to die, or do you want to help me send a message?"

"I'm gonna tear you limb from limb. There's no talking your way out of it."

"You're the one with the dot on your head now, so I'd suggest you reconsider."

"That's not how this works."

"I'm not playing by the rules anymore if you haven't figured that out already."

He keeps coming at me, arms wide like a blood-thirsty gorilla. *Fuck fuck fuck.* I aim for his knee and fire.

He cries out and his leg buckles, sending him to the floor. Injured or not, he's enormous. I might be faster and smarter, but he's stronger. So I move fast. I strike him with the butt of my gun and use his break in balance to shove him to the ground, belly down. He grunts when I wrench his arm behind him, exacerbating the pain where the bullets are still lodged in his thick shoulder muscles.

"Time to finish our little chat," I say, pressing the gun barrel to his temple.

"Fuck you," he wheezes.

I change the angle of the gun, adding pressure so he feels the fear of the inevitable. "Last call, Crow."

He exhales roughly a few times. "What's it matter? Jay's gonna kill me after this anyway."

"I don't have time to listen to you wrestle with your mortality, Crow. *Last call.*"

He gnashes his teeth and curses again with less force.

I take that as surrender.

"This is mercy," I say.

"I don't want your fucking mercy!"

I reposition my knee above his bloodied hand and add pressure. He shudders from the pain.

I lean in and lower my voice. "Listen carefully. They're going to find you here eventually, and you're going to relay a little message for me. Tell Jay to forget my name. Tell her to forget the girl. Because if she doesn't, everyone she sends for me is going to wish for the mercy I'm showing you right now."

He huffs in and out, his breathing labored. Even as the vow violates everything about the way I've lived these past few years, I know it's true. I can't let these bastards have her. The worst thing she ever did was fall in love with me, and that's not a reason to die.

"Who is she to you?"

"All you need to know is that she's mine, and I'm not backing down."

I leave Crow hogtied in Mateus's bedroom. On my way to hijack the Hummer for my ride back to town, I see Karina's red sedan idling up the road. I jog toward it, praying to hell there wasn't a fourth member of Crow's crew who could have gotten to her. Relief floods me when the driver's door swings open and she emerges.

"Karina. What are you doing here?"

"Get in. Hurry. Mateus is waiting for us."

Not wanting to waste time, I get in and she hits the gas, jolting us forward. A few minutes later, we're at the edge of town. The streets are busy with a weekend market. Lots of eyes, but lots of opportunities to go unnoticed too.

I see Mateus leaned against his car as Karina parks nearby. He doesn't pay me a second glance. He goes to Karina and all but rips her out of the car and hauls her into his arms. "Karina," he whispers into her wavy black hair.

I glance back to the crowd, scanning it for the one familiar face I'm eager to find.

"Where's Isabel?"

Mateus looks up, his forehead creased with worry. "I did as you asked, Tristan. I would have kept her with me otherwise."

"It's fine," I say, though I'm sure an apology is in order since I strongly considered killing him not so long ago. My distrust of him could have cost Isabel her life, a possibility that won't be ruled out until I find her safe.

I reach into my bag. He tenses until I retrieve the frame. "Here," I say, handing it to him. "You probably won't be able to go back for a while. I figured you'd want this."

He takes it without a word, opens and closes it quickly. Then he looks up and slowly reaches out his hand. I pause to consider the gesture and what it means. A reaffirmation of a relationship built on blood and revenge. Then I lift my arm and our palms meet and mold.

It's as close to forgiveness as we'll get for now.

"Where will you go now?" he asks.

I glance back to the crowd. "Time to disappear."

He takes the keys from Karina and hands them to me. "For your getaway."

"Thanks," I say.

"Thank you for not shooting me."

Karina's eyes grow wide and angry. "What? You were going to shoot him?"

Mateus hushes her. "It's nothing. I promise you."

"It's nothing? He is your friend, Mateus."

His lips thin. "He is," he says quietly. He reaches for the door of the Envemo and ushers Karina inside.

9

ISABEL

The air, weighted with three hundred years of desperate prayer, smells of old wood and the soot of scented candles. The heavily painted figure of the Messiah stands at the center of the church, silent and still, offering his open arms to the devout. The needy. The desperate.

The half-blind priest bolts the front door and gestures to the back of the church. "*Me siga.*"

I offer him a weak smile, ready to follow him to the only place I thought to hide when Tristan sent me off. With no hesitation, Padre Antonio agreed to give us shelter here tonight. He asked for nothing in return. Even as I am growing to distrust nearly everyone, I have faith in his genuine kindness.

Seeming to sense my somber mood, he pauses and touches my arm gently. His skin is dry and warm to the touch. The simple kindness wraps around me, threatening to unravel my quickly fraying emotions. I blink back tears.

He hushes me and speaks softly in Portuguese. "Rest here, Isabel. Come back when you are ready." Without another word, he walks away, leaving me alone with my thoughts in the empty hall.

I haven't stepped foot in a place of worship for years. Not since Grace's funeral. My parents all but turned their backs on Tristan's tragedy, and in turn, I turned my back on the traditions of our faith.

Still, something faint rings inside me. I can't remember a time when I've needed hope more.

Careful not to disturb the silence, I move up the narrow aisle. Whatever drew me to the church gate yesterday with Tristan on my heels compels me now into the pew and onto my knees. I lean forward, anxiety tight in my belly. The lacquered wood is warm under my palms and against my forehead. A small comfort. I exhale heavily, racked with worry and fatigue.

This unexpected journey with Tristan, fighting for our lives and more, has turned me inside out. It's made me raw and weak and aimless. Yet even as I long for the safety and security I took for granted every day before, I can't deny wanting to save Tristan from this nightmare too. I have no idea how I can, though. I've never felt more powerless in my life, flung from place to place, kept in the dark by the lover of my past.

How can the broken man I still care for beyond reason be the one to save me? Can he even save himself?

I'm miles from Tristan, but I pray he hears me.

Please.

Please come back to me. Please live.

Please fight for us… Survive for us… Remember us…

Over and over, I whisper my deepest pleas. All the while, visions of the horrific acts I witnessed earlier consume me. I grip the back of the pew tightly, refusing to believe the same fate could come upon Tristan. He's too strong. Too determined. Too broken to let them win…

I squeeze my eyes against tears. He's not dead. I'd feel it if he were. I'd know. There'd be an earthquake in my soul. Some kind of sign.

I look up at the cartoonish figure before me. No change in his peaceful countenance. I don't bow my head again, because this is no longer a quiet prayer. I'm as desperate now as all the troubled, poor, and sick souls who've passed through these doors and bruised their knees on the crude floor.

"Help me save him," I utter amidst the quiet crackle of candles. "Tell me what to do."

A door slams in the back. I grip the pew with knuckle-whitening force. My heart stutters and then launches into wild beats. Then I hear his voice mingled with the priest's.

"Tristan."

I scramble to my feet as he appears from the hallway. He's disheveled and dirty and bloody, but sweet mercy, he's alive.

I run toward him and throw my arms around him. "You're alive." The word tears like a sob from my throat.

"You're safe," he whispers against my hair, holding me almost painfully tight against him.

I mold myself to him as if the surface of my body needs proof of his existence. The more we touch, the more real this is. He catches me closer still.

Only then do I remember the barriers that still exist between us. The reality that came between us last time we were this close. I untangle from our embrace and take a small step back.

"Sorry. I just… I thought you were dead. I was so scared."

"Not today."

His hands fall to his sides. Then I realize the blood he's covered in is his own. A strip of cloth is wound tightly around his upper arm, seeping red and wet. I blink rapidly over my tears and swallow down all the emotion that wants to bubble up.

"You're hurt."

"It's okay. It's nothing."

"Nothing? You're bleeding, Tristan. You need a doctor."

He laughs lightly. "Hardly. I should clean it though."

I take his hand and lead him back down the hallway to the room the priest promised was ours for the night. The back of the church consists of a desk in the corner, several wooden shelves with old musty books, and a small twin bed that seems freshly made. Before I can ask for cleaning supplies, Antonio emerges from a tiny bathroom with a bowl of water, gauze, and disinfectant gathered up in his arms.

I rush to him. "Here. Let me help you."

I take the supplies and lay them out on the desk with shaking hands.

"He is your friend?" He speaks in a hushed tone that only I can hear.

His expression is pinched with concern. I can't imagine how this looks to him. He must know we're in trouble—or that Tristan is. I glance back to Tristan, who is looking out the windows.

"He's a friend, yes. Thank you for everything," I answer quietly.

"Here." Tristan comes closer, reaching into his bag with his wounded arm and withdrawing a brick of *reals*.

The father steps back like the offering might burn him. "No, no."

"Tristan, he doesn't want it. Come sit so I can dress your wound."

Tristan stares at the old man, his gaze stoic. "No one can know we're here. Do you understand?" His Portuguese is heavily nuanced with his American accent.

The father waves his hand again and shakes his head. "You are safe here. I can assure you. I will leave you now. I will bring you food in the morning. Yes?"

Tristan's frown deepens, but I step between them and place a hand on the priest's shoulder.

"Thank you. We are so grateful."

The old man offers me an uneasy smile. Tristan makes him nervous, but I'm beginning to understand why. This is life and death now.

"I will come check on you in the morning," Antonio says before shuffling out, leaving us alone once more.

"I should have had you give it to him." Tristan drops the money onto the desk and tugs his T-shirt over his head, leaving only the bloody dressing on his arm.

"He doesn't need a bribe. He only wants to help."

"We'll see," he mutters. "Are you sure you can handle this?" He glances down and slowly begins unwrapping the dressing.

I swallow hard. Blood has never made me squeamish, but seeing

Tristan hurt seems to trigger physical pain of my own. I feel it on the surface of my skin, a painful prickling in my fingertips.

"If you're not going to see a doctor and get this taken care of properly, then I don't suppose I have much choice."

"You know why we can't."

"I know," I say, resigned to these new circumstances by which we're bound. I recognize we're in a space where life and death supersede creature comforts. Like a hospital. A hotel. A home.

I collect a cloth and dip it into the warm water. Carefully I work to get the wound clean, hoping to minimize Tristan's discomfort, though he seems barely affected.

"That looks better."

"Told you it'd be fine. Just grazed me."

I roll my eyes, because even though the damage is clean and less gory, the bullet that "grazed" him took a long trail of flesh with it. Even now, I can see it'll be another scar that no amount of care can prevent. Yet nothing about this seems to give Tristan pause.

"Who were those men, Tristan? Why did Mateus call them your comrades?"

He gazes toward the ceiling as I dab antiseptic on the wound. He doesn't flinch or speak.

"I don't understand why they want me dead. What could I have done to bring all this on?"

"I'm guessing you didn't do anything. But sometimes innocent people can get caught in the crossfire if they're standing too close to the bad guys."

He washes his hands and face in the bowl. I place a fresh bandage on his arm as he does, satisfied that the gash is protected for now.

"Your father is obviously connected," he continues. "Is there anyone else close to you who could be in trouble?"

I frown. "My father has a desk job. He's not out in the field."

"That doesn't mean anything. He can piss people off from his desk. You have no idea what kind of situations he could be involved with."

I press my lips tightly together. What Tristan's saying could be true.

My father could never talk much about his work due to the confidential nature of it. I grew up knowing this, but nothing about his nine-to-five routine ever bled into our home life to make me think he was into bad things. Certainly nothing akin to the hell I've experienced today.

"It's been a long day." Tristan's tone betrays his fatigue.

His eyes are tired but still vibrant. Full of life and the glimmer of determination I recognized as he sent me off with Mateus. He seemed different then. Less heartless captor. More… *Tristan.*

He sighs and runs his fingertips over my hands, taking them into his. "What would you have done…if I didn't come back?"

I worry the inside of my lip and try to maintain a brave face, but the possibility of losing him all over again is too fresh. Never mind how I may not have been able to escape with my life when a vehicle full of men with guns were on the hunt for me.

I look away, not trusting myself not to break my composure. "Honestly, I don't know."

He pushes my hair over my shoulder, his touch unexpectedly tender. "Me neither," he says softly.

He weaves his fingers into my hair and drags them gently over my scalp and down my neck. I close my eyes at the sheer relief of his touch. I hear the rough slide of his body coming off the desk, feel the warmth of his proximity. We're so close that his masculine and earthy scent hits my senses.

When he leans in, I can feel his breath and then the tip of his nose across my cheek. I'm trembling, uncertain if I can handle the sensations his closeness brings. When his lips trail my jaw, my breath hitches.

"Tristan… What are you doing?"

He skims his hands down my arms, splays his palms across my back, and brings me tighter and closer against him.

"I'm remembering you."

He spins us and lifts me onto the desk, spreading my legs to take the space between them. He steals my next sharp intake of breath with a rough kiss. That quickly, he's all over my senses. His hands are everywhere, and so are mine. Raking over his broad shoulders, kissing his jagged scars with my fingertips, reclaiming him, one inch at a time.

His stubble scrapes my lips. "Can't stop. Not this time."

"No." God, if he stops now, I'll never survive.

I've been held on the brink for far too long. Starved of Tristan and all the things his touch once inspired. Passion on my skin. Faith in my heart. A future with him in it.

He pulls my shirt over my head and leans in quickly to reclaim my mouth. The kiss is almost bruising in its intensity, but I revel in it. I unhook my bra, let it fall to the floor, and hoist myself closer so our bare chests meet. Close enough to feel the tick-tock rhythm of his heart.

Our exploring touches fill the minutes. My ragged breaths turn to whimpers. Where I was tentative before, I'm frantic now. I press my nails into his flesh, silently begging for more.

He palms my breasts, squeezing and stroking the tender tips until I'm pulsing with desire.

"I need to taste you." He tucks his hand under the waistband of my shorts, new heat in his eyes.

How many times had I fantasized about this moment since he left? Those words on his lips, that promise lingering in the air between us?

I nod breathlessly, my lips tingling and my skin on fire.

Inch by inch, he draws my shorts down my thighs, baring me completely.

Then his lips are soft and slow, leaving a wet trail over my breasts, down my belly, and over the tiny jewel at my navel, almost all the way to the place where I throb for him.

His next touch is featherlight as he opens me under his hungry gaze. He's fixated on the space between us. I whimper when he bends, and his exhale barely kisses my flesh. I curl my hands over the edge of the desk. I'm afraid to move another inch, lest he change his mind and leave me this way, so vulnerable and needy.

But he doesn't back away. He leans in, nudges me wider with his broad shoulders, and consumes my flesh with his mouth. The delicious contact pulls another helpless cry from my lips.

"Do you have any idea what this does to me, Isabel? Being this close to you. Tasting you. Knowing the sounds you make…"

He pauses only a moment before coming at me again. Tasting and taking and tormenting with every wicked lash of his tongue. The more he gives me, the more I need. I'm greedy, ravenous for as much of him as he'll offer. As if his instincts are linked to mine, he licks me harder, grips me tighter. I fist his hair and struggle to keep up with the sharp incline of sensation.

I'm so close, my hips lifting into his ministrations, when he straightens abruptly. He curves his hand behind my neck and brings us together. "I want the rest of you." The sound is gritty and molten. Rock and fire.

I reach for the button of his jeans and wrap my legs around his narrow hips.

He kisses me hard, flooding my mouth with the taste of me and this unhinged lust we're drowning in. He presses his erection against my sex.

"Isabel…" He cups my cheek, forcing my stare to his. "It's not going to be the same. You need to know that."

A few heavy seconds pass between us. I believe him and I don't. I care, and the next second, I'm convinced I don't. I shake my head as much as his grip on me will allow. "I don't care."

His eyes darken with lust and restraint I'm not sure he'll be able to maintain. Yet he holds back, seemingly unable to take us further. Why?

Because this is more than our two bodies seeking sexual relief. This is my war-torn heart colliding with the reality of our present turmoil. No matter how hard I pray, I'll never have the Tristan I fell in love with. The man before me—the one who took the slice of a bullet fighting off those men today—is the only one I'll ever know again.

I exhale a shaky breath, drag my gaze down his scarred chest and back to his haunted eyes. "I'm not the same. I've changed too."

Maybe not on the outside. Maybe not in the ways that matter to a man like Tristan. But at this moment, we're matched in our intensity. In our brokenness. We're both empty and unwilling to survive another minute without being filled. What's this life if we can't fill the emptiness with each other?

I reach for him, but he takes my arm and shifts me off the desk. His next kiss is different. Sweet and savage. Tender and unapologetic. As if he's already asking permission for what will happen next. Turning me swiftly to face the table, he holds my wrist behind my back.

His breath is warm at my ear. "Like this."

I inhale a quick breath to feed the adrenaline spike he's inspired. I nod. And then I can feel him guiding my legs apart, pushing inside me, filling me. I tense and release, surrendering to the breathtaking feeling. I moan and let my head fall back against his shoulder. He's a wall of muscle behind me, every inch of his strength governed by the act of consuming the space between us and intimately joining us.

He releases my arm and bands my hips so I feel every inch of his next thrusts.

I slap my hands on the desk, using its steadiness for leverage. A wild heat races across my skin, but the fire burning on the inside is raging, consuming the last of my inhibitions. Obliterating the fear. Calling back memories I've kept at a distance for too long.

His free hand roams my flesh, plucking at my breast and then tormenting the place his mouth abandoned with a series of strokes over my clit that inspire even more primal sounds from me. I surrender to his rugged pace and race toward the firestorm of the orgasm I know is coming.

"Tristan… Tristan… *Tristan.*"

Every iteration of his name on my lips is louder, heavier, matching his drives. The sound is both demand for more and dedication to the climb that isn't even bliss. It's air. It's blood. It's us. Whatever is left of us now…

That truth sinks into my skin, melting into the places that Tristan has already set on fire until there's no place else to go.

His tortured groan, his teeth bared and sinking into my shoulder, and the clawing need to release… Everything comes together to push me over.

"Tristan!"

I scream it until he slaps his hand over my mouth, buries himself to the hilt, and muffles the pinnacle moment until I'm wilted and reduced to a series of long, delirious moans into his hot palm.

We collapse together. Me over the desk. He against my back. He surprises me by pushing deeper still. I gasp, and he sighs with such audible satisfaction that my heart squeezes in my chest.

Already I know I need this to mean more to him.

I've changed, but I'm wired to love Tristan. My love for him will never stop seeking its reflection. Until he says it again, I'll survive on those little sounds and the glints of affection in his eyes before they darken with truth I've yet to truly understand.

The warm night and our passion cool on our skin. Tristan lifts, and I turn to see him walking away toward the bathroom, zipping himself away. He returns with a warm cloth and offers it to me.

"Sorry, I—"

"It's fine. I have it covered." I take the cloth with a shaky hand.

His brows come together a second before he turns away again. He riffles through his bag for another T-shirt as I attempt to put myself together. Physically, I'm there. Dressed. Heart and brain functioning at a semi-normal pattern again. But I still feel scattered all over the room. Vulnerable. A mess of craving and splintered memories.

"What now?"

He glances toward the bed. "Rest, I suppose. We should leave early."

I take his hand in mine. Unexpected relief floods me when he doesn't reject the contact.

"Lie down with me."

"I wasn't vigilant enough before and nearly got us killed. I'm not letting that happen again."

"You need to sleep too."

He threads our fingers tighter. "I'll be fine. I can keep watch until daybreak. Then we'll get out of here."

"Please," I whisper. "Just a few minutes."

He takes a deep breath and touches my face gently. "What is it about you?"

I smile, unable to ignore the little flutter of happiness his words give me.

We move together to the little bed. There's barely enough room for one, but I don't care. I make it work and use it as an excuse to tangle myself in his familiar warmth. I'm scared to death of losing the magic between us. I just want a few minutes. Then I know I'll want more.

The church is quiet, save a few concerning creaks that soon become normal sounds. Wind. Tree branches scratching the roof. I sigh and try to turn off the fear that doesn't ever seem to go away altogether now. I nuzzle against Tristan's chest and let his scent chase it away a little more.

"Tristan?"

He hums and tucks me a little closer.

"What if they don't stop looking for us?"

He's quiet for so long that tendrils of sleep begin to wrap around my thoughts before I hear him finally speak.

"They won't."

10

TRISTAN

Gunshots. They're whizzing by and dropping men to the ground all around me. They're punching into my flesh. They're killing me.

The voices shouting are a tangle of English and the Arabic I've yet to pick up. I can't make sense of anything past the panic and the agony and the instinct to get the fuck out of here as fast as I can.

But every time I get up, I stumble back down, lightheaded and dodging the bullets that are still flying, puncturing the dusty walls of this hut. I lie on my stomach while hot rays of sunlight pour through the crude window openings until the room begins to cool and all I can see is the bright white overwhelming my vision.

"Stone! Stone!"

Faces imprint in flashes on the white. Men like me. Fear and fire in their eyes. Then they're gone and my whole body is vibrating. I'm moving. Strip after strip of fluorescent lights fly by above me. I can't tell if I'm chasing the lights or running from them.

"You're going to be all right. Just stay with me. Keep your eyes open." A man in green scrubs places a clear plastic mask over my face. "Just breathe,

Tristan."

I suck in a half breath that shoots pain down every limb. I try to cry out, but everything disappears, and I'm transported somewhere else.

A brushed metal table beams light into my eyes from the industrial lamp swaying above us. A woman with piercing blue eyes and red hair pulled tight from her fair-skinned face sits across from me in a blue pin-striped business suit.

"I'm Jay. I'll be your contact moving forward."

I look down at myself. I'm in street clothes. I can feel the bandages wrinkling against my skin underneath. The pain is gone, replaced by a muddy sort of consciousness. I'm pretty sure this isn't a dream, though. I think I'm alive.

"How did I get here?"

"You had some of the military's best doctors caring for you. You were put into a deep coma while you recovered."

"Is that why I feel... My head. It's like everything is cloudy."

Jay offers a tight smile. I can't tell if it's sympathetic or something else. "You will have a difficult time accessing your memory. Don't try to fight it, Tristan."

"I don't understand."

"The trauma from the mission combined with the induced coma you were in for several weeks resulted in what we call dissociative fugue. Your memory is..." She drums her fingers on her knee, averting her gaze for only a moment. "Think of it as a fresh start. For the sake of your safety and everyone involved, it's probably for the best that things turned out this way."

I wince. "Everyone involved?"

"If it weren't for the valuable skills you demonstrated over the past few years, I'm not sure you'd be given this opportunity. Several people lost their lives. There's a lot of blood on your hands, Tristan." She's quiet for a moment. "Take this for what it is. A second chance."

I press the heels of my hands to my eyes and rub vigorously. Maybe this is a dream. Everything is so confusing. The things she's saying don't match the synapses firing in my brain. Something's off. Something's wrong. Really wrong.

"What do I do now?"

"You won't be safe in the US for a while. We've set you up with a place just outside of Rio de Janeiro. You can heal and rest there. Then I'll be in touch

when we have a job for you."

"*A job?*"

She's silent a moment. "The second chance doesn't come without cost."

Jay's laser focus from across the table makes me uncomfortable, like she can see all the things that won't come into view for me right now.

"*What do you need me to do?*"

"*You'll take assignments that only someone entirely off the grid can take. You'll need to take every precaution to keep yourself safe after a hit. We won't be there to support you unless we absolutely need another agent involved. You'll receive all the pertinent information, and then you'll be compensated when the work is done. No paperwork. No red tape.*"

My mouth is dry. I think it's the pain medication that's making all this feel so surreal and out of reach. I take a drink from the water glass in front of me.

"*Listen, I just want to go home.*"

Jay leans in. Her eyes are cold, like deep ocean water.

"*Where's home, Tristan?*"

I jerk awake. Isabel is asleep beside me. Peaceful. Damn near angelic in the wake of the nightmare. A mix of relief and gut-wrenching fear washes over me. Fear that I'll fail her—both of us—if I can't keep her safe. I rise gingerly from the bed so as not to rouse her and go to my bag. I pull out my laptop, sit at the desk, and open the protected chat. Jay's unanswered messages stare back at me.

I'm a grown man. I've killed more men than I can count, but somehow I can hardly bring myself to acknowledge or challenge her. We both know what's gone down. Soon enough she'll know even more, once someone discovers Crow and gets him out of the impossible bind I left him in.

The cursor blinks, taunting me. With no one to report back, she could believe I'm dead, but she's too smart for that.

I begin typing.

> RED: You'll have to do
> better than that.

A few minutes pass with no reply. I look out the window. Early dawn is approaching. We'll have to leave soon, before the streets come back to life. The sound of a return message draws my attention back to the screen.

JAY: You're making a mistake.

I grimace, as pissed off as ever. Three years of clean, quiet, anonymous hits, and now I'm her mark.

RED: So are you.

JAY: Bring her in and we can talk.

She knows as well as I do that will never happen. Either some part of her wants to salvage the relationship, or Isabel's death is more of a priority than I realized. My money is on the latter.

I hear a rustle outside the window. I grab my gun and steal a glance at Isabel, oblivious in her slumber.

There's a soft rap at the door. "Isabel."

I rise at the muffled sound of the priest's voice. I open the door a crack to find him standing there with a cloth-covered basket. He lifts it. "Breakfast for you."

I reach out and take it, noting the unease and exhaustion on the old man's features.

I'm ready to close the door, when he lifts his hand, stopping me. "I was awake all night watching the street. The same black truck passes back and forth every hour or so." His lips press together in a worried line. "It doesn't feel right to me."

I poke my head around the door. The street is quiet. "When's the last time you saw the car?"

"Twenty minutes."

"Did they see you?"

He shrugs. "Not many people notice an old man like me."

"We'll leave soon. Thanks for this."

He nods and waves a silent farewell. After ensuring Isabel is still sleeping, I slip outside.

I take my phone out and hesitate over Mateus's number before dialing. It rings only once.

"Tristan. Is she okay?"

"We're fine. For now."

"What's happened?"

I hesitate over my next words. "Do you remember what you said about letting things go…to get what you really want?"

He's quiet for a moment. "You're sending her home."

"I'll get her out of Petrópolis, but I'm running out of time. They're closing in." I hesitate. "Can you help me get her out of Brazil?"

"I'll do anything you ask of me, Tristan. That's not the question."

"What's the damn question, Mateus? Help me or don't."

"The question is whether you trust me to."

ISABEL

Tristan's memory might be lost, but I swear I can still see vengeance haunting his eyes where I used to see his joy. He woke me this morning quickly and quietly. Danger wasn't on our heels, but we're on the move. To where, he won't say. I pick at the moist bread Antonio brought to us as we drive from one town to the next.

"Are you upset with me?"

His brows knit firmly together. "Why would I be upset with you?"

"I don't know. Last night happened. Guys can be weird after that."

"Guys?" He shoots me a narrow look.

I huff out a sigh. "Never mind."

Silence stretches between us for a long time before he finally speaks again.

"I enjoyed last night. Doesn't change the fact that today is a new day, we're in danger, and I needed to get you out of there. Your friendly neighborhood priest was on the lookout all night. Jay's people weren't far."

"Who's Jay?"

"Former employer," he says flatly.

I lean forward, my jaw slack. "Are you kidding me? You work for the monsters who are trying to kill us?"

The muscle in his jaw ticks. "I'm a contractor. We're having a disagreement about the terms of our arrangement."

I stare in stunned disbelief. Then…suddenly…it all makes sense. The blocks of cash. The guns and willingness to use them to any end. Tristan's near-complete disregard for human life. I push his tender moments out of the picture because they cloud the view. And it's all coming into focus.

Your comrades.

Someone wants you dead.

I know the price on her head. What's mine?

A rush of enlightenment crashes over me as we make a turn down a narrow, paved road. It's leading us toward an open field and tarmac. There are a few small planes and a helicopter parked around an old hangar. A larger, sleeker jet sits at the center of the tarmac, its boarding door open with stairs leading up to it. A young man is pacing beside it, stopping as Tristan parks.

"Come on," he says.

I get out of the car as he pops the trunk. "Where are we going?"

"Not we. You."

The man comes our way, extending his hand to Tristan. "You must be Mateus's friend. I'm Leo, your pilot." He nods to me. "*Senhorita.*"

Tristan shakes his hand before grabbing my backpack and slamming the trunk shut.

"Leo's going to fly you to Panama."

"Panama?" My eyes widen.

"They'll be expecting you to try to get a flight out of Rio or São Paulo. They'll pluck you from security or God knows what else. It's too risky."

"Okay." I try to will my voice not to shake.

"You'll be able to get to Panama City in the jet without refueling. Leo will take care of customs. But this is important. As soon as you get there, you're going to buy a ticket to DC. No stops. And use cash in case they're tracking your cards. I can't risk you getting on their radar before you're in the air. Understand?"

My breathing ticks up rapidly. This is too much too fast. I can't think anything through. All I can do is trust Tristan, and he's scaring the hell out of me with this plan. I don't even like flying.

"What about you? I can't just leave you here."

"I can't protect you here. It'll be easier for you to get back home without me. They're going to be expecting both of us."

"I'm not leaving without you. I don't care what you say." I cross my arms and prepare to hold my ground. I can't leave him… I can't let him go again.

Leo's eyes widen a fraction. "Let me know when you're ready. I'll wait for you."

"She's ready," Tristan answers for me. He hands the man my backpack.

I try to grab it back, but Leo is already moving toward the plane and out of earshot. My nostrils flare. "Enough of this shit, Tristan. You need to give me answers. I've waited long enough."

"I told you. The less you know, the better."

"You mean I shouldn't know what kind of man you are?"

Tristan's jaw is tight. "What kind of man am I, Isabel?"

I hold his steady stare, uncertain if I'm actually ready for the truth. "Tell me why you came for me that day."

He steps closer, dominating my personal space. That quickly, I'm caught in a tornado of our intense sexual attraction and the inherent fear Tristan inspires at moments like these.

"You want to know the truth?" His voice is dangerously low.

Lust pulses through me at the most inopportune time. Maybe if I kiss him, he won't have to tell me what I fear to be true. I fist my hand in his shirt. It steadies me on shaky legs and binds him to me in some small way, regardless of what he's about to say.

He touches my chin, guiding all my attention to the silvery sky reflecting in his eyes.

"Three years ago, the Tristan you knew died. Now I take jobs that only a dead man can take. Back in Rio, I was sent to kill you. I would have been paid handsomely for it. I was ready to pull the trigger, until you said my name."

"On the street?"

He shakes his head. "I was in your apartment after you turned away Kolt. You were in bed taking care of things he badly wanted to. I was so close to going through with it, but something held me back. Then you said my name, and... I just couldn't do it." He brings his hand to my face, drawing his thumb across my cheek tenderly. "Because I didn't, there's a bounty on both our heads. And if you don't get on that plane right now, they're going to finish the job I wouldn't."

The tears I've been holding back spill over. Hot, thick tears that threaten a torrent of sobs to follow. This can't be real. This can't be happening.

"You need to go now." He pulls away, steps away, looks away.

I tighten my fist in his shirt, but he's unclenching my grip. Putting distance between us. I fight him, but I know it's useless.

He tried to kill me.

He kept me alive.

He tied me to the goddamn bed.

He killed a man who would have killed me first if given the chance.

He's not my Tristan anymore.

He's a shadow.

He's indelibly imprinted on me.

In my blurred periphery, I see Leo coming closer. Time is running out. I need more time with Tristan to figure all this out.

"When will I see you again?"

He glances to Leo and back to me. "There will be someone to meet you at Dulles. An old acquaintance."

"How will I know him?"

"Trust me, you'll be able to spot him in a crowd. He'll take you to your father as soon as it's safe."

"No." I can't hide the agony wrapped around that one word.

His hardened expression softens.

"Go… Please, Isabel. Just go."

THE RED
LEDGER

part 2

1

ISABEL

Washington, DC

There's a saying in Brazil. *A esperança é a última que morre.*

Hope is the last one to die.

The sentiment resonates with me now more than ever as I lurch forward and clutch the armrest. The Boeing 737 touches down and brakes gradually toward the end of the runway. The flight attendant's voice crackles through the speaker system as she welcomes us in heavily accented English to Dulles International Airport.

I'm back in the United States. I'm home. This should give me solace, but the unexpected homecoming is shadowed by the fact that I'm running for my life, and once more, I'm without Tristan.

Less than twenty-four hours ago, he ordered me onto a private jet with no reassurances that we'd reunite. His only instructions were to get back to DC while raising as little suspicion as possible.

Now I'm exhausted and alone. It all feels so hopeless.

Yet hope is what I cling to as I file off the plane with the other passengers and head toward customs. I have no luggage. Only the contents of my backpack. Soiled clothes, some cash, and two passports. One gained me safe passage into Rio de Janeiro a year and a half ago. The other was pressed into my palm by Leo, the pilot who flew me from Brazil to Panama, insisting it would get me into the States undetected.

On any given day, I'm Isabel Foster. But today, as I walk toward US customs, I'm Isa Santos. An American woman returning from a girls' trip to Panama. I clutch the customs declaration form and pray I don't end up in prison as I approach the window separating me and the customs officer. He slides my fake passport through the scanner without making eye contact.

"How long were you in Panama?"

"Two weeks," I say.

"Business or pleasure?"

"Pleasure." I smile and invoke a mental image of me on the beach with a tropical drink in my hand to help sell the lie.

"Where did you stay?"

"San Blas."

He glances between my passport, his computer screen, and me. My palms are slick with nervous sweat. I may heave and confess everything if he takes much longer.

I distract myself by studying his badge and wondering what kind of man Officer LeBaron is. He looks to be in his forties. Kind eyes. Crew cut. I wonder if he used to be a cop. Or maybe he wanted to be, and this is where he ended up instead. Does he enjoy the power trip of deciding the fate of people seeking entry into the country? Is he having a bad day? What's he going to do when he finds out I'm a fraud?

I jolt at the abrupt sound of him stamping my forms and filing them away. Only then does he offer a smile, as if he's been purposefully holding it back all this time.

"Welcome home, Ms. Santos."

I try not to appear as enormously relieved as I am. "Thanks."

I collect my passport and head toward the airport exit, filled with new apprehension as the security doors open automatically to a large crowd waiting to greet other travelers.

Tristan told me someone would meet me here and somehow I'd know who it would be. I hesitate past the doors and search the crowd for anyone notable or familiar. My attention snags on a tall man standing on his own near the exit. He's wearing jeans and a black suit jacket over a tuxedo T-shirt. His short dreads stick straight up, making him appear even taller. He's holding a sign in front of him that reads *Santos*.

I walk up to him slowly.

"Hi… I'm not sure, but I think you might be my ride."

"Nice. You must be Saint."

I blink up at him. He must be the wrong guy.

Then he points to the sign. "Santos… Saint. Get it? That's what he calls you anyway. Wouldn't tell me your name."

"Oh, you can call me Isabel."

He lifts an eyebrow. "All right, then." He hesitates a moment before extending his hand. "I'm Makanga. Everyone calls me the Postman."

"Why?"

He smiles broadly, his teeth beaming white. "I deliver things."

"What kinds of things?"

He looks toward the ceiling. "Ah, let's see. Expensive things. Dangerous things. Really important things." He looks down again. "Like you."

He winks and nods toward the conveyer that is depositing bags onto the belt. "You got luggage?"

"No. Just this." I shrug my shoulder, and my backpack swings forward.

Intrigue glints in his amber eyes. "Let's go, then."

I follow him into the parking garage until we reach a two-door sedan. Its black paint is faded in several spots, and large Chinese characters line the top half of the windshield. He reaches for the missing passenger handle and yanks on a bent wire that unlatches the door.

He sweeps his hand toward the open door, gesturing for me to get in.

I hesitate. "I can just take a cab. Really."

He laughs. "Betsy's not in the best shape, but she's a safe ride. Promise."

My life's been turned upside down over the past five days. I wouldn't have ever gotten into a strange car with a strange man in Rio or anywhere else before. Somehow I'm chucking all the normal rules out and operating on instincts now. Tristan is distant and nothing like the man I remember him being, but despite the chaos we've been through, I trust him. I trust him to keep me alive. And I don't get the feeling that Makanga poses a threat to my existence.

So I get into his car, which smells vaguely of grapefruit and coconut oil and is mercifully void of guns or anything indicating its owner is a violent person.

A few minutes later we're heading down the highway. The sky is a wintery gray. The car heater is at full blast, reminding me that I'm definitely not in Rio anymore.

"So where are we going?" I ask.

"Red gave me instructions to keep an eye on you until further notice. So you can crash at my place until I hear otherwise."

I contemplate his offer and try to imagine what I might be getting myself into by staying with him. I know nothing about this man.

"Listen, my parents live in Alexandria. Otherwise I have a friend I can stay with in Arlington. You don't need to put me up."

He shakes his head with a smile. "You must be new at this criminal underworld thing. You can't be telling people your name and where you live. You don't even know me."

My jaw falls open. "I'm *not* a criminal."

He barely masks a smirk. "All right, all right. Didn't mean to offend. Just figured you were into something if Red's giving you a *nom de guerre* and all that."

I finger the St. Paul medallion around my neck and stare at the trees and office parks whizzing by. Whether I like it or not, I've become part of Tristan's world. And Tristan's world is probably chock-full of people who deal in aliases, debts and favors, and all manner of illegal activity required to meet a desired end. Including cold-blooded murder.

The truth remains that Tristan was hired to kill me. Never mind that he didn't. He kills people for a *living*. What could have led the brilliant, passionate man I once knew to such a violent and heartless existence?

I glance over at Makanga again, my suspicions renewed that anyone in Tristan's circle of acquaintances likely subscribes to the same code of conduct. As harmless as Makanga seems, I'd feel safer on my own.

"I appreciate the offer, but I'd rather stay with my friend in Arlington. I don't think Tristan will mind as long as I stay under the radar."

I should go see my parents. They think I'm lost in Rio, or worse. I can't imagine the agony they're going through not knowing whether I'm alive or dead, but reuniting too soon could put us all in danger. For now, I trust Brienne will take me in and stay discreet. We spent four years of college rooming together, a bond that has kept us in touch despite being in different countries living very different lives.

Makanga clucks his tongue and shakes his head. "I think he'll mind paying me when he finds out I didn't do my job."

I think for a moment before unzipping my backpack and withdrawing a stack of bills Tristan gave me before our hasty escape from Mateus's compound.

"Will this help?"

Makanga grins a little and turns his focus back to the road. "I believe it will. Where to, Ms. Santos?"

"The Clarendon. North Herndon Street."

Twenty minutes later we're taking the exit to Brienne's. I release a breath I didn't realize I'd been holding, relieved that he's definitely taking me there. I'm wiped out and need a friend, not a stranger pretending to babysit me.

As Makanga pulls up to the front of Brienne's apartment building, I peer up at the enormous complex. Everything is well lit. New construction. Clean lines and order. Safe. Nothing like Rio.

"Thanks." I hand Makanga his promised fee.

"One sec." He leans over and unlatches the glove compartment.

The door *thunks* open, revealing two handguns and a cell phone. He takes the phone out and offers it to me. "This shouldn't be traceable. Trash your old one if you have it. My number is in there already if you need anything."

I take it hesitantly and put it into my bag. "I should be fine." I hope I'm right, though my track record of properly estimating the danger I'm in isn't stellar lately.

He tosses the cash into the glove compartment and slams it shut. "Pleasure doing business with you, Isabel. Do me a favor and try to stay out of trouble. And if trouble comes to you, call me. I don't live too far from here."

"Got it. Thanks."

My muscles tense when I leave the vehicle and the cool March air wraps around me. Somewhere between my fatigue and swimming thoughts, I find myself missing Rio—all its imperfections, the beautiful chaos. The pulse of the city like a heartbeat of a lover. Slow and steady one moment. Rapid-fire the next. Then memories of Tristan's greedy touches and possessive thrusts hit my senses in an unexpected rush.

I sigh and push the heavy door to the building open. I put the memories away and resolve to lock them up tight until I find my bearings again.

I scan the postboxes in the entryway and double check the apartment number.

Brienne Wu #717

I check my phone on the elevator ride up and locate my contacts. I only have one. *Postman.* Nothing for Tristan. After what we've just been through, I have a hard time imagining him anywhere else but fighting for his life somewhere in Brazil, where people are still trying to hunt us down.

The elevator stops and dings at the seventh floor. Once at Brienne's door, I knock loudly and wait. Today is Sunday, so hopefully I'll catch her home. If not, I briefly consider napping outside her door until she returns. This endless day is wearing on me to the point of pain. I need sleep.

I fantasize about that possibility only a moment before Brienne opens the door.

"Oh my God!" she screams and bounds into the hallway to hug me. "What the fuck are you doing here? It's not even my birthday."

She pulls back, her expression reflecting her surprise and then confusion as she looks me up and down.

"Are you okay? You look like hell."

"Not really. And I know." I sigh. "Sorry for dropping in on you like this. I was hoping I could stay with you for a few days until I figure out my next move."

"Definitely. Come in."

We go in. I let my bag drop to the floor. This isn't home, but being here is suddenly the most comfort I've had in days. The relief hits me hard. I linger there a moment and take it all in.

"Isabel, what's going on?"

"I've been traveling all day," I say weakly. *Running. Surviving. Praying…*

"Come on." She takes my hand. "I've got wine."

One glass of wine, and I'll be unconscious. "I'd love to get cleaned up first."

"Sure thing." She ushers me toward the guest bedroom and the bathroom across the hall. "Make yourself at home," she says softly, though I can see the desire to pry burning behind her kindness.

Even as I step into the blessedly hot shower, I'm not sure how much of Brienne's curiosity I'll be able to satisfy. I'll need a story that doesn't make her want to call the authorities, or my parents, the second I leave the room.

I run through my options until the water turns cold. If only I could wash away this new reality. The one where I can't go home. Can't go back to my life in Rio. Can't leave this building without constantly looking over my shoulder.

I turn off the shower, wrap a towel around me, and venture toward Brienne's room, hoping to snag some clothes. When I walk through the doorway, she's there, picking up clothes from the floor of her messy bedroom.

"Do you mind if I borrow a few things? I wasn't able to bring much with me."

Concern shadows her bright gaze. "Of course. Whatever you need."

We riffle through some of her drawers for jeans, some warmer tops than what I brought with me, and a silky pajama set that I slip into right away.

I deposit the rest with my things and join her in the living room where she's unscrewing a cheap bottle of wine.

"So are you going to tell me what's going on?"

I accept a glass and find a spot on the couch, trying to ignore how the rest of the apartment is especially unkempt. She was never this messy of a roommate, but I have no room to talk. My present life is in total shambles.

"You're probably not going to believe it," I say.

"Hit me with it."

I take a sip of my wine. "Tristan… He found me."

She stares at me in silence, blinking several times before she speaks. "Tristan. As in, *the* Tristan?"

I nod.

"And what? He's in DC, so you came home?"

"No, we reconnected in Rio." I chew at the inside of my lip and hope the fact that I'm leaving out ninety-five percent of the story isn't overly obvious.

She blows out a breath. "Are you back together?"

"Kind of." By circumstance, mostly. But who knows when or if I'll ever see him again.

She puts her wineglass down. "Explain to me what 'kind of' means. He broke up with you. I mean, he *broke* you. I watched it go down, remember? You were a wreck."

"He's different," I say cryptically. "We're different. Everything is."

Her eyes go wide. "Let me get this straight. He ditched all your well-laid plans for a happily ever after, joined the military, and then ghosted you after sending you a fucking letter. No forwarding address. No hope of reconciliation. You remember all this, right?"

I gulp down a huge mouthful of wine. I haven't forgotten. For years, Tristan has taken up more space in my thoughts than he really deserved. I should have gotten over him a long time ago. I had…somewhat. I'd been with other people. I'd *attempted* to move on, but he's always been the reason why I couldn't fall hard for anyone else.

"Anyway. What's going on with you? How's work?"

"You're deflecting. I'm not letting you off that easy."

I offer her a weak smile. "I'm exhausted. I just want to hear about someone else's problems for a few minutes."

She sighs. "Fine. But then you're telling me everything."

TRISTAN

"You did *what?*"

If I could reach through the phone right now, Makanga wouldn't have a prayer.

"I dropped her at her friend's apartment. I scoped it out. Nice neighborhood. Looked fine for a night."

I grab the keys from the valet at the parking garage outside Dulles, pop the trunk of the black coupe I arranged, and deposit my bag.

"That's not what I fucking paid you for. I paid you to keep an eye on her until I got here."

"Well, she pays more than you do, Red. And she's fine. She promised to lie low. You can track her phone anyway. What's the big deal?"

"Never mind." I cuss under my breath and promptly end the call.

When I sent Isabel off on a jet to Panama, I knew I'd have to make a choice. Stay in Brazil and deal with Jay's backup team, or follow Isabel back to DC, where they'd eventually discover her hiding out. Staying in Brazil meant fighting a war I could very likely lose. I can't protect her if I'm a corpse rotting in the jungle, and Jay leaves nothing to chance. On the rare occasions I was sidelined on a job, she had a dozen more like me on standby ready to pick up where I left off, which is likely why Crow was tailing me. I don't imagine Jay has many unsatisfied customers.

If Isabel's not already on Jay's radar, she will be soon. Her first instinct upon recognizing me was to follow me through the streets of Rio and into a dangerous alleyway, so I had reason to question her impulses when she landed back home. More times than not, she does whatever she feels is right, which could quickly land her in trouble.

I open up the app on my phone that indicates Isabel's location. Relieved, I map my way to her friend's apartment, eager to finish the last leg of a very long journey back to the States.

I've been on plenty of assignments but haven't spent time in this part of the country since my memory went dark. Maybe that's why Jay never sent me here. Maybe she couldn't risk the familiarity of the place triggering something in me.

I contemplate that as I drive down the highway. What if I remember more? What if Isabel can break it open now that we're both here?

Is that even what I want?

I turn the car radio down completely, removing the distraction so I can focus on the visuals. The endless horizon of the highway is dotted with luxury cars and semis. I turn onto the exit that will take me to my destination, hoping for something. Suddenly every building and shop and street sign holds the promise of remembrance but offers none.

The brightly lit entrance of the Clarendon comes into view, and all I can feel is a prickling anticipation to see Isabel. All I can picture is her face when I said goodbye to her. The regret I feel for doing it is uncomfortable, but I'm all the more glad to be reconciling the distance now.

I park, enter the apartment building, and call the number for the phone I had Makanga set up for her. She picks up after the second ring.

"Hello?" she answers tentatively.

"It's me, Tristan. What floor are you on?"

She's silent a moment.

"Who is it?" a voice says in the background.

"It's Tristan," she whispers.

Fucking hell. "Isabel. The apartment number."

"Seven seventeen."

I hang up without another word. The twenty-four-hour lag between our arrivals was apparently too long. She's already spilled details to her friend. I know it.

I arrive on the seventh floor. The door is open before I knock. Isabel is there, and before I can say anything, she pulls me inside and slams her body against mine. Twines her arms around my neck. Presses her face against my skin.

The door clicks shut behind us. Her friend is inside on the couch, watching us intently. I hesitate a couple of seconds before slowly returning the embrace. I'm too tired to pretend it's not a welcome sensation. Like our last night in Brazil hasn't been replaying in my mind since I watched her take off without me. Isabel is under my skin, and I'm not sure any amount of insubordination will change that. She holds me tighter, sinks in deeper, touches places inside me that I forgot existed.

"You don't follow instructions very well," I murmur, breathing her in as I wait for a snarky comeback.

"If you want me to follow orders, you'd better be here to enforce them."

"Why do you think I'm here?"

She looks up at me like she can't believe I'm real. "Why didn't you tell me you were coming?"

"I wasn't sure I was."

I can see the impact of the admission in the slight pinch of her features and the cooling of her affection as she steps away. She turns toward our host.

"Tristan, this is Brienne."

Brienne waves her hand from her post on the couch. "Heard a lot about you."

"Really?" I shoot a narrow look at Isabel.

She returns it with a tight smile. "You were kind of a theme in my life before I moved to Brazil."

"A recurring theme, as it were," Brienne says, crossing her arms like she might have something more to say on the subject. "I think you have explaining to do."

She's a petite woman with dark eyes and smooth olive skin. Her hair is long and straight, falling past her shoulders the same way Isabel's does.

I look to Isabel again, wondering how much she may have told her friend about the man I've become and the danger she's fallen into.

Isabel clears her throat. "Can we talk for a minute?"

"Sure."

She takes my hand and leads me into the apartment, closing the door behind us after we enter what appears to be a guest bedroom. Her things are in a neat pile at the foot of the bed. I log all the details. The basic layout of the two-bedroom apartment. The impressive view out the window. The clean, modern decor. The accommodations aren't cheap.

"What did you tell her?"

"I told her we met up in Rio a little while ago and took a trip outside the city last week. Said we ran into some trouble with the locals and I had to fly home in a rush. She bought all of it."

"And why are you here and not with your parents?"

She flinches. "It's too dangerous, Tristan. You know that."

"Yes, I know that. What does *she* know?"

"Oh, I just said my parents didn't know about any of it yet. Told her that I haven't ruled out going back to Rio and I didn't want to worry them if I could avoid it. Obviously she wants me to stay, and she said I can hang out here as long as I want to. Or indefinitely. We lived together for four years."

"Which is why you shouldn't be here. As soon as Jay's people figure out you're back in the States, they'll scour all your contacts in the city. They'll find you here."

"I'm not staying with some stranger, okay?" She throws her hands up and sits on the edge of the unmade bed, her head falling into her hands. "We've been on the run for days, Tristan, and this is the first time

I've felt safe."

"You feel comfortable. It's not the same." When she doesn't respond after a while, I sit beside her. The bed dips under my weight, shifting her closer to me so our sides touch. I curl my arm around her, keeping her there. "We'll stay here for now, all right? And tomorrow we'll reach out to your father and see if he knows anything that can help."

She lifts her gaze to mine. I can see the gratitude swimming in those hazel depths. I touch her silky cheek, draw the backs of my fingers along her jaw. My gaze settles on her mouth. The magnetic force that draws me to this woman time and again lures me forward until our lips meet. The kiss is homecoming and desire and the smallest physical manifestation of all the things she makes me feel.

When I finally pull away, a few tears have fallen, leaving shimmery trails down her cheeks. I want to brush them away and reassure her. Except my reassurances are worthless until I can stop the people who want us dead.

2

ISABEL

I wake to sirens wailing down the street. My heart slams against my ribs as the sound fades out. I breathe a sigh of relief and remember I'm at Brienne's. Tristan's side of the bed is empty. Despite my disorientation, I know he was here. He wasn't a dream.

I lift my head to the sound of a keyboard clicking. He's sitting in a chair beside the window, dressed in dark jeans and a black T-shirt, his bare feet propped on the sill. His expression is pensive, his gaze intent on his laptop screen. Through the window, past parks and the Potomac, the National Cathedral is nestled into a backdrop of greenery, just visible through an early morning fog.

A contented smile tugs at my lips. I can't help but appreciate the visual and entertain a little fantasy that this is normal. A lazy morning at our place. This could have been us…

Despite how he left me so utterly heartbroken, I haven't been able to give up the dream we once shared. Having him back in my life, being reunited with the physical man, only reminds me how he's always personified everything attractive to me. Somehow it's all been amplified in the six years we've spent apart. His confident stride. His penetrating stare. The masculine yet graceful lines of his body, as if he'd been carved into being.

I imagine a sculptor chiseling away, revealing the man Tristan was meant to be from the block of stone that held him. Maybe there was more yet to reveal. Maybe holding on to the man he was all those years ago is hurting us both. He can never be that man again. His experiences the past six years have fed the darkness in him, but they've also led him back to me. I can't acknowledge one circumstance without the other. I have to learn to accept this reality.

He doesn't seem to notice my appraisal of him until the sheets whisper with my movement. He turns his head, his serious expression softening.

"Morning, stranger," I say, still groggy from sleep.

His eyes take a quick pass over my supine position before locking with mine. "Morning," he says quietly.

I regret that he barely touched me last night. Moments after I nestled against his side, he fell into a deep sleep. One that, mercifully, wasn't marred with nightmares like the one I'd witnessed at Mateus's. I followed him down, needing to rest my soul as much as my body in those quiet hours. Having Tristan with me again does something to my soul. No matter what we're facing, being in his presence again puts things right.

"You should get ready. We have a date."

I smile at the prospect of finally leaving Brienne's apartment. A date with Tristan sounds promising too. "I thought you'd never ask. Where are we going?"

"I made contact with your father. Anonymously of course. Said I had a tip for him and needed to meet."

I sit up. My heart picks up speed again as if there's another blaring siren coming my way.

"Are you sure we should do that?"

"It should be fine. I'll be there."

I nod and brace myself for what's to come. Except I never really know. With Tristan, I dive in headfirst and contemplate the risks afterward. I wasn't so different before, but now our snap decisions tip the scales between life or death. Every move matters.

Antsy to see my father, I shower and dress in record time. I emerge to find Brienne and Tristan in the living room, a tense silence filling the space.

"Everything okay?"

"Everything's fine," Tristan answers. "You ready to go?"

Brienne rolls her eyes and heads down the hallway. "See you guys later."

"What was that about?" I ask as we leave the apartment.

"Nothing."

Tristan's curt reply closes the subject, though I intend to press Brienne on it the next chance I get.

A sharp wind whips through the ground-floor breezeway as we make our way to the street. Tristan's car is a new, sporty BMW, a nice improvement from my last ride.

"How do you know Makanga, anyway?"

"We've done business before. Not in DC." Tristan merges with the street traffic and drives us toward a park on the outskirts of town where my father will be waiting for me.

A pang of anxiety hits me about our impending rendezvous, so I attempt to distract myself.

"Is he a friend?"

"No friends, remember," he says without emotion. "But he's reliable most of the time."

"You didn't want to tell him my name."

"That's because I don't trust anyone." He turns left, his wrist resting casually on the wheel as if he's made this drive a thousand times.

"You don't trust him, but you expected me to feel good about staying with him for an unforeseen amount of time?"

He lifts an eyebrow and glances at me before returning his attention to the road. "You trying to pick a fight over this?"

"No," I say quietly and look out the window. I don't know why

I'm pressing the issue, except that there's still so much I don't know.

"I didn't trust Mateus either," he says, "but I let him get you out of there. I did what I had to do. When you're on the run and living off the grid, the rules are different, Isabel. Every bond can be broken. Family, friends, lovers. It doesn't matter. We do what we need to survive."

Something cold wraps around my heart with his words. I'm not Tristan's friend. I'm barely his lover. And no matter what I am to him, everything is conditional.

Every bond can be broken.

Tristan parks on the street and surveys the area. It's noon. Despite the chill, a few people are bundled up on benches, eating their lunches. Others run along the path that follows the river. No one seems suspicious.

Then I see my father. His back is to us. He's gazing out over the choppy water, hands in his pockets.

My heart lurches. I want to run and tell him everything, but a part of me is terrified that he'll be upset with this mess I've gotten myself into. I look over to Tristan, whose attention has fixed on my father as well.

"What are you going to tell him?"

Tristan slides his gaze to mine. "Nothing. He won't know I'm here. It's all you."

I exhale a shaky breath. "Okay. That makes sense, I guess. What should I ask him? Anything specific?"

Of course, I'll want to just blurt out what the past week has been like, but I'm not sure when I'll get the chance to see him again. This meeting isn't about sentiment. I came here to find out the truth, and my father might be the only person who can get us closer to it.

"You should ask if he has enemies, people who would want to hurt you to get to him. He might be working on something that's gone sideways and implicated him in a more personal way."

I mentally log the request. Morgan Foster hasn't gotten to where he's at by betraying confidences or clearances. He never discussed his work at home. I'm not sure he would even if he could. He's always been private. But I've got to try.

"What about the notebook? The one you told me to give him if you didn't find me at the church that night?"

Tristan goes still. "I'd like that back if you don't mind."

"What is it?"

He sweeps his gaze across the park once more. "You should tell your father the truth. You may not get it from him, but at this point, there's nothing to lose by him knowing what's happened. The more information he has, the more he'll know what to look for if he actually plans to help us."

"Then why can't he see the notebook now?"

He turns to me, his expression hardened. "Because as long as I'm breathing, it's my business, not his. It's insurance. Something I thought might help you if Crow managed to kill me."

"Who's Crow?"

His lips tighten into a grim line. "He's a pain in my ass. Another contractor."

"He's an assassin. He kills people for a living."

His silence answers for him.

"Do you know a lot of people like him?"

"Some," he says. "Mostly others in the organization. Jay calls us Company Eleven. Sometimes our paths crossed."

"How does it work?"

He juts his chin toward my father's stoic figure in the distance. "He's waiting for you."

"I'm waiting too. Tell me." I fold my arms over my chest.

Tristan thrums his fingers on the steering wheel. "After I got settled in Rio, I got my first message from Jay. We communicate through a protected chat. It's always the same thing. She sends me a file on the hit. Name, location, optimal time to execute, and any pertinent details or hindrances I should know before going in. If I ever feel like I need to know more, I have to dig for it myself, which I've gotten pretty good at. I figure out all the logistics on my own—travel, surveillance, bribes—and report back when it's done. She wires the funds by the time I land back home. The fee plus incidentals."

I study his stolid features, as disbelieving as ever that this was his existence. His normal. "Just like that."

He hesitates a beat. "Just like that."

"How much would you have gotten paid to kill me?"

My father's begun to pace a short path, back and forth, looking between the gray sky and the pavement. Still, I wait for Tristan's answer.

"Thirty thousand dollars," he says without making eye contact.

I'm not sure why I wanted to know, but now that I do, the reality of it hits me in an odd way. Someone was willing to pay thirty thousand dollars to make sure I died.

Thirty thousand dollars is the price of someone's life, regardless of what they've done or not done, regardless of who they'll leave behind...

The truth is crushing, but I find myself seeking more of it. More of the painful, terrible truth.

I close my hand around the door handle. "Where will you be?"

He finally meets my eyes. "I'll be right here watching you the whole time."

I leave the vehicle and walk toward my father. Within seconds, I'm within earshot, but I can't bring myself to call out to him. I don't have to. He turns, and recognition lights up his eyes. He takes a few large strides toward me.

Wordlessly, he pulls me into a crushing embrace.

I can feel his heart hammering. The strength of his embrace is home—the safe place I was so determined to run from once upon a time. I exhale a shaky breath as we break away, blinking away the emotion burning behind my eyes.

He holds me by the shoulders, seeming to do the same. "What happened? Why didn't you come straight home? I don't think I've slept since the police told us you were missing. I know your mother hasn't."

"It's a long story. It had to be this way. I'm sorry."

Every worry line in his face is more pronounced than ever. "We should have never let you go there."

I close my eyes with a sigh. My parents argued with me endlessly about going to Rio. But they'd argued against me being with Tristan too. They argued about the hour-long bus ride into Baltimore. Every nagging objection was a strip of rope around my freedom until I was ready to snap.

"Nothing could have made me stay," I finally say. "Not after Tristan."

He can't mask his grimace. "For Christ's sake, Isabel. You need to let him go. All he ever brought you was heartache. Let him *go*." He shakes me slightly with that last demand.

As if any amount of time or manner of well-meaning advice could change my heart.

"He found me." My admission is nearly carried away by the breeze.

He freezes. "Tristan?"

"Do you know what happened to him?"

He takes a step back, breaking contact. Several seconds pass as he seems to absorb this new information.

"Why would I?"

"He's different, Dad. He's in trouble, and so am I."

He searches my gaze, his posture rigid. "What kind of trouble?"

"He…" I swallow hard. This is the moment I've dreaded. Admitting the awful truth of what's come to pass. Tristan's role in it is salt on the wound. "He was hired to kill me."

My father pales. "Are you serious?"

Something seems to click, an unspoken understanding that things are more dire than he realized.

"Once he found out who I was, we took off. He got me out of Brazil. I used a fake passport to get home, but he's worried they're not going to give up that easily. We need to find out who's behind all this."

He flickers his gaze to mine. "Are you sure this isn't some game?"

"Dad, this isn't a game. People are dead. I've seen things…"

I close my eyes against the terrible memories. My thoughts pivot to the men guarding the gates of Mateus's compound. Sharp bolts of sound. Instant results. White rocks bleeding red.

When I open my eyes, his are wide with panic. "Isabel, let's get you home. We can figure this out there."

"Wait." I step back. I can't bring myself to tell him I can't go with him. Not yet. "Who would want to hurt me? Someone wants me dead. Do you have an enemy, someone who may be trying to get to you through me?"

His brows furrow. "No. I mean…" His focus darts around as if he's pinging between all the possibilities. "I've always been very careful. Hell, I don't even wear a wedding ring so no one assumes I have a family at home. If someone intended to send a message, I'd have gotten it by now. Why anyone would want to hurt you is madness."

Maybe so, but that doesn't change the fact that I'm still running for my life from the people who turned Tristan into the killer he's become.

"Do you have any idea what happened to Tristan after he enlisted?"

My father's frown deepens. "If he's in trouble, he can fend for himself. All that matters is you're safe now. You're home, and I can take care of the rest."

His indifference toward Tristan riles me.

"We're tied up in this together now. I'm not coming home until I know why he was sent for me."

He hesitates. "He's here with you? Where is he?"

"Close," I say hesitantly.

He works his jaw. "Listen, he's gotten himself mixed up with the wrong people. That's not your fault."

"It's not his fault either."

"Stop defending him, Isabel. For God's sake, when are you ever going to get it through your head? The kid is a loser. He was on the wrong path long before he met you. I did what I could, but—"

"Stop it!"

I huff out a few shaky breaths. Familiar anxiety ripples through my limbs. Suddenly I'm eighteen again, defending myself. Defending Tristan.

I love him. They can't keep us apart. It's my life.

The old song weaves into this new dilemma.

My father stills, his gaze searching mine. Defiance meeting defiance. Finally he breaks his stare and pinches the bridge of his nose.

"I looked him up in the database at work after he broke things off with you. You were miserable. I thought maybe I could track him down and give you some solace. He went on a few deployments overseas. His last mission in Afghanistan was a bloodbath. He got out of it alive, and then he transitioned out. I figured he'd lost a limb or something bad enough that it'd just end up breaking your heart all over again."

A cold, sobering wind rushes between us. Gratitude and grief hold me up. An enduring sadness with what's come to pass. Relief that Tristan's fate wasn't even worse.

"He lost his memory, Dad. He doesn't remember anything before that last mission. He doesn't remember *me*."

He winces. "That can't be true."

"I believe him," I say. "If I hadn't recognized him, I think he would have killed me. Whatever they did to him, they turned him into a killer. And because he didn't go through with it, they're after both of us."

"Who? Who's they?"

"I'm still trying to figure that out. Tristan has a contact in the organization. A manager, I guess. Her name is Jay. He doesn't know much else about them other than she calls them Company Eleven. He gets dossiers on hits and is wired the money when it's done." I'm heartbroken all over again as I utter the words aloud. "I have a feeling he was pretty good at his job."

My father rakes his fingers along the side of his short, silvering hair, betraying his anxiety. "Christ."

My thoughts drift to the red notebook. I'd found it in my things on the flight back to DC. I'd studied the names in it, each with a number beside it. Dozens of them were scratched onto the lined pages in his script. He might call it insurance, but I'm pretty sure it's a ledger of all the people he's been hired to kill.

"Will you look into it more?"

"Of course. I'll find anything I can. For now, let's get you home. Lucia is worried sick. I haven't seen her this way since Mariana…"

He closes his eyes, and instantly I know. If my mother thinks her daughter is dead, she's reliving the worst kind of pain.

I take my father's hand and squeeze it firmly. "Tell her I'm fine. I am. But I can't come home yet. I have to lie low until we figure out what's going on."

His eyes go wide with panic. "Isabel, no. You have to come home."

"If someone is still looking for me, it's the first place they'll go," I say, mimicking Tristan's warning.

"Then they don't know who they're dealing with." Something about the finality in my father's tone gives me pause. He's gone from concerned father to something else. A man to be reckoned with.

I withdraw a piece of paper from my jacket and hand it to him. "This is the number you can reach me at. If you find anything—"

"You can rest assured I'm going to get to the bottom of this, Isabel." He clutches the paper tightly in his hand, not speaking for a long time. "How am I supposed to let you go back to him after what you've just told me?"

I think through a dozen reassurances. Most he won't believe. That Tristan would never hurt me. That he'll keep me safe. Everything boils down to the same thing. It's my choice. My life. My trust. My mistake.

He already knows this.

I reach for him. I'm not sure he's ever hugged me so tightly or for so long.

"I need you to be careful, Isabel. Be smart."

"I will," I whisper. "I promise."

When we pull away after several minutes, I can't mistake the tears in his eyes.

"Bye, Dad."

3

TRISTAN

I watch as Morgan gets into his car on the opposite side of the park and speeds off. The meeting with Isabel could have played out a few ways. I'm glad I didn't need to intervene. I step out and meet Isabel as she approaches the car.

"How did it go?"

"Fine." The look on her face isn't promising.

"Fine?"

"He doesn't know much, but he seems determined to find out."

"You asked him—"

"Everything you said, yes. He's too careful to have enemies. At least any that he knows of. No one's reached out to him."

"What else?"

She bites her lip. "He said he knew about your mission. The one that went wrong. He called it a bloodbath. Said you transitioned out afterwards and that was it. He…"

"He what?"

"He still hates you, I think."

I roll that around in my head. With Isabel's life at stake, I wasn't expecting her father to be clinging to old grudges. "He said that?"

"He didn't have to," she murmurs.

She tightens her hold around her midsection as a strong gust of wind rolls in.

I resist the urge to tuck her against me and warm her. I don't trust myself to touch her. Lying beside her last night was almost more than I could bear. Thankfully the day's exhaustion pulled me under before I could act on any of the sordid thoughts that come to mind every time she's within reach.

"He knows you're with me?"

"Yes, I told him."

"If he let you leave, he can't hate me that much."

She sighs heavily. "I think he could see in my eyes that this was serious. I mean, he's been wondering if I've been dead this whole time."

"And you believed him? Everything he said?"

She nods wordlessly.

We should drive off and get out of sight. I have no idea where we'll go next. I'm not ready to hole up in the apartment again yet.

I'm too edgy after what Isabel's told me. I never pegged her for gullible, so when she tells me she believes her father is clueless about who's put the hit out on her, I'm not sure what to think. As connected as Morgan Foster is within the CIA, he's the natural choice.

I kick one of the tires. "He has to know *something*."

She crosses her arms and leans against the hood. "I'm sure if he knows anything that would get me out of this mess, he'd tell me. He seemed shocked. In disbelief. It's a sentiment I'm familiar with lately. I recognized it when I saw it."

I hesitate to reiterate my rule about trusting people—a rule that doesn't have exceptions. I have little doubt that some of the people in my book were marked by someone who claimed to love them.

She straightens and comes to me. Strands of her hair play in the breeze, and her cheeks and nose are pink. She looks mussed and natural—uniquely beautiful in the most unexpected moments.

"What now?"

"I can't go back to the apartment right now," I say.

"Do you detest her that much?"

I laugh roughly. "You should ask her the same question."

She frowns. "Did she say something to you?"

"Yeah, I'm a real piece of shit for breaking your heart the way I did, and if I even think about hurting you again, she's going to hunt me down and castrate me." I lift my eyebrows and put on a fake smile.

She sighs. "Listen, Brienne's just being protective. She was there for me during a difficult time. She takes it personally that I'm with you again."

"Whatever," I mutter. "As far as I'm concerned, the less time we spend there, the better."

She seems thoughtful a moment. Then she reaches out her hand. "Give me the keys."

I don't budge. "Why?"

"You don't want to go back to Brienne's. I have a better idea. Let's go for a drive."

"Where?"

She closes the small space between us, pouting prettily while running her hands down my arms.

"What are you doing?"

She lifts on her toes and barely brushes her lips over mine, blindsiding me as she slips her hand into my jacket pocket.

"Stealing your keys," she whispers with a smirk.

Little things start to register as soon as we exit the highway. The neighborhoods on the outskirts of Baltimore leave much to be desired. We're a far cry from Rio's favelas, but whatever street sense I've retained tells me that we need to be on guard more here than we were in Arlington. Isabel takes a few more turns. The way she stretches her neck forward and squints toward the numbers on the houses tells me we're close.

"It's one of these," she says.

My palms sweat, and I'm starting to regret the decision to let Isabel take us here. But, like her, I'm curious. A little too restless to see if being in my old neighborhood will bring back more memories. Maybe a few that aren't so heart-wrenching.

We pass an abandoned bus stall. A convenience store with a yellow awning and a few people lingering under it. Closely set houses go on and on until she slows to a stop in front of one. She puts the car into park, and we both stare out the passenger-side window.

I know this is it. The house is a few paces off the street, distinguishable from its neighbors only by the red eviction notice stapled to the door, almost obscured by a board nailed across it. Somehow I just *know* I've scaled the front steps a thousand times. Heard the door creak every time I opened it. Shivered when the air inside wasn't as warm as it should be on cold winter days.

I get out and scan up and down the street. Kids with backpacks walk by in groups. School must have just let out. Isabel comes near, welcome warmth at my side. A few people look at us but move on, unconcerned by our presence.

As I stare at the abandoned place, gunshots fire through my memories. Sickness permeates my gut, yet I crave more. Something more than visions of my mother's bloody body in the street. More than my screams.

I move forward, no longer tentative. I make soundless steps, the whooshing of my own breathing and heartbeat drowning out the finer details. At the door, I slam my foot against the board, cracking it.

"Tristan!" Isabel's concerned voice fades into the background.

Without hesitating, I kick it again. I don't care. I've got to get in. I bash the door twice more until the jamb cracks and it swings open with a high-pitched scrape. I duck under the busted board.

One step inside, and I'm paralyzed.

Being here feels like a dream—one where I'm drawn forward into a place I've never been, but somehow I know all the rooms. Not that there are many. A kitchen with filthy linoleum and a rotten odor to match. A narrow hallway that leads to a bedroom. I can't tell what color the carpet is supposed to be. Cheap yellowing curtains are bunched in the window that offers a view of the next house a few feet away. It's dark. Cracking paint spiders the dirty walls.

I turn when I hear Isabel catch up. Her eyes are wide, a deep green in this light. Anxiety rolls off her. She's worried we'll get caught. I know in my bones that no one around here cares about us or this place.

"This was my room."

She wrings her fingers together and nods quickly.

I look around again, disgusted. Granted, it's been six years, but the house couldn't have looked much better when I called it home.

I walk to the window. Nothing to see, but hell, it's a window. Dust is caked on the sill. Isabel is beside me again, resting her head against my arm. Our fingers intertwine, palms meet. I reach for the comfort her touch brings, but embarrassment overwhelms everything.

"Either there's something really wrong with me, Isabel, or there's something wrong with you."

Her dark brows draw together.

I'm sick with this place and the fact that she's here. That she was *ever* here. "Why would you be here with me? How could you stand it?"

Her lips part, her countenance awash with innocence and understanding at once. "Because I loved you. I wanted to be with you more than anyone else. All the time. It didn't matter where we were."

I clench my jaw. Nothing's changed. I'm the worst person she could have possibly brought back into her life. I'm convinced of it. "I've never been good for you."

She squeezes my hand. "Maybe I was good for you, though."

"That's not enough. There's no reason for you to sink this low. You should have left me..." I drop my hand from hers and pace away, clawing my fingernails across my scalp. The discomfort brings me back. Out of the dream. Into the sobering present. "You should have left me before I left you. You brought this on yourself. God, Isabel... What were you thinking?"

She comes close again, reaching for me, but I brush her away. I can't handle her touch. Her eyes glisten and her lips tremble.

"I wish I could fucking burn this place down."

Her face is tight with pain. "Not me," she whispers. "You can wish it away all you want. But this was *real*, Tristan. We were real. I didn't care about what you had or didn't have. We were with each other for the only reasons that mattered. We filled a space inside each other that only we could. Okay? And it didn't matter what side of town you were from."

"And what about now? What about the fact that I fucking kill people for a living and you're teaching English to school kids? How much further apart can we fall before you give up?"

She doesn't answer, so I press on.

"Because I know you haven't yet. When are you going to give up?" I shove a hard hand through my hair again. "I wish we'd never…"

I stop myself and try to scour the images of her naked body writhing under my tongue. It's impossible. I'll have those memories forever. I'm certain of it. They're burned in. Same way I'm certain they're burned into her. Same way the man I was keeps taking up space in her heart.

"Let's go." I walk swiftly out.

"Tristan, wait."

I don't wait. I hurry back to the street. A few more people meander by. No sign of the local authorities. As I suspected, no one cares about the busted door or our brief tour of the slum I once called home. I get to the driver's side and realize Isabel still has the keys.

She meets me there. "Tristan, you're upset. You shouldn't drive like this."

"Give me the fucking keys."

Her eyes narrow into angry slits. "Just because you're hurting, it doesn't give you the right to be such an asshole."

With that, she slaps the keys into my palm and circles the vehicle.

We get in, and I gun the engine, too eager to put this shithole in my rearview.

"Turn left at the next stop sign."

"I know the way back," I snap.

On the hour ride home, we don't speak. The radio plays quietly, but my thoughts are too loud to notice. Isabel's posture is tense. She doesn't make eye contact, which is fine. I'm not in the mood to make her feel better. I'm too wrapped up in my own confused emotions.

We park and go up to the apartment. Inside, Brienne is nestled on the couch with large headphones covering her ears, deep in virtual battle.

I pause near the doorway. "I'm going for a drive."

Isabel turns back, her shoulders soften. "Tristan…"

I want to stay and make things right with her. But the part of me that needs to pace and be pissed off wins.

"Here." I take her phone out of her coat pocket and program my number into it. "Call me if you need me."

"Where are you going?"

"Just for a drive to clear my head, all right? I'll be back soon."

We're a few inches apart, close enough to feel the effect she has on me. I can't spend another night that way. And sleep won't save me this time.

"I'll see you later, Isabel."

4

ISABEL

I wake up abruptly. No sirens. No jarring sounds. The bed is empty, and somehow I know Tristan never made it home. I scramble for my phone. I'm ready to start thinking the worst when I see a text from him.

Taking care of a few things today.
See you tonight.

I don't bother acknowledging his message or asking for details he'll never share. This is who he is. Cryptic and moody. Tender one minute, indifferent the next. Two steps forward, one step back.

Our detour to his old place seemed like progress until he lashed out. I've never seen him so rattled, so vulnerable. Watching recognition hit his features was both heartening and heartbreaking. Not only because of the words he hurled at me but the loneliness hidden in them. The utter emptiness around them. I can be there for him, but I'll never know what this must be like.

How much of his memory was triggered in those moments? I

worry he's rethinking how much more he wants to relive. Especially if he's intent on keeping me at arm's length or disappearing for hours or days at a time, leaving me to wonder where he is or if he's even alive.

I navigate to a second message from a familiar DC number. My father's.

Checking in to make sure you're okay.

I type out a quick reply.

I'm fine. Did you find anything?

Three little dots animating below the message indicate he's typing. The small connection makes me smile. He may hate Tristan and most of my life choices, but he's still my dad. I've still missed him, and of all people, I'm grateful to have him fighting for me and trying to find the truth.

Working on it.

I'm hit with disappointment. Either nothing has turned up, or he's not sharing it with me. A moment passes until he's typing again.

*Tristan attended a rehab center for vets
after the army. No other trace of him after.*

I fall back on the pillow and let this new information sink in. Tristan never mentioned a rehab center. I don't think he remembers anything about his recovery. Maybe this could get me closer to finding out how he ended up in the clutches of Jay and in the company of assassins.

I get up, get dressed, and go make coffee. As I wait for it to brew, I find Brienne's laptop. I open it, pull up a new browser window, and type in a search for veteran rehabilitation centers near the DC area, assuming he came here afterward. A handful pop up, all government-run VA clinics and offices. All but one. Trinity House. I click on the website and am presented with a large photo of several smiling men and women sitting around a courtyard. *Helping our service men and women transition into civilian life.* I read their mission statement and learn that they're privately funded with a waiting list for new clients. They seem nothing like the run-of-the-mill government programs typically offered to returning vets.

I try to imagine a broken and battered Tristan coming to a place like that. Knowing nothing of his past. Having no one to turn to for support, financial or otherwise. If he was this close, I could have been there for him. And I would have. My heart hurts when I think of it.

I shoot off a quick text to my father.

Trinity House?

I put my phone back in my pocket and go to the coffeemaker, willing it to create its liquid magic a little quicker.

I hear Brienne's shuffling footsteps behind me. Her face is swollen from sleep. Her hair leaves much to be desired, and she's wearing an old GW hoodie that I've seen her in at least a few hundred times.

"What's up, roomie?"

She groans and takes two large mugs out of the cupboard, sliding one toward me. "Bree need coffee."

I chuckle as she takes the half-full pot out of its cradle and fills both our mugs. She returns it, and the coffeemaker resumes its percolating gurgles.

"What are you up to today?" I finally ask.

She goes to the refrigerator and pours some flavored creamer into her mug. "I have the week off, and my favorite thing to do is nothing, so that's what I'm up to."

My phone buzzes, and I take it out of my pocket. A one-word reply from my father's number.

Yes.

Then, a moment later.

Mom wants to see you.

I look up at Brienne. "I have to go out and run a few errands. Want to come with?"

She narrows her eyes slightly. "Who's going to take us? Tristan? Where is he, anyway?"

Her question is valid. I'm not sure how I'll get to the rehab center or how I'll disguise any of what I plan to do as "errands." Brienne doesn't have a car, I'm out of cash, and my credit cards are off-limits. I may not be out of favors though.

"No, Tristan's not around today," I say absently. I search for Makanga's number on the phone and type out a quick text.

Can you give me a ride?

Brienne moves to the couch and settles in her nest, covering herself in a throw blanket. I follow her over. I have one knee on the couch when my phone rings. Makanga's number displays.

I hold up a finger, indicating I'll be back, and answer the call.

"Hey," I say.

"Someone called an Uber," he says, his deep voice dry with humor.

I laugh. "It's just a quick trip. An hour there and back."

"What's Red doing?"

"He's doing his own thing today. Can you help me out?"

"Fine, but my rate's gone up."

I roll my eyes. "I think the enormous stack of cash I gave you the other day ought to cover me for today."

He exhales a sigh. "Yeah, all right. Be there in five."

"Thanks."

I hang up. By the time I return to Brienne, she's already lost in another round of Fortnite. Her empty cup has joined the other dirty dishes on the coffee table. Her eyes are glued to the television, seemingly oblivious to me.

I want to drag her out of the apartment so we can catch up more. So I can feel like a normal person for a minute, but I know it'll only complicate things for me. So I put it off for another time.

"I'm running out, Bree. I'll see you in a bit."

She flips me a peace sign without breaking her trance with the screen.

On the outside, the Trinity House doesn't seem as magical as the website suggests. Set between two storefronts with simple signage—a small banner in the window—the place seems unremarkable.

"I'll be right back," I say. "I shouldn't be long."

Makanga pulls a grapefruit out of the center console and starts to peel it. "Take your time. I'll be here."

I push through the center's double doors and see a couple of middle-aged men sitting in the waiting room. A young woman sits at the reception desk.

"How can I help you?"

"I'm trying to find out some information about a man who was in your program a few years ago."

Her lips form a small pout. "I'm sorry. I can't share patient information. It's company policy."

"I understand." I'm not ready to give up yet, though. "It's actually really important. He's been missing, and I'm trying to help his family track down anything I can find about where he might have gone."

She hums and looks around her desk, as if the answers might be there. She doesn't seem extremely bright. Then her eyes light up.

"Would you like to talk to the director? She's almost always traveling, but she's here today. Maybe she could help?"

I release an audible sigh. "That would be amazing. Thank you so much."

She lifts a pen attached to the clipboard between us and taps on the paper with it. "Can you just sign in here? She should be with you shortly."

I take the pen and begin to write *Isab*—

I freeze.

I finish writing *Isabel*...and then scrawl *Santos* for my last name.

I drop the pen and find a seat in the waiting room. I wonder where the courtyard is and whether Tristan spent much time here before starting his new life. Several minutes later the receptionist calls my name, leads me deeper into the building, and pauses outside the director's office.

She raps lightly on the door, and the redhead seated behind an exceptionally clean desk turns away from her computer screen and rises. I take a couple of steps inside.

"Hi," I say, suddenly paralyzed by the intense blue-eyed stare she's pinned on me.

She offers an outstretched hand. "I'm Jude McKenna. You must be Isabel." Her fingers are cold, and her grip is solid. "Have a seat."

The receptionist disappears, leaving the door ajar, and we both sit. The office seems new with clean beige walls and matching rugs. The woman before me doesn't blend in with her surroundings though. Her hair is pulled back into a severe bun, which does little to diminish her natural beauty. Impeccably dressed, she could be a model straight out of a women's work fashion catalogue with her fitted trousers and turtleneck blouse. She belongs in the Capitol building, not here.

"How can I help you? Kelly said you were inquiring about a patient."

"Yes, I am." A knot of anxiety lodges in my throat. I'm at a loss for words. This all suddenly feels wrong.

"His name?"

I blink rapidly. "Um, Tristan Stone."

Her nostrils flare slightly. "Doesn't ring a bell. Are you family?"

"No."

"Girlfriend?"

My jaw opens, and then I clamp it shut. She smiles, but it soon disappears. She turns toward her computer and clicks her mouse a few times. The privacy screen keeps me from seeing anything she's doing.

"Have you checked with the VA?"

I swallow over the anxiety building with each passing second. "No, he came here. I know he did."

"And then...you lost touch?"

"Right. He just kind of disappeared after he came back from his last deployment. I thought maybe you could tell me something. Last-known address. Anything, really."

She turns away from the screen and faces me again. "If it were a police matter, I could help. But unfortunately I can't share patient information with you." She pauses a moment, and then her voice softens slightly. "I can tell you that our center specifically caters to veterans dealing with the worst kinds of trauma. Sometimes the only path forward is to start over."

I stare into my lap and try to mask the blow of those words, because nothing could describe Tristan better. He'd suffered the worst kind of trauma. And he thought the only choice was to start over...as a trained killer. Except I suspect that path chose him, not the other way around.

I lift my gaze. "I suppose you're right. I'm sorry to have wasted your time." I stand to go. This woman's vibe is unsettling. Everything about the meeting is. I already feel as if I've said too much. Shared too much. What if I've left a trail somehow? What if the people who want me dead find out I was here?

"Miss Foster?"

My grip tightens on the door. Suddenly I can hardly breathe. The sound of my name—my *real* name—has sucked all the oxygen out of the room. All my instincts are screaming for me to get out of here.

She looks me over thoroughly. "I can have Kelly try to track him down. If she makes contact, she could let him know someone is looking for him if you think that might help."

"Sure," I say quickly just to end the conversation. "That would be wonderful."

"Just leave your contact info with her on your way out."

"I'll be sure to." I return her polite smile and hurry down the hall.

I don't bother leaving my info at the front desk. I see Makanga outside, his body reclined in the seat, apparently napping. I go to the car and yank hard on the wire. Makanga bolts up and reaches over, letting me in.

I drop into the seat and slam the door behind me. "Fix your fucking car."

"I guess it didn't go so well in there."

"Just… Let's go."

As he starts the engine and puts us into motion, I catch Director McKenna's figure hovering just beyond the doors, watching us drive away.

5

TRISTAN

Isabel is bait. Temptation of the best and worst kind. Ignoring my past was easy enough when I didn't have a beautiful, charismatic woman luring me into it. Hell, maybe she's a siren leading me to my death—or at least much further down the rabbit hole than I ever imagined I'd go.

As soon as I begin to doubt the journey, curiosity tests the edges of my resolve and I find myself reaching for more. I'm compelled to rip away the gauze that's made everything dark and fuzzy for so long. Which is exactly why I'm sitting outside the Patriot's Fare Restaurant & Bar waiting for Zachary Brennan to get off his shift. If I bail, his wife will tell him an old buddy stopped by looking for him. He'll never know for sure it was me. And I'll never know about the massacre that sent us both home three years ago.

I spent most of the night driving around DC. I stopped at a few monuments. Admired them in their illuminated wonder. Drifted back into my own turmoil and drove some more. Then I stopped at a little diner to recaffeinate and did what I probably should have done a long time ago. I pulled up an internet search for Tristan Stone.

What I found was sparse. My mother's obituary, a graduation roster from my high school, and an article about an ambush on a Special Forces unit stationed in Afghanistan. Only two men walked away from it alive. Tristan Stone and Zachary Brennan.

Even if I hadn't seen his photo in the article, I feel as if I'd know Brennan's face. He has a large build but a humble stride as he heads toward his pickup truck in the parking lot behind the restaurant. I push off my car and meet him as he's fumbling with his keys.

"Brennan?"

He looks up, his eyes wide. He freezes and blinks a few times. "Holy shit. Holy *shit*!" He laughs and then covers his mouth with his hand. "I can't believe it's you, man. Where the hell have you been?"

I force a smile, which isn't extremely difficult since Brennan seems pleased as punch to see me. I wasn't sure what to expect.

"It's been a while," I simply say.

"Yeah, sure has." His mirth fades a little. "Shit, last time I saw you, I thought we were both finished."

I look down a moment and back up, studying his features. "You want to grab a beer or something?"

"Hell yeah." He lifts his chin toward the restaurant. Its faded blue paint is peeling off the wood in places. "I know the owner here. He'll hook us up."

I follow him inside, and we settle at a small table near the back of the restaurant. An older man with a thick midsection and an apron tied around it comes up to our table.

"You back again already?"

Brennan laughs. "Met an old friend outside. Wanted to buy him a drink. Abe, this is Corporal Tristan Stone. We served together a few years back."

The older man jolts back. "Hell, beers on the house, then. Thank you for your service, young man."

I shake his meaty hand, feeling like a fraud as I do. Nothing I've done since my time overseas has been deserving of pride.

Brennan orders our beers and the man disappears.

"So how have you been, man?"

I let out a nervous laugh. Jesus, fuck. How do I even start to answer that? I can't pretend that anything about my life has been normal. I wouldn't know where to begin, so I have to come clean with him. Now or never.

"This is probably going to sound…odd."

His buddy brings our beers and a bowl of peanuts. "Here you go, fellas. Hey, thanks again. I mean it." He pats me hard on the arm, and I harness all my willpower not to glare so he'll leave us—*me*—alone. I force another smile and avert my gaze, hoping he'll go away.

As he does, Brennan pops a peanut in his mouth. "Sorry. Abe gets excited sometimes. When I told him I did a tour in Afghanistan, he hired me on the spot. He's got a thing for vets."

I lift an eyebrow, and he laughs.

"I'm serious. He goes around town and harasses people when their flags get too tattered. Buys them new ones if they won't replace them on their own. I've never met a bigger patriot. Honest to God."

"I bet."

I don't understand patriotism, though I'm certain another part of me probably did. Or maybe I put my body in harm's way for some other reason. To seek revenge for my mother's senseless death by making my country's enemy my own. Or maybe my years in the military converted me into a flag-loving patriot, someone worthy of his friend's pride.

Brennan interrupts our brief derailment. "So, you were saying…"

"I was wondering if we could talk about the last mission… The details are kind of foggy for me."

For the first time since I've been in his presence, he frowns. He curves a hand around the back of his neck and rubs back and forth.

"That was a long time ago, Stone. I don't really feel like digging up old graves, you know?"

"I know, but whatever happened over there really messed me up. I have severe memory loss. I'm just trying to put the pieces back together."

His exhale whooshes out. "Damn. I'm sorry, man. I had no idea.

They wouldn't let me see you after. Then you transitioned out, and I couldn't track you down." He's quiet a moment. "Honestly, I wasn't sure I wanted to."

You have a lot of blood on your hands.

Jay's words rattle through me. I take a swig of beer and contemplate leaving.

Instead, I level my gaze to his. "You don't have to spare my feelings. Just tell me what happened."

Did I really need to know?

He takes a deep breath and then a long pull off his beer. "Jesus Christ, you're gonna give me nightmares for a month." He drags his hand down his face and then nods, as if he's giving himself a pep talk to even begin.

He doesn't realize the things I've done since are probably far worse than whatever he's about to reveal.

Rolling his shoulders, he begins. "We were stationed at Camp Dwyer, but we set up an outpost near one of the local towns to keep a closer eye on things. The valley was a shitstorm, especially with the harvest coming up."

"The opium harvest."

Fields of red flowers. As far as the eye could see. I blink away the vision and wait for Brennan's words to fill in the empty space around it.

"Right. Prettiest place in the country. Most dangerous too. The higher-ups, they just wanted us to keep peace with the farmers. Impossible when we're two steps away from burning their whole fucking opium crop. So the local Taliban's taking a cut to protect the farmers whether they want it or not. Funds their activities real nice, and of course it's a good excuse to shoot at us."

"Right." I don't remember being in the thick of it, but I'm familiar with how the local drug trade funds all kinds of extremist organizations. Rio was on the same plan without the religious zealotry.

"Rahul Khan was our man," he continues.

I roll the name around my head, but it doesn't hit any pegs.

"Who was he?"

"The local commander. Kingpin, whatever. He'd been gaining a lot of ground in Helmand. That meant we were losing it. Not what we were sent there to do."

He starts picking at the label on the bottle, and I have a feeling the story is about to get bloodier.

"Then what," I press.

He exhales. "We came up with a plan. Khan had a drug depot nearby. Taking it out would send a message to the farmers without fucking with their livelihoods, and we'd take back some control. We couldn't just waltz up to it, of course. So we picked up a tip from a local guy named Javeed." He shakes his head. "I'll never forget that fucking name."

"Why?"

"He's the one who told us how we could get to the drug depot through the caves and underground tunnels. Drew us a map. Told us exactly when Khan would be vulnerable. Planned the whole damn operation for us."

"Let me guess. He led us right to trouble."

"I was your superior. I could have shut it all down. But once we started talking it out, you were dead set on taking this guy down. Everyone was right there with you." He pauses a beat. "We all agreed you and I would go through the tunnels. It was going to be quick. In and out. Take Khan out, come back, and then see if his people would scatter. We'd reevaluate whether or not to bring any more heat once we got back."

"Why me?"

"Your Arabic was shit, but that didn't matter. We weren't going there to talk. You were a good shot. Almost as good as me. More importantly, all you had to do was look at the map once and you'd be able to get us there and back faster than anyone in the unit."

I nod. "That makes sense."

He leans in. "You could remember anything, Stone. Numbers, directions, maps. You never wrote a damn thing down. I can't believe you don't remember what happened that day."

Whatever happened that blighted my memory of that day and everything before it hadn't changed my inherent abilities—abilities that made me valuable to people like Jay.

"I can't explain it," I say. "I wish I could. I guess that's why I'm here."

That was the truth.

"We got to the depot just before dawn. Khan was right where Javeed said he'd be. Pop pop. Done. We high-fived and got the fuck out of there before anyone was on to us. It was pitch black in the tunnels, but you led us back through them like nothing."

A few empty seconds pass, and I wait for him to finish.

"Turns out Javeed was jockeying for Khan's position. He led us right to him. Meanwhile, he tipped Khan off that we were preparing an offensive that morning. That's why security was light. By the time we got back… Fuck," he mutters quietly, pinching the bridge of his nose.

I echo the sentiment in my head but push him harder. "What happened?"

"When we got near the entrance of the tunnel, we could hear gunfire, but it seemed like it was fading away. You ran right into it before I could stop you. Another envoy from Dwyer showed up and chased the rest of them off before I could get to you. You were fading by then. I thought I'd lost you."

"And everyone else?"

He shook his head, his eyes haunted with the horrors he must have seen. That was enough.

"I'm sorry." I feel idiotic saying it.

"Me too. It's not something I'll ever forget. I'm damn glad you can't remember it, but at least now you know."

Several minutes of silence pass. Brennan waves Abe over, and he brings another round of beers. I don't need it, but I'm sure Brennan does after what he's just recounted.

"Your wife was really nice. When I tracked down your address, I stopped by there first to see if you were around."

He smiles. "Thanks, man. Angel's the best. No one was happier when I became a civilian again. She put up with enough while I was in."

He looks wistful for a minute, and I can tell he's smitten. Lovestruck is about as foreign to me as patriotism, but I recognize it when I see it.

"How about you? Did you and your girl ever figure things out?"

My jaw falls a fraction. "Isabel?"

He snaps and points at me. "That's it. Isabel. She had you twisted up. I remember it now."

"I think that might have been the other way around. We weren't together."

"Everyone had their ups and downs, Stone. There was always a chance we weren't coming home or that we'd get cheated on or heartbroken. So we'd screw things up before life screwed us. Didn't stop you from talking about her all the damn time. I'm pretty sure you wrote her a letter once a week and set it on fire before you could send it. Hell, you had her picture on your wall as long as I could remember."

I stare at him in stunned silence. Moments ago, he described what was likely the most horrific scene I'd ever experienced. It didn't feel good, but learning that I was still in love with Isabel after I'd broken things off… That's got my heart in my throat. Brennan seems to realize this.

"Do you remember her? Isabel?"

I drum my fingers on the table nervously. "No, not really. But we reconnected."

Brennan's face is awash with pity. "Wow. That sucks."

"What?"

"You came home and didn't even remember her? I can't imagine. She must be special if she took you back after all that."

Isabel is special. My instincts knew it the second she said my name. We may be mired in heartache and peril, but Brennan's just given me one more reason to protect her.

I need to get back to her before things get worse.

I rise and reach out to shake his hand. "I should let you get back to Angel. Thanks for everything. I know it'll never be enough, but I am sorry. I really wish things had been different. I'm sorry to make you go through it all again."

He stands and offers a smile that doesn't meet his eyes. "We can't bring them back. But we survived, and as shitty as that feels sometimes, it reminds me to be grateful for whatever I've got. Because nothing's promised." He shakes his head slightly. "Nothing's promised."

6

ISABEL

"What does it mean…that lettering on the car?"

Makanga squints out the window of the barbeque place we've stopped at for lunch.

"Means fall down a thousand times, get up a thousand and one. At least that's what the Cambodian lady I bought it from said. Works for me."

Sounds like my new life motto, so it works for me too. I swallow the last of my pulled pork sandwich and reach for my phone. No messages from Tristan. I'm still shaken from my run-in with the director. I want to tell him about it, but I'm also not sure how he'll react. One step into his old house put him in a place dark enough that he couldn't stay with me last night. I worry what this new discovery will mean for us.

"Did you find what you were looking for?"

I contemplate Makanga's question. "Yes and no."

"What's that mean?"

"I may have found something I wasn't looking for."

"All right." He leans back in his chair and tosses his napkin on his finished plate. "Where to next?"

I quirk an eyebrow. "You're not going to try raising your rates on me again, are you?"

He chuckles. "Nah. I figure you'll make it up to me later."

When I freeze, his brows come together.

"That's not what I meant." He waves his hand. "Not at all. I know you're Red's girl. I just meant, you know, sometimes we have to help each other out. Maybe one of these days, I'll need a favor from you. Plus, I don't have anything going on today, and I want to make sure you stay out of trouble."

I relax and choose to believe him. "Thanks."

The waitress brings our check, and Makanga takes it. We exchange a look like he's logging this with the rest of my debt.

"What makes you think I'm with Tristan anyway?"

I'm not really sure what to call us. There's no mainstream term for the circumstances that have thrust us back into each other's lives.

Makanga drops some cash into the check holder. "I've known him a little while. Red's not exactly a passionate guy. He's…" He smirks. "Well, he's all business, you know? With you, it just seems like something else is driving him. Like he's ready to go to war for you or something."

I avert my eyes and try to hide how true his words are.

"Maybe he already has," Makanga says with even more certainty.

Tristan hasn't exactly professed his love to me, but he's protected me. He followed me here. I believe he wants me safe, even for his own selfish reasons, which I can't deny are significant. The attraction aside, I'm the only reliable person from his past.

I decide to sidestep Makanga's presumptions about Tristan.

"Do you think you could take me to my parents' place?"

Makanga clucks his tongue. "Eh, not sure about that. Red didn't want me taking you there until it was safe."

"My father works for the CIA. He wouldn't ask me to come home unless he knew it was safe."

"Shit," he mutters under his breath as he slides his gaze to his sorry excuse for a car.

Everything is just as I remembered. The Midday Lane of my childhood
is freshly paved, curving through our quiet suburban neighborhood.
On either side, brick colonials are set back on quarter-acre lots. Ours
is painted yellow with a red door at the end of the walk. The yard is
manicured, though spring has yet to bring the trees and grass back to
life.

"You just going to walk right in?" Makanga scans our surroundings
from our parking spot across the street.

I look around, feeling much like Tristan as I do. I expect to see
danger, or feel it, but I don't. "I guess so," I say hesitantly.

"I'd wait for you, but I think Betsy might be a little out of place
here."

"I'll be fine. Maybe Tristan can pick me up later." I look down at
my phone, unsure if that's even a possibility. Tristan has no idea I've been
out and about.

I tuck the phone back into my pocket, thank Makanga, and make
my way to the front door. I ring the bell once. Twice. No answer. Over
my shoulder, I spot Makanga still idling, waiting like a worrisome parent
for me to get inside safe.

I circle to the back and try the door, but it's locked. Finally, I bang
on the door, and my mother comes into view. Her eyes are wide with
worry. Her dark-brown hair is falling in wisps around her face, fluttering
as she walks briskly toward me. She flings open the door.

"Isabel!"

She meets me at the threshold, grabs me, and traps me in a hug
so tight it's difficult to breathe. "You're home. Thank you, Jesus, you're
home. My baby." She rocks me as if I still were a child. "I should have
never let you go," she whispers shakily.

I choke back emotion at being in my mother's arms. Once upon a
time, this was the safest place to be. The place where tears turned into
giggles. The place I could always run to for comfort and soft words...
in simpler times.

She pulls away with tears in her eyes. "Come in. Quick. It's freezing."

She ushers me inside and into the kitchen. She's in jeans and a loose top with a beige pashmina wrapped around her shoulders. The skin around her eyes is dark, evidence of what likely have been many sleepless nights worrying about me. She doesn't look well.

Seeing her this way, I'm steeped in an emotion stronger than my fear—newfound guilt that I left DC for such a dangerous and unpredictable place. I even find myself acknowledging the heartache my determined love affair with Tristan caused her.

"I didn't think you'd come here," she says.

"Dad said you wanted to see me."

She glances out the window and then back to me. "I thought we could at least meet somewhere. He told me everything that happened. I just felt like I had to see you to believe you were truly okay. This has been awful. When they told me you were missing…" Her eyes glimmer with tears.

"I'm okay now, I promise," I say softly.

"I know, but sometimes it's hard to convince myself when everyone else thinks you're still missing. I have to pretend like you are, and then I start worrying that something's happened to you. These people…" Her tears spill over. "My God, this is all my fault."

"Mom, this isn't your fault."

She shakes her head stiffly, wiping at her eyes as she does. "You don't understand, Isabel. This world is full of hateful people. Monsters who thrive on vengeance and stealing people away from the ones they love. They could have taken you."

Her elegant features collapse with a silent sob.

"Mom, no." I go to her and bring my arms around her shaking frame.

"They took Mariana. Not you too."

I hold her closer and tighter, the seed of worry growing. She's not making sense. I glance around the kitchen expecting to see an empty wine bottle or something. Only her cold tea and dishes from yesterday's meals stacked in the sink. Maybe she's taken something, or maybe she needs to.

"I'm home now, okay? No one can hurt me," I say in a soothing voice. "Do you want to lie down or have some tea?"

After a few moments, she seems to calm herself. "I'm fine. Come."

I follow her into the library, a quaint sitting room where I'd spent many hours curled up in the window seat, watching cars go by between the pages of a book. She draws the curtains, and we get settled in two comfortable chairs. She seems to have composed herself. Her eyes are only slightly red.

We share the kind of tense, knowing smile worn by two people who've just endured something truly grueling. Even though we've been thousands of miles apart, I'm certain we both have. I've missed our regular phone calls. I've missed a lot of things...

"How is Tristan?"

I shrug slightly. "Fine, I guess. Different."

Moody. Intense. Impossibly sexy.

Her lips draw tight, and I can see her wheels turning. My mother never hated Tristan, but she hadn't exactly warmed to him either.

"I wasn't sure what to think when Morgan said you were with him. It's been so long."

"I know. It's not like I ever really stopped thinking about him though."

"What about Kolt?"

I rise and walk to the fireplace. The mantel is lined with old family photos. My parents' wedding photo among them.

"Kolt always wanted more than I could really give him. He wanted a part of me that I'd already given to someone else."

I turn back, expecting to see her disappointment, but her expression is calm and lacks the judgment I'm used to seeing whenever conversations revolve around Tristan.

"Does that disappoint you?" I ask for good measure.

"You've never disappointed me, Isabel. If anything, I've disappointed you. God knows if we hadn't resisted so much when it came to Tristan, maybe none of this would have happened."

She gives voice to a thought I've had many times since Tristan came back into my world. What if we'd been met with less opposition from the start? What if he hadn't fulfilled their every wish by leaving and ending things?

All the wondering leads me to the same place it always does. What if Tristan hadn't come back into my life ever again? And that seems like the worst *what if* of all.

TRISTAN

I've been parked down the street for over two hours. Long enough to see Isabel's father pull into the driveway and walk inside. Long enough to talk myself out of storming into her parents' home and fulfilling their worst nightmares—kidnapping their daughter all over again in the name of keeping her safe. I can't leave, though.

Seeing her phone location hovering over this location inspired a rush of anger, followed by a swift compulsion to get here straight from my meeting with Brennan.

Now that darkness has fallen, I make my move. I duck into the shadows of the trees that line the edge of the property. Much of the first floor is lit up, but I can't spot them inside. The curtains are drawn in one room. *The library.*

A gust of wind sets a chime on their back patio jangling loudly, drawing my attention. The porch light illuminates a bare stone patio and the faint outline of an oak tree near the corner of the house. One of its branches leans unnaturally toward the structure, creating a perfect ladder to the second floor. *To Isabel's room.*

I don't understand how, but I know this house. After all that's happened to me, somehow it's still mapped in my brain. I can feel it. Warm inside. Smooth wooden floors on the bottom. Clean, plush carpeting on the top. Books on the shelves. Photos on the walls. Smells of food and flowers. Smells that a home should have. A real home.

I refuse to let my thoughts return to the house in Baltimore. I sped away from there determined never to think of that damned place again. Of course that means denying the time Isabel spent there with me, which isn't exactly fair.

I step away from the nagging guilt and go to the base of the tree. I wedge my foot into the narrow valley of the trunk and propel myself onto the arching branch. A few feet away from what I'm convinced is her bedroom window, I shimmy along its sturdy length, feeling ridiculous but strangely compelled to find her on the other side. Once I'm closer, I reach forward and try the window but find it locked.

Damn it.

Straddling the branch, I withdraw my phone.

Isabel.

Are you talking to me now?

I will if you come upstairs.

I hope to hell she comes up alone. The last thing I want to do is climb back down this tree, and I'm feeling anything but stable waiting on it. A few minutes pass. As soon as I consider going back down, the bedroom light switches on. Isabel's figure appears through the sheer, willowy curtains. She turns around but halts at the door when I rap my knuckles on the glass. She turns back and quickly unlatches the window and pushes it up.

"Tristan, what the hell are you doing?"

I don't answer her as I slip through the opening and shut the window behind me. When I turn, she's already a few steps away, locking the door. The distance irritates me. Because after one look at her, I realize I miss her. The same way I missed her when I watched her plane take off for Panama.

Too much space or time between us feels like a bridge we have to keep journeying over again and again. I can read it in her careful stare, her hesitant posture. She's gauging my mood, wondering whether I'll cross the space and touch her or offer the smallest reassurance that she's still important to me. That I still want to kiss her and make love to her more than I want to protect her from the foolish affection she has for me.

Foolish? No, real. I can finally accept it was real for me too. The day I lost my memory, I was in love with Isabel Foster. She was red flowers and desert air and my last breath before everything went dark. Three years later, I've opened my eyes for what feels like the first time since, and she's all I can see.

She finally breaks the silence. "How did you know how to get up here?"

"I don't know. I just remembered, I guess. Did I used to sneak up here a lot or something?"

Her lips curve a little. "Until we got caught. Then my dad threatened to cut down the tree until I swore I'd never let it happen again."

I laugh, but she presses a finger to her lips. "My parents are on high alert. We have to be quiet or—"

I take two long strides and press my lips to hers, silencing her surprised squeak. I cradle her against me and push my fingers into her hair, angling her how I need her. And hell, I need her. She melts, and I go deeper. Savoring all the soft recesses of her mouth. Binding her tighter to me. My instincts scream for more, but I know it's never going to be enough. Not until she's preaching my name again.

I force myself to tear from her lips, even though I'm hard and completely unwilling to stop touching her or fantasizing about all the things our bodies could do. She doesn't help, guiding her fingertips along my unshaven jawline.

"Tristan, don't stop."

"We have to. Getting caught may have different consequences this time."

She kisses the corner of my lip. "We'll be quiet."

I laugh softly. "You are *not* quiet."

Color rises to her cheeks. I skim my knuckles across her warm skin, reliving the moment that has her embarrassed. "If you had any idea how many times I've heard your voice in my head saying my name, Isabel, you'd be blushing twice as hard."

"I'm not blushing," she says, patting her cheeks.

I step away and catch my breath, something I'm going to have to get used to if I don't stop this thing between us. I'm not sure she'll ever stop affecting me the way she does.

"We should head back, Isabel."

The heat in her eyes cools. "I can't. My mom…"

"What's wrong?"

"I don't know. She's different. When I first got here, she was so upset, talking nonsense. She seemed to get it together after a while. I told her everything that happened. But I'm worried about her."

"She's upset over all of this. That's to be expected," I say.

"You don't understand. This is her worst nightmare. Worse than her worst nightmare."

"Then the best thing you can do is keep yourself out of harm's way. Your father is here for her. That's got to be enough."

"Tristan…" She walks past me and drops onto the edge of her bed.

She sighs, but I can't be sure it's resignation. Exhaustion, maybe. Maybe if I hadn't lost my shit at my old house and dropped her off at Brienne's with barely a word, she wouldn't have felt compelled to go off on her own. Now here we are.

"Isabel," I say softly.

She lifts her wordless gaze to mine.

"We keep doing this to each other, you know."

"What?"

"Second guessing each other. Then leaving each other behind when we're trying to move in the same direction."

Her shoulders soften, as if some of her defenses are already coming down. "Believe it or not, we weren't always like this, Tristan. Not until you left, anyway."

I lower into a chair in front of her writing desk and face her. She scoots back on the bed and props herself up against the wall with her knees tucked to her chest. She seems in no rush to leave, and against my better judgment, a part of me wants to stay too.

"What was I like…before?"

I'm almost afraid to hear the answer, but we've come this far. Brennan didn't think I was too awful, judging by his warm reception and willingness to relive some of his worst memories for my sake.

She rests her chin on her knee, eyeing me calmly. "Are you sure you want to know?"

I trail my thumb up and down the wooden arm of the chair and think of our trip to my old house. She didn't deserve the reaction I gave her, and I don't blame her for being wary of a repeat episode.

"This isn't easy for me. Believe it or not, I'm trying pretty hard to keep an open mind and not freak the fuck out every time I get hit with something vaguely familiar. For years, I convinced myself I didn't care about whatever happened in the past. Promised myself I'd never give in to the temptation to seek it out. Now being here, being with you… It's like I'm rewiring my brain to accept things I never thought I could. And sometimes I'm an asshole about it."

"I'm trying to help." Her voice is so genuine, her expression filled more with concern than pity.

"I know you are. I'm trying to let you."

"Why didn't you ever try to find out who you were?"

I look out the window. The leafless branches scrape against the house. The truth is, I could have found out. The search was at the tip of my fingertips any day of the week, but I'd valiantly resisted. Until now.

"I figured enough people's lives had been shattered because of me. I knew if I started digging for answers, more people I cared about would get hurt and I'd probably end up dead."

She's quiet a moment. "What about the people in your book? You took those jobs and didn't think twice. Lives were shattered."

I did think twice. I contemplated Jay's first assignment a lot longer than she wanted me to. I did my research on the mark and sat with my doubts for days until she demanded action. Then something became clear. If I was going to play this game with Jay, survive as one of her hired guns, I couldn't be the judge. I had to point and shoot. Erase the humanity from all of it. There was no other way.

I lean forward, rest my arms on my knees, and release a tired sigh. How could I explain it to someone like Isabel, with such a pure and patient heart?

"Did you ever hear about that experiment a long time ago where they withheld human contact from babies? No talking, no eye contact, no affection."

Sadness swims in her eyes. "I have. It's awful to think about."

"When I got to Rio, I had nothing. I had Jay, and our conversation had been so brief, the only thing I knew walking away from that was she was going to give me this chance—the only chance I'd ever get—but if I fucked it up, I was probably going to wind up dead or in prison."

"What does that have to do with the experiment?"

"I was kind of like a grown-up version of one of those babies. Isolated, deprived, trapped in a situation I was too vulnerable to find my way out of. The only person who cared I existed was Jay, and she gave me just what I needed to survive. An occupation, an income, a way to stay alive. Not a single shred of warmth or compassion to reassure me that I was a human being. Because to her, I wasn't. And little by little, whatever humanity existed in the man you used to know ceased to exist. With every hit, I had to give more of it up until there was nothing left."

Tears glisten in her eyes. Releasing her knees from her chest, she crawls to the edge of the bed. She swings her legs down to rest between mine and takes my hands in hers.

"I wasn't there for you when you needed someone to care about you, but I *did* care. All that time. Sometimes I would hate you and curse you for leaving me the way you did, but I could never bring myself to believe that you'd done it to truly hurt me. It just felt like you were... *lost.* By the time I realized how lost you'd become, I couldn't find you. I would have never given up on us." She squeezes my hands, and it feels like she's got another hand around my heart, massaging the dead thing back to life. "You were right, Tristan. I still haven't given up."

It's too much. Too much truth and heaviness. I don't know how to be human and acknowledge one of the scariest emotions on the map—her love for me. I don't know how to reassure her, even though a part of me undeniably wants to know what it's like to truly accept her affection without the debilitating fear that we'll be doomed if I let it go too far.

So I unlatch our hands and pretend to stretch. I even smile a little and hope she doesn't feel rebuffed. This halfway is progress, because a bigger part of me wants to fly out the window and disappear into the night. Back to the darkness I know so well.

She watches me carefully, and I'm convinced she's just read my mind.

"At the beginning, maybe you were more…like this." She gestures with a flick of her hand in my direction.

I cock an eyebrow. "Huh?"

"You asked me what you were like before. You were more like you are now. Guarded. A little resentful, maybe. You didn't like me very much, or at least you didn't act like you did. I think in your eyes, I was just some rich girl trying to fill out her college résumé by helping out at a disadvantaged school."

"Were you?"

She smirks. "I could have filled out my résumé without taking a bus to Baltimore twice a week."

"Then why did you do it?"

She glances toward the locked door. "I lived a sheltered life for a long time. I was tired of being careful all the time. After Mariana died, my mother couldn't let me out of her sight. By the time I turned sixteen, I couldn't take it anymore. I was suffocating here."

"Who's Mariana?"

She stares at me thoughtfully before pointing to the photo on her bureau. Two toddlers with big brown eyes and wavy brown hair wear matching pink dresses and broad, nearly identical smiles.

"Your sister."

"Twin sister," she says lightly. "Sometimes I forget this is all new for you."

"Are you sick of repeating yourself?"

She smiles a little and looks down. "No. I want to help you remember things, or at least understand what's missing." She looks to the photo again. "Mariana got sick when we were really young. Leukemia. She died when I was three. I don't really remember her. I was too young to see how it changed my parents, but they were always so much more protective over me than my friends' parents, and I figured that was why."

"I'm sorry." Even though she's not grief-stricken, it feels like the appropriate thing to say.

And here, in her room where I'd sneaked through the window who knows how many nights to be with her, I'm compelled to be better for her. Better than I was yesterday. Better than the man who was too afraid to stay in her life and face the pain instead of running to the desert to bury it.

I cross my legs at the ankle and lean back, ready to listen to as much as she'll tell me.

7

ISABEL

The doorbell rings, jarring me awake beside Tristan. I fell asleep in his arms last night, very likely midsentence. For some reason, mentioning Mariana sparked his interest not just in the tragedy of losing my sister too soon but in everything else. He asked me about my family. About college at George Washington and teaching English in Rio. About my love of dabbling in all the languages I haven't found the time to truly master yet.

Every once in a while, his lips would find mine—deliberate, searing kisses that spoke a language filled with all the things he couldn't tell me, either because he couldn't or he wouldn't. I wished his kisses would take us further. But beyond the occasional roaming hand and teasing touch, he showed impressive restraint against my whispered pleas, even though I could feel exactly how our closeness affected him too.

I haven't won the war with Tristan, but I know I haven't lost it. I feel him breaking down, showing what he's capable of. Compassion, empathy, tenderness, remorse.

His confession last night is a fresh wound I'll wear on my heart the way he wears his scars on his skin. Somehow his pain has always been mine. He was reborn into this new life a grown man, one with vulnerabilities so raw and deep he may as well have been a child. I'm more determined than ever to help him find his way home. I pray that home is me, *us*...

I'm unmoving beside him now, listening. My mother opens the front door, her polite voice distinct but not her words. Then a male voice, just clear enough that my heart stops. I sit up in bed.

"What is it?" Tristan's voice is a sleepy rasp that makes me want to curl up against him and forget the world.

Instead, I scramble to the door and open it to hear better.

"I'm sorry for the intrusion, Mrs. Foster. I got here as fast as I could. I told the local authorities everything I could but figured I might be more use here." He pauses. "I'm Kolt, by the way. I don't know how much Isabel told you about me."

Kolt's voice drifts off. I grip the edge of the doorway. Hearing him takes me back to the life we once shared. To the day everything changed. *Everything.*

"She mentioned you, yes." My mother's voice is hesitant but firm.

She doesn't want him to know I'm home. Tristan's sudden presence behind me and gentle hold on my arm communicates the same thing. I bite my lip, suppressing the urge to run downstairs and announce that I'm alive to the man who deserves to know.

"I appreciate you coming, but this isn't a very good time. You must be exhausted. Maybe you could come by tomorrow after you've had some rest," my mother says.

"Is everything okay?" My father's serious tenor carries through the foyer and up the stairs.

"It's fine, Morgan. This is Kolt. Isabel's friend from the English school."

"Can you tell us anything about what happened before she disappeared?"

"Morgan, not now—"

"In light of the current circumstances, I think he can answer some questions for us." My father's clipped tone leaves no question.

"I don't know much," Kolt says. "The day she disappeared, we were having lunch at our usual spot. She seemed really distracted. We were going to have dinner that night and talk things over."

"What things?" my father asks.

Kolt hesitates a few seconds. "We were going to talk about our relationship. Where we wanted things to go, I guess. But we never had a chance. She took off, and I didn't see her at the school for the rest of the day. She didn't answer my calls. Her apartment was empty when I went by. I notified the police after she didn't come to work the next day."

I curse inwardly and open the door wider. Tristan's grip stiffens, halting my forward progress. I turn, pleading with him with a look.

No, he mouths.

"He deserves to know," I whisper.

"I don't trust him."

Kolt's done nothing to betray my trust. This is something else. Something I wasn't sure Tristan was capable of until now. This is jealousy.

"That's not why you don't want me to talk to him."

"Do not go down there, Isabel."

I set my jaw firmly. "Let. Me. Go."

His chest moves steadily under his tense breathing. For a moment, I think I'll have to wrestle free, but he surprises me by letting go.

We stand there a moment in silent opposition. The last thing I want to do is hurt him when we're finding our way back to each other, but Kolt didn't ask to have me ripped out of his life. Guilt on top of guilt compounds on me, but Kolt's voice downstairs prompts me into motion.

"I'm sorry for just dropping in on you like this. I can come back tomorrow."

"Sure," my mom answers. "I think that would be best."

I hurry down the stairs, my heart flying as Kolt's figure comes into full view. He looks like hell—skin dull, hair unstyled and sticking up in places it shouldn't, his button-down a wrinkled mess. I've no doubt he traveled all night and came directly here.

"Isabel." My name breaks on his lips. "You're here."

I halt at the foot of the stairs. He steps between my parents. When he reaches for me, I can't deny him. He clutches me firmly against his chest and buries his nose in my hair.

So much more than my absence has come between us. He has no idea I've been falling in love with Tristan all over again. Still, Kolt is the closest friend I've had for months. The cute coworker who kept me smiling and laughing until he became the lover who warmed my bed on lonely nights. Then I disappeared without a trace and followed Tristan into the jungles of Brazil. I've thought of Kolt from time to time, but the guilt of leaving him so suddenly has never been this heavy.

And he's right. Only days ago we were negotiating the terms of our relationship—a relationship I was reluctant to define and eager to diffuse.

"I'm sorry," I whisper. "So sorry."

He looks into my eyes, cradling my face in his cool palm. "What's going on?"

"It's complicated. I can't explain it all right now. I just needed you to know I was okay."

"Why didn't you tell me you were leaving?"

I shake my head tightly. "I couldn't. I just couldn't."

He opens his mouth to speak, but his attention is taken away. Creaks down the stairs have my heart plummeting to my stomach. I press my palms against Kolt's chest, loosening his grasp. He backs off slightly, very likely distracted by the man behind me.

Tristan drops from the last step with a notable thud.

Stoic, deadly Tristan has arrived. Everyone in the room seems to feel it. Except when I chance a look at him, his eyes are fixed on me as if no one else exists.

"Hi there, I'm Kolt." Kolt extends his hand.

Tristan regards him coolly, making no effort to return the gesture. Undeniably, he's dark and damaged in ways he never was before. Somehow that makes him even more beautiful to me, though. And somehow all the other people in the room bring this truth into stark relief. Kolt is inches away, yet I'm drawn to Tristan so strongly, I worry Kolt must feel it too. That energy that hums between us, nearly palpable in its intensity.

"This is Tristan," I say lightly, as if introducing the love of my life to the friend I've been casually fucking is the most normal thing in the world.

"There are matters at play here that you don't understand and you don't need to understand," Tristan says without ceremony. "Isabel's in danger, and no one can know that she is here. Can you keep your mouth shut?"

Kolt grimaces. "Excuse me?"

"I said can you keep your—"

"Do you know who you're talking to?" Kolt leans in, his words and body language offering a challenge that has me in an instant panic. He has no idea who he's dealing with.

"Kolt, please don't."

I reach for him, but he brushes me off like a fly trying to distract him from more important things and shoots daggers at Tristan.

Tristan reacts, grasping my hand in his. He takes a threatening step toward Kolt, wedging his body between us. I wrap my free hand around his bicep and squeeze, a silent plea for him to exercise restraint when I'm worried all he wants to do is write Kolt's name in his little red book just for breathing.

"I know exactly who you are. You're Kolt Mirchoff. Harvard University dropout, class of '18. Your family's made a fortune slinging legal drugs through one of the biggest pharmaceutical companies in the world. You've got too much money on your hands and all the time in the world to piss it away."

"I didn't drop out. I'm on a leave of absence. And my family's business doesn't have anything to do with what's going on with Isabel right now."

"Maybe not. But you need to get out of my face before they think you've gone missing too."

Kolt slides his gaze from Tristan to me and back again. "I'm not going anywhere unless Isabel says so."

Tristan brings his face dangerously close to Kolt's. "You've been fucking with the wrong girl, Mirchoff. She's not in love with you."

My father's face reddens with anger. "That's about enough of that."

Thankfully, my mother gets between the two men before my father can. "Kolt, Isabel needs her rest. It's been a long journey for her too. Come, I'll walk you out and we can talk."

Just like that, my mother manages to pull Kolt away from the house and lead him down the front path, but not before he pins me with a look filled with such confusion and defeat.

I resist the urge to go to him and apologize once more, but Tristan's not wrong. I'm not in love with Kolt. I never could be. If Tristan hadn't shown up on the street that afternoon, I would have explained it to Kolt that night. We can never be what he wants us to be.

He turns away, but the crushed look in his eyes won't leave my memory anytime soon. My mother's voice disappears when my father shuts the door behind them.

"Happy now?" Tristan works his jaw, doing nothing to mask his frustration. "I know you'll do whatever you damn well please, but may I suggest we leave before someone finds out you're here? The probability of that just increased substantially."

I meet his challenging stare, all too ready to defy him.

"He's right."

We both turn toward my father's voice. "But first I'd like a few words with you, Mr. Stone."

Tristan's anger seems to cool. Or maybe it goes inward. Something about his energy and posture changes. He's black ice on a cold night. Dangerous if ignored. Of all people, my father might understand this.

"I'm going to get some things from my room. Give me five minutes," I say.

Tristan nods but doesn't look my way. He follows my father into his office and closes the French doors behind them.

I watch them a moment through the glass. Tristan's rigid stance, my father circling his desk and dropping into his chair. I could watch and wonder, but I'll have to pull it out of Tristan later. Our safety may be an issue, but right now, I'm more concerned about getting Tristan out of the house before someone snaps.

I don't waste time. I go upstairs, tear open boxes from my old apartment that I'd stored in my closet, and put together a bag of warmer clothes so I can return Brienne's. I have no idea why I kept so much stuff. I lived on next to nothing in Rio. A simpler life. A richer life. I'll tell my mother to donate the rest before I go.

I hear the front door open and shut and, a few seconds later, my mother's voice in the kitchen. Then Tristan's and my father's join hers. I hurry, gather the last little things, and take a last look around my room, certain I won't be seeing it again for a while. I've said goodbye to this place before, but I could always come back.

So much has changed...

TRISTAN

I'm a clusterfuck of emotion. I have no idea what to do with any of it. I brew over all the ways this is Isabel's fault as we speed toward Brienne's apartment in tense silence. I could blame her all day long, but I'm the one who's given her this much power over me. I've been giving in to her little invitations to be the Tristan she used to know. The man who cared and felt things. The naïve, fucked-up kid from the slums of Baltimore whose heart beat to love one woman. This one particularly infuriating woman.

I am *not* that kid. I slam the door behind us with that thought, grateful to find the living area void of her screen-obsessed friend. I'm not sure I could pretend to care that I'm being a rude houseguest.

Isabel bends over the coffee table and lifts up a note. "She went out. Be back soon."

"Great." I go to the fridge, pull out a bottle of water, and wham the door shut.

"Are you going to talk to me, or are you going to keep slamming things around like a toddler?"

She's right in front of me when I spin around.

"Am I going to *talk* to you? What good would that do?"

I advance on her with no regard for how thin my self-control is at this moment. When she stumbles backward, I catch her. I tuck my hand into the band of her jeans and roughly tug her toward me. She huffs out a breath as our chests clash. My lips hover over hers. The hunger I have for her claws at me—a gnawing, nagging hunger that doesn't let up no matter how much I tell myself she's got unfinished business with the guy I watched grope her not that long ago.

"Tristan...I'd love to talk this out, but—"

"But what?"

She licks her bottom lip. The movement shoots straight to my groin. A fresh hit of lust razors through me. Her eyes have that hazy look that tells me we're already on the same page. Needing her to this degree is akin to a thousand tiny blades under my skin, but I'm still pissed about her insolent behavior, not to mention the way she all but ran into another man's arms.

"What makes you think I'd give you the satisfaction?"

I revel in landing the blow. Then I regret it when the lusty fog in her eyes is replaced with the pain I've inflicted. Because I feel things now, and I'm irrationally resentful that I do.

"You're entangled, Isabel."

She rests her forehead on my shoulder. "Despite what you saw, you have to understand that Kolt is more a friend than anything else. If you could see past your jealousy, you'd understand that leaving him in the dark would be cruel."

I let her go. "Jealousy?"

"That's what that pissing contest in the foyer was, wasn't it? What else would you call it?"

"That was me crushing any hope he had of getting you back. For his safety and yours, I needed him to back off."

She lifts her hand to my face, caressing over my tight jaw. The silent gesture seems to call me on my bullshit. I'm obviously jealous, which is so foreign and unsettling, I have no idea what to do with that emotion either.

"Would you rather I pretend like I don't care if he puts his hands on you?"

"You're making excuses. Kolt isn't your enemy or mine."

"Maybe not, but he's your lover."

"He was," she says quietly, not meeting my eyes.

I wrestle with her confirmation of what I already suspected to be true. I saw them together in Rio. That was before I cared, though. Before I committed to saving her life, not ending it. I touch her chin and force her gaze up, hoping to see the truth in it. I'm putting my life on the line for her. I need to know.

"What exactly does this guy mean to you?"

She steps away, disconnecting us. I hate the sudden distance between us as much as I hate this conversation. Why the hell did he have to show up?

I pace toward the living room window. It's a clear day. Views like this are always peaceful from a distance. The chaos lives under the trees, inside the buildings, down on the streets. That's where we are now, existing in the quiet, invisible chaos of life.

"I care about Kolt, but we were never really a couple."

She's a few feet away, arms crossed defensively, making me wonder what she has to defend.

"He was starting to have feelings for me," she says. "Deeper feelings I couldn't reciprocate because I was still so wrapped up in losing you. I wasn't ready to be in a relationship with him. I didn't know if I ever would be, and that's what we were going to talk about the night I left with you. Leading him on wasn't fair to him, but disappearing without a trace and letting him believe the worst wasn't fair either."

"Doesn't change the fact that he knows you're alive. He knows you're back in DC. He could tell someone, and all the pains Mateus and I took to get you here undetected will have been wasted."

"I don't think they will be."

"Let's hope not. Your mother assured me she'd do everything she could to keep this quiet."

Isabel stares down at the floor, dragging her toe along a seam in the tile. "What did you and my father talk about?"

"He asked where we were staying. Offered to help us find a place to hide out for a while."

"What did you tell him?"

"I told him that I'd keep you safe and I didn't need his help."

She rolls her eyes. "Amazingly, nothing has changed between you."

"If it's the difference between me keeping you safe and you being dead, what choice does he have?"

"Not much, I suppose."

"We have to get out of here, Isabel. We can't stay anywhere too long. We have to keep moving."

"I know." She glances at the couch, and I can read her thoughts.

"Write her a note if you want. We can't wait for her."

She doesn't answer and disappears into the bedroom. Meanwhile, I open my laptop and scope out hotels downtown. We'll have to put DC behind us soon, but not before I get more answers. Meeting with Brennan filled in some of the blanks on what happened, but I'm no closer to figuring out why someone wants Isabel dead. Morgan had assured me, though, that he would follow every lead until he got to the bottom of it.

Isabel comes back and drops a note on the table. "I'm ready," she says. "Where are we going?"

"I booked a room at the St. Regis. We can stay there for a few days."

"I have to tell you something."

I close my laptop and look up.

"My dad told me that after you transitioned out of the military, you went to a rehabilitation center for vets here in DC called Trinity House."

"And?"

"I went there yesterday. They wouldn't give me any information or even acknowledge that you went there, but I met with the director."

She twists her fingers. Dread pools in my gut.

"And?"

"At first, I thought I must have imagined it, but I didn't. I know I didn't. I wrote Isabel Santos on the sign-in sheet, and I was on my way to leave and she called me Miss Foster. She knew my name, Tristan."

My heart slows to a near stop. "You're sure."

"I'm sure. I don't know how she knew my name, but she looked at me like she wanted to turn me inside out. I don't know how else to describe it. That's how it felt. She creeped me out, and I got out of there as fast as I could."

"Why the hell didn't you tell me this earlier?"

She throws her hands up. "I went to my parents right after, and then you showed up at my window, and we started talking about everything else. Never mind that I can't think straight when you're touching me."

"Fuck." *Fuck!*

I go into the bedroom and pull my own bag together. When I come back, Isabel's eyes are wide and she's clutching the strap of her backpack like a life preserver.

"What did she look like?"

She blinks up at me. "What?"

"The woman. What did she look like?"

"Professional. Maybe early thirties."

"Her face, Isabel."

"She was fair skinned. Red hair. She wore it pulled back tight. Blue eyes. Like, a deep, dark blue."

I harness the lecture she deserves, because nothing matters more than getting out of this building and back on the move. I grab her arm and lead her to the door. "Let's go. Right now."

8

ISABEL

We get into Tristan's car. Everything about our situation is stressing me out, but Tristan's new tension threatens to push me over the edge. My heart beats fast with fresh anxiety. Going to the Trinity House was a mistake. I realize that now.

"What's going on, Tristan?"

He starts the car, and the heater blasts cold air on us.

"That woman you met with was Jay."

I'm momentarily paralyzed by this information. "What? Are you sure?"

"I have no recollection of going to that place. I do remember her, though. The woman you described sounds exactly like the first memory I have."

This can't be real. Could I have really walked directly into the lion's den, the office of the woman who sent the directive to kill me?

"That would explain how she knew me."

"What was her name?"

"Jude McKenna."

"Look her up. I'll know her face."

I reach for my phone when Brienne knocks on the window. I fumble with the buttons on the door and roll down the window.

Brienne leans in. "Hey, where you guys off to? You never came back last night."

"I decided to visit my parents, and we ended up staying the night. Sorry, I should have called to give you a heads-up we wouldn't be back."

"No worries. Hey, I got takeout. Chicken tikka masala. Your favorite." She smiles and holds up a bag of stacked Styrofoam containers. It smells delicious.

"Thanks, but—"

A whizzing bolt of sound. Tristan's window spiders around a massive gap in the glass.

Another whiz, and the crack of her face against the car door.

Blood. So much blood.

I try to scream, but nothing comes out.

A third sound and a fourth. Rapid-fire *thunk*s hitting the car, jolting Brienne's lifeless body on its way to the ground.

Tristan grabs me by the shoulder and yanks me down. My temple hits the center console. He jams the gas pedal to the floor, and we lurch forward. I can't breathe. Can't speak.

Finally an agonizing cry tears from my throat. I bring my hand to my mouth to muffle the screams that want to come with it. My fingers are lathered in red. Thick, warm red.

"Tristan," I sob.

"You're okay. Just breathe, Isabel."

The car jerks around a turn. Then another. We're going fast. The windshield is splattered with Brienne's blood and brain matter. Through it I can make out the sky and the blur of passing buildings.

This isn't happening. This isn't happening. This isn't happening.

The mantra runs on a loop in my brain. Then I'm whispering it. Praying it's true each time it passes my lips.

Brienne didn't just die in front of me.

We didn't just leave her in the street.

No one wants me dead.

Tristan didn't try to kill me.

I'm safe.

I roll the tape backward, further and further, until I'm home. Young enough to appreciate all the attention my parents gave me. Ignorant of the desire to leave and brave the world on my own.

I don't know how much time has passed when the car finally stops. Tristan puts it in park and gets out.

Don't leave me.

I can't seem to speak. I reach for the empty seat and skim my palm over its warmth.

Need you.

A gust of cold air rushes over me. I'm shaking all over. Tristan pulls me straight again and lifts me into his arms through the passenger side.

"Come on. You're okay. I've got you."

His voice is soothing. So kind and reassuring, I'm tempted to believe my mantra. We're safe. I collapse against him.

"What the fuck happened?" Makanga's in the doorway of a house I don't recognize, stepping aside as Tristan takes us inside.

"I need to get her cleaned up."

Makanga doesn't answer, but Tristan follows him through a bedroom and into a bathroom. He sets me down on the toilet seat and turns on the shower. The flimsy yellow shower curtain billows gently as the water heats up.

"Tristan. What the fuck?"

"Not now," Tristan snaps.

Makanga's eyes are wide, his warmth and humor gone. Nothing seems real right now, but he doesn't feel like a friend anymore.

"You blast in here with no warning, and your girl is covered in someone's vital fluids. You want to hang here, you have to tell me what's up."

Tristan closes his eyes for a brief moment and then opens them. "Give me five minutes. Can you wait five fucking minutes so I can get her cleaned up?"

Makanga disappears, closing the door loudly behind us.

I don't want to be here.

Tristan lifts my shirt over my head. I let him undress me the rest of the way. I'm shaking so badly, I'm not sure the warm water will even help. Tristan helps me into the shower, steadying me with his strong hands. I suck in a breath as the sharp sting of the spray hits my skin. I've never felt this numb, but the water feels like daggers all of a sudden.

"You okay?"

I look up from the pink water pooling around my feet and into Tristan's eyes. Silvery blue and round with concern. His lips pull taut, like he already knows I can't possibly be okay. I may never be okay again.

He pulls his shirt over his head and goes for the button on his jeans.

"No." The single word croaks past my lips.

He stills.

"Talk to him. I'll be all right."

"Are you sure?"

I nod, reach for a bottle of shampoo, and squeeze some ivory liquid into my palm. I want Tristan with me, but I don't want to linger here. It doesn't feel right.

"I'll be back in a minute with some clothes."

I duck my head under the water, appreciating the harsh water pressure now that it's coaxing the debris out of my hair. More pink swirls. More evidence of Brienne's life-force gone. She's gone.

Just like that.

I wash quickly, scrub my skin and scalp and close my eyes so I don't have to see what's breaking loose and swirling down the drain. But closing my eyes brings the horror of what happened flashing behind my eyelids.

The nausea hits me fiercely. I wring my hair, turn off the shower, and find a towel below the sink to wrap myself in. Seconds later I'm kneeling in front of the toilet, letting the sickness take hold of me. I heave and heave until my stomach finally expels its bile.

Then all I can do is cry.

TRISTAN

My fault. All my fucking fault.

I can't dwell on all the missteps that brought us here. All I can think about is our next move. Jay knows way more than I thought she did, and that changes everything.

I bring Isabel's bag inside. Makanga is sitting in his lounger, pinning me with a hard stare.

"What?"

"Five minutes are up," he says.

"I need a night here to regroup. She just saw her friend get murdered."

"Since when do you care?"

"What's your fucking problem?"

Makanga stands up abruptly. "My problem is that you're changing the game. The people who come into my life may not be noble, but they're consistent. You? You're getting soft over some girl, which is dangerously inconsistent with the guy I used to know. And that tells me that you're getting into something that maybe you don't have much control over."

"So you're saying you won't help me because I'm not consistently heartless enough for you? She's in shock, for Christ's sake. I can't bring her out like this. You want to cut me a break?"

Makanga's expression softens a fraction. "Listen, Isabel's a nice girl. I don't think she's headed down the right path getting mixed up with you, but that's not my business. Her friend getting murdered? Not my business either. I deliver shit and do some light babysitting, but you're bringing heat to my house. That's my business."

He might be right. About everything. My contacts here are few, and I may have pulled my last favor by showing up here. I also don't want to bring trouble to his door.

"I'll get her calmed down and we'll go," I finally say.

We both turn when sounds of her agonizing sobs carry down the hallway.

Makanga's shoulders slump. "Listen, you can stay tonight…"

I don't let him finish. I'm moving toward her, ready to fix this however I can.

It takes two more hours for me get Isabel dry and dressed, hold her until she stops crying and shaking, and clean all the evidence of the horrific act she witnessed off my car. We don't speak on the drive to the hotel. I park in a nearby garage since a valet's likely to be concerned about my missing driver's-side window and the bullet punctures in the side door.

We cross the street to the hotel, walk through the automatic doors, and enter the St. Regis's luxurious lobby. Isabel looks like hell, and I'm not sure I look much better, but thankfully my money's as green as everyone else's.

I walk us to an empty sitting area. "Wait here, all right?"

She clutches my hand in a death grip.

"I'm going to be right over there checking us in. I don't want anyone to think something's wrong, okay? Can you wait for me?"

She swallows hard, slowly releases her grip, and drops on the pale-blue velvet couch. Her red-rimmed eyes remain locked on me.

I give her an extra few seconds before I leave, to make sure she isn't going to freak out. I wouldn't blame her if she did, but this hotel has to be our sanctuary for the next couple of days at least. I don't want to raise suspicions right out of the gate.

At the front desk, the concierge upgrades us to an executive suite that will give us some room to move around. With Isabel's fragile emotional state, I don't want her to get stir-crazy and bolt. She doesn't know it yet, but I'll have to leave her at some point. I don't know how I'm going to pull that off yet. I manage a smile when I look her way as the man hands me the key cards and rambles on in his best customer-service tenor about the amenities I don't especially care about.

I hand him a hundred-dollar bill when he finishes.

"What's this for, sir?"

"I need a bottle of Leblon and a bowl of limes delivered to the room as soon as you can."

He lifts his eyebrows. "I will do my best, sir."

"Do better than your best," I say before turning back for Isabel.

After a short elevator ride to our floor, I get her settled in the room. She says she can't sleep yet, so I run her a hot bath using the hotel shampoo to make bubbles. The bathroom is muggy and smells like lavender when there's a knock at the door. Room service brings in a bucket of ice, an unopened bottle of my favorite cachaça, and an ample serving of sliced limes as requested. I tip the man and turn to Isabel sitting on the edge of the bed.

She's little more than catatonic, her eyes glossy and far away. She's propped up with her hands as if she can barely support the weight of her own body. I coax her into the bathroom and undress her again. This time she's not shaking. We're not in a hurry, so I go slow, whispering my lips over her skin every once in a while. Her forehead, her palms, the place above her knees, silently kissing the wounds she's sustained on the inside.

Even in this traumatic state, she's still beautiful. Soft and warm. Delicate and full in all the right places. I resist the urge to drag her into my lap and kiss her until she's breathless and thoroughly distracted from all this misery. God knows I could use a diversion too, but she's undeniably fragile. The rum will have to do.

She submerges in the tub and closes her eyes with a sigh. I leave and return with two tumblers of rum on ice, three juiced limes floating in each.

"Here." I offer one to her.

She clutches the cool glass with both hands and takes a swallow, exhaling softly. I arrange myself on the floor, my back to the wall so I face her.

"Thank you," she says.

She drapes one wet arm on the lip of the tub. I take it and slide my fingertips from her palm up her forearm. The simple touch holds so much. Forgiveness, solidarity, regret…

"You don't ever have to thank me," I say. "For anything ever again, actually."

"This isn't your fault." Fresh tears gleam in her eyes. "I insisted we stay there."

"Isabel, no. Don't do this to yourself."

In no way was today's bloodshed her fault. I sent her to DC to keep her safe. I promised to protect her, which I barely managed to do today. I'm damn lucky she's alive.

I clutch her hand tightly and slug down a mouthful of rum, eager to take the edge off that unsettling thought and this whole day.

I learned to let go of my guilt a long time ago. For the people I was hired to kill and for anyone else who got in the way. But the vision of Isabel meeting the same fate as Brienne has me faintly nauseated. I can't lose her. I refuse to accept the possibility.

"I miss Rio," she whispers, sidelining my thoughts. With one finger, she dunks her limes under the ice in a hypnotic rhythm.

"Me too."

I've never missed a place. Never found myself in a new city that made me want to uproot and start over. But now I miss the island-dotted view of the ocean from my abandoned apartment in Ipanema. I miss the heat, even the chaos in the streets.

"We can't stay in DC much longer."

She nods, sad understanding in her eyes.

"Where do you want to go?"

This hunt for a phantom enemy isn't leading us in any particular direction. If we need to disappear, at least we have an open road in front of us. Whether we like it or not, we're in this together for the foreseeable future.

"Someplace warm, I think." She finishes her drink and looks up at the ceiling. She seems more relaxed now.

"That sounds good to me."

Our fingers lace and stroke lazily against one another. When her eyes start closing for longer stretches, I pull the plug to the drain and get her dry and into bed. Tucking her close to me, I hope for dreams to quell the nightmare we survived today.

9

ISABEL

Harsh sunshine pours in through the window. The golden rays glint off the handgun set on the small table in the corner of the room. Memories rain down, funneling into my sharpening consciousness. Brienne. The explosion of blood. Makanga's wary face as we left the brief haven of his place. I press the heels of my hands against my eyes, refusing to let the agony take hold of me. I'm not sure my heart can survive another day of it.

Now that the shock has finally worn off, staying steeped in my anguish isn't possible. Mourning Brienne's death will have to fit into the empty places between seeking out the truth and running for our lives. I can't wallow like this for days. Friends won't bring casseroles to the house. No one will give me time and space to process this new emptiness.

This is my life now…

I get up and go to the chair beside the table and stare at the weapon. I study its dark metal tones and mold my hand around its cool, textured grip. Its heft alone is intimidating, never mind its purpose.

I think back to when Tristan pushed a gun into my hand with his blessing to use it against Mateus if I needed to. Everything was happening so fast, but even in the milliseconds between dodging Jay's henchmen and speeding toward town, I recognized that I couldn't do what Tristan expected me to. I was more likely to let myself be killed than put myself to the test of taking someone else's life.

I bring the gun into my lap, supporting its weight with my other hand. I trace its lines and mechanisms, delicately familiarizing myself with it as if it were a wild creature that could turn violent on me at any moment. Inherently, I know I have to push my fear of it away if I'm to ever wield its power to my own benefit.

But to what end... To protect? To kill?

The pad of my index finger rests on the curved trigger. A smooth, almost welcoming resting place. *Pull and release. Done.*

Emotion clogs my throat. I flinch when the bathroom door opens. Tristan stands frozen before me.

His dark hair is slicked back. His lips are parted, eyes fixed on the gun in my lap.

"You okay?"

I move my finger away from the trigger, not trusting my nerves. He walks over to me, his bare feet soundless on the hotel carpet. The towel wrapped around his lower half splits over his thigh as he crouches in front of me.

"What are you doing with that?"

I shake my head and swallow hard. I have no business with this gun, but I feel so powerless over my life, a part of me wonders if making this weapon an extension of myself could change that.

Tristan eases the gun out of my hands and places it back on the table.

"Is that what you use? You know, when you kill someone?"

His brows draw together slightly. "It's quick," he says, his voice low. "I'm not into prolonged torture."

I nod as if I get it, but I don't.

"The names in your book... Are they all dead?"

He's silent a moment. "Yeah."

"I want to know who killed Brienne." My voice breaks over her name. "Then I want to find that person so I can see how it feels to balance the injustice of an innocent life being taken."

"Are you in the revenge business now?"

A hot tear travels down my cheek. "Why shouldn't I be?"

"Because it's not who you are."

I straighten my shoulders. "It's who you are. Or have you grown a conscience since you decided not to kill me?"

He sighs and takes my hands in his, massaging them. "Sometimes people get caught in the crossfire, Isabel. I know that better than anyone. We need to focus on who hired me to kill you." He hesitates, looking down a moment before meeting my eyes again. "I need to talk to Jay. I looked her up. It's definitely her."

More tears fall. Hateful, angry tears. I cover the tops of his hands with mine and squeeze. "She's a monster for what she did to you."

"But she's a monster I know."

"She wants us both dead. Why would you go to her?"

The corner of his mouth lifts into a wry grin. "You walked right into the dragon's lair, Isabel. Why can't I?"

"I'm so scared," I speak through my tears. "I can't lose you."

Something shadows his eyes. His smile fades. His lips part slightly. I want to touch them, trace their etched fullness with mine, drown in his kisses that feel like so much more than the melding of mouths.

"You won't lose me, Isabel. We're in this together now. Just you and me."

Just you and me.

His gritty words are a touch of salve on what feels like never-ending pain. I close my eyes, letting the tears cool on my cheeks. I tunnel my fingers into his damp hair as he feathers warm kisses across my bare legs and our intertwined hands.

When the brush of lips gives way to his teeth and tongue, I let my head fall back with a sigh. The sensations spider out, creating a heat that's almost painful in its intensity.

"Make me believe it, Tristan." I whisper the plea. "Make me feel it."

He nips at my inner thigh. I gasp and look down to where he's soothing the same place with his flattened tongue. Our gazes lock. Suddenly the desire we've been feeding and tempting and sidestepping all this time feels different. Like we're not fighting what could be but denying what simply is.

I'm done with denying. Done with fear. My heart knocks against my ribs, hard enough that I feel the pulse of it everywhere. He rises and brings me up with him. As we move together, I slant my lips over his, moaning into the contact. His answering kiss isn't patient or careful, as if something's unleashed in him the same way it has in me.

I'm overwhelmed with a sudden frenzy to take this further. To find a place safe from the passing of time and the danger that seems to close in on us every day. To be consumed by this unstoppable desire.

He nudges us to the bed, and we tumble down together. Our hands are everywhere. He tugs my shirt off with one unapologetic sweep.

"We can stop." His words don't match his movements. Every tender touch has an edge. A ridge of teeth. The blunt edge of his nails down my thighs locked tight around his hips. "If it's too much, tell me now." His voice is thready with restraint.

"No… I need this."

I need too much. I need to feel something other than this fear. This valley of darkness in my soul growing wider with every fresh tragedy, every harrowing realization of what the world is truly made of. Tristan may be covered in its shadows, but we're in this together… I can live in the margins if I have him with me. If we can have this…

Tristan holds his weight above me, dragging hungry kisses down my neck and along my shoulder. I arch and tug at his waist, eager to feel the heavy press of him, all his harnessed strength.

Licking along my collarbone, he drifts his mouth to the small charm resting in the well below my neck.

"My miracle," he whispers when he gets back to my ear. "My saint…"

I can't wait anymore. I push my panties down, and he drags them the rest of the way. I reach for the knot where his towel is tucked in, and it falls away, the sensation of terry cloth replaced by the rough hair on his legs as I lock my thighs around him. The searing heat of his erection slides up my belly. He glances down between us, repeating the motion until I'm trembling.

He pins my hip to the mattress with one hand, stilling my impatient gyrations.

"I can't risk getting you pregnant, Isabel. I wasn't thinking straight last time."

I blink up into his eyes. Something about the fact that he was too consumed to take care last time makes me even crazier with need. Once upon a time, I'd fantasized about having Tristan's babies, being his wife, sharing every experience life would give us. I could have never expected this life...

"I told you, I've got it covered. For the next three years, actually," I admit, thanks to the contraceptive implant hidden in my arm. "There's nothing to worry about."

He exhales roughly. "Sounds perfect."

He closes in for another kiss, his relief palpable. I share his relief. I fall into it. I cry out with it when he finally pushes inside me. So close. As close as two people can be. I clench around him, savoring our union and aching for more.

He sets a deep, drowsy rhythm between us. And as the real world drifts away, Tristan fills the frame. The Tristan who's not the same but somehow *more*. Ruthless and hardened, he's claiming space in my heart like a warrior protecting what's always been his. Our bonds, our wounds, and our memories—they wind us tighter day by day.

Over and over I breathe his name into the space between our lips. I revel in his weight and the pressure building with each passing minute. I feel every ridge, every slide, every clutch and drag and pulse of flesh. But the higher we climb, the fewer places I have to hide.

Flashes of violence and death seep in and swim among my thoughts. My mind has become a dark ocean, soothing and rhythmic one moment, angrily revealing its monsters the next.

I squeeze my eyes shut, hoping to force the visions away.

"Isabel."

I open my eyes to Tristan's. I don't have to say anything. One shared look, and he seems to know.

"Look at me... Stay with me..."

I gasp when he roots deeper. The breathtaking sensation and his lust-painted features command my attention, magnetize all my roaming thoughts to the physical act and the invisible vibrations around my heart, where he's owning me a little bit more.

Look at me. Say my name. He murmurs the demands against my mouth. Takes me up and away, closer to the peak.

Trust me. Be with me. Remember me, Isabel...

I do, I am, and I could never forget...

My eyes drift closed. I'm shaking again. So close... He's all cool ocean, but my heart knows the monsters lurk on the other side of this bliss.

He takes my hands and clutches them tightly above my head.

He kisses me hard. Rocks into me harder. Takes and takes and forces me to take too. He drains my thoughts until all that's left is the raw feeling of our bodies crashing together.

"Let go, Isabel," he says. "Let go with me."

And then I do.

TRISTAN

I haven't existed the past three years without the pleasure of female company from time to time. I never walked away feeling anything more than basic physical satisfaction, though. Nothing like how I feel now.

I'm sitting in the chair where I found Isabel holding my gun in her lap not that long ago. She's asleep now, curled up like a baby bird in a warm nest of soft, white hotel sheets. I'm completely preoccupied with her and this odd afterglow. Utterly blown away by this bone-deep compulsion I have to build a bulletproof wall around her and fight this war for the rest of our lives if it means keeping her safe forever.

Every day, I find myself needing her more and seeing it mirrored in her eyes. A runaway train I have no hope of slowing down.

She doesn't know it yet, but I'm going to find the motherfucker who killed her friend and put his name in my book along with anyone else who dares come after her. Chances are high I may already know who it is.

Jay's the key. Jude. Whatever name she uses, whatever bullshit organization she hides behind, she's the heartless bitch who yanks on Company Eleven's reins. I'm done running. Done playing this game like I'm a mark she'll have cornered in a matter of time. Fuck that. If Isabel can get to her, so can I.

The problem is I can't leave Isabel alone right now. She's too emotional, too raw. I shouldn't and won't leave her to her own devices. One look at her with her hands wrapped around my gun struck fear in my heart that I still can't shake. If she's harboring any thoughts of hurting herself or anyone else, she can't be left alone.

I quietly open my laptop, track down Lucia Foster's information, and shoot off a message. If all goes to plan, she'll be here by tonight to keep Isabel from climbing the walls while I'm gone.

I pull up a few more searches and retreat to the hallway to make some calls, including one to Trinity House with an inquiry about Director McKenna's availability this week. She's at a conference for the next few days in New York. If it's not bullshit, I plan to find her there.

I make another call to Morgan.

"I need to know more about Jude McKenna," I say when he picks up.

"Who's she?"

"She's the director at the Trinity House, which I'm pretty sure is a front. In real life, she manages the group I've been working for."

He's quiet a moment. "Are you sure about this?"

"I'm positive," I say, hoping to convey the seriousness of my request for intel. I can hack my way into plenty of resources, but Morgan has clearances that give him access to significantly more. "If I can get to her,

I can figure out who put the hit out on Isabel."

"Give me a minute," he mutters.

I hear a door close through the phone and then the clicking of keys.

"Jude Ellen McKenna. Thirty-four. West Point after graduation. Four years in the army. Two years with the DEA. And she's been managing Trinity House ever since."

"Interesting transition," I say dryly.

"No kidding. I'll send you her address. I can apply for a tap on her phone."

"No." Something tightens in my gut. Instinct.

"No?"

"A tap could raise red flags. I don't know how deep this goes, and I don't want to spook her."

He's silent on the other end of the phone. "How is Isabel doing? We heard about Brienne. Does she know?"

I pinch the bridge of my nose. "She knows. She saw everything." I'd pay a king's ransom to erase the terror in her eyes. Even when we were making love—and that's sure as hell what it felt like we were doing—I could see her struggling to keep the memories at bay.

Morgan exhales heavily. "Goddamnit."

I pace down the empty hotel hallway. "You should take extra precautions. If they found us there, they'll be watching your place."

"It's already taken care of."

"Good. I'll be in touch," I say before hanging up and heading back to the room.

When I open the door, Isabel is pacing, tears in her eyes.

My heart falls like a rock into my stomach. "Shit, I'm sorry. You were sleeping, so I made some calls in the hallway. I was right here."

I go to her, but she tenses, pressing her tight fists against my chest, fire in her eyes. I don't let it keep me from wrapping my arms around her. Breathing her in. Whispering apologies in her ear until she softens against me.

"I'm right here. I won't leave you," I promise, knowing I'll have to break it too soon.

We make love again, and it's no less intense. Every time we're together, I'm caught in that strange place between my past and my reality. She's brand-new and familiar at once. Discovery and memory fusing into one intoxicating, boundary-shattering experience.

I lie beside her as we catch our breath and I wait for my heart to find a normal rhythm. Her arms are above her head, resting on the lone pillow that wasn't tossed to the floor. The narrow line of calligraphy trailing up her ribcage catches my eye.

I roll to my side and prop my head on my elbow to study it closer. She peeks out from under her arm. "What?"

"I was just wondering about this." I brush my thumb up the ink and caress her breast while I'm there.

एकं जीवनम्, एकः अवसरः

She hums softly and tangles our fingers together. "One life. One chance. It's Sanskrit."

I remember the first time I noticed it. Now I know what it's like to be the reason for her cries of pleasure, to be the man who makes her scream my name, not just the memory. Going through with the hit on her life seems unthinkable.

Her eyes close sleepily. "Reminds me not to let fear get in my way."

I'm glad she can't see the turmoil those words inspire. Thanks to me, whatever fears she had about the world before are likely a hundred times more terrifying now. Then again, maybe she's braver than she realizes. Maybe knowing what she's truly capable of can crush more of the fear that once held her back. We'll find out soon enough, but I'm not ready to go there yet. I'm more than content to stay in this post-fuck haze for as long as I can.

I lower my head to nibble on her shoulder. "You're beautiful."

She turns into my chest and nuzzles against me. "You're trying to get laid again."

I drape my arm around her and hold her to me, unwilling to argue.

"Do I fuck the same?"

Her lips quirk up a little. Seeing her smile releases another hit of endorphins into my already thoroughly blissed out bloodstream.

"Kind of."

"Kind of?"

She shrugs. "I can tell you've had experience."

"Oh." I hesitate. "Does that bother you?"

Hopefully not, since I can't do a damn thing to undo it.

She draws a ring around one of my scars—an old one that's faded white but is unmistakably from an ugly bullet puncture. "All things considered, no."

I exhale a measure of relief. True enough, we're alive. Presently safe. Not much room to complain. At least not when it comes to the way our bodies seem made for each other.

We linger that way for a long time. Not talking. Just breathing. Touching. Drifting in and out of sleep. When I glance at the clock for the last time, I remind myself that we can't stay this way forever, no matter how much I may want to.

I get up and shower while she orders room service. When I emerge, she's bundled in her robe that seems to swallow her up, eating a bowl of macaroni and cheese. I steal a couple of bites before I towel dry and get dressed.

"Where are you going?"

I don't answer her right away. I can sense our perfect day is about to come to a grinding halt.

"Tristan?"

I toss some of my things into a bag. "Jay's going to New York. I'm going to meet her there and get some answers."

Her fork clangs against the dish. "You said you weren't going to leave."

I sit across from her, grateful when she lets me take her hand. "I know I did. Your mom is going to stay here with you while I'm gone, though. I won't be long. Two days at most."

She doesn't acknowledge this as she gets up and begins pacing between the two rooms of the suite.

"Isabel…"

She halts and pins me with a taut look. "What?"

I sigh. "Listen, I get it. Every time I'm not with you lately, it gives me a goddamn heart attack. But we can't stay holed up here forever. I need to get to Jay before she realizes I'm coming for her. Then I'm coming back to you and we're going to get out of here. I promise."

She worries her lower lip and continues pacing.

I get up and stop her, bracing my hands on her arms.

"Look at me. Do you think I've made it this far being careless?"

"But she made you this way. The people she controls are just like you."

I shake my head. "No, Isabel. I'm better than they are."

She searches my gaze, seeming to slowly accept that this might be true. Granted, I haven't come in contact with everyone in Jay's employ, but I have a pretty good idea of where I stand next to the ones I have.

"And for the record, she didn't make me. She used me. I learned some tricks of the trade, sure, but she doesn't get to take credit for the nuts and bolts of who I am."

She looks down. "I just don't know what to say."

"You don't have to say anything. Just know that when you're strong for me, you're strong for both of us. Just you and me. Remember?"

She glances up, her eyes gleaming in the darkening room. "I remember," she whispers shakily.

We both turn at a knock on the door. We won't be alone after this, so I steal this last moment to kiss her. A soft, chaste kiss. A promise that I *will* come back to her.

10

ISABEL

Tristan leaves, and heroically, I don't make a scene, even though I'm worried I'll turn to dust if anything happens to him.

He'll be fine. He's strong. Dangerous. Cunning.

Two days. I can handle that, I reassure myself.

I join my mother in the living area of the suite. The suitcases she rolled in are open on the ground, filled with clothes, makeup, and several small black pouches and cases.

"What is all this, Mom? It's two days. You look like you're moving in."

"It's not for me." She smiles thinly. She's more put together than I saw her the other day. Her makeup is fresh. Her hair is blown out. She looks like she's dressed to kick ass in tight leather pants and a deep-maroon shirt tucked under the waistband.

"I travel light these days. I don't need all this."

She sits down on the couch, patting the place beside her. "Let's talk."

I peer down at the luggage and join her. Her bent knee takes the space on the cushion between us. She takes my hand and squeezes.

"I heard about Brienne. I'm so sorry, sweetheart."

I try to ignore the way my throat constricts. I refuse to cry.

"You don't have to talk about it," she says gently. "But now at least you know the kind of people we're dealing with. You've seen what they're capable of."

I still at her even tone.

"They murdered two guards where we were staying in Brazil. I know they won't hesitate."

She pauses. "I'm not sure how to say this delicately."

"Say what?"

"You need to disappear. At least for a little while."

"Tristan said we need to move on soon. I get it."

She shakes her head tightly. "I'm not sure you do. There's no place you can go as Isabel Foster without them finding you. This is more serious than anyone realized. They're not going to stop this hunt until they find you." She clutches my hand firmly. "I'd rather bury your name than your body, Isabel. I'd never survive it."

I simply stare at her in stunned silence. "What are you saying?"

She reaches into one of the suitcases, retrieves a manila folder, and places her hand on it as if she's taking an oath.

"What is that?"

"This… This is a new life to take the place of the one you'll need to give up."

I shake my head in disbelief, but she keeps going, her voice lapsing with emotion every so often.

"A birth certificate. Social security number. Passport. Bank accounts with all the money you'll need for a while."

I bolt up and back away. "Mom, what the hell?"

Her expression hardens. She speaks through gritted teeth. "Isabel, I will *not* let them take you from me too."

Exasperated, I throw my hands up. "This isn't about Mariana, Mom."

She sets the folder aside and stands, her hands in tight fists. "This has everything to do with Mariana. Why do you think I always hovered? Why do you think I protected you at every turn? Fought to keep you home until you fought me back so hard, all I could do was let you go. They killed her, and I never knew if they would come for you next."

My breathing is erratic. I miss Tristan. Need his arms. His reassurance.

"You sound crazy. You're not making sense. She had leukemia. There was nothing you could do."

She closes her eyes, exhales heavily, and walks to the window. "You don't know the whole story, Isabel."

"Then tell me, because you're scaring me with all this. I know this is bad. Really fucking bad. But you're talking about…basically…*killing* me." I can't hide the panic in my voice.

"I know what I'm asking. And the choice is yours. I'm just giving you everything you'll need if you decide this is what you want. There's not much time."

I cross my arms, darting my gaze from the manila folder to her position by the window. "How did you get all those documents? Did you already talk to Tristan about this?"

"Tristan doesn't know," she says matter-of-factly.

"Mom… What's going on?"

She lowers her head, eyes closed, as if she's remembering.

"You remember when Papa was still here?"

"Of course." I have vague memories of my grandfather. When my father brought my mother to the United States with him, he also secured a visa for my grandfather. He moved back to Honduras a couple of years after Mariana passed away. We spoke by phone sometimes, but I haven't seen him in years.

"He helped us when Mariana was very sick. Before you and Mariana were born, he'd been working at a research facility just outside of Boston. The relationship with the company soured after a few years. Papa disagreed with some of their practices. They wanted him to skew his research to benefit the company, and he disagreed. Adamantly. When he left, he published a paper on it in one of the popular medical journals. There was an investigation. The company had to pay fines, but they persevered."

"What does this have to do with Mariana?"

She comes back to the couch and sits. "We were desperate, Isabel. You can't understand the lengths a person will go to for their child. We would have done anything to make her well. None of the treatments were working." Her lips tremble slightly. "Papa's old company was working on an experimental drug. It was still in trials. Papa went to them."

"But there was bad blood between them."

"He agreed to retract his statements, reimburse the fines, even if it bankrupted him. Anything if it would help Mariana."

My jaw falls slightly. "So you agreed."

"We signed waivers, a stack of nondisclosures that would protect them if anything were to go wrong. We would have signed anything."

I feel sick, but go to her and clutch her hand, needing to hear the rest.

"She died two days after the first treatment." She exhales shakily. "We couldn't save her, but they stole the only time we had left."

I'm stunned, repainting the story in my mind with this new information.

"You really think they killed her?"

My mother lifts her now stony gaze to mine. "They were unreachable. Even before she'd passed, they wouldn't answer our calls. After she died, Papa received a sympathy card from the man he betrayed with the paper he published. Just his signature. He knew then it was justice for what he'd done."

I shake my head in disbelief. "That was over twenty years ago. Even if what you're saying is true, if they killed her to get back at Papa…"

"Isabel, why would someone want you dead?"

I scramble for possibilities, an exercise that always seems to draw up fruitless conclusions. "Maybe Dad is involved in something."

She crushes my hand in hers. "Sweetheart, no."

TRISTAN

I spent the night scoping out Jay's apartment in the city. After dawn broke, I followed her to the airport, checked the times for her flight to New York City, and promptly headed back to the apartment, arriving just after her scheduled takeoff.

Considering she was the manager of a high-profile mercenary ring, her security system was surprisingly easy to hack. Within twenty minutes, I was able to bypass the system, and now I'm standing in her immaculate luxury apartment. Not a thing out of place. Not even a coffee cup in the sink. I drag my finger along the granite countertop separating the living room from the kitchen. Not a speck of dust.

I journey down the hall to her bedroom. Not a wrinkle to be found. I lift the corner of the bedspread to find the sheets tucked in tightly the way every cadet would be taught.

I open the bedside drawer to find a handful of over-the-counter medications, including a few sleep aids. Nothing else. Her closet is meticulously arranged. Light blouses to dark, all grouped by garment type and color according to the spectrum. If I thought I had OCD tendencies, Jay had me beat hands down. Either that, or she didn't really live here.

I go to the second bedroom. A glass-top IKEA desk is set in the corner, flanked by three short filing cabinets. If she doesn't live here, she definitely works here.

I pick the lock of the first cabinet, its contents surprisingly sparse, with only a dozen or so files set in the hanging folders.

RED - Stone, Tristan

I withdraw the file that catches my eye first and sift through the first few pages. My enlistment paperwork. Grades and assessments on my skills and basic aptitude. What appears to be a thick stapled brief of the mission in Helmand that Brennan told me about. I skim over it, matching up his account to the official report. Oddly, nothing seems to slant toward my gross negligence.

I was your superior. I could have shut it all down.

Brennan's words ring through my memory. Then Jay's.

A lot of blood on your hands.

I move on to a stack of slick photos. They're gory and probably would not affect me at all if they didn't depict the wounds my body sustained. Nine gunshots. I've counted them more than once. I should have died.

I turn them over, and my focus shifts to the first page of medical records. As I begin reading, a subtle but sharp ring emits from the entryway. The tinny sound of tile being struck by a dime—the one I strategically placed on the door handle in the event Jay decided to come back home.

I set the file down and stand, drawing my gun as I do. Without a sound, I glide to the side of the doorway to wait and listen. The quiet click of the door closing. Jay's heels across the kitchen floor. The static of fear and danger in the air. The shit I live for.

"Check the bedrooms," she murmurs.

The almost imperceptible sound of footsteps on carpet gets closer and disappears when her associate steps into her bedroom. Anticipation sizzles in my blood, tingles in my fingertips as I ready myself to face Jay and whoever has come to protect her. Have I ever looked forward to an introduction more?

I hear him again, along with his measured exhale. I tuck my gun back in and wait.

Come to Daddy.

He steps into the room, gun first. I clench the barrel and twist it hard with my left hand. His finger cracks, and then so does his face as it makes sharp and repeated contact with my right.

He stumbles into the room and throws punches I deftly avoid. In the milliseconds before his face starts gushing blood, I realize he's not anyone I know from Company Eleven. I'm almost disappointed, but it makes disposing of him less complicated.

I take two fists of his jacket and knee him in the groin. He doubles over with a painful grunt. It's the last sound he makes before I jack my knee up into his jaw. His head jerks toward the ceiling with a snap, and he falls to the floor in an awkward heap. A few heavy seconds pass.

"Web? Do you have him?"

Jay's alarmed voice echoes down the hall. I can taste her panic from here. I step around the lifeless body. I'm jonesing to see her fear up close.

"Web?"

I edge down the hallway. Then I see her ahead of me, dressed in her navy pantsuit, a pistol hanging by her side. Her eyes widen a second before she raises it.

"Don't," I say loudly.

She freezes but keeps the gun aimed at me.

"I don't want to hurt you." I lie with my whole body, from the words on my lips to my unnaturally relaxed stance, even though I'm ready to duck and draw.

Her jaw is tight. Her cheeks are flushed.

I raise my hands in mock surrender. "Jay, I just want to talk."

I say her name like it means something. Like I'm glad she's here. Truly, I am. I'm even more satisfied with how restless her hands are on the gun. She doesn't want to kill me. Yet.

"Should I call you Jude?"

Her nostrils flare. "I should shoot you."

I smile a little. "Isn't that below your pay grade?"

"It is, in fact."

I take a slow step toward her.

"Don't. Just stay there, Tristan."

"How am I supposed to tell you what you need to know when you've got that thing pointed at me?"

She lets out a nervous laugh. "Do you expect me to trust you now?"

"I'm not pointing a gun at *you*. That's a pretty good display of trust, don't you think?"

"This isn't a fair fight, and you know it," she utters.

She's right. I don't care what training she has. I'm at an advantage.

Physically outmatched, if she's not willing to shoot me, she's fucked. Of course, she may not want to shoot me, but I'm not ruling out the possibility.

"I trusted you for three years, Jay. Never asked questions. Never said no."

A tense silence stretches between us. This twisted partnership between us weighs it down. The camaraderie that grew around succeeding and surviving her missions.

"I'm aware of our track record, Tristan."

"So you're saying it doesn't count for anything?"

She works her jaw. "You were paid to do a job."

"*You* were paid. I changed my mind. There's a difference."

"Our credibility was at stake. It is *still* at stake."

My lips curl with a sneer. "Your credibility? Are you serious?"

"You've been paid very well thanks to the credibility of the organization as a whole. You gave me no choice."

I take another step toward her. She flexes around the grip.

"What about Crow?"

"He was in the area," she says flatly.

I don't believe her. "He was following me the whole fucking time."

"I often use fail-safes. You know this."

True enough, I'd been backup on a few particularly important assignments. Sometimes the first line botched the job. But this was different.

"A twenty-five-year-old schoolteacher? You think I needed a fail-safe for her?"

"It was important. The client was eager. I've told you all of this."

I narrow my eyes. "Who is it? Who's this VIP client you need to please so badly?"

"You know I can't tell you that."

I laugh because she's consistent to a fault. "I bet you're employee of the month every damn month."

Then something changes in her countenance. I've hit a nerve. Touched on some truth.

I come closer. She steps back, keeping steady on her black pumps.

"I'm not going to hurt you," I say in a quiet, firm voice. A voice she can trust.

"You kill people for a living, so you'll have to excuse me if I don't buy it."

I keep walking toward her. She raises the gun a fraction. I pause before continuing my advance. She's flushed again, her hands shaking.

"I'm not going to hurt you," I say again. "I just need to know."

"Red, just stop right there."

I slow to a stop. She can almost touch my chest with the muzzle. I don't focus on that. I narrow my gaze to hers.

"You saved me, you know."

Doubt has cast a pretty big shadow on that possibility recently, but I spent a long time believing Jay had a hand in giving me the only life I could have. I reach for gratitude and try to communicate it in the tense space between us.

"I just want to talk… Without you pointing a gun at my heart," I add gently.

She's only half-lowered the gun when I grab her wrist, duck to the side, and wrench it from her. She screams. The sound comes to an abrupt halt when I wrap my hand around the delicate column of her neck. Her eyes go wide when I grip hard enough to cut off her air supply.

"Who wants her dead?" I growl with far less finesse. I am the monster she knows me to be.

She tries to shake her head, but her skin is already rising from pink to purplish-red.

"You going to tell me or not?"

She closes her eyes. Damn. Employee of the month indeed. Her lips tremble, and the rest of her limbs do too as she claws at my grip. Then I realize she's pulling the same card. Banking on some unspoken connection or sense of loyalty between us so I'll stop.

But, like she said, I kill people for a living. The prospect of ending her life doesn't make me squeamish. I can win this round, even if it costs me information I badly need. Seconds pass. Precious life-saving seconds.

Yes. Her lips mouth the word. A couple more seconds, and her now bloodshot eyes go wide again. The real panic is setting in.

"Yes? Is that what you said?"

She has a death grip on my forearm. Her nails dig into my flesh, but I don't care. I hate her. The part of me that can watch her die without remorse is the part she made—the killer in me who she shaped and encouraged until I was barely human.

When she starts to go weak, I snap out of my vengeful thoughts enough to loosen my hold on her throat. Just enough to let air flow. She drags in a desperate breath.

"Tristan."

"Wrong name. Tell me who put the hit out on her."

"I don't know."

I don't waste a minute. I grip her throat again, more tightly than before.

She's clawing at me again like she wants to talk, so I give her a little space to. She sucks in a series of ragged breaths before speaking.

"I don't deal directly with the clients. I'm only the manager, Tristan."

"Who does?"

"He's a shadow, Tristan. You'll never find him."

I bring my face close to hers. "Did you forget?" My voice is barely above a whisper. "I am a shadow, Jay. You killed me. I can see pretty well in the dark now."

Tenderly, I run my thumb over the place where the integrity of her windpipe would give with some focused pressure. "What's his name? Your boss."

She swallows, wincing over the discomfort it brings her. "Soloman."

I lift an eyebrow. "Tell me more about Soloman."

"He's got clients all over the world. There's no amount of money you could offer that would turn this around. He only takes the most expensive jobs, or the most difficult. Governments, Forbes 500, well-funded militias, the deepest pockets."

"Then why Isabel?"

She blinks. Tears gleam in her eyes. Tears of fear. Tears of impending death.

"I don't know, Tristan. I don't know. He wanted you and said it was important, so I sent Crow as backup because he was close."

I drag my fingertips along the back of her neck. She starts talking rapidly again.

"I can find out. I don't know how, but I'll try. Please, Tristan. Let me at least try."

"I'm not feeling merciful. Didn't you talk to Crow? I thought I made it clear."

Her lips tremble. "I got your message."

"I was hoping you would. It took extra effort to keep him alive. You didn't take it to heart, though. You killed Isabel's friend, and now I'm really pissed off."

"It was supposed to be her."

I shake my head and *tsk* softly. "You're lucky it wasn't. You'd already be dead."

She exhales a ragged breath full of her own fear. I look her over. She could intimidate Isabel from behind her desk, but now she's nothing more than a twig I can't wait to snap.

"Who was it? The one who killed her friend?"

She hesitates a second before nodding toward the hallway. "You've already been introduced."

I make a small sound of surprise. "I didn't recognize him."

"He's new. Like you were once."

I'm thoughtful a moment but can't bring myself to get emotional over it. I made choices. So did he.

Tires squeal outside. We both peer through the bay windows in the front. Two black SUVs park abruptly along the curb. She looks back to me.

"They're here for you."

"I guess I should get going," I say casually, even though I'm more than aware of the clock ticking until I'm outnumbered.

A furious tremble takes over her body. "Tristan, please. I'll get you the name. I can't get Soloman to stop looking for you, but I can get you the name. I know I can. You have to trust me."

The car doors shut, and several men start toward the apartment.

"Tristan, please..."

The itch to put a permanent end to her tearful pleas is strong, a reflex away. But something holds me back. Whatever exists between us was forged in blood and lies. I know that violence and betrayal begets more violence and betrayal.

"I'll find you again, Jay," I promise, because the business between us is far from over.

"I won't give you a reason to. I'll get you the name."

No matter what she says, I know I'll be seeing her again.

11

ISABEL

I stand before the mirror, trying to decide how I feel about anything, let alone this new look.

My mother smooths her hand over my hair, slick now from being stripped of its natural color and heavily conditioned. I run my hands through it experimentally, testing out how it feels and falls. My simple no-style length has been artfully chopped into an edgier bob. Bleached blond, a little wavy and messy, the overall look is dramatically different but satisfyingly on trend, which was nothing I ever cared about before. I tug at the clean-cut tips that fall just past my jawline.

"Remember how you used to threaten me if I ever dyed my hair?"

She smirks. "If J.Lo can pull it off, so can you. You're beautiful, Isabel. I really like it. Do you?"

I think I do.

She puts her arm around me and tugs me against her side. "Are you ready?"

Our eyes meet in the mirror.

Am I ready?

For this new life?

For death?

I'll only be dying on paper, of course, but it's enough to make me feel ill when I really take it in. People I know will mourn. They'll remember the twenty-five years of my life and bemoan that I was taken too soon. Then they'll forget me over time. I'll be memories in photographs. No one will know I've started over except my parents and Papa, who's using his contacts in South America to stage a death that will hopefully deter or at least delay the people who've been after me.

Mom won't tell me how he'll do it or where the documents for my new identity came from. She assures me everything will make sense once I get to my destination. The important thing is getting there. Crossing this threshold as soon as possible.

I fold my hands across my torso, running my fingers over the exposed ink peeking out from under my sports bra. *One life…* What if one life becomes two?

I shake off the thought, because it doesn't matter. If they want me dead, I'll die. And then I'll start anew.

We go back to the suitcases. Mom has packed them with my new wardrobe and anything else I may need on the road. Everything's brand-new with tags. Lots of black. Tight jeans and formfitting shirts. Boots and a pair of Converse just like the pair I left behind in Rio. She said she wanted me to feel strong and beautiful. A new me.

I feel new. Beautiful, *okay*. Strong, *working on it*.

She crouches over one full bag and zips it up tight and then the other. I'm leaving before it gets dark. Nervous energy courses through me. I can't believe I'm doing this. But it feels like Rio. Like Tristan. The thing I need to do…

Mom stands and lifts the heaviest bag to rest on its rollers. The manila folder with my new identification is on the couch where we left it, along with a debit card loaded with all the money I'll need to get set up someplace new and keys to the car that'll take me there.

"Are you sure you don't want to wait for Tristan?"

This is your new life. You decide who you want in it, she said when we went through all the documents and mapped out the plan.

Ten days ago, Tristan crash-landed back into my world. Ten days ago, I stepped out of the safety and security of my life and blindly ran with him into another chapter, not truly understanding what I'd be leaving behind. I've been careening through it all, clinging to Tristan to anchor me and make sense of it.

Of course I want to wait for him. I'm undeniably in love with him. I'd be content to curl up with him in this hotel room for the rest of my days and forget the rest of the world exists. When he touches me, my pain goes someplace else. When he leaves, I'm a mess. I'm scared to death of everything. And this is why I can't wait.

Facing the unknown future is terrifying, but it's the only way forward. Wishing for things to be the way they once were would be a futile waste of energy with danger on my heels and a band of faceless enemies committed to securing my destruction.

This truth is fortifying in its own way. I'm choosing the point where my old life ends and my new life begins on my own terms, in my own way. I'm drawing this mark on the timeline of my life alone.

I love Tristan, and I trust he'll find me when he's meant to.

TRISTAN

I managed to escape Jay's apartment without clashing with the men outside. I had to steal a car to do it, but I managed. I'm relieved and unsure. Motivated by the information I now have—a stack of folders with all the hit men who are a leash tug away from carrying out Jay's, or Soloman's, bidding.

I never really considered the hierarchy of things before. Jay was God. The gauzy vision in the sky that ruled my world. Knowing someone wields power above her, someone who sought me out for this hit, unnerves me.

Jay's semblant commitment to help has me knotted up too. I should have killed her, but I let her go with a bruised neck and mercy I swore

I'd never give her.

I'm not used to hesitating. But ever since I decided not to pull the trigger on Isabel, I've been doing a lot more of that.

Still, I killed a man back there. Doing so evened the score, except I'm not celebrating it. I won't come home to Isabel a hero tonight. She'll think of the notebook and carry the weight of my decision and blame herself for the words she spoke in the depths of her misery.

On my way to our floor, I decide I won't tell her. God knows, she's dealing with enough gravity right now. I hover the key card over the sensor and walk inside, expecting to see her with her mother, maybe watching TV or talking over room service and a stiff drink. But the room is dark.

I flip on the lights. The room's been cleaned. It's bare of any signs of her. My heart's in my throat as I walk the three rooms, confirming she's gone. I double back to the bedroom and look around frantically, when something catches my eye.

In two long strides I'm at the bedside table. I pick up the notebook. Its worn leather slides against my fingertips.

She's gone. Really gone.

An icy fear works its way through me when I think of her out in the world, alone, when she's just now begun to understand what a savage place it can be.

"Fuck!"

I hurl the notebook across the room. It bounces off the wall and drops to the floor, both dull sounds that do nothing to represent my current frustration.

I walk over to retrieve it, noting how the leather straps come loose along with one of the pages. I open it and pull free the torn-out paper. Scrawled with someone else's handwriting, it's not like the others. I know it's Isabel's instantly by the feminine swoop of the letters.

St. Joan of Arc, New Orleans

The loose page was wedged above the last entry I'd made several weeks ago. A narco in Miami who very likely had it coming. Below his name is another. One I didn't write. One that's been etched into my brain since she called out my name...

Isabel Foster

A short dash takes the place where I'd have logged my fee had I gone through with it.

Seeing her name written among the dead sends my anxiety into overload. Worry spikes through my gut until I'm pacing along the bed, trying to figure out how the fuck this went down. What does this mean? Where the fuck *is* she?

Why... Why is her name here? Written in the same feminine script.

I stop in place. As I drag my thumb over the ink, the fury in my veins lowers to a simmer. The rage and the worry turn into something else.

Hope.

THE RED
LEDGER

part 3

1

ISABEL

New Orleans

Ribbons of passion and song seep through the closed doors of St. Joan of Arc Catholic Church into the empty street. A woman inside is singing, the soulful sound lifted up by the accompanying piano and drums. Making my post my pew, I hum the familiar hymn until the lyrics to the refrain come back to me.

> *All that we have and all that we offer*
> *Comes from a heart both frightened and free.*

I briefly consider going inside, but for now I'm content to wait where I am, a block off the Mississippi River. The immediate neighborhood is unremarkable—modest houses, an adjacent school, and a warehouse with commercial space a few feet down the street where I'm now parked.

After an all-night drive from DC, I traveled the long stretch of highway that took me over Lake Pontchartrain and into the city at dawn. Already the sultry spring air is a welcome change from the chilly capital. I close my eyes and melt into the supple leather seat of the blue SUV that's been my home since my mother pushed the keys into my hand and we said our tearful goodbyes. Only goodbye for now, I think, as I feel exhaustion tug at me.

"Hey."

A loud voice and the sudden rapping on the windshield jolts me upright. I brace my hand on the center console and open my eyes at the same time. A heavily muscled man with a shaved head, his shirt damp with sweat, is standing just beyond my rolled-down window. My heart threatens to beat out of my chest. I scramble to open the console and whip out the pistol I have hidden there.

"Whoa, whoa." The man backs up a couple of steps with his hands raised.

I blink rapidly and try to steady the full-body panic vibrating through me. On second glance, he looks a little less menacing. More like a forty-something gym rat out on his morning run. His skin is like mine, sandy brown. His eyes a shade darker, wide and honest.

"I'm not going to hurt you, all right? I noticed your out-of-town plates, saw you sleeping here, and wanted to make sure you were okay."

"I'm fine."

"Do you need help?"

"No, I don't need help," I snap. Why would he think I need help? Do I look that bad? I catch my reflection in the rearview mirror. My skin is dull, and the bags under my eyes seem to reflect the toll of this latest leg of my journey.

I untangle my hand from the weapon. My adrenaline is still pumping hard, but I try to suppress the feeling of immediate danger.

"Sorry. I've been driving all night. I'm just tired. I'm waiting for someone."

I glance at the still-closed doors of the church. The Sunday service should be wrapping up soon.

"With a gun?"

"It's for protection. You scared the shit out of me."

He drops his arms and pinches the center of his branded T-shirt, tugging it off his damp skin a few times. "You worried about someone in particular or just everyone?" His chest moves with labored breaths, more from physical exertion than the fact I considered shooting him a few seconds ago, I'm guessing.

He points toward my lap when I don't respond. "Believe it or not, you don't need that."

Why can't he take a hint? I'm not interested in company. Can't he read the sign on my forehead: *Crazy, exhausted woman with a handgun. Back off.*

"Thanks, but you don't know anything about what I need or don't need."

"I know you're scared to death. Probably a little too punchy to have a weapon like that within reach. You almost shot me for knocking on your window. Doesn't that concern you?"

Jesus. If I wanted a sermon, I would have attended the service. I clunk the gun back into the center console and slam it shut. "I don't even know how to use it. Does that make you feel better?"

"Not really."

"Listen, I have to go." I look to the church again, relieved when I see the doors open and patrons spilling out onto the steps. "Sorry," I say again for good measure as I get out of the vehicle and move away from the man.

Approaching the church steps, I try to ignore the knot of anxiety I've been holding on to about meeting a different stranger altogether— the mysterious woman my mother assured me would help me get settled here in the city.

Martine Benoit looks just like the picture Mom gave me. A few inches shorter than me, she's petite with curves that fill out her bright floral sheath dress, her feet adorned with bright-red patent leather pumps. The heavy rouge on her cheeks and heavily dyed blond hair betray a woman clinging to her youth. She lingers near the entrance with the reverend and two other women who look to be around my age.

The sparse crowd thins quickly, narrowing my window for making contact. I push my doubts aside and climb the steps to her.

"Let us know what you need for the dinner. I'm sure the girls would love to help," she says.

The reverend takes her hand and holds it in both of his. "That would be wonderful. Your generosity is always a blessing."

His gaze flickers to mine, and Martine's follows.

She looks me up and down before smiling. "Isabel."

I hesitate a few paces away, but she waves me forward.

"Come. Reverend Stephens, this is Isabel. She'll be staying with us."

I go to them, and as he takes my hand, I experience for myself his warmth and gentle strength.

"It's a pleasure to meet you, Isabel. You are welcome here anytime. Consider this an extended home."

"Thank you," I say, uneasy with how quickly I'm being swept into a world of people I don't know.

The knot in my belly tightens when I think of Tristan. I miss him. I'd much rather have him at my side than force myself into these new circumstances. But I have to be strong. Have to find my own way for now.

The reverend nods to each of us. "You ladies have a blessed day."

Martine and the two girls flanking her murmur reciprocations before turning their attention to me.

"You made good time," Martine says with a painted smile. "Lucia said to expect you tonight at the earliest."

"I decided to drive straight through," I admit. I didn't relish the miles I was putting between Tristan and me, nor was I overly anxious to make this first move into my new life. Mostly, I couldn't see myself staying at a hotel anywhere between here and there and feeling comfortable enough to actually rest.

"I'm Skye." One of the young women waves her fingers. Her hair is pure fire, a natural bright auburn that's braided down her back.

"Skye and Zeda are sisters at the house. They'll help you get settled."

House? Sisters?

I register a needle of concern that my mother has committed me to some sort of convent for wayward women.

Martine gestures to Zeda. She's tall with deep-brown skin and features made even more striking by her short hair. She could easily model the runways of Milan, but the distance she keeps from the others and her untrusting eyes tells me that's not the path she's been on.

"Good to meet you," she says without much warmth.

"You must be exhausted, child. Come." Martine hooks an arm into mine, and together we descend the steps.

Except our journey is leading us right back to the man I hoped would go away. He saunters across the street, his muscles flagrantly on display, his lips curved slightly.

"Noam." Martine sings his name.

"Morning." He leans in to kiss her cheek. "I'm sweaty."

She shushes him. "I wouldn't know you any other way. Meet our new sister, Isabel."

His gaze lingers on Zeda a moment before locking with mine. "Isabel. Pleasure to formally meet you. I'm Noam Namir."

"Noam owns the Krav Maga center over there." She points down Cambronne to a plain-looking building with metal siding and a few windows.

"You're welcome anytime, Isabel. I'd love to have you. No charge."

"I'll think about it," I say tightly.

The exhaustion is no doubt making me edgy. His aggressive concern for me is difficult to accept, though. All of this is. Martine's motherly clutch on my arm. Her flock of "sisters" who probably already know things about this arrangement and me that I wish no one did. Even the reverend who reminded me of Father Antonio back in Brazil, an open heart and a kind smile.

"The house isn't far. We can walk," Martine says. "It's a fine day."

I stiffen. "I have my car. I can meet you there if you give me the address."

She waves her hand. "It's only a few blocks. Noam, you can drive

Isabel's car up the street for us, couldn't you?"

"Sure."

"Wait—"

Martine squeezes my arm gently. "Noam is with us. Your things are safe with him. Plus, I was hoping we could chat."

I don't feel as if I'm being given much choice, but my mother ensured me that Martine could be trusted. She's an old friend. A dear and well-connected friend whom she never spoke of until she was handing me a new life in a new place—a place where the people who want me dead will hopefully never find me.

I take my keys out and hand them to Noam.

"I'll be over in a few." He winks.

He jogs over to my car as Martine leads us toward our destination.

Skye and Zeda walk ahead of us. Their quicker pace soon makes it impossible for them to hear us.

"You poor thing, you must be terrified," Martine mutters.

We share a look, but I'm at a loss for what to say.

Am I terrified? All things considered, yes, terrified sums up my current state of mind pretty well.

"Your mother told me everything," she continues. She shakes her head as if something unpleasant has just passed through her thoughts. "Even if she hadn't, I could see it on your face the minute I saw you. It may take some time for you to believe it, but you'll be safe with us. I promise you that."

"Thank you."

I am thankful. Even if I'm scared and uncomfortable. Noam drives by in my SUV, honking as he passes.

"You know him pretty well?"

"I have known Noam for many years. He's part of the fabric of our little community here. He watches out for the girls. More importantly, he helps them watch out for themselves. You should go to him." She gives my upper arm a harsh squeeze. "Put some muscle behind your fear and it'll become something else. Something you can face."

I nod a little as we turn onto a much busier St. Charles Avenue.

Majestic live oaks line both sides, bathing our path in shade.

"But first, we'll show you around, and you can get some sleep. You can breathe easy now. No more running."

The farther we walk, the better I feel. Our conversation melts away, replaced by the flow of cars up and down the street. The rhythmic clopping of Martine's heels on the sidewalk. The hum and periodic ding of the street car moving past us down the median. I feel as if I've stepped into another world. An offbeat kind of place that—despite its grit and oddities—feels almost magical. And the woman beside me may be my fairy godmother.

I'm ready to chide myself for these sleep-deprived thoughts when we slow in front of a sprawling old house with an ornate facade. I take in its features—a welcoming wraparound porch, tall bay windows, and a second-floor balcony. Lush greenery, a long drive where my car is already parked, and a wide wrought-iron gate separate it from the street. A castle too, I think, fully surrendering to the fairy tale now.

Two golden emblems are set within the gate's rails—the serif letter "H" with a double ringed oval running through its center and enclosing the upper half of the letter. Wrought-iron fleur-de-lis and swirling vines curl around them, reaching all the way to the top of the center pickets that are artfully coiled above the others.

Martine punches a code into the box beside the door latch. It buzzes, and the door slowly opens with a groan.

"This is the house?" I wonder aloud, doing little to hide my awe of the place.

Martine smiles and leads me down the path. "Welcome to Halo."

TRISTAN

I wait at a café across the street from the car repair place and stare at my phone, rereading the headline that hit the national news circuit this morning.

Missing American Teacher Found Dead in Rio

The article goes on to explain how the body of Isabel Foster, an English teacher in Brazil who disappeared ten days ago, was found dumped on the outskirts of the city, so unrecognizable that dental records had to be referenced to confirm her identity.

Someone's helped Isabel disappear, and for once, it wasn't me. While her father has resources, I'm skeptical he's used them to fake his daughter's death.

Then there's Lucia…

I'm halfway through my second cup of coffee when she passes through the door.

I study her. Her rigid posture and confident gait. Her hand steady on her purse.

"I got your message," she says almost breathlessly as she takes the opposite chair.

"Is she safe?"

She meets my eyes. "She's safe."

"Who is she with?"

She quietly assesses me. Like Isabel, her beauty is a distraction from whatever lies beneath. I have every intention of unearthing at least a few of her secrets today.

"Tristan, what do you truly want from her?"

"I want her out of harm's way."

She cants her head as if she doesn't believe me.

"I would never hurt her." Unnerved, I make the vow with more force.

"If she has to start over—and she does—she has the right to do it alone."

Her words are a swift punch to my heart, the same broken organ that Isabel's brought back to life. I exhale slowly, trying like hell not to show how her words affect me. Maybe I'd read things wrong with Isabel. Misunderstood her affection for something entirely different in our desperate circumstances. Or maybe after Brienne, there's simply nothing left to salvage.

"She cares for you." Lucia interrupts my spinning thoughts.

Flattening her palms on the table, she leans in. "What I'm asking is if you care for her past your sense of obligation to keep her safe."

"Of course," I say without hesitation.

"Have you told her that?"

I hesitate. "I... Lucia, we've been through hell. When was I supposed to tell her?"

"You're sleeping with her, aren't you?"

I work my jaw and look away. True enough. Our intimate moments have been heavy with all the things I haven't said, things I don't know how to express. I trusted she could sense it without me having to say the words.

"We've been a little distracted."

"You're making excuses."

Her mother's not giving me an inch of forgiveness. When I invited her here to talk, I was expecting to press her for information about Isabel's situation, not state my intentions to earn it.

I swipe the coffee stirrer and trap it between my teeth, grinding absently. What do I say? How do I get back to Isabel with her mother guarding the gates?

I cycle through my options. Lie, manipulate, threaten, kill. I can't handle this like a mercenary, though. I need to think like the human being Lucia expects me to be if I'm going to have any kind of presence in her daughter's life.

"I think you want me to say that I'm in love with Isabel and I should have told her that at some point while we've been running for our lives. Maybe I should have, but the truth is, I don't know what that feels like yet. I'm not normal. I'm not like this Kolt guy."

"He's not good for her," she says abruptly.

I stare, hoping to unlock her cryptic look and the meaning behind her statement. Her trying to steer Kolt away at the door the other day and her swift intervention between us had taken me off guard. She knows things about him.

"Why do you say that?"

"His family... They're not good people."

I didn't expect they would be. Anyone with that much money and influence has secrets. Not the good kind.

She drums her fingers and looks out the window. "Did she tell you about Mariana?"

"Leukemia."

She nods tightly. "I want to tell you things, Tristan. I want to arm you with everything you need to know, but I need to trust you. You may think you care for her now, but what if that changes and she's left even more vulnerable because of the things you know? I *have* to trust you."

Possibilities whirl through my brain, and suddenly I'm fiending for the information she has. I was not wrong about Lucia. Her eyes are shadowed with secrets untold. Her desire for trust is evenly matched. I need her to tell me every useful nugget of information that will bring Isabel back into my world.

"You probably never approved of me. Never liked me or whatever Isabel and I shared."

She sighs. "Tristan, you were both very young. We had dreams for her."

"I got in the way of those dreams."

"You did. Then you broke her heart. And here we are."

"There's no point in holding it against me now. I'm not that person anymore. I don't know why I left her, but if I hadn't, I'd have a normal life. I'd have my memories. Now all I have is her. I know I've never deserved her, but I need you to understand that I will never hurt her. She cares about my life more than I do, and I'd gladly sacrifice it to keep her safe."

The silence stretches between us for a long time.

"She needed to take this trip on her own, Tristan. Between the things she saw in Brazil and losing Brienne, she's unsteady. She wants to find her balance and not feel like she'll lose it the minute you walk out the door. I kept her sheltered for too long."

"She told me," I say.

She twists her wedding ring absently, shifting the modest diamond back and forth on her finger. "When she'd had enough and finally struck out on her own, I was so scared for her. But I can't deny that a part of me was proud too. I've seen the horrors that human beings can bring on each other. A parent never wants her child exposed to those things, but Isabel was hungry for life and I couldn't hold her back." She closes her eyes briefly. "Nothing could have prepared her for what's come to pass, but she's capable. I know she is."

Lucia's impassioned speech resonates. If I could keep Isabel isolated from the big, bad world for the rest of my life, I would. She's strong enough to face it, but she'd have a much better chance of surviving it with me by her side. Of all people, her overprotective mother should realize this.

"So you thought this was a good time to let her spread her wings and fly solo. When her life is on the line. When she's a fucking target."

"Feeling like she can't manage on her own is dangerous too. If she's made to feel weak, she'll be weak. If she knows you'll always be there to catch her, she'll never be able to catch herself. This is more than the immediate threat, Tristan. This is going to be a long road for her."

"Hopefully it is."

"She's in good hands, I assure you."

I lean in, pinning her with a look full of steely determination. "You do realize that I'm going to do whatever it takes to find my way back to her. No matter what you say. If you decide to help me or not."

"I know that," she utters quietly.

"Then, please, for the love of your daughter, tell me what you know."

She takes a deep breath, as if she's deciding at this moment that she will.

"Mariana did not expire in a natural way. She was given an experimental drug that ended her life two days after it was administered. My father, Gabriel Martinez, begged for help from the people who'd been developing the drug, despite the bad blood between them. They were…estranged, bitter enemies. But a child's life hung in the balance. They could have saved Mariana. Instead they chose to settle the score, robbing us of the time we had left."

The photo in Isabel's room flashes in my mind. Then Isabel's sad but accepting account of her sister's untimely death. "She doesn't know."

"I raised Isabel hoping she'd never need to know these things, but she understands the men who took her sister's last days are the ones who now want her dead. I explained everything when I came to the hotel."

I worry now that inviting Lucia to stay with her was my worst misstep yet. Not only did she help Isabel disappear, but her involvement runs deeper than I could have imagined. Either that or she's completely crazy. All of this could be the paranoid delusions of a grieving parent who needed someone to blame.

"If they settled the score twenty years ago, what's changed? Why would they be after Isabel all of a sudden?"

"The grief was too much. My father didn't know what to do with it, and neither did I. We had to fight for her in our own way." She levels a tired gaze at me, some of her earlier sternness seeming to ease. "We chipped away little by little, exposing information about their company, their finances, figuring out their connections. Over the years, the company grew, merged with others. Their interests expanded. Their power stretched so far and so fast, we could hardly keep up."

"Wait a minute. Who are *they*?"

"Today, *they* are Chalys Pharmaceuticals. You may recognize the name."

My blood turns to ice. My heart's in my throat, and my hands turn to hardened fists. Jesus, they've been right there the whole time. Under my nose. In her goddamn *bed*. The pendulum in my chest has turned into a murder weapon, wreaking havoc on my insides. I can't breathe right. Can't see properly through this sudden rage.

"They couldn't have sent him there for her." *I'll kill him...*

"He could have been there by chance. I never made the connection between Kolt and Chalys until Isabel went missing and his full name came across in the police reports. He was the last person to see her, so I looked him up, hoping to find out more about him. Then I realized who his mother was. Gillian Mirchoff. She and her brother took over operations for Chalys and its subsidiaries a decade ago. I would have gone and gotten Isabel out of there myself if I'd known."

I pound my fist on the table. "Why else would he have been there if not to kill her?"

"Because he can do whatever he wants, and Rio's a playground for the young and the rich. Besides, why would his family risk putting blood on his hands when they could pay someone like you to do it?"

I stand abruptly. The chair groans against the tile floor. I pace to the opposite side of the café and back again.

"He loves her," she says when I'm near again. "I'm sure of it. Not just from the way he acted the other day. Isabel and I spoke often. He's been in her life for months. He wanted her to come to Boston with him after the school year ended. Mentioning her to his family could have spurred all of this. I can't be sure."

I keep pacing, trying to tamp down my violent thoughts. Isabel's penchant for walking directly into danger and surviving is nothing short of astounding. I'm past furious for Isabel making her well-being known to Kolt the other day. If she hadn't, he'd believe today's headline as pure fact. She'd be dead to him. Lost forever.

"Tristan, sit down. Please."

I return and drop angrily into the seat. "Why doesn't Morgan do something about this?"

"Because he doesn't know." Her admission falls like a stone between us.

I still. My bloody thoughts clear. "Are you kidding me?"

"He's never known," she says.

"They killed his daughter. How can he not know that?"

"We signed away our rights, Tristan. We had no recourse against them. Until my father knew for certain it was foul play, we let Morgan believe it was her time. We were so heartbroken already, after months of treatments and not knowing if she could get better. If he'd known what really happened, it would have destroyed what was left of our family. He would have never forgiven me."

"It wasn't your fault."

"It's always someone's fault," she whispers.

"He could have helped nail them for what they did."

She shakes her head. "He's bound to the law, and these people are above the law."

"Well, you certainly could have told me. I've been in DC for days trying to find more information, and you've been sitting on it this whole time."

"I had to make arrangements. Do my own due diligence. I just needed you to keep her safe while I figured out a more permanent solution."

"You mean killing her."

She exhales a sigh and rubs her forehead. "We can bring her back to life just as easily. Trust me, this is far from over."

I'm roiling. Vexed in more directions than I can count. Pissed at myself for having so narrow a view that I let Isabel slip through my fingers. I'd been so focused on Morgan, I'd ignored Isabel's concerns about her mother's behavior. If Lucia was able to fake her daughter's death and hide her away, I have to question what else she's capable of.

"Who is she with?"

My jaw is locked tight. I pin her with a look, daring her to challenge my final request for the information I came here for. Acting like a decent human being for her sake was just that. An act. I'm ready to buy a ticket to hell for Isabel. I wouldn't hurt her mother, but I'm silently imploring her not to get in my way.

"She's with a friend," she says, pursing her lips as if that's all she'll tell me.

"In New Orleans?"

Her expression remains impassive save a small twitch at the corner of her mouth. "She told you."

"She left a note. Are you surprised?"

"No, I don't suppose I am." She rises, her hand firm on her purse once more. "If she wants to be found, that's where you'll find her."

2

ISABEL

Halo, as Martine calls it, is more than a picturesque estate along one of New Orleans's historic arteries. It's a haven. As soon as I step through the front door and into the foyer warmed by the spring sunshine pouring in through the bay windows, I can feel it. A sense of home that has nothing to do with this brief reprieve from imminent danger. The worn floors creak under our footsteps as Martine gives me a tour through the rooms.

As she describes them, the local cadence of her voice becomes more obvious. Every room is welcoming. Clean but lived in. The dining room, which holds an extended rustic table that could seat more than a dozen, flows into an impressively large kitchen equipped with modern appliances and wrapped by exposed brick, creating a feeling of comfort and hominess.

"The bedrooms are upstairs." She gestures to the narrow staircase in the hallway.

I follow her up, running my hand along the thick railing. The bones of the house are strong, and I get the sense it's been stripped down and thoroughly restored while preserving all the heart of the place.

We pass several bedrooms and pause at the last doorway. "This is your room. Skye and Zeda are next door."

She steps aside and waves me in. The bedroom is small but cozy. My suitcases are just inside the door. A full-size bed is set against a wall and flanked by a bedside table and an antique chest of drawers. An oval mirror hangs on another wall. I share a brief look with my tired reflection before going to the window that takes up nearly the full height of the wall and faces the back of the house. Below is a stone courtyard surrounded by a variety of leafy trees and bushes, some already flowering with white blossoms. Skye and Zeda are sitting with a couple of other women around a painted picnic table. Some are smoking. Most are laughing, though I can't tell what they're talking about.

"How many people are staying here?"

"Seven right now, including you. Sisters come and go. Most usually stay just the once and move on when they're ready. Our door is always open, though. This will always be your home for as long as you need it."

"Why do you call it Halo?"

My curiosity is burning about this place and its steward, this strangely magnetic woman.

"Halo isn't the house, Isabel. It's a mission." As she stands beside me, the afternoon light reflects on her fair skin, exposing every smudge of rouge, every imperfection. "We exist to illuminate the truth. The truth in ourselves first." She touches her chest. "Then we cast light on the people who threaten our well-being." She follows my gaze to the courtyard below. "We take women in and we help them onto a better path. Any age, any background, under any circumstances. Prostitution, violent relationships, drugs." She lifts her gaze to mine. "We offer protection…asylum from those who would do us harm, mentally or physically."

Asylum is the word that rocks me. More than a place, it's a state of being. Here I somehow feel out of reach from the people who would have killed me if they'd gotten a clear shot.

Martine's intent is so matter-of-fact, I have a hard time accepting it.

Have I lost trust so quickly? Or is the picture she's painting too altruistic even for me to buy into? How can any place, any entity, have such pure intentions?

"How do you sustain all this?" I gesture around the room. Maintaining a house like this with only one occupant would be expensive. How can she afford to support so many others?

"Halo sustains itself in its own way. But we don't ask for money from within. All we ask for is an open mind. A willingness to consider our doctrine and a chance to be a part of something bigger. A band of light that reaches all corners of the globe."

I tense a little. A doctrine?

"So you're like…missionaries?"

Maybe my earlier assumption about the nunnery was right. I've found myself brought to my knees in desperate prayer more than ever lately, but I've also faced death and seen the horrible acts human beings are capable of up close and personal. I'm not ready to hear anyone's doctrine with my own faith on such shaky ground.

"Missionaries in that we have a mission. A fluid one at times. We must evolve as the world around us changes. We aren't faith-based. However, I find that light travels well through those channels. Not all of course, but there are plenty of kind souls left in the world. People like the reverend. People like Noam."

"Light… What do you mean by that?"

"Information, mostly." She takes my hand gently in hers. "Don't worry about any of that, though. For now, we focus on you."

I laugh. "Where would someone start? My life—if I can even call it that anymore—is a complete mess."

"You've been on the run."

I nod. "Not long. But it feels like a lot longer."

She frowns. "Running is a hard place to be. You may feel alone with what you're going through, but you're not. When you're running away from something, remember you're also running *to* something."

"I wish I knew what that something was." Because right now this journey feels like a never-ending road paved with unknowns and lined with heart-wrenching pit stops.

"Maybe we can help you figure that out. Show you ways to tap into your power when it feels as if you have none, and then help you use that power to fight back and win. Not just to survive, Isabel, but to thrive and cast light on the darkest corners of your life. You have the power to do that."

I swallow over the emotion constricting my throat. The weight of the past two weeks threatens to crash down on me. "I can see now why my mother wanted me to come."

"When your mother reached out to me, I accepted without hesitation. Lucia's been vital to our work for many years."

I still. "Really?"

She nods. "After your sister passed, our paths crossed. Halo was just beginning to take shape, and she told me about your grandfather and what happened to Mariana. We've been helping each other ever since."

"I never knew about Halo. She never mentioned you either."

"I don't think our work was something she ever wished to burden you with." She touches my shoulder. "Circumstances have changed. But perhaps this was fateful that you would find your way here."

Perhaps.

Her eyes soften with quiet understanding. "For now, just rest, Isabel."

By the time I wake up, the sky has grown dark. I should feel rested, but the exhaustion is still heavy on me. Weighing down my limbs as I force myself upright. Lingering in my bones as I unzip one of my suitcases and pull out fresh clothes and some toiletries.

I shower in the little bathroom across from my room. When I emerge, I hear female voices down the hall. Delicious aromas waft upstairs from the kitchen, tempting me. My stomach growls, but I'm not sure I'm recharged enough to face the rest of Halo's tenants just yet.

Instead I spend the next hour or so reorganizing my things into drawers and the bedroom closet. Doing so reminds me of my first days at college. Brienne and I had become fast friends. She was honest and real, and I could always just *be* around her without pretense. She didn't drain me or expect me to be someone else. And she didn't expect me to be whole again after Tristan had broken me.

Because of those times and countless others, we could flow in and out of each other's lives knowing that we could always count on that solid foundation of friendship.

By the time my second suitcase is emptied, tears are streaming down my face. I still can't believe she's gone. Because of me. If I hadn't gone to her, she'd still be alive.

"Hey."

I whip around to find Skye in the doorway. I wipe my tears quickly.

She comes in holding a plate in her hands. "Dinner's ready. I brought you up a plate in case you wanted to eat in here tonight."

I accept it. "Thanks. I was going to go down later to see if there were leftovers."

"When Martine cooks, there usually aren't leftovers. But there's always takeout. It's hard to get a bad meal in this town."

The food smells amazing, and my growling stomach can't disagree. I take a seat on the bed and dive into the rice dish. It's an explosion of flavor on my tongue, and I don't hesitate to go in for another bite and another.

"Wow, girl. When's the last time you ate?"

I catch my breath a moment. "Drive-through on my way into town. I didn't mean to sleep so long."

Skye flops her body over the end of the bed. A bite of the moistest cornbread I've ever had distracts me from the pretty girl edging her way into my personal space.

"My God, this is good."

"I figured you wouldn't be able to resist." She smiles. "So what's your story anyway?"

"My story?"

"Everyone at Halo has a story. But Martine knows you, so you must have a good one. We're all dying to know."

I eat my next few bites a little slower, the immediate pangs of hunger having subsided. Skye seems like a nice girl, but the last thing I want to do is recount the past two weeks of hell.

"Where are you from?" she asks next, showing her persistence.

I set the empty plate aside and lean against the headboard. "DC. How about you?"

"Houston."

"What brings *you* to Halo?"

She props her head up on her elbow. "The short version? A life on the streets."

"And the long version?"

"I came to New Orleans with my pimp a few years ago. He heard there was money to be made in the Quarter, and I was his best girl. Got me dancing in one of the clubs and wanted me to push drugs to the johns too. One of the johns got mad when I wouldn't snort coke off his dick one night. Made a big show about it like I was rejecting him or something. Charlie was into all kinds of shit by then. High all the time. He beat the hell out of me after. Didn't touch my face, of course, but I ended up in the hospital with internal bleeding. When he came to pick me up, one of the nurses who'd been taking care of me turned him away. Threatened to call the cops if he came back. Of course, I freaked out because he was my whole life. Didn't matter that he almost killed me. I thought I loved him. Why else would I do all those things for him?"

She traces her fingers over the quilt stitching on the bedspread. I bite my lip, not knowing the right words to say. Skye's story is heart-wrenching and, for the moment, pulls me out of my own malaise.

"The nurse told me about this house where you can go and stay free," she continues. "Free food, a clean room, other girls like me who are trying to start over from bad situations. Said the woman who ran it had some good connections and could get me a real job. Help me start over."

"Martine."

Martine's the one who's brought us all here, like a beacon of hope.

She nods. "It was scary at the time because I didn't know what it'd be like here. If it didn't work out, Charlie probably would hurt me really bad if I had to go back to him."

"Looks like it worked out," I say softly.

"I've been here for a couple years."

"What do you do now?"

She shrugs. "Odd jobs here and there. But mostly I help Martine." She straightens on the bed before I can question her further. "Hey, do you want to come with me and Zeda to Noam's class in the morning?"

I hesitate. "I'm not sure I'm ready for that."

"Come on. It's fun."

I sigh and decide to hear her out. "What kinds of things do you do?"

"You learn how to kick ass. Shoot, you should see Zeda go at it with him. He's been training her for like six months. She's lethal."

"What about you? Are you lethal too?"

Something mysterious flashes behind her eyes, a coy little smile lifting her lips. "I can be. But when it comes to Noam's classes, I do it for a while, and then I pussy out so I can just watch him. I mean, have you seen him?"

I laugh at her obvious enthusiasm about his physique. "I have. He's very fit."

"He's more than that. He's like my Israeli knight in shining armor. You know he'd beat the hell out of anyone who came at us." She lifts her shoulder, a starry look in her eye. "I don't know. I just haven't met a lot of guys who don't use their strength to push women around. Sometimes I'm a little in awe of him."

My heart goes out to her. She looks my age, but she sounds so young too. Like a lovesick teenager—one whose heart should be hardened against the world for everything she's endured.

"There are more guys out there like him," I say reassuringly.

"Yeah, probably," she says.

"You seem…" I bite my lip, not sure how to say what I want to. "I guess you seem really positive for everything you've been through."

"I've never been this happy in my life." She swirls her auburn braid around her index finger until the tail whacks her chest. "My mom kicked me out when I was thirteen. I quit school and started hooking for cash just to live. With everything I went through from then to now, I'm lucky to be alive. It's more than just feeling safe here, though I do. I get to be a part of something bigger. I never thought I'd get to do something like that."

Her energy seems to brighten my own and lift me out of my fatigue some.

"Anyway, I'm sure you're tired from your trip. I'll come grab you around nine if I don't see you at breakfast, okay? Just wear, like, whatever you want. Noam doesn't have many rules except he wants you to break a sweat. Not usually an issue."

I open my mouth to protest.

She lifts her finger. "Just give it a try once, okay? Trust me. It's worth it."

I slouch in my spot on the bed, feeling completely won over by this glowing redhead, even though Noam's the last person I want to face in the morning.

TRISTAN

I hit the highway not long after my meeting with Lucia. I don't put much stock in the "good hands" she claims Isabel is now in. Not to mention I'm eager to see her for myself.

Going the speed limit the whole way brings me into New Orleans's Garden District just past midnight. I paid extra to have the rental manager meet me this late at the house—a small two-bedroom furnished and stocked with groceries for the week.

The rental boasts views of one of the city's historic cemeteries and easy access to the streetcar that will take me right into the Quarter at all hours. I don't care about any of that as I check the app on my phone for any sign of life from Isabel's phone. The circular locator arrow spins endlessly, giving me no confirmation that she's in the area.

I toss it aside and open my laptop. As it loads, I start some coffee, needing a boost while I figure out tomorrow's plan. Munching on a pastry, I watch the pot brew and let my thoughts drift to Isabel—the driving force behind everything now. Lucia's earlier challenge kept circling back to me on the drive. Unease curled through me every time it did. Regret that I should have tried to explain how important Isabel was becoming to me while she was still with me. Frustration that I lack the emotional tools to express myself to her the way she deserves.

Because Isabel had opened more than her heart to me. She let me into her body. We shared an act that wasn't reserved for people in love, but she's obviously in love with me. Why couldn't I have given her an inkling of reciprocity when it's her feelings for me that saved her life? And mine…

I fill a mug when the pot is half full and take the first scalding swallow, chasing the fatigue.

Yes, Isabel saved my life in some ways. Being on Jay's hit list isn't the retirement I was hoping for, but I'm not sure anything could convince me to go back to doling out dark justice for money I don't need. I'll take a life on the run with Isabel if that's where this is going.

A ding from my computer draws my attention back to the living room. I drop into the couch and pull it onto my lap.

CROW45: I heard you ran into Jay.

I hover my fingers over the keys. If the chat handle is any indicator, Crow managed to get out of the bind I left him in. Alive.

RED: How's your hand?

CROW45: Fuck you.

I smile. At least I know who I'm really talking to. Contractors in Company Eleven making contact is rare. We know *of* each other and little more. I'm unsure why Crow would reach out now, and I'm hesitant to encourage an exchange without knowing his intentions. So I wait patiently for him to continue the conversation I never asked for.

CROW45: I left the Company.

"Interesting," I mutter to no one. Who knows whether he's telling me the truth or not, though.

RED: Why?

CROW45: You think I was going to let her kill me?

I thought I tied those knots pretty tight. Either he got away on his own, met a very forgiving clean-up crew, or overpowered them before they could take him out. Still, Jay received the message and he knows about my run-in with her, which means he's been in contact with the Company one way or the other.

RED: What do you want?

CROW45: A resource.

RED: I'm not your friend.

CROW45: I fucking know that. This is business.

I should end the chat. Crow's not like me. The old me or the new me. We're in this life for different reasons. Even if he's not trying to lure me out for Jay's sake, I have nothing to gain by maintaining contact. I'm ready to close out the screen when another message pops up.

CROW45: I have info on Soloman.

RED: How?

CROW45: My family has their fingers in some of the same pots. How do you think I got into this shit? This is bigger than Jay. Bigger than Soloman. Think BIG.

Undeniably, I'm intrigued. I know he's thinking big dollar signs. I'm thinking payback. Freedom. Being able to give Isabel a life where she doesn't have to look over her shoulder. I'm not even sure it's possible, but knowing more about the organization behind all the hits could *make* it possible.

RED: Still in the revenge game?

CROW45: $$$$$

I laugh to myself because Crow's so predictable. And Makanga wasn't wrong. There's something safe in consistency, no matter how fucked up the person is. I don't care about money, but Crow doesn't know that.

RED: I'm listening.

CROW45: Let's meet.

RED: I'm busy.

CROW45: I don't trust this chat.

RED: I don't trust you.

CROW45: I'll be in New York for
the next month. Let me know
when you want to talk.

I stare at the blinking cursor for a minute and close the window. Crow's successfully dangled a carrot in front of me. I'm interested in what he knows. I'm not wild about getting lured into his family's mob den and risking my life for information that may not even exist, though.

So for now I push Crow's offer out of my head and spend the next hour or so mapping out a plan to find Isabel, starting with the best clue I have. The church on the corner of Cambronne and Burthe.

3

ISABEL

I'm ready to hit the bench with Skye after forty minutes of warm-ups. Wandering away from the others not long ago earned her some mild harassing from Noam. I refuse to give up, though, which is difficult to do when he's pushing everyone so hard—Zeda and me and a few other people I don't recognize from the house. I'm pouring sweat and now holding planks that have me trembling.

When the count expires, I drop to the mat, desperate for the reprieve and seriously questioning my decision to come.

"Okay, now we battle, folks." He picks up a couple of black leather punch pads.

Zeda and another student do the same as they pair up with the others. Noam comes right for me.

He slaps the pads together like they're boxing gloves. "Come on, Izzy. Let's do this. It'll be fun."

I suppress a groan and crawl upright once more. I face him with a grimace and every nonverbal cue I can muster to communicate my lack of enthusiasm. He ignores them all with a smug smile and a bounce in his step.

"Show me what you've got."

He crouches a little, holding the pads toward me as targets. I ball my fists and hit one after the other, concentrating hard on not missing as he shifts around.

"All right, now rotate your shoulders. Bend your knees a little."

I struggle to modify my motions on top of everything else.

"Harder."

I clench my jaw. My whole body hurts, never mind the sting in my hands. So I ignore him. A bit more of this and he'll leave me alone.

"Harder," he says again.

Then he uses a break in between my jabs to tap one of the pads on my cheek. Not overly hard, but the impact mimics a slap. A patronizing offense.

My nostrils flare. Heat rushes to my already burning cheeks.

He licks his lower lip and flashes a crooked grin. "There we go. That's the fire I want." He gestures for me to come at him again, so I do. I punch until I worry about the integrity of my wrists.

"That's it," he says. "Continuous motion. Put your instincts to work. Never give me a chance to put you on the defensive."

He sneaks in another tap to my face that makes me want to scream but instead inspires me to retaliate until he's forced several steps back.

My arms are ready to give out when he makes us stop. "Nice work," he says, tossing the pads to the ground.

"Now I'm going to come at you. Remember, I'm not your benevolent fitness instructor. I'm a bad guy. Show me what you would do."

My heart is already beating too fast. "Wait, what?"

He doesn't respond, but his expression flattens into a serious one. Then he comes closer. I seem frozen in place until he grips my arms firmly. I twist and wrestle an arm free to slap at his face, but he ducks and dodges and pushes me backward. In one swift move, he nudges me off balance and knocks my leg out from under me so I slam down on my back with a hard *humph*.

I lay there fighting tears. He stands next to me, hand out. His expression all peppy again.

"You want to learn how to do that to me?"

I catch my breath a moment before taking his hand and letting him hoist me upright. Everyone around us is engaged in their own "battles," but Skye is watching every move between us. I can't decide if I'm more embarrassed or pissed off.

"You've got a hundred pounds of muscle on me. Not exactly a fair fight, but I hope it felt good."

"Don't get confused. You can absolutely overpower me."

"Go to hell," I mutter under my breath.

He frowns. "Excuse me?"

I turn away and head for the door, my pride hurt and my muscles screaming.

"Hey, wait."

I don't wait. I push open the heavy door and start moving in the direction of the house. I hope no one wants to attack me on the way, because I have nothing left to fight anyone off.

"Isabel, wait up."

He circles in front of me and halts my forward progress.

I shoot him a glare. "Listen, I know Halo is all about saving people, and that's great. But I don't need you to save me, okay? Whatever you do here, I'm not into it."

"So you think you're going to rely on that shitty pistol to fight off the bad guys?"

I cross my arms tightly. "Maybe I will."

"Well you're not getting it back from me until you let me show you how to fight and properly defend yourself."

I pause. "You took it?"

He shrugs, his lips thin with determination. "Maybe I did, maybe I didn't."

"That's mine."

"Then earn it. Be back here tomorrow morning, and be ready to get your ass bruised some more."

I unfold my arms. "I'm not going to let you toss me around your mats to impress your friends."

"They're students, and they're used to getting a few bumps and bruises because that's what it's like when someone is seriously trying to hurt you."

I'm silent and unwilling to acknowledge the truth in this. I'm not worried about the bruises as much as being in the crosshairs of a gun. Nothing about Noam's class is going to keep me safe from a bullet.

He looks past me toward the studio, his posture and features softening as his focus drifts back to me. "Isabel, I don't know what's going on with you, but I know you're scared. I've seen that look before, and I just want to make it go away. That's what I do. I can't promise it's going to be easy or that you'll always be in the right headspace for it, but I can promise that it'll be worth it." He rubs my shoulder briefly. "Sorry for knocking you around. I just wanted to motivate you a little bit."

"Is this enough fire for you?" I try for a snappy tone, but I feel my anger fading.

"Yeah. I want you to use it on the mat, not for cussing me out."

I sigh. "Listen, I've been through a lot lately. I'm just not sure this is the right time for me to do this."

"Let me prove you wrong. I think you need this. Meet me tomorrow at eleven when the studio is empty. There's less pressure outside of a class."

I consider his offer and let his words sink in. What he sees behind my edgy tone and jumpy instincts is real. I'm trying like hell to be brave, but I'm scared too. And I'm so tired of being afraid.

"Fine," I finally say, the word barely audible.

"Yeah?"

My acceptance is met with another winning smile from the man I'm confident will push me well past my physical limits.

"You want to finish up? I'll take it easier on you."

I shake my head, knowing my spirit's a little too broken to return. "I'm good for today. I'll see you tomorrow."

I pass him and start back toward the house. I could wait for Skye, but I'm craving some alone time. I'm unsettled and missing home. For once, home isn't a place. Home is anything familiar that holds the faintest measure of comfort. My mom. Rio. Tristan…

Up ahead, the church consumes the corner of the block. The street is quiet except for the sound of a barge chugging down the river nearby.

I halt in front of the steps and consider a dozen reasons not to go inside. I'm tired and grumpy. Sweaty. My legs might not even carry me up the steps. More, I don't want to risk seeing the kind reverend, even though he offered his sanctuary as an extended home. I'm seeking peace, not friendship. Reassurance in my heart, a voiceless knowing that all will be well.

I lumber up the steps and hesitate just outside the entrance. The doors are closed, but they're really open. Lost souls are always welcome. I rest my hand on the tall wooden door and then slide it down to the thick metal handle.

I listen. All I hear is silence and the call to find some peace inside.

Then the hurried shuffle of footsteps behind me. Then my name.

TRISTAN

"Isabel?"

It's her. It has to be her.

The woman ahead of me turns abruptly, removing all doubt.

"It's you." The confirmation is a mix of shock and awe as I rake her in, cataloging all the ways she's changed since I last saw her.

Her hair, much shorter and now blond, is dramatically different.

She's flushed, and I'm pretty sure I know why. I first spotted her coming out of the fitness center moments ago, bickering with a forty-something meathead before I could intervene.

I wasn't about to let her out of my sight. Now here she is, taking up the whole view.

Her eyes are the same greenish-brown almonds. Dark lashes set against her perfect skin. The flash of fear in her eyes quickly morphs into something else the minute she recognizes me. Something much more powerful than relief. I recognize it, because it's pulling through me like a riptide.

On the outside, I'm frozen in place, worried about everything that's going on in her head. Feeling like I can't pick up where we left off, my hands in her hair, my mouth on hers.

"You came," she whispers.

"Of course." I never gave myself any other choice.

Her hand stills on the door like she's about to go inside the church. Instead, she lets go and comes closer, touching my chest. The contact resonates throughout my body.

I grasp her hand, molding her palm against my heart.

She accepts my embrace, circling her arm around my middle, resting her head against me as I hold her to me.

"I missed you," she whispers. "So much."

I close my eyes as a barrage of questions burn through me. *Why did you leave me? Who are you with?* Then the demands. *Disappear with me. Trust me.*

I guide her chin up, ready to start my interrogation. She exhales a shaky breath and brushes some wayward hairs from her face. "I'm a mess. I'm sorry."

"As if I care."

Her skin aglow with sweat only makes me want to kiss it, lick it, and take in as much essence as her body will offer—the magic potion that kindles the faintest memories of the intimacy we once shared. Probably the best memories I had before they were all stolen away.

I brush my fingers across her cheek. My muscles grow taut with effort not to haul her against me again like I'm some kind of feral beast. I should have more control over my impulses, but no matter how often I tell this to myself, I'm no less compelled to touch her.

Heavy silence stretches between us. Still, she doesn't speak. Doesn't let on to what brought her here or why she ran from me.

"I got your note," I finally say.

She offers a short nod before stepping out of our embrace

completely. She takes a seat on the steps, closing her eyes and arrowing her fingers through her new hair.

I follow her down. "I like the new look."

She smiles weakly. "Thanks. I'm getting used to it. I still don't recognize myself when I look in the mirror."

"I almost didn't." I guide one of her hands in mine. "Why did you leave?"

She's quiet for a long moment. "When my mom came to the hotel, we talked."

"About Mariana."

She looks up, her features pinched. "How do you know?"

"I reached out to Lucia after you disappeared. She told me about your grandfather and your sister. And Kolt."

She stills. "Kolt?"

One look and I realize she has no idea. Of all the things Lucia decided to share, she didn't bother sticking a fork in the last little pockets of Isabel's affection for a man who may very well have been sent to Rio to kill her.

I shake my head with a tense laugh. "If what your mother says is true, then your friend Kolt's family is behind Mariana's death."

She pales and stares straight ahead. "That's impossible."

"Why?"

"I know what you're thinking. Kolt wouldn't hurt me."

"Are you sure about that?"

Because if she's not, I'm going to kill him. I'll do it for free and take immense pleasure in it.

"I'm not that naïve, Tristan. We knew each other for months. I'd have sensed if he were *that* disingenuous."

"You couldn't manage to fall in love with him all that time. Maybe that's why."

She breaks her thoughtful composure with a burst of laughter.

"What?"

"If anyone could fall into bed with someone who wanted her dead, I guess it'd be me."

An unpleasant feeling curls through me with her meaning. I don't like being lumped into that group.

"Whoever in his family paid for the hit may think you're dead, but they may not. Especially if Kolt's involved. Plus the Company knows we're on the run. Whether they choose to share that with their client and claim it's a case closed, we can't be sure. Faking your death may have bought us a little time or none at all."

"You saw the news, I guess."

I nod. "I'll admit your mother's reach caught me by surprise."

"You're not the only one. She's kept so much from me for so long. If it weren't for the extreme circumstances we're dealing with, I'd have taken more time to hold it against her."

True enough, we don't have a lot of time for grudges—at least not with people who are on our side of the battle line.

"Why did she send you here?"

"I'm staying with a friend of hers. Martine. I guess they've known each other a while. I hadn't met her before, but she seems like she really wants to help."

I glide my fingers back and forth through hers, relishing the physical connection, not wanting it to end.

"I rented a place not far from here. You can stay with me."

A knot forms in my stomach when she's quiet for too long. Three days have passed since she disappeared, and I've come too far to risk losing her again.

"If you want me to leave you alone, you're going to have to try harder," I mutter in a low tone.

She tightens her hand around mine. "You didn't ask for me to come back into your life."

I still. "What's that supposed to mean?"

"I wanted you to find me, Tristan. You have no idea how much. That's why I left the note. But if me dying on paper meant I could live without you protecting me, then it solved a problem for you too. You wouldn't need to worry about me anymore."

I hook her knees and spin her toward me so we're facing each other. "This was your way of letting me off the hook?"

She lifts her shoulder, avoiding eye contact. "Maybe. People are trying to kill you because of me. It's not like we always see eye to eye, either. Wouldn't your life be easier without me in it?"

"Isabel. Just…" I work my jaw, needing her to stop painting this picture of us because it's all wrong. "Stop it, all right? I care about you. Is it not obvious?"

She lifts her gaze to mine, trapping her lower lip between her teeth. Lucia's challenge comes back to me.

"A declaration of love? Is that what you want from me?"

"No. I'm not asking for that," she answers softly, her cheeks turning pink as if the mere suggestion embarrasses her.

"You make me feel a lot of things." I curve my hand around her nape, swiping along her silken cheek as I go. "Fear's not common for me, but with you it's real. I'm afraid I'm going to lose you and have to live the rest of my life knowing that I failed you."

"That's what I'm saying. I don't want you to carry that burden."

I pinch my brows together. "You think that's it? That I've got some kind of bodyguard complex that's overridden everything else all of a sudden? I spent three years waking up in the morning and checking my messages to find out who I had to kill next. It took something pretty intense for me to figure out what I was missing. *You*, Isabel."

She chews her lip harder, her eyes gleaming.

"I don't know how to feel things like normal people do, but I know I miss you when we're apart. I'm jealous when someone wants any part of you that I've already decided I can't share. When you smile, I'm ready to move mountains to see you happy. This is all new, and it scares the hell out of me." I struggle to form the next words. "I don't just *feel* these things because of you. I feel them *through* you, Isabel. When you hurt, I fucking bleed. When you love, you show me how. That's the only way I know how to explain it. I can't do any of that when you're not with me."

Her breaths come faster. Her eyes are glassy. And it resonates through me too, a strange cocktail of emotion. Vulnerability and frustration and passion so strong it makes me want to draw her to me, kiss her hard, and never let go.

I guide her closer and lower my mouth to hers, because I don't know what more I can say…

The sounds of shoes scuffing up the steps stops me the second before we touch. We both turn toward the slight woman with a tail of long red hair climbing the steps.

"Hey, Isabel, you okay?"

When I let my hand slip from Isabel, she rises abruptly.

"I'm fine."

I follow her up and take a better look at the girl. She's dressed in a tight tank top and running shorts that reveal her pale, toned legs. She's young but has an air of fearlessness about her that makes me think she's had to have her own back more than a few times.

"This is Skye. She's staying at Martine's too," Isabel finally says.

I force a polite smile. "I'm Tristan."

Skye looks me over, her eyes sharp and assessing before softening when they land on Isabel. "We should head back."

Isabel nods. "Sure. I'll be right behind you."

Skye doesn't make any moves to leave, though. It's obvious she thinks I pose a threat. My instinct is to be blunt and tell the girl to carry on her way. This is my territory. None of her damn business. But I sense Isabel may not want to make waves with her new housemates—or host, for that matter.

I turn my body toward her. "Maybe we can meet up later." By maybe, I mean definitely. And by later, I mean as soon as possible. But I'm using soft language for the sake of Skye. "I'd like to talk to you about a few things."

"Okay." Her smile is genuine this time, and the relief almost knocks me down.

"Can you do me a favor and turn on your phone?"

Her eyes widen. "Oh…sure."

Another wave of relief hits with the reassurance that I'll be able to track her down more easily. One of these days I'll come clean about it, but for now, I can't risk her slipping off my radar again.

I can barely bring myself to let her leave me now. I resist the almost searing urge to kiss her despite this watchdog girl invading our personal space. Instead I give her hand a little squeeze and watch her walk down to the street with Skye.

Wherever she's staying is within walking distance, but I follow well behind them until I see her turn down another street, then another, determined to find out where she's calling home these days.

After a few blocks and a short walk down the streetcar route, they stop at the gate of an old antebellum mansion. The kind that is so impressive in its style and grandeur that it makes a person wonder what kind of important person lives there. This one is no different.

4

ISABEL

Thankfully Skye didn't question me too hard about Tristan on the walk back to the house. Trying to explain that we were once in a relationship and he followed me here after I disappeared wouldn't sound great to someone like her who sees most men as predators. Tristan's not a predator. At least not to me. He is more committed than I'd given him credit for, though.

Just you and me...

After I left DC, I agonized over the small vow we made. I questioned what it really meant to him and if the words were more to keep me from running off or downward spiraling during one of the blackest moments of my life. The more I questioned it, the more I convinced myself that Tristan's feelings for me can't possibly be anything close to what I feel for him. After all, I have the benefit of years of missing him. And these memories, so deeply ingrained in me, evade him.

But if what he said on the church steps is true...

For being ill-equipped emotionally, he couldn't have expressed himself much better. I wasn't expecting him to tell me he loved me.

Obviously I love him. I've hardly made that a secret, even as the meaning behind the sentiment evolves as I come to know the new Tristan better.

But what he shared means so much more.

Still reeling from the weight of it all, I shower, dress, and power up the phone Tristan gave me. Knowing Tristan would likely track me through it, my mother gave me another one before I left DC, and that's the one I kept on during the drive in case of an emergency. The subtle distress in his expression when he asked me to turn on my phone removed all doubt. He definitely tried to track me.

I don't plan on leaving Martine's yet, but I can give him some reassurance that I'm here, safe.

The phone dings when two old messages from Tristan load.

Tell me you're okay.

Then…

I'll see you soon.

I smile a little at the determined tone I can hear behind his words. Doubting that he'd find his way to me seems foolish now. Maybe selfish, too, when I consider my own unsteadiness and how being here, away, was intended to cure that. To what end? Only to find myself back in his arms, the warm embrace of his protection and affection?

I'm still shaky from the morning's session at Noam's, and my body is demanding food. I go downstairs, pick up an apple from the countertop bowl, and take a loud bite.

"There you are." Skye enters the room with a spring in her step.

"I'm starving," I muffle as I look through the pantry cabinet.

She opens the refrigerator and pulls out a small baking dish covered in foil. "Noam's classes will do that. You want some jambalaya?" Under the foil is more of the delicious rice dish I sampled last night.

"Oh yeah."

She warms up two dishes of jambalaya, and we take them to the dining room table.

"You want to go out tonight? See the town a little?"

I stall and take a big bite of food because the possibility of seeing Tristan later is heavy in my thoughts. I miss him more than I'll admit to anyone. I crave more of his touches, more of his heart-wrenching honesty.

"I'll probably stay in. But thanks."

She pins me with a stare as her mouth works her food. "You have plans?"

"I didn't say that."

"You've been different since I saw you with that guy. I feel like you don't want me to know why he's here."

I try to shrug off her comments. "That's reaching a little. I don't understand why it's any of your business anyway."

"Transparency is important here. We don't keep secrets. Especially ones that could put anyone else in the house in danger."

"I'm not putting anyone in danger."

"Then who is he?"

I drop my fork on my plate and attempt to calm my nerves. I appreciate Skye's play at friendship, but my need for space is sudden and unmistakable.

"Listen, Martine knows what I'm dealing with right now. That has to be enough. I can assure you that Tristan isn't a threat to anyone here or me."

I start to get up when she catches my hand.

"Wait. Just... I'm sorry."

Her pretty blue eyes seem to implore me to stay.

Reluctant, I lower into my seat again.

"Let me explain a few things." She takes a deep breath before continuing. "It was hard for me at first to talk to people about the life

I'd come from. It was humiliating. I felt so worthless, like no one could possibly understand how a person could fall so low."

I replay her story and how she shared it with me so easily. I hadn't thought any less of her. If anything, I considered her incredibly brave for stepping away from the only life she'd known, not fully trusting where a new path would take her.

"I don't think that about you," I say gently.

"I appreciate it. I need you to know, though, that whatever you're dealing with, you can tell me, and I won't judge you. I promise, I'm nothing but open ears and bottomless acceptance. I'm ready to make this shit right."

"You can't make this right."

She folds her arms and leans in. "Try me." Her determined posture doesn't sway. "Martine says you're running. Who are you running from? Is it him?"

I wince. "No. Tristan's been with me through all of this. I just... I don't know why I left DC without him." I close my eyes a moment before opening them again. "I've seen a lot of people die the past two weeks. I came here hoping that if I disappeared for good, no one else would have to die because of me."

Skye's tenacity simmers a little, seeming to make room for me to tell her more if it'll calm her down.

"Tristan is dangerous. But not to me. Someone—a company from my family's past—hired him to kill me. He didn't. We've both been on the run since. I think the heat is off for now, but we have no way of knowing yet."

The muscles in her jaw flex and release. "Okay. We got this. Hold that thought."

She takes our empty plates into the kitchen, clanks them in the sink, and comes back a few seconds later with a notebook, pen, and her phone.

"Who is this company?"

"Skye... You don't need to get involved in this. This is my mess."

She rolls her eyes with a groan. "Ask me what happened to Charlie."

I hesitate. "Your old pimp?"

"Ask me what happened to him." She purses her lips firmly.

"What happened to him?"

"He's serving ten to fifteen for possession and assault. Ask me what happened to the owner of the club who took a cut off every 'private dance' I gave there knowing full well what was going down—and also looked the other way whenever Charlie decided to get physical."

"What happened?"

"He's running a clean operation now. Ask me why."

"Why?"

She leans in again, her eyes sparkling with something like quiet satisfaction. "Because if he doesn't, I'm releasing video and photos that show what really went down in that place. He'll lose his business and his freedom."

"Why should he have either?"

"He shouldn't, but someone else would take his place in the Quarter in a second, and nothing would change. Letting him stay means Halo gets twenty percent of the profits and the girls who work there don't have to worry about pushing drugs or offering anything more than a dance. They get benefits now too."

I attempt to process everything she's telling me. "So Halo deals in blackmail."

"Blackmail is too specific. We deal in information. The information I collected from Charlie when I pretended to go back to him put him in jail. The information I chose not to share with the police ensured the club owner got a slap on the wrist and a few fines. Now we have him by the balls and his business allows us to help more people. People like you."

My thoughts spin. "Martine put you up to all this?"

"Martine has a heart of gold, but I wouldn't fuck with her. She's been doing this so long, she can outmaneuver anyone. She may not have dirt on everyone, but she either knows someone who does or can dig it up with very little effort. And once she's got it…" She shakes her head, her lips curving into a smug smirk. "Watch out."

TRISTAN

After pouring my heart out to her on the church steps, I thought Isabel would have wanted to meet yesterday. Instead she texted me hours later and asked me to meet her after her morning class.

Entertaining this unwelcome distance and her decision to stay with a woman I don't trust requires patience I don't have. Still, I used the extra time to get what little rest my body would give me. Too often I jolted awake with nightmares that the sniper who took out Brienne took Isabel from me too. That it was her blood splattered across my car. Her life-force stolen. The last of my humanity snuffed out right along with her.

I shake off the disturbing visions as I park across from the fitness center, ready to intercept her as soon as her class ends. I can see Isabel through the window standing across from the man I recognize from yesterday. He's gesturing as he speaks. Then he takes a step back and suddenly comes toward her in a series of offensive motions that have her flat on her back.

I climb out of the car and get to the door in a matter of seconds. I swing it open just as he pulls her upright again.

"You don't have time to think through the moves," the man says. "You have to feel it. Always be on the offensive. Always moving. That's the *retzev*." He pauses, noticing me. "Can I help you?"

Isabel turns. Her face flushes a little more. "Tristan." She walks toward me, leaving him behind. "Is everything okay?"

"Yeah. Sorry, I saw him slam you down, and I obviously came right in to kill him."

She poorly masks a grin, glancing back to the man and then to me. "That's Noam. He's just showing me some self-defense stuff. He thinks pissing me off is a good motivational tool."

I lock eyes with the man. His arms are crossed and his pectorals are puffed up. He's gone from upbeat to threatening with his body language alone.

"Why does everyone around here look at me like I'm trying to hurt you, Isabel?"

She toys with the hem of my shirt. "I'm not sure if you realize this, Tristan, but you don't blend in as well as you think you do. And the vibe you give off isn't usually very friendly."

"Is there a problem, Izzy?" The man approaches us, flanking her.

His nickname for her feels like an icepick through my whole body.

"She says you're pissing her off," I say, baiting him.

"That's between her and me."

"Not really," I offer quickly.

"This is a private class—"

"Guys, stop. It's fine. Everyone is fine. Tristan, do you mind waiting for me until I'm done?"

I break the staring contest with Noam to look down at her hand, now warm against my chest. I grasp it and kiss her knuckles before finally releasing her.

"I'll wait right here," I say before shooting a flat *don't-fuck-with-me* look to her instructor.

She returns to the mat, and he trails behind her. His lips are pulled into a grim line as he joins her in the middle of the room.

"You good?" he mutters quietly.

"I'm fine. What's next?"

He slides his gaze to me and back to her before continuing. "Soft points."

"What are those?"

"Points on the body that are vulnerable no matter how big someone is. No matter how much muscle they've got. Thumbs in the eyes. The nose is easily broken." He pinches his own. "The throat is delicate. A knee to the groin works like a charm. Got it?"

"Easy enough."

"Good." He waves her forward. "Come at me."

She stands unmoving for a few seconds. "I don't want to hurt you, though."

He smiles, and even though I share his amusement, I'd also like to see her crush one of his soft points when he's not paying attention.

The next thirty minutes pass much the same. Lessons, trials, and correcting. Until Isabel's clearly wiped out and Noam's broken a sweat. I'd like to continue hating him, but the more I watch, the more I approve. He's fair when he needs to be and appropriately aggressive when demonstrating what she could be up against with someone his size. This is a simulation, but it's far better than trying to break boards with her fists. He's arming her with skills she could use, and she very likely will. Because her mother was right. This journey is far from over.

When they finish, she walks over to me, breathless. She probably thinks she looks like a mess again, but to me she's vital and thrumming with energy I want to feed on until we're both as spent as she looks.

"I'm going to get cleaned up in the locker room. Give me ten minutes, okay?"

"I'll be here."

Once she's gone, Noam wanders closer. I rise as he does. He takes a towel off a nearby hook and wipes his face.

"How do you know Isabel?" he asks.

"You mean *Izzy*?"

He cocks his brow. "I call her that to get her riled up, and it works. Don't tell me that's your nickname for her."

"Not a chance."

She's Isabel to me. My saint. She's not a nickname.

"So what are you? Her boyfriend?"

Another diminutive term that doesn't suit us. But I simply reply, "Something like that."

He doesn't look relieved. "I hope you're not the reason she pulls weapons on total strangers."

I flinch, a faint movement under my eye.

"That's how I met her. She was dozing off in her car. I startled her when I was passing by, and she pulled a pistol on me before she realized I wasn't a threat."

"I haven't taught her how to shoot yet. I probably should."

He laughs. "I wouldn't rush it."

"This is important. What you're doing here with her."

His humor fades. "I think it is too. She's going to be banged up a little bit, but it'll be worth it when she feels like she can hold her own."

"Agreed."

He glances to the door she left through and then back to me. "Listen, most of the girls that stay with Martine are trying to get away from trouble. I just need to know if you're the trouble she's hiding from."

"Does it look like she's hiding from me?"

He purses his lips. "Not exactly. But she's obviously shell-shocked. What happened to her?"

I shouldn't tell him a damn thing because it's none of his business. But maybe if he understands a measure of the gravity Isabel's faced, he'll be in a better position to truly help her.

"We've been on the run. Trouble finally caught up to us. They killed her friend." I pause. "Right in front of her."

His expression sobers. "Got it."

When she returns, fresh faced with damp hair, we both stare. She's wearing a black tank top that hugs her perfect tits. The tight jeans set low on her hips reveal the barest sliver of skin there. With the new hair and a pair of low-ankled black Converse, she's owning her new look and displaying a shade of confidence I haven't seen in her before.

She gives me a concerned look. "What?"

"When did you turn into a badass?"

She laughs and rakes a hand through her hair.

"Tomorrow? Same time?" Noam interrupts.

"Uh, sure," she says, her shoulders set with new determination.

If she's made to feel weak, she'll be weak.

I never meant to make her feel that way. Isabel's not weak. She never was. But now, this new emboldened version of her is gradually blowing me away.

We leave Noam's. She walks ahead of me toward the passenger side of my car, giving me a delicious view.

"What now?" she asks.

She reaches for the door when my patience finally expires. I curve my hand at her hip, spin her, and give her a gentle shove against the car. I take in her shaky exhale and parted lips. Then I lean in until I can smell the soap on her skin.

"I'm going to kiss you now." My voice is like gravel. Any space between us feels like an affront.

But there *is* space between us—an unspoken chasm I have to journey across to get us back to where we were. In the space of waiting for permission to reclaim her lips, she grabs my waist and guides our bodies together in one hungry tug. A bolt of lust arrows right to my groin. I make certain she feels it when I crowd her harder against the curve of the coupe. She gasps, and I entertain a vision of taking her right here. I'd never do it, but God I want to.

She feathers her fingertips near the band of my jeans, tangles in my hair with her other hand. I angle and taste and take…and fuck me, her mouth is heaven. A room in heaven just for me made of vanilla and soft skin and every sound she's ever made.

Suddenly three days without feeling her against me has become the longest dry spell I've ever known. I'm all hot-blooded male without a dash of reason until a car roars down the cross street, abrasive enough to jar me faintly into the present.

I withdraw just enough to catch my breath but not a fraction more. I'm still fixed on her swollen, pouty lips and her wild breathing.

"Isabel…" I cup her cheek. I grimace at the willpower needed to keep from tearing her skin-tight clothes off.

"I know," she whispers.

She doesn't know. She won't know until I discover new ways to make her scream my name. As my imagination starts sprinting in a dozen of those directions, I can feel her pulling back, pushing me away. Concern and a dark cloud of thoughts I can't read cool her features. The bastard in me wants to kiss away her change of heart. The better man she's turning me into follows her lead as I attempt to temper my own raging impulses.

"We should talk," she says shakily.

We probably should. Maybe I can blindfold myself while we do. Or handcuff myself to the opposite side of whatever room we occupy to keep from touching her. Only then can I imagine being able to untangle my thoughts from the promises of pleasure tied to every curve of her body.

Jesus, I've endured things that would kill other men. Why can't I get a handle on myself when it comes to her?

For now I close my eyes and take a deep breath that stings my lungs because I want more than this tepid air. I want *her* air.

5

ISABEL

Nothing would be easier than melting into the sweet, dark oblivion of Tristan's touch. If nothing larger loomed, I'd have stayed in DC and drowned myself in moments like these. I'd have cocooned myself in Tristan's protective embrace instead of taking to the road on my own, getting my ass kicked by Noam every day, and falling asleep in a house of well-meaning strangers for the sake of forward motion. I came here to find a path that wouldn't end in more ugly death.

Because I can't run anymore if we don't have something better to run to. That much I know. For the first time since all this madness started, I recognize a glimmer of hope. An inkling of light seeping in. The only question is whether Tristan can be a part of it. He's wired to maneuver and fight and kill. The plan Skye and I drew up until the wee hours doesn't include much of that.

So when Tristan and I settle at a table at Cooter Brown's, the local tavern a few blocks away, the plan I was so committed to hours ago dies in my throat. We order, and when Tristan shoots an expectant look my way, I muster up the words I need.

"I have an idea about how to end all this."

His eyebrows shoot up his forehead, but he doesn't say anything. He rubs his thumb along his lower lip rhythmically. The tiny movement is distracting and nerve-racking.

"I don't want any more people to die," I say.

His answering look is full of doubt and quiet understanding, like one a parent gives a child who hasn't yet experienced the world.

"What's your plan?"

"To blackmail Kolt's family into calling this off." There. I said it.

"Tell me this doesn't have anything to do with Kolt."

"No, I don't think he'd be much help. I spent some time researching Chalys Pharmaceuticals last night, though. His grandfather owns the company. Kolt's mother and uncle run it."

"We don't know who hired me yet. Who are you going to blackmail? Better yet, how?"

I'm grateful when the server brings our lunch. I pop a fried shrimp in my mouth and replay last night's conversation in my head.

"We haven't exactly planned it down to the letter yet, but—"

"Who's we?"

I huff. "You have a lot of questions."

"Well, you came here to talk, and I have a feeling you're trying to convince me to step back so we can handle this your way, which I'm not crazy about. But I'm hearing you out. So just tell me."

"Skye and I talked things through last night. Martine too."

"Great," he snips before pulling his mouth into a taut line.

"I trust them."

He curses under his breath and rubs at the creases across his forehead. "Two steps forward, one step back."

I rest my fork on my plate and fight to stay in control of my emotions. He said he'd hear me out, so he's going to.

"Martine has connections all over the country. All over the world. At all levels of society. She doesn't have enough dirt on the family to turn this around. But Kolt's uncle, Vince Boswell, is the president of the company. He has a reputation that could work in our favor."

He stills. "What kind of reputation?"

I gnaw at the inside of my lip to the point of pain. "He's unmarried. Untethered. He's all business, which is why they've been able to expand the family's interests into so many different industries so quickly."

"And…"

"He has a weakness for high-priced call girls."

"If you think exposing that to the public will make a pinch of difference, you're crazy."

"I know it won't. They can bury that news easily. And who cares? He's not cheating on his wife. But it's a way to lure him in. We could get him vulnerable. Get him to tell us whatever he knows. Maybe even get information off his laptop, which could be a potential goldmine. And of course we'd get everything on video. Enough to scare him into calling off the hit."

"No."

I wilt. "Tristan, you haven't even heard me out."

"I don't care who Martine knows. Your friend Skye can't pass for a high-end hooker. She's got streets written all over her."

"I know. She has serious triggers with men too." I take hold of my lip again and brace myself for his reaction to what I'm about to say. "What about me?"

He stills and levels me with his silver stare. "Fuck no."

"I think it could work. Vince never met me in person. I have a really different look now. With the right makeup and maybe contacts, I don't think I'd be recognizable. Especially if he has a few drinks first."

Tristan's features are all hard planes. "I have a better idea."

"What? Kill everyone instead?"

He jams the toothpick from his sandwich between his teeth and stares out the window, telling me that was definitely his "better idea."

"Sorry, but I don't consider your experience as a trained killer an asset in this situation. If you really want to be with me, Tristan, you have to know I can't live like that. I don't care if we spend the rest of our lives on the run if that's what we have to do, but to know that you'll keep doing *that*…" I swallow and push the horror of it all down. "Taking lives and never asking questions. I can't accept it."

He doesn't answer me. A few tense minutes pass before he picks up his sandwich and proceeds to eat, ignoring my plea and my plan. The thought that he'd want to keep on that path makes me too ill to touch the rest of my lunch. What if these breakthroughs in emotion have more to do with our animal attraction than an actual shift in his priorities?

I can find it in my heart to forgive the killer Jay made him, but I don't think I can forgive keeping that part of himself alive. Of course, I wish our enemies would disappear too. Days ago I held Tristan's gun in my lap and, deep in my grief, fantasized about what it might be like to take an eye for an eye. In the same moment, I recognized I wasn't capable of carrying through with anything so heinous. He knows it too. So does Noam. Apparently I have gun-shy innocence written all over my face.

Several minutes pass in tense silence.

"I'll drive you back," he says gruffly after we get the check.

I pack up my picked-over meal and hope to have an appetite for it later. As Tristan takes us through the oak-lined streets toward Martine's, I reflect on the total roller coaster this day has been. I went from hopeful to empowered to set ablaze to utterly defeated.

As we drive, I worry the Tristan I have been falling in love with is still the Tristan who could kill me in the blink of an eye. Somehow he's convinced me that he could be different. A man I could give my heart to again.

He rolls in front of the house, slowing to a stop.

"I'll see you later," I mutter, not sure when or if I want to see him again after today's conversation.

But when I reach for the handle, he reaches across for my hand, stopping me.

"Don't go yet."

That contact between us feels right, even when everything else between us feels wrong. The flickers of vulnerability where I saw hardened defiance before give me hope.

"I didn't choose this life." His tenor is soft, but the heaviness of his words fills the small space.

"I know you didn't, Tristan."

"I've seen things and done things I wish I could forget. I've made a small fortune from it, and every cent of it is red with the blood of others. Good people, bad people. Doesn't matter. It was all wrong. Until you, I never hesitated before. Couldn't let myself fail. Somehow, contemplating a different kind of life felt just as scary as carrying on the way I was. How miserable is that?"

I don't answer him but clutch his hand tighter.

"If I never write another name into that fucking notebook, I almost think I could forgive myself one day."

"Then don't," I whisper. *Please don't...*

"I can't rule it out."

Disappointment rolls through me like a drowning wave. Our gazes lock, and I'm certain my heart falling to the floor can be seen on my face.

"Isabel... I'll never take another job again. But if someone gets in my way or if someone threatens you... If it's a matter of eliminating someone else to save you, I'll always make the right choice. I'll always protect you. And if that makes me a killer that you can't be with, all I can do is try to change your mind, try to convince you that sometimes it's kill or be killed, and hope for your forgiveness if circumstances come to that."

The drowning wave ebbs away and is replaced with relief and a prevailing sadness that this life could be my life always. Running, fighting, and facing death over and over again until I'm numb to it. As naïve as I've been, I can't deny that Tristan has killed people who would have otherwise killed me. How many, I don't know, and I'm fearful to ask.

Would I change that? Would I sacrifice my life for any of the monsters who would have killed me without regret? Who killed Brienne?

No. I'd choose to live. To survive. But I worry permission to protect is not all Tristan is asking for.

"I'm asking you to question your instinct to shoot first."

"And how am I supposed to ignore that instinct after all this time?"

"You're brilliant, Tristan. You always have been. You have tools at your disposal that aren't served behind a gun. We can figure this out without anyone else dying."

He looks past the iron gates to the house. Martine is sitting on the front porch with Zeda. I can see them through the trees, but they likely can't see us.

"I know you think I'm being altruistic and naïve," I say.

"You understand why it's hard for me to get behind this plan on multiple levels."

"I know. But what other options do we have? Keep running? Hiding? Never knowing if we need to be looking over our shoulders?"

"There are other options."

"Tristan…"

"That feeling you have that makes tears well up in your eyes at the thought of someone dying? I don't have that feeling. It doesn't exist in me. I can eliminate them until there's no one left who would dare hurt you."

Even as he says the words, I find myself swallowing over emotion thick in my throat. I trust this reaction is normal and his isn't. "It's Kolt's family. I would never wish that on him. Never."

"You don't know he's not involved."

I roll my eyes with a huff. "Jesus, Tristan, we've been over this."

"And we still don't know, do we?"

"And you don't know who *is* involved, and you're proposing that you, what, just fly up to Boston and start knocking people off until you get the one who ordered the hit?"

"I saw Jay. Before I had any idea you left me, of course." He smiles tightly. It's a smile made of discontent. "She knows she has to give me the name or I'm coming for her. I'll get it. Just…whatever plan you're hatching with them…wait until I know more, okay?"

I hesitate. I'm eager to move our plan into motion and be free of this invisible prison, but I can't deny that without knowing the true target, we run the risk of failure and nothing will have changed.

"I'll wait if you promise to help us."

He slides his gaze to me. Attraction and hope and fear that everything could come crumbling down around us at any moment fills the air between us.

"Is this an ultimatum?"

I squeeze his hand. "No… It's an invitation to show me the kind of man you can be."

TRISTAN

I let Isabel out of my sight for what feels like the hundredth time. I miss her and ache for her. Yet when I walk through the door of my rental, I'm relieved to be alone with the fucked-up person I've become and not have to spend another minute trying to convince her I'm worth being in her life.

She makes me feel things, and worse, she makes me see. She shows me the broken person I buried when I went to Rio and the savage I replaced him with. She touches scars I learned to ignore. She's ready to absolve me of all my crimes if it means I can change. How much blood on a person's hands is too much? At what point does redemption matter?

Of course, if I had a pinch of faith, I could try to talk myself into a place of hope. I could contemplate my soul. Figure out ways to stop the bleeding when life as I've known it has been a nonstop hemorrhage of murder and sin.

I don't especially want to kill people, but I can't deny that sometimes it's the easiest way to solve a problem. I don't trust Halo or her budding friendships in the organization or her plan. But massacring Kolt's family doesn't end the chaos. It would likely breed more. I still have the Company to deal with. And despite Lucia's connections—the extent of which I'm still trying to figure out—Isabel's family is at risk the longer this goes unresolved too.

I open my laptop, bring up the chat window, and type a message for Jay. I don't have much to threaten her with, especially since I failed to kill her once. I don't know what I could possibly offer her, so I go into the communication with no strategy other than trying not to show how I'm emotionally beating myself to death right now.

> **RED: Time's up.**

I start with a threat and hope for the best. Minutes pass. Nothing. I get up and pace around the house. It's a cute house. Almost cottage-like, except most of the blinds are drawn, making it dark and depressing. If Isabel were here, she'd make it moody and seductive and we could fuck for hours and I could pretend I didn't have this enormous mess to clean up. At least for a little while.

> **JAY: I can disclose the details whenever you're ready.**

There has to be a catch. Asking opens the door for her demand, though. So I wait.

> **JAY: One condition.**

> **RED: I'm not in the mood to negotiate.**

> **JAY: You're not in a position not to.**

I refuse to acknowledge that I owe her anything. I could kill her. That doesn't guarantee I'll get the information I need, though. Of course she'll have plenty more people guarding her place—if she'd even risk showing up there again. Then again, maybe I have an ace.

> **RED: I already know about Chalys.**

JAY: I know more.

Tempting. I'm tired and pissed off, so I finally do it. I ask.

RED: What do you want?

JAY: We want you to come
back to Company Eleven.

Dread roils my normally iron stomach.

RED: Not happening.

JAY: Sharing this information with you means
there will be losses
for us. You'll have a debt.

But I'll have my life. The only way to keep my secrets safe is for them to keep *me*. I've known this for a long time. It's why I kept the ledger. I can remember every name and number on it, but once I'm dead, it's gone forever. The trail of blood. The map of all my offenses.

RED: The girl?

JAY: You can bring her back
to life when you're ready.

Minutes go by. I need a drink. I wish I'd never initiated the chat and invited the demand I knew would come. Why ask a question when you don't want to hear the answer?

JAY: You're important to us.
Soloman wants you back.
You're the best we have.

RED: Flattery will get

you everywhere.

JAY: I'd have told you before
if you didn't already know it.

Jay spews lies, so the compliment does nothing for me. She's dictated my life for the past three years. I despise her. I despise the person I've become. The only patch of beauty in this bloody existence has been Isabel. Her inexplicable love for me. I have no authority on what's healthy in a relationship, but a cold-blooded killer falling hard and fast for a beautiful mark probably isn't anywhere in the realm of healthy.

I mull over Jay's proposition. If I accept—regardless of whether I intend to follow through—we could trap the right people and employ Isabel's developing blackmail plan, with my willingness to extinguish Boswell as a solid backup.

If I did follow through and let Jay bring me back into the fold of Company Eleven… My instincts scream no, but my brain keeps spinning despite the reluctance I feel in my bones.

With the Chalys feud neutralized, Isabel could get her life back, though. Maybe not the same life but one that could be normal given time. Maybe letting her go would break her heart all over again, but she'd be alive. Teaching. Putting her saint heart to work in the best ways she could. Not wasting her time in a rootless existence with me.

Then I could scratch Isabel Foster's name out of my book, and she could scratch my name out of her life.

I wouldn't have to spend my days protecting her with my life. But I could offer what's left of it to make sure no one ever tries to hurt her again.

Wouldn't that be simpler? Would it be worth it?

No, because selfishly I can't give her up. I'll never be able to bring myself to do it.

Regardless, I want whatever Jay knows. So I press her.

RED: Time to disclose.

JAY: Do I have your word, then?

RED: My word isn't worth
anything anymore.

A long pause.

JAY: There will be consequences
if you don't follow through. Don't make me
regret this.

RED: I know how this works.

JAY: Vince Boswell.

Isabel is on target. I'll give her that. But I'm not getting roped into Jay's bullshit deal for a name I already know.

RED: Tell me something I don't know, or this
conversation is over.

JAY: They sent his nephew to Rio to get close
to her and collect intel. He got too close, so they
enlisted us.

He fell for her. I knew it. I fucking *knew* it. I type hard on the keys with my next question.

RED: Why is she so
important to them?

JAY: Ask her mother. She's been meddling in
their affairs. Causing problems for quite some
time.

Been there. Done that.

RED: Anything else?

JAY: They know she's alive. This isn't over until one of us ends it.

So much for buying time. The only thing faking her death did was get the case off the Feds' radar, which I admit is one less concern since they'd be useless in bringing her justice. At least the kind of justice I'm after. The longer Isabel's name is in the media circuit, the more likely she is to be recognized, but her death is already old news.

RED: Give me a couple weeks.

JAY: Don't screw this up.

We're negotiating, always maneuvering, because that's the dance we know. But underneath it all, the real tension in our exchange exists because this is the last straw. Turning on a client simply isn't done, but if they want me back, they'll have to suffer the consequences. And if I don't go back, they'll be merciless in finding me.

I shouldn't have agreed without knowing if I could go through with it. The prospect of going back to my old life is both tortuous and comforting at once. Like Isabel, I've been tossed out of my comfort zone with all of this. But maybe it's a means to another end. A better way through this mess. Find Soloman. Root out the threat from the inside.

If I let them reel me back in, that's what I'll do. Of course, they'll expect that too.

6

ISABEL

I spend another morning at Noam's. I'm sore from the past couple of days' exertions and using my muscles more intensely than I'm used to. Today's lessons are more pragmatic than physical, though. He talks about using weapons of opportunity. Keys, pens, belts. Anything within reach in an emergency. He shows me how to disarm him of a fake gun and knife with fast, strategic movements. It takes me several tries, but I feel more confident with each iteration.

We review soft points and incorporate those offensives into the sequence, which is only loosely structured. Everything can change. Noam comes at me differently each time, and each time I have to react first. He never gives me time to think.

These lessons resonate maybe more than any of the others. I'm not worried about bar fights. I'm worried about the people who want me dead, and they won't come at me with their fists.

I walk back to the house feeling taxed but stronger. More capable. Like maybe one day soon I could hope to defend myself against the white-collar devil who wants me dead.

Vince Boswell is that devil.

Tristan texted me last night. Kolt's uncle is our mark. Putting a face and a name to the threat might feel better if I didn't have to find the nerve to seduce him. Tristan's not the only one tentative about that part of the plan. Skye insists I have it in me. A part of me does, sure. I know how to get a man's attention. But this one is the head of a billion-dollar corporate powerhouse and probably intimidating even in the most casual situations. That and he paid someone to kill me.

Still, I'm not sure I can trust anyone else to the task.

I shower and hurry to get dressed, knowing Tristan will be here soon. Martine gave her blessing when he requested a meeting. We're hurtling forward into this plan faster than I anticipated. Skye's not the only driving force, but her energy makes me nervous. She's hungry for justice, which I get. But I'm having a hard time catching up to her.

I clean up and head downstairs. Martine has an office in the back of the house. Murmurs of voices carry to the front when there's a hard rap at the front door.

I open it to find Tristan.

"Oh, hi. How'd you get past the gate?"

A coy grin. "I memorized the key tones when I dropped you off yesterday."

I lean against the jamb and cross my arms. "Aren't you tricky?"

He braces his hands on either side of the door, leaning in so I can smell him. That familiar scent—earth and spice and the love of my life—emanating off the man who's overwhelmed my senses for as long as I can remember.

"You didn't think I was going to let a fancy iron gate get between us, did you?"

"Of course not."

I don't think he'll let anything stand between us unless that's exactly what he wants.

"You going to let me in or what?" His tone is low, a threatening little tease.

I look him over because I can't help myself.

He's wearing his usual black T-shirt and jeans, both contouring attractively over his muscular frame. His dark-brown hair is messily parted and hangs over his forehead a little. He's clean-shaven—a rarity, because who has time for that when you're Tristan Red? I run my finger along the smooth edge of his jaw.

"You shaved."

He hums an affirmative, capturing my hand when it falls away. "You know this distance between us is like a slow death for me, right?"

I swallow hard and offer a small nod. I start to move to the side when he hooks his finger around my belt loop and tugs me a step closer.

"See me tonight," he murmurs.

My skin erupts with goosebumps. I recognize the heat in his eyes. The potent need that's gone unsatisfied for too long tugs at the already frayed threads holding me together.

Before I can say yes, I hear footsteps behind me.

"You must be Tristan."

Tristan straightens and lets me loose. I turn, and Martine greets him with a practiced smile. She looks as put together as ever. Today it's perfectly pressed cream slacks and a bright floral blouse with lavender and creamy swirls that ties everything together. No one would peg her for the mastermind that she is.

"And you must be Martine," he says coolly.

"I am. Welcome to Halo."

He returns her polite smile, but I can see he's holding back. Suspicious. Guarded as ever. I'm sure she knows too as she waves him inside and guides us to her office.

Skye is sitting on the edge of the desk and talking to Zeda.

"Have a seat," Martine says, taking hers behind her desk. She peers at her computer screen and clicks around a few times.

The office is painted a deep maroon, but white country-style furniture adorns the room, brightening it up. The walls are covered in vibrant abstracts and paintings of New Orleans's classic architecture.

Tristan leans against the wall by the doorway. I take the empty chair nearest to him.

"Isabel says you've isolated the target," Martine says almost absently. Skye and Zeda fix their stares on him.

"I have," he says.

Martine leans back in her chair and appraises him. "Perfect. There's a private event this weekend that I believe will work. It's at the Mercier Terrace Courtyard at the Ritz. The most important people in New Orleans will be there. I happen to know several, and a few happen to owe me favors."

"This is New Orleans. Not Boston," he says.

"Taking a weekend to indulge in the debauchery our fine city offers is rarely a hardship. Beyond that, the Boswells have been trying to expand into oil for some time. This event will be flush with oil money. Not to mention politicians, who are always helpful to the cause. And, of course, beautiful women."

"What's your plan?"

He crosses his arms, putting his strength on display, and a little bolt of possessive pride warms me.

"He'll book a room at the hotel, of course," Martine says. "Before he checks in, Zeda will sneak in and pose as a maid to get access to the suite."

"The whole place will be outfitted with surveillance," Zeda says with confidence. "We'll have audio and visual from multiple points. Plus we can inconspicuously plant whatever Isabel will need while we're there."

Tristan's features tighten at the sound of my name.

"Isabel will be a guest at the party on the terrace," Martine continues. "When the time is right, after Boswell's had a couple of drinks, I'll have someone introduce her if he hasn't already taken an interest in her."

Tristan straightens off the wall, letting his crossed arms fall to his sides. "No. We discussed this. It's not happening. Someone else can go."

Martine doesn't flinch. "Can I ask you something, Tristan? What exactly do you bring to this plan beyond a compulsion to protect Isabel?"

"Let's just say I've been around the block a few times."

"Yes," she gives him a quick once-over. "I'm aware of your skill set. It's your instincts that concern me. Isabel wanted your help, but I'm questioning if we really need it. If you allow your emotions to get in the way of what has to be done here, the whole plan is foiled. More damage will have been done than results achieved."

"I'm not emotional," he says in a clipped tone.

"Then let us do our jobs, and you do yours. We'll be in a nearby suite. We'll have eyes on the room the whole time. If anything goes wrong, you can be on standby to intervene if needed. And *only* if it's needed."

"You're going to send her in there to seduce and subdue him? That's a tall order for a school teacher."

Martine's eyes narrow slightly. "You underestimate her."

I stand up. "Can you two stop talking like I'm not even in the room? Listen, I'm nervous about this too, but I realize it should be me."

Tristan squares his body with mine. "Tell me how it'll go, then. You entice him to the room with the promise of sex. He starts trying to rip your clothes off. Then what do you do?"

"Slow things down." I share a quick look with Martine because we've already discussed the plan. And there's no way in hell I'm telling Tristan the whole plan. "It'll be enough for the cameras, but then I'll excuse myself to the bathroom or something before he can take things too far."

"What if you don't get that chance and he overpowers you?"

"I can defend myself."

"You're learning how, but you're not an expert, and you'll be panicking."

I close my eyes and stave off a flare of alarm with his warning. "For now, let's assume he won't be that aggressive. He should know how to take a hint. I'll ask him to get more comfortable while I'm in the bathroom, and when I get back, I'll be armed and he'll know it. Then I'll…"

I have a hard time envisioning the next part. The part where I stay strong enough to reveal myself to him—the girl he would have murdered—and confront him on the matter at hand. I'll have to issue the threat and be convincing about it. How those few minutes play out will be the difference between stopping this feud between our families, hopefully forever, and inciting more bloodshed.

"You'll do what, Isabel?" Tristan's voice is quiet but firm.

"I'll explain the terms and ask for his compliance."

He chuckles. "You'll ask."

"I will demand it while I'm pointing a gun at his chest. Is that better?"

He's quiet. "Much better."

Martine brings her hands together with a slap that makes me jump. "We have a plan, then. I'll get him the invite. In the meantime, we wait and prepare."

"Perfect." Skye bounces upright and shoots me a satisfied smile on her way out of the office.

Whether Tristan likes it or not, the conversation is over.

The rest of us follow except for Martine, who stays at her desk, working.

As we walk toward the front of the house, Skye says, "Zeda and I are going to Frenchmen Street for a few drinks tonight. Do you guys want to come?"

I look to Tristan, expecting him to shoot it down the way he's shot down everything else today. No to the plan. No to my involvement in the plan. No to never killing anyone again.

He blows out a tense exhale. "I guess I could use a drink since all I can think about now is another man trying to have sex with you."

"Great," Skye beams, effectively ignoring Tristan's grim mood. "We're heading out around ten."

TRISTAN

I'm used to adapting to my surroundings. Maneuvering around unexpected circumstances. Eliminating obstacles as I go. Because, in my line of work, nothing ever goes down the way it's supposed to. Never knowing what challenges I'll face keeps me sharp. Focused. Fluid. I get off on the threat of failure and beating the odds.

Nothing about this plan is getting me off. I'd rather put Isabel in a plastic bubble and lock her away until I can take care of things my way. I'll *still* take care of things my way if I need to, though. She and Martine don't need to know that as long as it looks like I'm bending to their grand plan.

As we drive toward our destination, I'm not sure if I've ever seen Isabel more relaxed—almost as if a physical weight has been lifted off her.

"What's on your mind?"

She sighs. "Just taking it all in, I guess."

"Have you ever been to New Orleans?"

Traffic slows as we turn off Elysian Fields Avenue on our way to Frenchmen. The streets are already busy with pedestrians. French-inspired row houses frame the narrow streets. Even as night falls, the pastel stucco fronts create an atmosphere that matches the revelry the city is known for.

"No, but that's not what I mean," she says.

I reach across and take her hand in mine, as if the contact will give me a better line into what she's thinking. "What do you mean?"

"Life is moving a million miles an hour. I don't have time to overthink anything. Or worry or hesitate. I'm more in the moment than I've ever been, which, oddly, might have been what I was hoping for when I moved to Rio to begin with." She pauses. "It's funny, but I think I might be getting used to it."

"Welcome to my world, I guess."

"I'm not sure I'd know what to do if things were normal."

"You'd have to get into something really intense like skydiving to keep your adrenaline up."

She laughs, and the sound feels like an explosion around my heart, melting the ice and tension there. We park a few blocks away from the Blue Nile because the street is already jammed with taxis and people partying in every available crevice.

I tense a little because this is the type of place where trouble hides under all the good fun everyone's having. Most of the people around us are here to either fight, fuck, or make a few bucks. Some are already wasted, and the rest aren't too far behind. We walk toward a blue-painted stretch of building with a neon crescent hanging above the doorway.

"This is the place," Isabel says over the chatter of people around us.

The doorman checks our IDs—both of which are fake for reasons the doorman would never guess. We both get stamped and walk inside the club that's surprisingly empty. She spots Skye and Zeda at a little bar table near the stage. Noam and a few others I don't recognize are with them. Isabel waves to them, but I coax her toward the bar, the urge to be antisocial too strong to resist.

"Want a drink?" I ask, gesturing to the bartender.

"Sure. Whatever you're having."

I order an Abita Amber and a Don Julio on the rocks with extra limes for her.

She laughs when the bartender slides it across the bar. "Are you trying to turn me into a cheap date?"

I grin. "Absolutely."

She takes a little sip of the tequila and wrinkles her nose. "Not bad."

We linger by the bar as the band on the stage warms up. Me on a stool, Isabel taking the space between my legs. Already I'm enjoying the relaxed atmosphere and our proximity. The ability to touch her whenever I want is a luxury I haven't been afforded lately. But tonight feels different, like she's letting her guard down for the first time since she left DC without me.

"We should at least say hi." Her attention wanders to her new friends and back to me.

Except the request can't distract me from my silent worship of her body in the little green wrap dress she's wearing. I grab her waist and inch her tighter to me, kissing her bare shoulder. "I'm here to be with you, not them."

Our noses graze. Our lips are close enough that I could take hers with no effort. We could be at the other table, and I wouldn't see anyone but her anyway. I wait for the heat in her eyes to match the fire coursing hot through my veins. She melts a little into my easy hold on her.

When the band kicks up, the club starts to fill in earnest and people crowd the stage.

"Will you at least dance with me?"

She shoots me an adorable little grin that almost tempts me.

"Not a chance," I say.

She pouts. "I'm not leaving you alone over here. Some hot girl is going to try to hit on you."

I laugh, her hint at jealousy throwing me.

"What about the overtly unfriendly vibe I give off?"

"I'm afraid that just adds to your sex appeal."

I grin broadly. "Really? Tell me more."

I coax her against me again, and she rests her hands on my shoulders. "You really need me to tell you how ruggedly handsome and utterly irresistible you are?"

"Can't you just show me instead?"

She rolls her eyes with a smile.

"It's a reasonable request," I press.

"Maybe I will if you dance with me."

As if on cue, the club fills with the urgent sounds of trumpets and trombones, percussion, and the upbeat harmony of voices belting out the tune. The show has officially begun. We'll have to yell to hear each other, so I lean in to kiss her, but she evades me, taking my hand and dragging me onto the dance floor instead.

I should have opted for the tequila because dancing isn't really my thing without it. Still, Isabel is so eager right now I can't say no. We snake through the crowd, making a space for ourselves among dozens of others. She sways to the music and twirls herself under my arm, so I spin her once more, making her dress flare.

The beat is steady and addictive, so loud that every single body in this place has got to feel it vibrating down to their toes. The whole crowd bounces and moves, staring up at the seven-man band who seem no less entertained on the stage.

The experience consumes the senses. Overwhelms in the best way. Like a rich meal. Like sex. Like Isabel happy…

When she leans into me, her back to my chest, and gyrates to the rhythm of the music, it's the best of everything. I can't remember a time when I've been happier.

Another hour passes that way. Song after wall-shaking song. Another drink for Isabel. Skye finds us in the crowd, and she and Isabel own a pocket of the dance floor for a good part of the set. I'm content to watch Isabel dance, and I'm *certain* she knows I'm watching her. I try to ignore that I may not be the only one lusting after her, but I console myself with the promise that I'll be the one she spends the night with.

When the band takes a break, she comes back to me. Her skin is glowing with sweat. Her cheeks and chest are rosy and warm.

"Hey," she says breathlessly.

"You having fun?"

"What do you think?"

I razor my teeth against my lower lip and drink her in. "I think I want to take you back to my place so we can get back to talking about how ruggedly handsome I am."

She laughs, and I catch her against me. She's so perfect right now, I don't want to change a thing.

"I love when you laugh. I feel it," I say quietly.

Her eyes dim a little. "I miss it."

Of course she does. That's what normal people do. Drink, laugh, have fun with their friends. Something twists painfully inside me when I realize her happiness here doesn't have to do with me. I'm just a witness to it. This is who Isabel is when she's not running for her life.

She brings her hand to my cheek, drawing my thoughts back to the moment we're sharing.

"Let's go home."

I can feel her raspy voice on the surface of my skin.

"My place."

She confirms with a quick nod. "Let me just tell Skye I'm heading out."

I watch her walk away and count the seconds until she gets back.

We're barely inside the front door, and she's wrapped around me. A desperate moan leaves her lips when our mouths collide. I hold nothing back because I'm starving for her. I'm fucking starving, and I didn't fully appreciate the gravity of it until this moment.

I crowd her against the door and tug her straps down, baring her breasts for my greedy touches. Tasting all of her becomes a race against an avalanche of desire. I pinch and bite at her nipples. I drag my nose up the graceful column of her neck to breathe and suck and taste her. Her sweat, her essence.

"My God…" I don't think I've ever been this hard in my life. I'm vibrating with a nearly violent need to fuck. And when I hold her against me, I feel her trembling too. I hike up her thigh so it slides against mine, opening her to more pressure.

"Tristan, I can't wait." Her voice breaks like she might cry.

"Me neither."

It's got to be here. Right now.

She claws at my shirt until it flies to the floor. Her fingernails slice down my shoulders when our bare chests meet. We'll be bruised and bloody by the time we're through, but that would be strangely right.

"I want you rough," I say. It's more a warning than a wish. I'm not sure I possess the restraint to have her any other way.

"Yes," she breathes.

"Hang on to me."

As I lift her up, she winds her arms and legs around my frame, giving me the few seconds I need to tear her panties at the side with a satisfying rip. When my fingers find her wet heat, I plunge and stroke until she's quivering and arching to deepen my touch.

My heart bangs like a barrel drum, thrumming through my whole body. *I'll want this forever...*

I free my cock from my jeans and drive into her, unable to stop the feral growl that tears from me when I do. It mingles with hers. The opening note of the fierce and greedy symphony that follows. The door thudding with every thrust. The soft slap of our bodies meeting. Her labored breathing. The throaty cries that pierce the air when I go deeper, take her harder.

I swallow them, breathe her air, fight off the urge to let go too soon. But taking her this way—rough and passionate—is a fast-burning sprint to the end. She's there too. Her body a taut bow ready to sail into oblivion.

Having her so close to the edge is almost enough.

"Isabel... Say you love me."

Those three little words ring through me, annoying in their simplicity. *I love you* was made for normal people with normal lives and normal problems. Still, I reach for it. I can't say it, but I need to hear it.

Her eyes flutter open and lock on me in the darkness. They glimmer with love and lust and the street light seeping in through the windows. Seeing her this way, my heart threatens to burst in my chest. She owns me. I know it before she says what I now desperately want to hear.

"I love you, Tristan," she whispers against my lips.

The next meeting of mouths is pure possession. I kiss her deeply and match my rhythm to it, because what I feel now is more like I-love-you's dark and fucked-up cousin. A raw, primal obsession. A twisting, grinding compulsion to sink into her so profoundly that reality has no choice but to bleed away and concede itself to our moment.

Just this... Just us...

She has to know I feel it too. All of it. Every drop of her love. She has to know...

I slide my fingers into her hair, fisting gently. I tighten my arm around her waist. My ability to maintain the punishing pace goes to war with the impending need to completely spend myself without taking us both to the ground.

Her fingernails dig deeper into my flesh. She goes rigid all around me, and her thready scream sets off my own climax, a fierce rush that causes my knees to buckle.

I recover enough to take us safely to the floor. She lies against my chest. Her breaths come in uneven pants. Our hearts are two jackrabbits slowing after a thrilling chase. And in that space, a kind of peace washes over me that scares me as much as it comforts me, because in this moment, I realize I'll never have it again without her.

7

ISABEL

I wake to an empty bed and the intermittent squeak of metal against metal coming from outside. I roll over. Through the blinds in the window that faces the porch, a broad shadow swings back and forth. Tristan. I check the digital clock on the bedside table. It's past ten o'clock. Thankfully Noam isn't expecting me today. I'm enjoying the sessions more, but I'm grateful for a break. I'm even more grateful for a pocket of time to get my head together before the Vince Boswell plan goes down.

I fall back into my pillow, unable to ignore the dread that slams down on me suddenly. I know what I need to do. Doesn't make facing it any easier. I can't run from this anymore. Last night was a potent diversion. The last time I felt that free was with Kolt, sipping caipirinhas and watching Rio come alive with Carnaval—the lights and heat and sexy rhythm of a rhumba infecting everyone with its addictive beats. I let it infect me too, the same way last night consumed my senses and ended with the most intense sex of my life.

Everything I held back with Kolt I give freely with Tristan. Love.

Passion. Every raw emotion flows uninhibited.

The night Tristan decided not to take my life, I turned Kolt away. If Tristan hadn't been so heavy in my heart, I might have chosen differently. Maybe Tristan would have too. Now here we are, steeped in a dangerous game of life and death. Cat and mouse. The hunted becoming the hunter.

A little of my dread lifts away because I know I can be strong. We can beat them. We can win.

I take my tumbling thoughts into the shower. When I emerge, I slip into last night's dress and find Tristan on the porch, coffee in hand, a faraway look in his eyes.

"Hey."

He looks at me, his expression almost eerily blank for a moment before he manages a small smile. "Morning."

"Is everything okay?"

"Yeah." He gets up. "Do you want to get breakfast?"

"Sure. I need to get some clothes from the house." I cross my arms and rub them with my hands to fight off the slight morning chill that feels like dew on my skin.

"Okay. I was hoping we could go someplace after."

"Where?"

I frown a little because he's so businesslike suddenly. Last night we were a couple in love. I was professing it in the throes of our passion. Passion like I've never felt before. He hasn't even touched me.

He tips his coffee mug to his lips once more. Only then do I recognize the puffiness under his eyes. We'd tumbled into bed together after recovering somewhere in the entryway last night, but he doesn't look like he's rested at all.

"Have you slept?" I ask.

He shrugs, avoiding my eyes. "I was thinking I could teach you how to shoot today. I know you're not especially keen on guns, but you should at least learn the basics so you can handle one confidently."

My muscles tense a little more, which has nothing to do with the temperature and all to do with the plan—the one that requires me to have a weapon to protect myself in the worst-case scenario.

I swallow hard. "Okay. That's probably a good idea."

I wait for him to touch me in any way. Instead, he opens the front door and we go back inside.

"There's an indoor shooting range near Noam's. We can grab breakfast close by and head over."

He puts his mug in the sink and grabs his jacket.

"Tristan."

He looks up wide-eyed, as if he might have forgotten I was here.

"Are you sure you're okay?"

"I'm fine. Why?"

"You seem kind of intense right now."

His rolls his shoulders a little. "Sorry. When I have a job to do, I make sure I'm ready for it before I head in. You're not ready yet." He comes close and gives me a peck on the cheek. "Let's go. Time to work."

Tristan drops me at Martine's so I can change. I'm able to dodge Skye and any interrogations she'll likely have ready when I see her next, even though "all business" Tristan is making me anxious. Still, he has a point. All the dread I'm feeling about dealing with Vince probably roots in doubting my ability to execute on the plan, which is to end this shit once and for all. Being able to pick up a gun and not feel like I'm a danger to myself with it would definitely help the cause.

Tristan and I eat breakfast quickly at a nearby café. We fill the brief time with small talk about New Orleans. I wouldn't mind spending more time here and exploring more of its hidden gems, but I have a feeling we'll need to move on after this weekend. I haven't talked about that part with Martine yet, but the last thing I want is to bring any of this mess to her doorstep.

Tristan checks us into the range, taking the lead since I have no idea what I'm doing. We use two guns Tristan already owns. A Sig Sauer for him and, for me, a Glock 19, which he assures me will be good due to its smaller size. He shows me how to load it and unload it several times until I'm comfortable with the routine of releasing the magazine and operating the slide catch.

He picks up his weapon and models how to hold it with both hands.

"Firm like a handshake, finger along the frame. Keep your grip high so it's easier to stabilize the muzzle on your target."

I mimic everything. His easy confidence here helps mine. Still, when we finally go into the stall, I'm shaking a little from anticipation and feeling so far outside my comfort zone.

He points to the target ahead of us, which is pretty close, because any real-life threat would be this close. I try not to think about that and instead focus on keeping a relaxed stance and controlling my breathing, which I can hear more acutely with the protective earmuffs on.

I raise the gun and line up the white dot to the bullseye on the target. I look to Tristan out of the corner of my eye, and he nods for me to go ahead.

I exhale slowly and empty my thoughts. My finger moves the trigger. There's a loud pop and a sharp jolt from the gun firing in my hands. My heart thumps rapidly.

With a broad smile, Tristan nods to the target, which I'd forgotten existed with all the adrenaline whizzing through my system. I zero in on the tiny hole just outside the bullseye.

I jump on my toes a little. He gives me the thumbs-up to keep going.

My next few shots aren't as gifted. I pout a little because the competitive part of me has decided it's important to impress Tristan. So I go through the magazine, increasingly intent on mastering the fine art of drilling the bullseye. I go through another, and another, until the paper is covered with pocks, several of them in the center circles, which pleases me.

After about twenty minutes, I'm a little exhausted. Maybe from concentrating, or inhaling gun smoke, or absorbing the nonstop rush that seems to happen behind a weapon like this.

I might feel more comfortable with the mechanics, but as we pay and head back to the car, I'm still uneasy with the power of it all. My attempt to wield a gun when Noam confronted me at my car seems even more absurd now. That missing pistol mysteriously reappeared in one of my dresser drawers yesterday, though, which must mean Noam trusts me to treat it more responsibly.

Maybe after today I can. Though, if I'm lucky, one day I'll never have a need.

"Do you feel better?" Tristan asks when we get back to the car and pull away.

"I guess so. I just have a hard time with the idea of it all," I say.

I stare at the houses we pass. Without discussing it, he's bringing me back to Martine's. My home for the time being.

"I know you do. Maybe after this is finished, you won't ever have to deal with it again."

Something about the way he says it bothers me. Like maybe I'll never have to deal with him again.

When he parks in front of Martine's, I want to press him more on his tone and the weird attitude he's had with me all day. Especially after last night, which was decidedly more than sex.

"I had an amazing night with you."

"Me too."

I catch a flicker of heat in his eyes before he looks away, out toward the road.

"I wish we had more nights like that."

That he doesn't answer. The engine is still humming. He's belted in, and for some reason, I feel like I should go. Our date is over.

"We should meet up Saturday morning to go over everything," he says. "Make sure we're all on the same page and you're as prepared as you need to be."

I stare at him, confused. "It's only Thursday. I'm not going to see you until then?"

His expression doesn't change. "I need some time to scope things out. Do what I do."

"But Martine—"

"I know you have faith in her, and I think her heart's in the right place. But trusting other people with the plan isn't how I stayed alive all this time."

"You trusted Jay."

He twists his lips slightly. "I relied on her direction. But when she handed out the assignments, I always did my homework."

And the final test was someone's death. Cold-blooded murder.

"And you were such a good student."

I catch the smallest twitch of muscle under his eye and a tenseness in his jaw as he looks away.

"I guess I should go, then," I say, my voice tight, inviting him to stop me. Because I don't want to leave like this. Missing him already is insane, especially since he's felt a million miles away all day, but I do.

"One more thing," he says. "You're not going to like it, but I think you should know. Just in case Kolt tries to come back into your life somehow and you decide to let him."

My brows furrow.

"When I talked to Jay to get more information about who hired the hit on you, she told me that Kolt's uncle sent him to Rio to get close to you."

My heart lurches into my throat, and my whole body turns cold. Curling my hands over the edges of the car seat, I try to ground myself. Replay the words. Kolt was sent to Rio. For me. I shake my head, unwilling to accept this new information.

"That can't be true."

"I'm not a fan of his, but I never brought him up before with Jay. I don't know why she would mention it unless it were true."

I look out the window toward the house, my thoughts a violent blur. Kolt's face. His cocky smile. His privilege. The way he always seemed out of place yet almost determined to stamp his presence wherever we were instead of blending into the richness of what already existed. Every memory is tainted. Stained with betrayal.

I bring my hand to my mouth and breathe deeply, staving off the nausea. I let him fuck me. I let him pretend to fall in love with me.

"Isabel..."

Tristan's voice is careful and tentative. So is his touch when he reaches for my hand. I rip it away. Because suddenly I hate him too. For telling me. For being right. For whatever smug satisfaction I know he's feeling right now. More than anything, I hate him for pulling away from me today when I gave him so much of myself last night.

I'm empty of trust. Bone dry.

"See you Saturday," I say as I open the door and step out.

"Isab—"

I slam the door and quickly start punching the code into the gate's box. He doesn't chase me. Doesn't call after me, which makes me even more miserable as I enter the house alone.

Skye wanders into the foyer looking like she just finished a class with Noam, a jar of peanut butter in her hand and a spoon in her mouth. Her eyes widen with concern.

"What's wrong?"

"Not now."

I contemplate locking myself in my room, but I'd be a caged animal. I'm too pissed off. I need to scream. Cry. Throw and break things.

I tear my fingers through my hair with a frustrated sound— something between a growl and a scream.

"Is it Tristan?"

"No," I snap and speed by her until I reach the back door. I rush down the steps into the courtyard.

It's mercifully empty. Quiet. Lush. I pace to the far end. Except there's nothing to throw here. Everything's too pretty to violate. I pace back. Skye's there waiting for me.

"Do I have to kill him?"

"I told you it's not Tristan."

"Then who is it?"

I walk around a little more, cursing Kolt and especially myself for being so stupid. So blindly naïve.

"Isabel. What's going on?"

I halt and turn to her. "Vince Boswell's nephew."

She scrunches up her face. Confusion. Yes, that's the face of my life. Warped confusion.

"They sent him to Rio to get close to me." I grind my teeth. Tristan was wise not to tell me this when I had a gun in my hand.

"Okay. So what? Their family is screwed up."

"I was sleeping with him for months!"

I groan loudly and pace off again. I can't believe it. How could Kolt do this to me? How could he convince me he cared? How could I have been so wrong to believe him? I didn't love him, but I cared about him. The chemistry was real enough. He'd been fun and charming and passionate, even if that passion wasn't always matched. We were lovers sometimes, but we were friends too.

Finally my anger begins to ebb away and the ugly tears come. I press the heels of my hands against my eyes, causing bright colors to flash behind them. I refuse to cry over this man, no matter how violated and foolish I feel.

I feel Skye's arms come around me in a gentle hug. She's so delicate compared to Tristan, but I feel her concern and do my best to hug her back. A silent thank-you for her support even though I'm a cluster of emotion right now.

She lets me go, her face still pinched with worry. "But what about Tristan? I know you're raging right now, but I'm confused."

I sigh and will the violent resentment to ease. Another deep breath tamps it down one percent.

"I've been in love with Tristan for six years. We were together, and then we spent a long time apart without contact. He just came back into my life recently." I skip the reason why, because saying everything out loud makes my life sound even more insane. "Kolt and I worked together in Rio."

"Kolt? That's his name?"

"Yeah."

"Fuck Kolt. I hate that name."

I let out a laugh because I know somewhere inside her she's

hatching a plan to ruin his whole existence. I think getting his family to stop trying to kill me will have to be enough.

"Unfortunately I did fuck him, and I really thought he was falling for me even though I was trying to put distance between us."

"Wait, you weren't into him, but you were messing around for months?"

"Not all the time. We hooked up sometimes. Weak moments, I guess. But I was still in love with Tristan. He left me really abruptly, and I was messed up from it."

She wrinkles her nose. "Fuck Tristan too."

I laugh again. "Skye… Ugh." I drag my hands down my face. "I'm mad at him for telling me. He was so cold this morning."

"You slept with him last night."

I roll my eyes at that. "Obviously we're sleeping together. He's Tristan. He's…" I wave my hands in tiny circles, trying to find the words to describe him. "He's the one. You know, the one who feels like a hit of heroin or something. He's always been that person for me. Even though he's massively different now and has done unthinkable things the past few years. Everything is so fucked up, but somehow I'm falling in love with him *more*. Except he's an enigma. He's missing so much. Not just our memories but basic emotions. He's this beautiful, brilliant man, but in some ways, he's only just now starting to figure out how to live. How to feel…"

She props her hand on her hip. "You're making me feel like I really have my life together, you know."

I crack a smile, grateful to at least have someone to talk to. Being alone in all of this would be ten times worse.

"So what now?"

She purses her lips. "Let's go shopping. You have a hot date with a bad man Saturday night."

TRISTAN

The Mercier Terrace is on the fourteenth floor. I survey the layout of the room, now empty save a few hotel staff setting up for the event. No one pays me any mind until I lock eyes with a woman fussing with one of the plants past the courtyard doors.

Zeda.

A minute later, she comes up to me.

"Fancy meeting you here," I say, taking in her maid's uniform. "Nice outfit."

"You're not exactly looking covert."

"I'm a wandering patron of the hotel. I got lost." I nod to the courtyard. "What's going on out there?"

"Just setting things up so we have eyes outside and can see her coming."

Some more workers come into the room and start moving tables around. She motions me to follow her into the hallway.

"He's booked the Vieux Carré suite. It's vacant until he arrives tomorrow, so we have the place to ourselves for a while. We'll be set up in the room across the hall."

"We?"

She walks ahead of me. "Skye and me. Martine will be overseeing things remotely. You're welcome to join us."

Once in front of the suite, she hovers her key over the sensor. It beeps with a green blink.

"That a master key?"

"Sure is."

Perfect.

We enter a sitting area that expands into an opulent bedroom. This is where Boswell will try to have his way with Isabel.

I shove away the jealousy the way I'm shoving everything else away—all the emotions Martine's worried will ruin Isabel's showdown with Boswell. Spending the day without Isabel has been its own kind of agony. Putting distance between us doesn't feel good, but right now, it's necessary.

Pretending I don't feel a damn thing is easier when I'm back in my routine. Assessing, calculating, hunting. Jury's still out on whether I'll be able to keep myself from pulling the trigger out of pure instinct.

Wasting no time, Zeda reveals a thin case concealed under her uniform and sets it on the coffee table. She unzips it and starts setting out several small cameras perfect for hiding in a room like this one.

"Where are you positioning them?"

"One in the corner by the curtains. Should give a good view of the bed. One at the desk. And one above the doorway so we can keep an eye on his bodyguard or anything else he does outside the bedroom."

"Bodyguard?"

"Private security company. They're local."

"Is Martine taking care of that?"

"Of course." She pulls a chair to the door, lifts herself onto it, and carefully places one of the tiny cameras by the door hinge.

I glance into her little case of goodies and spot a small roll of duct tape. From my jacket, I withdraw a tactical knife and the same gun Isabel practiced with at the range.

"Mind if I borrow your tape?"

She comes down from the chair and pauses, her eyes fixed on the weapons in my hands.

I lift them up innocently. "I'm planting them for her."

"Sure," she says, carrying the chair into the bedroom to reach the top folds of the curtain.

While she works on that, I go to work scoping out convenient places. All the while my thoughts circle around this plan. Around Isabel and how all this might go down. This is what I do, but Isabel isn't anything like me. She'll react differently. Since I can't take her out of the equation, I have to make damn sure I'm there and ready when she needs me.

When I return, Zeda is still busy at the curtains.

"She's got a knife under the coffee table and a Glock behind the toilet."

"Got it," she says with a strip of adhesive clenched between her teeth.

"What exactly do you do?"

"Same thing you do," she says, evading my question.

"I doubt that." Not even close.

"My brothers used to pick up old computers and TVs from the local junkyard. They'd bring them home and use the pieces to make their own computers or sell them to their friends. Kids who couldn't afford laptops or new phones."

"You learned all this from them."

"I needed something to do after Katrina wiped out everything we had. I got my GED and did a year at a trade school. Working for Martine is more lucrative obviously."

"How did you hook up with her?"

"Martine took me in after the storm. When our house flooded, my family and I got separated. When everything settled down, turns out I was the only one left. Everything we had was gone. Martine took a lot of people in then, but once she found out I was useful, I stayed and took on more work with her."

There's an edge to the way she talks about Martine. Like being in her employ is a matter of circumstance, not commitment.

"Seems like you're a pretty tight-knit group."

She ignores the bait and steps down, moving next to the desk lamp.

"Call me crazy, but you don't seem like the rest of them," I press.

"You mean I'm not an evangelist like Skye?"

I chuckle. "Right."

"She drinks the Kool-Aid."

"You don't?"

"I'm there to learn. There's no binding contract that you have to buy into their mission. So I don't. Martine knows I'm a skeptic, but she's determined. She keeps me busy, so, for now, I stay."

"What's the mission?"

She pauses. "Halo's mission is to collect information. The more important and connected the person, the more valuable the dirt. Martine banks it with the organization, and then they use it to manipulate people for strategic results. Sometimes the bad guys go to jail. Sometimes they can funnel some funds to the organization. Sometimes nothing happens and we wait."

"And you don't buy into any of this?"

She huffs quietly, remaining concentrated on her task. "Martine can't see the forest for the trees. A true missionary, she wants to save one soul at a time. It's like she's keeping count or something. But all it does is chip away at the edges of the bigger issues."

"Bigger issues like…?"

"Like this fucked-up world we live in. It's not the little people. Skye's pimp? He's part of a system that made his abuse of power possible. This Big Pharma guy?" She shakes her head. "We're getting warmer, but twisting him to keep Isabel safe doesn't do shit for all the people dying because of the drugs they're pushing."

"So you're suggesting we use the intel we get here to try to damage his company instead." I know it would never work, but I'm curious about her theories. Especially since Isabel's about to star in the movie they plan on banking until further notice.

"Nah. This Boswell guy is like the strip club down in the Quarter. Take 'em out, and someone new will be there setting up shop in the morning. The real problems run deeper."

Her focus on the systemic versus the isolated problems hits a nerve with me. Not like anything I've ever done was purpose-driven, but I haven't been operating much differently. Taking aim at people's individual grievances. Solving problems on a case-by-case basis.

Then I remember Crow's message. *Think big.* Maybe Martine's not the only one who's been thinking too small.

"Doesn't matter anyway," Zeda says before whipping a small laptop from her bag. "This will combine all the signals from the cameras and send it to the room we'll be in. Everything will be saved as it feeds in. We can edit the footage after to make it look however we want."

"Perfect."

She finishes syncing everything up and hides the machine in the far back of the entertainment center where Boswell will never notice it.

"Hey, can I borrow your key for a second? I'm going to check out the other room before I head out."

I hold my hand out for the key. She eyes me warily before pulling it from her apron pocket and handing it to me.

"Thanks." I leave quickly, not giving her time to change her mind.

The room across the hall is a smaller version of the suite but still finely appointed. I check out the windows and layout. Nothing of importance. I take out the RFID card duplicator hidden in my jacket, scan the master, and then program an extra key for myself. If Martine thinks she's the only one smart enough to get the keys to the kingdom, she's all wrong.

When I return, Zeda has another laptop open displaying the feeds from all the cameras, including the two from the courtyard and terrace rooms.

"Audio too?" I ask.

She clicks a few keys and brings up the waveform fluctuating from our voices. "Audio too."

Silently I thank Martine for organizing half the work for me. Because once Zeda leaves and we go our separate ways, I circle back to Boswell's suite. Using my new master key, I gain entrance and carefully tape a second computer to the bottom of the entertainment center. Installed with a packet sniffer, the machine will ensure that whatever feeds out to Zeda and Martine's operation will also feed out to me.

Several hours later, when I check into the room down the hall, all the camera and audio feeds are at my fingertips. All that's left to do is wait.

8

ISABEL

"I'm freaking out a little."

A little is an understatement. Anxiety is rocketing through me, and the more I try to subdue it, the stronger it holds me.

We're in the bathroom of the hotel room Martine secured for the night. Knowing it's directly across from Boswell's is reassuring, if anything is. At least I'll be close to help if this all goes sideways. I pray it doesn't.

"You look awesome." Skye smooths and straightens the sleek white cocktail dress.

Its formfitting high-quality material molds attractively over my curves. The deep V in the front puts some of my cleavage on display. My skin pops against the cream, as do my eyes when I place the bright-blue contacts over them. My makeup is heavy but subtle—smoky shadow around my eyes and nude glossy lips. Fake eyelashes make mine look thicker and fuller.

"Do you need this?" Skye touches the silver pendant at my clavicle. "It's kind of messing with the flow here." She gestures up and down the bared strip of torso the dress reveals. "Is it important?"

I hesitate. "Yes, it's important." I need every talisman and good omen I can get my hands on right now. St. Paul stays.

"Fine." She reaches around my neck, unhooks the chain, and circles it around my wrist a few times." She cocks her head with a satisfied smile. "There. Now it's important and won't distract him from appreciating all your assets. Plus, we can't have him thinking you're a goody-goody Catholic girl, can we?"

I doubt he would in this outfit. The reverend would have a heart attack.

I look in the mirror and glide my hands over my slick blond bob. Not a hair is out of place. "What if he recognizes me?" I barely recognize myself.

One of Skye's genuine blue eyes goes much wider than the other. "Are you kidding me? The contacts aren't even necessary. I'll be impressed if he remembers your name. He's going to be fantasizing about your tits the whole time."

She's probably right. But her assumption is a blast of both relief and fresh worry. I have no idea how aggressive he'll be or how adversely I'll react.

"I'm so on edge already. I feel like I'll jump out of my skin the second he touches me."

And he *is* going to touch me. He's going to go further than Tristan realizes, which is a betrayal for the cause that we'll have to work out later. Or not.

I haven't heard from Tristan since Thursday when he dropped the bomb about Kolt on me. Maybe he already senses there's more to the plan than we told him.

I check my watch. The rooftop party starts in an hour, and he's still not here.

Skye twists her lips and looks me over. "You do look really tense."

"That's because I am. I feel like I need a drink or a Valium or something."

"You can nurse a glass of champagne until he takes you to the room. No more."

"I know," I mutter. I don't like the anxiety, but it's better than dulling my instincts.

"Listen, you have to get out of your own head for a little while. At least until you have him where we want him."

I pace a little circle around the large marble bathroom, getting comfortable walking in the deep-red stilettos I bought for the occasion.

"How am I supposed to get out of my head, Skye? This man wants me dead. It's hard not to dwell on it."

She crosses her arms and leans her butt against the counter.

"How do you think I got through half the shit I did? Of all the men I was with, you know how many guys I actually wanted to fuck around with?"

"Not many, I'm sure."

"Exactly. You know how many kept coming back for more?"

I don't answer because I'd hate to know. The idea of her selling her body to live one step above the streets is awful to consider.

"Plenty did, Isabel," she continues matter-of-factly. "Because I was really good at pretending. I'd pretend that whoever I was with was going to see me for who I really was and take me away from that life. Didn't matter what they said or did or looked like. So I sold the lie to myself, and then I sold it back to them. I looked at every man I was with like he was the only one on the planet. Like for the next twenty minutes, I might not be able to breathe without his hands on me. And when I started to hate it, I told myself I loved it."

"I don't know if I can do that." Another jolt of anxiety razors through me, making my fingertips tingle. I'm going to have a panic attack and botch this whole thing.

Skye comes up to me and puts her hands on my arms. "Look at me. Breathe."

I take a few deep breaths and our eyes lock. My heart beats an odd rhythm.

"Just look at him like you look at Tristan."

Could I do that?

I don't know.

Maybe.

"Where is he?" I whisper, trying to keep my emotions in check.

"Don't worry about it. You know he's lurking around here somewhere."

"What if he isn't?" My heart starts scampering in my chest again at the prospect of his eternal absence.

What if he doesn't care what happens tonight? What if he's angry with me for how I messed everything up with Kolt?

She hushes my unspoken worries and leads me into the bedroom, where Zeda is sitting at the desk with two laptops showing feeds of the opposite suite. An hour ago, the rooms were empty. Now I can see the pixelated figure of a man in a suit walking back and forth, talking on the phone, disappearing from one view and entering another. It's Vince Boswell.

"Oh, God. He's here."

Skye squeezes my hand. "You've got this."

The party on the terrace is already bustling when I arrive a predetermined half hour late. The crowd is noticeably thicker in the courtyard than the adjoining terrace room, so I collect my first and only drink at the inside bar, swallow half of it down, and give myself a pep talk.

I can do this. I know what guys want. I know what they're thinking about when they're on the prowl. And while I'm not normally preoccupied with how I look, I'm acutely aware of my physical assets tonight. I'm not negotiating a merger. I'm trying to interest a man sexually. This is easy stuff.

With that affirmation in my head, I brave the courtyard. The space is beautiful and lush. Statues and greenery decorate the lightly colored terra-cotta walls. Servers mill between partygoers with glasses of champagne and drinks to order. Cocktail dresses and suits seem to be the going attire, so at least I fit in.

I scan the crowd for one of two faces. One is the club owner who runs Skye's old stomping grounds in the Quarter. He's been out of the game for a couple of years, but he has a reputation for introducing beautiful girls to important men, so he's at the party thanks to Martine. His job is to casually get me on Boswell's radar if I can't manage it myself.

I spot them both sitting at one of the outdoor lounge areas, talking casually to one another. I look away quickly, suddenly terrified Boswell will see me, which is the entire point of being here. Except I'm not sure I can breathe. I walk to the far corner of the courtyard and have another swig of my champagne. My glass is nearly empty already, which wasn't the plan. I'm sure my adrenaline can offset a second round.

I look up and try to forget where I am for a minute. The navy-blue sky swirls with featherlike clouds. A few stars prickle the darkness. It's a cool night, but I can't afford to cover up. Not tonight.

My thoughts drift to Tristan. Silent, absent Tristan. I replayed the night we spent on Frenchmen Street over and over. The unapologetic intensity of it. I let my guard down, but maybe I showed him too much. Hadn't we been baring souls since we got here?

"You look lost."

A man's subtle New England cadence clearly stands out in the sea of local accents in the conversations around me. The sound makes the hair on the back of my neck stand up. Still, I manage to glance over my shoulder and feign surprise.

"Excuse me?"

He's dressed in a dark navy-blue suit and a white collared shirt unbuttoned casually at the neck. He lifts his lowball to his lips, revealing the expensive diamond-studded watch adorning his wrist.

"I said you look lost," he says after a swallow, "over here all by yourself."

I quickly sense I'm being hunted. I turn to fully face him, and his attention goes where I expect it to—down the front of my dress. He doesn't honor me with a quick return to my eyes. Instead he lingers there, licking his bottom lip like I'm a piece of meat, before slowly returning his gaze to mine.

I practice Skye's advice and pretend he's Tristan for a moment. If Tristan looked at me like that, my clothes would fall off.

"I have this rule at social engagements," he says. "I can't let a beautiful woman suffer one of these parties alone. I have to come rescue her."

"That's very noble of you."

He smirks. "Thank you."

"Am I suffering, though?"

He cocks his head. "I definitely am. There's only so much networking I can stomach before I need to have a real conversation with someone."

"So you picked me?"

"There is absolutely no one else here I would bother with."

I laugh lightly because Vince Boswell is unexpectedly charming. And in a sudden and disturbing moment that I mask with a coy smile, I realize that he reminds me of Kolt too. Expensive and cultured and carefree. Vince is tall with pale-blue eyes. His tanned skin is mottled with dozens of freckles. He shows his age with his slick scalp and lines spidering from the edges of his eyes. He's too old for me, but he's undoubtedly attractive.

"What brings you to the party?"

I give myself a beat to recall my story. "I was supposed to meet a friend, but something came up once I got here." I shrug. "So here I am."

"This is a pretty exclusive get together. What exactly do you do?"

I hold his gaze for a long moment. "I'm a student."

He nods quietly, looking me over again.

"Do you have a name?"

"Do I need one?"

He chuckles. "I have a few more people I need to say hello to before I get out of here. But I don't want to let you out of my sight. Might be less awkward if I could introduce you."

I break his stare and scan the crowd, as if I'm considering his offer. Finally, I extend my hand. "I'm Michaela."

He takes it and, instead of shaking it, brings the back of my hand to his lips. "I'm Vince," he murmurs before kissing the skin, keeping his eyes trained on me.

I let my lips part and hold his heated stare. A little surge of triumph ripples through me. I have him. As long as I don't mess it up while he keeps me on his arm tonight, I think I have him.

He turns my wrist before letting go. The pendant shimmers against my skin. An irrational fear strikes through me that somehow this will be the thing that tips him off that I'm not who I claim to be. That I'm not the type of girl he could bring into his bed for a night of no-strings sex.

He lifts his gaze. "You religious?"

I pause and do my best to appear unaffected. "I know who to call when I'm in trouble."

With that, he laughs and slides my hand in his. "I like you, Michaela. Come on, I want you to meet the senator."

Another glass of champagne and almost an hour later, Vince's hand rests possessively at the small of my back as if we're a couple already. His charm slips away when he talks business. He seems especially passionate about legislation that affects the pharmaceutical industry. Thankfully, he's got a friend in Senator Williams, who's just secured a campaign donation for what would support an average middle-class family for a year.

I listen and learn but keep my interactions to small talk. No one cares about a pretty girl in a grad program at Tulane unless they plan to sleep with her later, which rules out everyone but Vince.

When we're finally alone again, he lowers his mouth to my ear. "I'm ready to get the hell out of here. How about you?"

His lips brush against my ear seductively. I shiver, because that's what I do when Tristan does it. I close my eyes and lean into Vince a little, hinting at the desire for more contact.

"I think that sounds like a great idea," I say.

"How much?"

My breath hitches. I look up at him. Martine and I never discussed a rate. I was going with the pretty girl act, not the hired hooker act. I wouldn't even know a figure to toss out.

He shakes his head. "Forget it. You can tell me when we get to the room. Charge me double. I don't fucking care."

"Are you staying here?" I ask dumbly, my voice breathy and soft.

He nods. "We don't even need to leave the floor."

He takes my hand, and I follow. After a short journey out of the event room and down the hall, we're at his door. An imposing man stands nearby, barely looking at us. Then Vince opens the door and gestures for me to go inside. I walk in slowly. The sitting area is dark, but I can make out the basics. Beige walls and beige carpet. Local artwork and expensive upholstery. I slow in front of the French doors that lead from the sitting area into the lit bedroom.

He comes behind me, molding his hands to my hips and nuzzling into my neck.

"How much, baby? I'll make sure my guy has the cash by the time we're done."

In the time between leaving the party with him and being in his room, I came up with a work-around to the payment situation. One that I hoped would segue nicely into the plan.

I turn slowly in his arms and rest my palms on his chest. "I don't want you to pay me."

He frowns. "I'd feel better if I did. I'm sure we can come up with something reasonable."

I toy with the buttons on his crisp shirt and bite my lip. "What are you into, Vince?"

He exhales slowly, cinching our torsos closer. "A few things. You seem like a good girl, though. I don't want to scare you."

I peer at him through my eyelashes. "That's the thing... I kind of like to be scared."

He doesn't speak. Scarcely breathes. Doesn't stop his slow journey over my dress until he gets to my ass. He cups my cheeks and adds pressure so I can feel his growing erection.

I scream on the inside. I close my eyes and bite my lip harder, turning the outward reaction into something sexy and needy, when all my instincts are telling me to run out of here.

"I can do that for you, Michaela. I don't do safewords or any of that shit, though. Because once I start, I'm not going to stop. Can you handle that?"

Anxiety zings through my veins. When I'm certain the fear hits my eyes, I realize it's the kind of fear he enjoys. Because he smiles and slides his fingers into my hair, twisting them through the strands until I wince.

"You like it rough, baby?"

I nod quickly, breathing fast. I'm scared, but he thinks those outward reactions are a result of my deviant desire. He thinks I'm turned on.

It's a perfect misunderstanding.

Soon I'm shaking in his arms. Because I'm about to ask him to do unthinkable things to me. My lips part, and my voice trembles when I finally find it.

"I want you to hurt me."

TRISTAN

I force myself to blink when my eyes start to burn. I feel like I could crack the computer screen displaying the feed to Boswell's room with how intensely I'm staring at it.

She didn't just say what I think she said. She didn't just ask this sick fuck to hurt her. On purpose. Consensually.

Yet I'm sure she did when he suddenly goes from sweet and soft on her to pushing her into the bedroom. She stumbles on the bench in front of the bed. He catches her. By the throat.

I hear her struggle to inhale before he leans in and kisses her. When he lets go, she drops down hard.

"Slow it down," I growl. "Slow it the *fuck* down."

That's what she said she was going to do once she got this far. But I fear that was never the plan.

The nightmare visions of what he might do next are reeling too fast for me to thoroughly process. For all my practicing detached emotion the past couple days, I'm a total fucking head case right now.

Then he slaps her across the face, and I worry I might black out from pure rage. Rage so raw and violent, I know it's breached a new category of feeling. I grab my gun and stand up. I take long strides to the door, my vision already red with all the blood I'm going to shed once I get in there.

Kill. I'm going to fucking kill him.

Another slap draws my attention back to the screen. She screams and scrambles away. He follows her onto the bed.

"This what you want? You want me to rough you up a little first, baby?"

"Yeah."

I hear her voice. So small and afraid. She doesn't want this, yet it's exactly what she's asking for. I squeeze the grip of the gun, relishing the bite of the jagged metal pattern into my palms.

When he hauls back and hits her again, he does it with enough force that her whole body spins. Then he's behind her, fisting her hair and muttering something in her ear as he mauls her breasts through her dress. When he jerks her head back, she lets out a wail. And that's when I know.

I'll never be the Tristan she wants. I'll only ever be the one who kills.

Taking lives is her limit. Risking hers is mine.

An odd peace comes with this realization. Because it means I don't have to hesitate. I don't have to apologize. All I have to do is save her. She's already decided the rest.

Everything shifts into focus because I'm seeing it through the scope I'm already accustomed to.

Knowing what I need to do, I leave my room down the hall and approach the heavily muscled man guarding Boswell's door several feet away.

"I need to get in there now," I say.

His expression doesn't change. "No one gets in there until I get the signal."

"The signal?"

He nods. Martine. What a prize she is, letting her friend's daughter get beaten up for some bullshit incriminating video.

I nod in mock agreement and look away a second before using my fist to crack his nose. He throws a punch, clipping my jaw and pushing me against the wall. But my next three hits come too fast for him to dodge or react to. The fourth one ends the fight. He drops to the rug, knocked out for the foreseeable future. I'll have to deal with him later because too much time has already gone by. Isabel's alone in there with a goddamn monster.

I slap the key I made over the sensor until it beeps.

When I go inside, I hear nothing except heavy breathing. Then a painful grunt. Hidden in the darkness of the sitting room, I lift my gun and go deeper into the suite until I can see more. Boswell is holding himself up against the wall, one hand on his groin, the other cradling his bloody face. His nose is gushing.

"Fucking bitch. Take my money and get out of here," he says with a garbled voice.

I take another silent step forward, and Isabel comes into view. She's in the bathroom doorway pointing the gun I left for her right at him. The adjoining room is dark, so neither of them know I'm here.

"I don't want your money." Isabel's voice is slow and hoarse. "I want my life back. The one you almost took from me."

He winces. "What?"

"You sent Kolt for me."

His eyes harden with recognition. "Jesus Christ. It's you."

"It's me. And this is going to stop. Tonight. I'm not running from you anymore."

He doesn't speak.

"Everything you did was on camera," she says. "Unless you want the senator to find out how you treat your women, I'd suggest you put all of this to bed. Call off the hit. Let us move on with our lives."

He's calculating. I can see it in his eyes. All the potential losses. All the ways he can manipulate to get what he wants.

He straightens off the wall, though not easily. "Isabel Foster died in Rio last week. How'd you pull that off?"

"I didn't have anything to do with that."

"Lucia and Gabriel were getting fancy again? Why am I not surprised?" He sneers, though the motion causes him to wince.

"This feud has to stop before more people get hurt."

"Did you give your mother the same speech? Because she's been fucking with my family for years. She's got people breaking into our accounting firm to hack files. Setting off alarms at our properties. She never fucking stops."

"You killed my sister," she whispers.

"She was already dying! They insisted on the treatment. They begged for it. Your sister had an adverse reaction, and your crazy fucking mother hasn't let it go. My father did her a favor she didn't deserve after your grandfather nearly tanked our company."

"So you tried to kill me? That was your solution?"

He pauses. "Lucia has her priorities. I have mine. She's obviously dedicated to destroying us, and I have to protect my company. She wasn't leaving me a lot of options. For what it's worth, hiring the hit on you wasn't my first choice." He strips off his shirt and uses it to sop up the blood. "Kolt wasn't supposed to fall for you. I guess I can see firsthand now why he did."

"Promise me this is over."

He pins her with a hard look. "Call off your mother and her band of do-gooders, and we'll call this water under the bridge."

"This isn't a negotiation," she says.

"Then shoot me if that's what you want to do."

Something flickers in his eyes when he says it. Isabel rearranges her hold on the gun the way I taught her. Something knots in my gut, though. Boswell's challenge is like a shockwave through the room that we all feel. We all know deep down she can't do it.

He tosses his shirt to the floor and takes a step toward her.

"Stay there," she says firmly.

"I don't think you really want to do this, Isabel. You're a good girl.

We can figure this out." His tone is calm and gentling.

Her arms start to waver. Shit. She knows how to hold a gun, but she can't pull the trigger.

Before he has a chance to get any closer, I step out from the shadows and move through the doors.

"Hold it right there."

Boswell jolts back, his eyes wide. "Who the fuck are you?"

"Someone you can't intimidate. Back up."

He lifts up his arms and starts taking steps back. His breathing ticks up. I can almost smell the fear on him. An unpleasant odor that comes from a human body when it realizes it's facing death. He reeks of it suddenly.

"This shit is over. You'll wish the video was the worst of it, because if any harm comes on her after this, you're going to have to deal with me. And I don't hesitate. I. Don't. Care."

His back hits the wall again. I crowd him, my gun aimed between his eyes.

"I'll come for you first," I say quietly. "It won't be quick, but it'll be thorough. I'll enjoy it, I promise you. And when I'm done, I'm coming for your father and your sister. And then that pretty boy nephew of yours. Until I've wiped out so many of you that no one knows who Isabel Foster is or why one of you thought it'd be a good idea to kill her. Do you understand what I'm telling you?"

He swallows hard. "Yeah."

"Do you realize I would much rather kill you right now than ask for your cooperation?"

He hesitates and then nods slowly.

"Good."

As vicious as I'm feeling right now, I don't want to kill someone in front of Isabel. Even if she left now, she'd know I did it. Just being in her presence, I can register the horror she'd feel, and I can't deal with it.

I turn Boswell around and bind his hands with the stash of zip ties I keep in my jacket.

"Your bodyguard took the night off, so don't bother yelling for him. No cops. Figure out how to patch yourself up, get your ass on a plane back to Boston, and call off the hit. I'll know if you don't."

"Consider it done," he says with a grunt as I haul him toward the bathroom.

Isabel steps out of the way, and we pass through.

"On your knees." I kick the back of one so he drops down with a *humph.*

I yank his bound hands toward the toilet pipe and hook a couple more plastic loops through it so he's tethered there, hopefully until maid service arrives in the morning.

"Boswell."

He snaps his head up, looking like a beaten dog on the floor with his wounded, hateful eyes and bloody face. I really hope I never have to see it again. I hope he doesn't give me a reason to.

"Are we clear?"

"I get it, all right?" he says. "It's over."

9

ISABEL

Tristan slams the bathroom door shut and pauses when he sees me.

"You okay?"

"I'm okay," I croak. I try swallowing over the tears that want to break free, but my throat is too sore from Boswell's viselike grip on it.

Adrenaline is flooding my system. I don't even want to think about what would have happened if Tristan hadn't shown up.

When I knew we had enough damaging behavior captured on video… No. When I knew I had enough of Boswell's blows, I finally fought back. My invitation to play rough was met with more than I anticipated. The last hit had my ears ringing. That's when I realized he could knock me out and this would be over. At least for me. Not knowing if anyone had my back but Zeda, anything could have happened.

In an instant, I called on my instincts and everything I'd learned. I hit him in the nose as hard as I could with the heel of my hand. He came after me, tried subduing me until I got an angle to his groin and managed to scramble to the bathroom for the hidden gun Zeda told me was waiting for me if I needed it.

Having the weapon in my hand gave me a short-lived sense of relief. Once I pointed it at him, he seemed to surrender. But the gun was no good if I couldn't pull the trigger.

As soon as Tristan showed up in my periphery, I knew he wouldn't hesitate. I wasn't sure what scared me more. The prospect of Tristan following through on my empty threat or having to fight Boswell off myself.

"Let's go." Tristan's voice is clipped as he moves into the sitting room. He reaches under the entertainment system and withdraws a tiny laptop.

"What's that?"

"Insurance," he says.

I follow him out of the room and into the empty hallway.

"I have to get my things," I say. And check on Skye and Zeda.

He opens the door to their suite with a plain white key that I don't ask about. Because Boswell's bodyguard is slumped on the floor when we walk in.

I look at Tristan, new panic sliding through my veins. "Is he dead?"

"Zeda and Skye must have dragged him in here after I knocked him out. They probably bailed when they saw me go in for you. Get your shit and let's go before he comes to."

I run to the bathroom, but it's empty. Everything's been cleared out. The laptops, my bags, everything.

"Everything's gone."

He takes my hand and drags me out and down the hallway to a third room. There, he puts his laptop and the smaller one into his backpack.

"Service elevator," he says.

We hurry down the hallway to it. Once inside, he hits the button for the bottom floor. I'm breathing hard. I'm scared and want this to be over. I want to be somewhere safe. Somewhere really far from Vince Boswell.

Tristan touches my chin, slanting my face to see both sides of it. "You're already bruising."

I can feel it too. The ache in my jaw. The heat on my cheek. The swelling in my lips.

He looks away like the sight of me physically hurts him.

The elevator deposits us near a restaurant in the back of the hotel. Tristan turns and leads us out the first entrance. His car is parked on a side street.

We get in, and the second my back hits the leather seat, the tears start burning behind my eyes and then course down my cheeks. I'm shaking, trying like hell not to break into a fit of sobs as Tristan drives. I don't care where we're going, because being alone with Tristan again floods me with relief like I've never known.

But he doesn't reach for me. Doesn't say a word. He's cold, and I'm desperate for his warmth after what I've been through.

More tears fall. "You hate me."

"I'm nowhere close to hating you."

We're back on St. Charles, and Halo is only a few minutes away. I can feel it before we park that he intends to leave me here. I tighten my grip on the door handle.

When he parks in front of the house, the silence is brutal.

"Tristan…" My voice is watery, but I will myself to be stronger. "I'm sorry."

He's quiet for a long time, staring out the windshield, his expression taut with unspoken thoughts. For all my wanting independence, I'm ready to run away with Tristan. Anything to end this distance between us.

"Will you talk to me, please?" I beg.

He shakes his head slightly. "You did what you felt you needed to do. I did the same thing," he finally says.

"But you're upset with me."

He pulls his lips tight. "There are some things I need to take care of, Isabel. You're going to be on your own for a while. I think you should get out of New Orleans. I don't trust that Martine can keep you safe here. Not now."

"What do you need to take care of?"

He avoids my question with more silence. I wish I could reach into his mind and draw out all the things he's thinking.

"They're bringing me back in," he says.

The air leaves my lungs. My limbs turn cold.

"Jay?"

"I agreed to go back if they gave me intel on Boswell. That's how I found out about Kolt."

"But you can't go back. You said you'd stop taking jobs."

"What does it matter?" He pins me with a cold look. "Let's face it. You can't be with someone like me."

"That's not true."

"You said it yourself. You want your life back. Pretty soon, you'll be able to have it. Just lie low for another few weeks. I'll make sure the heat is off, and Lucia can figure out how to bring you back to life. Mistaken identity or something."

My jaw falls. I can't believe what he's saying.

"Why are you doing this?"

"Because you can't change who you are any more than I can change who I am." He closes his eyes a moment, breathing out through his nose. "What you did today was brave. Stupid, but brave. Martine was right about one thing. I underestimated you. But you've already seen enough carnage to last a lifetime. You have a lot more to offer this world than being some bastard's punching bag to bait him into a corner. You did what you had to do to end this. Now it's over and you can go home."

"I don't want my old life back if I can't have you." Fresh tears roll down my cheeks.

He sees them and looks away.

"I have to go back. It's not negotiable. If I bail, they'll come after you and we're back to square one."

I can't believe it. He sold his freedom. For mine...

"Where will you go?"

"I'm going to New York. I'll check in from there."

"You can take me with you."

He shakes his head. "It's not safe."

"Is it any safer leaving me here?"

He hesitates. "Martine has connections. She can hide you someplace else until the coast is clear."

His complacency about leaving me behind ratchets up my panic.

"Tristan, no. I shouldn't have left you in DC. It was a mistake, and maybe this whole plan with Boswell was a mistake too. But what you're saying is crazy. You're being rash." I'm talking fast, nearly spinning out with racing thoughts.

"Isabel... You don't need to apologize. You just have to accept this for what it is. We both do."

I'm tempted to beg, but I know it won't change his mind. He's made it up. He made it up days ago when I felt the shift between us.

So I decide to fight dirty, because that's what he would do.

"If you're going back to Jay, then maybe I will too. I know where to find her."

He shoots me his cold, silver stare. "You stay the fuck away from that place. Do you hear me?"

"Then take me with you."

He grits his teeth. "Goddamnit, Isabel. I can't do that."

"Why not?"

"Because I can't keep my hands off you. And that's not good for either of us."

"I think it's just fine."

"Jesus, Isabel, you really think you can live this life? You think you can love an assassin? Someone who kills other people for a living?"

He gestures between us, as if he's disgusted that I could even consider it.

"I already do."

He grips his hands on the steering wheel. "You don't belong in this life," he says quietly.

"I belong with you, Tristan. We can figure the rest out. I promise."

Frustration and desperation swim in my veins when he shows no signs of giving in to my pleas.

"Tell me you don't love me," I challenge. Because even if he can't say it... Even if it's strange and foreign... I know he does.

He looks out the window, his jaw tense. "You know I can't do that, Isabel."

Several agonizing seconds pass before our gazes lock. I meet his steely stare with a determined one of my own. I won't give in. I won't give up on us.

"Fine," he finally says.

Fine? My heart does a pole vault.

"You're hell-bent on ruining your life, one way or the other, right? Whether it's with me or throwing yourself into absurdly dangerous situations. So let's see how long you last."

I'm hurting and wrung out, but his relenting gives me a surge of hope. Because as long as we're together, I can try to change his mind.

I smile even though it hurts. Tristan is an unwelcoming wall of tension, but nothing can stop me from leaning across the car and kissing him square on the mouth. The contact soothes my battered nerves.

"I love you, Tristan." I say it against his lips and pray he doesn't push me away. Because the distance he wants to put between us will destroy me. Truly and completely. Beyond a shadow of a doubt, it will.

When our mouths drift apart, he feathers his fingers over my aching cheek. His gaze travels slowly along all the places he caresses.

In his reverent touch, I see his heart. His resentment. His confusion. The love he doesn't know how to accept.

"Get your things," he says. "It's going to be a long drive."

Continue The Red Ledger with

RECALL

Available November 13, 2018

ALSO BY

MEREDITH WILD

THE RED LEDGER

Reborn

Recall (November 13, 2018)

THE HACKER SERIES

Hardwired

Hardpressed

Hardline

Hard Limit

Hard Love

THE BRIDGE SERIES

On My Knees

Into the Fire

Over the Edge

ACKNOWLEDGMENTS

December 2, 2014, I woke up from a nap with an intense dream in my head. The notes I took all that time ago would eventually become the first scene of *Reborn*. To be publishing this book almost four years later is literally a dream come true!

So many people have helped me bring this first volume of Tristan and Isabel's story to the world.

To those who have given their time and thoughtful feedback to help me make this book the very best it could be—my husband and first reader Jonathan, my editor Scott Saunders, my story consultant Remi Ibraheem, and my beta readers, Cleida, Carol, Amber, Krystin, Megan, Delanea, Linda, Martha, Melissa, Lauren, Stephanie, Beatrice, Cathy, April, Jordan, Jamie, Elyn, Sue, Kika, Danielle, and Kristin... Thank you!

To my sprint ladies for giving me critical motivational pushes and support the whole way—Angel Payne, Victoria Blue, Mia Michelle... Thank you!

To Solange, my constant cheerleader for this little dream of a book... Thank you!

To everyone on the Waterhouse Press team who has taken special care of this project every little step of the way... Thank you!

To my readers and amazing Team Wild crew, you have embraced the concept for *The Red Ledger* since the moment I decided to bring it out of hiding. Thank you for your daily support and bringing so much joy to my world as an author. I can't wait to share *Recall* with you very soon!

ABOUT THE AUTHOR

Meredith Wild is a #1 *New York Times, USA Today,* and international bestselling author. After publishing her debut novel, *Hardwired,* in September 2013, Wild used her ten years of experience as a tech entrepreneur to push the boundaries of her "self-published" status, becoming stocked in brick-and-mortar bookstore chains nationwide and forging relationships with major retailers.

In 2014, Wild founded her own imprint, Waterhouse Press, under which she hit #1 on the *New York Times* and *Wall Street Journal* bestseller lists. She has been featured on *CBS This Morning* and the *Today Show,* and in the *New York Times,* the *Hollywood Reporter, Publishers Weekly,* and the *Examiner.* Her foreign rights have been sold in twenty-two languages.